Reckless

Devon Hartford

COPYRIGHT NOTICE

Want to get an email when the sequel is released?

Sign up here:

http://eepurl.com/B7crf

"Storytelling is wakeful dreaming.

Writing is the harnessing of our dreams with words."

—Devon Hartford

DEDICATION

To every person who reached out to me online to say hello and to encourage me to keep doing what I was doing. You know who you are, and I want to sincerely thank you, AGAIN! :-D

Without your support, I might never have finished this book on time.

Now it's yours to enjoy!

Prologue

CHRISTOS

THREE MONTHS EARLIER...

I couldn't bear to look at Samantha. Naked heartbreak strained her face.

Because of me.

At the end of my first day back at SDU, two cops stuffed me in the back of a police cruiser right in front of her. I felt like a complete douche nugget. You can romanticize it all you want, but getting arrested fucking sucks. Who wants to go to jail, really? I'd been locked up enough times to know.

Samantha tried to catch my attention as the cruiser drove me away, but I avoided her eyes.

I felt bad, but I was too embarrassed to look at her, no matter how many points I'd scored by cleaning up the coffee cesspool in her car before the cops showed up. I grinned to myself. That shit had been rank, but enduring the smell was a small price to pay for more time with Samantha.

The cop car pulled onto the freeway, taking the Five south toward downtown. Traffic was heavy. I'd have plenty of time to mull things over.

I wasn't sure who was pressing charges against me, but my bet was that fat red-faced fuck who'd been harassing Samantha on the way to campus in the a.m. He tries to jump me, and I'm the one hauled downtown?

Fuck that shit.

I exhaled heavily and pushed away my irritation.

For a guy my size, the back of a squad car was cramped quarters. I wanted to slouch down and get comfortable on the bench seat, but with the cuffs on, it wasn't doable. Instead, I leaned my shoulder against the door and rested my head against the glass.

Watching the familiar landmarks sail past should've been comforting. The mural with the waves and surfers on the storage building in Pacific Beach was pretty nice. But my favorite was always the huge mural of humpback whales on the side of the Chevrolet dealership. Those painted whales swam in a vast emerald ocean, elegant symbols of graceful mobility and independence.

Sadly, the artsy roadside surroundings, the blue skies overhead, and the Pacific Ocean a hop-skip to my right were now an infinite distance from my grasp. They taunted me with promises of fleeting freedom, a stark contrast to my current situation.

Screw it. I wasn't letting the cage of this squad car trap my spirit. My mind was free to roam and seek safe harbor.

A smile crept across my face as I pictured Samantha in my mind's eye. Not the downer moment when she'd panicked at the sight of the cops cuffing me, but all the magic moments before that, since this morning.

Like when I'd bumped into her coming out of the Student Center bookstore and she laughed when I told her my name was Adonis. I think that made her the first chick who'd ever openly mocked my middle name. Most girls melted when I said it, like I was some kind of celebrity movie star. Sure, I'd gotten giggles galore and countless stripper laughs from all kinds of bar babes in the past, but not Samantha's sour-faced disdain. I kind of liked it. She was all spark and no bullshit.

It helped she was epic hot. Too bad she couldn't see it for herself. But it was clear as day to me. Underneath her self-doubt, she was super-nova, incendiary hot. My lips curled in my trademarked cocky smirk. I could handle it. I liked fire.

Getting burned let you know you were alive.

The funny thing about Samantha was that, even though she was a total hottie, she was a complete spaz. Her firestorm emotions constantly tore up her good looks, turning her face purse-dog ugly half the time. Like when fatty had tried to climb into her VW on the way to campus, the look on her face had been the visual equivalent of nails grinding across a chalkboard. Totally heinous. But it was only temporary.

I dug the honest flow of Samantha's emotions. It was way better than the contrived gamesmanship of Tiffany and her loony sorority friends with their Halloween-mask sincerity.

Samantha's naked honesty and tumultuous emotions made me want to protect her that much more. She was some kind of rare and unique truth.

When she was calm, she was undeniably the most beautiful woman on the planet. I don't say that shit lightly. I've been with more than enough hotties to know.

But with Samantha, it went far beyond her looks.

I'd totally flipped for her the moment I'd laid eyes on her. Even with her funky dress and that coffee smell and her jangling nerves, something about Samantha shone right into me like a beacon. Call it her spirit, her essence, I don't fucking know. But sure as shit, I'd never felt anything like it coming off of any other chicks I'd ever met.

Samantha was in a class of her own.

She had a calming effect on me, like everything in the world had fallen into place at last, and the human race could kick back and sip Mai Tais into eternity. This was a unique experience for me. Ever since my mom had left my dad, my life had been a scattered vortex of recklessness. Peace and calmness were strangers to me. Daily disaster and emotional chaos were my resting state.

There was *one* memory of perfect calmness that I cherished, and I turned to it whenever my head was spinning out of control. It reminded me of the calmness my life *could* have, if only I could figure out how to hold onto it for longer than a minute or two at a time.

It'd happened two or three years ago, on a surfing trip down in Baja with Jake and some of our buddies.

We'd camped overnight on the beach, and I'd hit the waves first thing in the morning, before everyone else was awake. They were sleeping off the cases of Coronas everyone had pounded the night before. For whatever reason, I'd gone easy on the brews and was ready for an early start.

After I'd paddled out for the seventh time, I'd been sitting on my board in meditative silence, alone, lolling on a glassy ocean, waiting between sets, feet dangling in the tropical water while a perfect sunrise soaked the horizon. The entire world had felt like everything was as it should be, the way nature intended. For the first time since my mom had left my dad, I'd felt perfect, total calmness. For a fleeting moment.

Then it was gone.

Samantha had brought that peaceful feeling back ten times over. I'd felt it continuously since meeting her, and it spiked whenever I was in her presence. Too bad the cops trashed my vibe the second they took me away. Fucking five-oh. I shook my head.

Samantha…

I needed more of her. I was hooked. I mean, *junkie* hooked. She gave me something I couldn't give myself, no matter how hard I'd tried.

Samantha…

Bouncing around inside the rolling jail with the two cops sitting in front of me suddenly yanked me painfully out of my private reverie.

Bars, handcuffs, no escape.

I struggled to keep my feelings for Samantha protected from my grim predicament. I didn't want my current situation tarnishing my memories of her in any way. After taking a deep, calming breath, I dove back into comforting reminiscence.

I recalled Samantha's surprise when we'd first locked eyes in Life Drawing class. Watching her struggle not to stare at my package while she'd been drawing me naked was probably the comedy highlight of my year. She'd been ready to boil over with embarrassment.

Despite her nearly perpetual awkwardness, I totally dug her, no matter how off-kilter her mood.

Stalking her at the Eleanor M. Westbrook art museum was probably the calmest I'd seen her. The deserted museum was a quiet and relaxing cocoon, making it easy to let your guard down. I'm sure Samantha was so busy marveling at the paintings, her worries had fallen away. I knew the experience well. I felt it every time I went to a great art museum myself, and slid into the colors and shapes of the paintings, escaping my own inner turmoil for brief moments.

While Samantha had stood mesmerized in front of my grandfather's painting, Shrouded Paradise, I witnessed her truest beauty come out of hiding for the first time, like some timid field mouse sniffing the air for danger. That crazy beauty was such a fragile, fleeting thing, like a snowflake or a perfect sunset. You could only appreciate it if you stopped yourself and really took it in before it was gone, maybe forever.

I wanted desperately to protect Samantha from whatever haunted her because I knew her insecurity ran deep, just like mine. The only difference between me and her was that I hid it, and she didn't.

I couldn't decide if she was the bravest person I'd ever met, or the craziest.

It didn't matter.

I wanted to wash away her tears and fears so that the amazing young woman I sensed beneath her teenaged anxiety could finally emerge.

I already knew beyond all doubt that I would do anything to help Samantha find her way in life.

The fact I was parked in the back of a squad car because of her, ten hours after we'd met, was living proof.

I sighed heavily again, my heart accelerating while my chest tightened around it. Man, I knew Samantha was going to be trouble for me. Maybe even more trouble than where I was heading in this black-and-white. I grinned to myself. The good news was, this shit was temporary.

I looked forward to finding out how much trouble Samantha could be the second I got out of whatever steaming mess I'd tripped into with the cops.

Because whatever was brewing between me and Samantha felt permanent.

Eternal.

Chapter 1

SAMANTHA

PRESENT DAY

I still couldn't get over how hot Christos was. His tattooed arms flexed hypnotically and his body gyrated only inches from mine.

"Oh, it's so wet," Christos said.

"Can you get it in all the way?" I asked nervously.

"It's so tight. I don't know if it'll fit."

"Push it in all the way. Go deep."

"Are you sure?"

"I've waited long enough. Just do it."

"Okay, but I'll go slow, just in case." He eased it in. All the way.

"Oooh, yeah," I purred, "I think that's going to do it. Just like that. Smooth and easy." I totally needed this. I'd been waiting for what seemed like my entire life.

"You like it when I do this, don't you?" he smirked.

"Why wouldn't I?" I grinned back.

"I don't know, I thought maybe you were afraid it would ruin things. You want me to go faster?"

"Yes. Do it, Christos. I trust you. As fast as you can."

His entire body flexed in a choreographed symphony of poetic movement. "Like this?"

"Oh yes, Christos. Just like that. Harder."

Things were so wet down there, it made a sucking sound as it went in and out, in and out.

"Here it comes!" he grunted. "It's gonna pop!"

"Faster! Harder! Keep it in deep or it'll gush everywhere!"

"Now!"

"Yes, that's it! Flush it!"

I pressed the lever while Christos gave the rubber plunger a final thrust into the toilet bowl. The water swirled and gurgled. "We did it!" I squealed.

He high-fived me as my toilet bowl finally drained.

"What've you been throwing in that thing?" he asked skeptically. "Paper towels? It's not a garbage disposal."

"I don't know, regular stuff?"

"Regular stuff doesn't clog the pipes."

I wiped sweat from my brow. This conversation was making me feel guilty of some sort of heinous pooping problem. I needed to steer the heat onto a likely target. "Maybe my neighbor's pet elephant has been sneaking into my bathroom in the middle of the night and is clogging up my pipes with its elephant dumps?"

"I'll totally buy that if you can convince me how the elephant gets past your bedroom door without you noticing."

"It tiptoes?"

Christos lifted a doubtful eyebrow.

"Elephants are very light on their feet. It probably wears ballet slippers, which are perfect for sneaking around."

Christos' eyebrow ratcheted up another notch.

"Have you ever *worn* ballet slippers?" I demanded. "They're ninja stealthy."

Christos' other eyebrow joined its twin.

"I swear! It wasn't me! It flushed fine before I went to D.C.!"

Christos smiled broadly, finally letting me off the hook.

"Jerk!" I tiptoed and kissed him on the cheek. "Anyway, thank you for helping."

"My pleasure." Wrapping an arm around my shoulder, he kissed me affectionately on the cheek. "While I'm at it, do you have any toilet bowl cleaner?"

"What for?" I asked.

"May as well give the bowl a quick once-over while I'm already in here."

I grabbed a bottle of toilet bowl cleaner from under the sink. He squirted a blue ring under the rim and went to work.

"Christos, why is it I get all turned on when I see you scrubbing things?"

"All women have an elbow-grease fetish." He cocked his head and flashed his now-legendary dimpled grin. "It's a proven fact." Christos put the bowl brush away and washed his hands. After toweling them dry, he leaned toward me, wrapping his arms around my waist. "Now that I've got you all worked up…" he said suggestively.

"Christos," I rolled my eyes demurely, "Romeo and Kamiko are going to be here any minute. We don't have time to fool around. I still haven't picked out an outfit." Earlier, Christos had told me he had a surprise New Year's Eve destination in store for all of us. I couldn't wait to find out what it was.

"You'll be gorgeous no matter what you wear," he said, suddenly dipping me like a ballroom dancer.

"Oh!" I gasped.

He grinned.

I gazed into his liquid blue eyes. They bathed me in the light of his love.

He leaned toward me, licking his lips. "*Agápi mou,*" he murmured.

Phew! His fluid Greek accent melted me every time. My mouth parted as our lips met like lost lovers. We hadn't kissed in, oh, I don't know, about thirty minutes. My soul was parched and needed another drink from his sensual fountain. Christos poured himself into our kiss, his tongue caressing the sensitive spot under my upper lip before sliding across my teeth, then deeper into my mouth. My head started to spin.

I didn't realize my bathroom could be this sexy. The next thing I knew, Christos had pulled me back to standing from our ballroom dip. His palms slid down my back and cupped my ass, huge hands squeezing hypnotically. Jolts of pleasure fingered up into my pelvis. Oh god. How did this man do this to me? I hooked my leg around the back of his, pulling him into me.

"Mmmm," he moaned. "Aggressive. I don't remember this behavior. Do I know you?"

I dropped my leg. "Stop, Christos," I giggled.

"No, don't stop. I like it when you do that."

"You do?" Feeling shy, I studied the barbed tattoo that wired around one of his forearms, tracing it lightly with my fingernail.

"Yeah. It's okay to be confident. I don't mind one bit." He grinned and slid a thumb across my cheek lovingly. "Let go, *agápi mou.* You're safe with me."

I gazed up into his eyes.

"Let your hands roam freely, Samantha. Explore my body with

your fingertips. Your touch is electric, and powers my heart."

I grimaced, but laughed and bonked my forehead against his chest. "I'm not San Diego Gas & Electric, Christos."

"You sure?" he smiled confidently. "You totally light up my life, Samantha."

"Oh, that's terrible," I giggled, swatting his rock-hard shoulder.

"And you love it." He flipped on his thousand-watt dimpled grin.

He was right. I did love it. And I loved him. I lowered my lashes, suddenly shy again. I snuggled my cheek into the black long-sleeve V-neck sweater covering his muscular chest. He was so completely manly, every woman's fantasy, and he had given himself to me. I'd won the biggest lottery on the planet and had my dream-man all to myself. What more could a girl want?

I inhaled his fresh-washed scent. I could never tell if he wore some sort of exotic cologne, or if that was his natural smell. If it wasn't cologne, somebody needed to bottle it. They'd make millions. "I love you, Christos," I whispered, hugging him.

He caressed my neck with one hand while hugging me into his warm embrace with the other. "I love you too, Samantha."

SAMANTHA

Christos and I hadn't had any sort of intense sexual activity since before winter break.

Sure, I'd thought about sneaking into the guest bedroom while he'd slept at my parents' house on a nightly basis. But somehow, the idea of rattling the walls with my wails of ecstasy while Mom and Dad were one room away had spoiled my mood.

Imagine that.

Shudder.

Since arriving in San Diego yesterday, we'd had plenty of first- and second-base hits in the bedroom, but no home runs. I was still somewhat off my game, no pun intended, after dealing with the whole Taylor Lamberth scenario back in D.C. Going to her lawyer and giving my deposition wasn't exactly sexy or arousing, but it was the right thing to do. Christos totally understood. He always did.

Besides, merely being in D.C. had brought my old demons

creeping back.

Bitch. Slut. Whore...

Fortunately, with the loving presence of Christos in my life, my old emotional wounds had started to heal over. I imagined in time, the scars would fade permanently, but it would take more than a few weeks.

Emo. Goth. Witch. Sorceress. Suicide Watch...

I couldn't wait to get rid of those demons.

Now, wrapped protectively in his arms after conquering my toilet monster, I felt completely at peace. I was totally in love with him. There was no doubt about it. I had been crazy to think Christos was *anything* like Damian.

So, why did my love for Christos worry me so much?

The only answer that came to mind was that I risked losing him. I supposed that was the price we all paid for love, tolerating the terrible possibility that it could be torn from us in the blink of an eye.

I couldn't decide what would be worse: never having had Christos in my life at all, or losing him after what we'd been through together. The sudden sinking feeling in the pit of my stomach was evidence that losing him would be far, far worse. I was instantly nauseous, despite Christos' protective embrace. He couldn't protect me from unexpected things that happened to *him*.

I tried to ignore the pressing conviction that I might lose Christos forever. Ugh. I didn't want to think about it. I took a deep, cleansing breath, intending to sweep away my mental gremlins.

"Is something bothering you, *agápi mou*?" Christos asked, concern in his voice.

I didn't want to ruin our mood. It was New Year's Eve, and Christos had some awesome surprise awaiting me. "Oh," I said dismissively, "it's nothing." I smiled up at him. "I'm fine, as long as I have you."

He gazed down at me. The look of love I saw shining in his eyes was overwhelming.

CHRISTOS

THREE MONTHS EARLIER...

Afternoon traffic was so bad, it was taking forever to get to the jailhouse downtown.

The cops in the front seat chatted away in low voices, their conversation blending with the squawking Motorola two-way radio bolted to the dash.

Their irritating camaraderie slowly prodded away my good mood. The rugged steel cage between me and them made it seem like I was on the wrong side of a horror movie screen. Officers Happy and Go Lucky got to laugh it up and have a good time while I was tortured by circumstance. Not that I was mad at them. I didn't know them from nobody.

I tried to focus on thoughts of Samantha again, but the dude cop was so fucking grating, he shredded my happy place with his verbal meat grinder. He smiled constantly, but it was that snarl-smile you see on psychos. I felt bad for his partner sitting next to him, for his wife, his kids, his friends, his unborn grandchildren; whoever the fuck had to put up with him.

I sighed heavily again.

"You gonna catch the Chargers' game at the Q on Monday?" the female cop asked Snarl-Smile. Her hand rested casually on the steering wheel, like she was driving to the beach on a Sunday. Too bad we weren't.

"Bet your ass," Snarl-Smile replied enthusiastically through his mustache. "I've had season tix for five years. Haven't missed a game. The Chargers are going to slaughter the Texans. I've got extra seats, if you want to come out."

"You bleed blue and gold, Ruiz," the female cop chuckled.

"Bleed, nothin'. I've got lightning bolts shooting through my veins. I'm like the God of Thunder and shit."

They went on like this for some time, with Ruiz growing increasingly louder as he extolled the winning season the Chargers had waiting for them this year. Listening to his voice was like working in a hammer factory or sitting in the middle of a hand-grenade fight. His cackle-laugh went hyena when he recounted the final moments of the Raiders' game at the end of last year's season.

I pictured myself bending the bars between me and him like I was the Incredible Fucking Hulk. I'd choke him out until his eyes popped clear of his skull. Based on his partner's forced smile, I think she might have thanked me. How did she put up with this guy day-to-day? Maybe earplugs were standard issue for duty officers with assbag partners.

The squad car exited onto the gridded downtown streets and we pulled into the garage at the San Diego Central Jail. Same as I remembered. It looked like a fancy office building on the outside. You might easily mistake it for a place where people in suits and slacks made money hand over fist. That was a lie. On the inside, from what I remembered, it was getting old. Too dark, too dreary, too dirty. I guess that was fitting. The peeling paint and cement decor went with the broken-down people inside.

When Ruiz opened my door, I gave him a friendly nod and a flat smirk, letting him know I wasn't going to hassle him. He wasn't worth the trouble. We both knew he held the leash. I stood up to my full height.

"You're a big one, aren't you," Ruiz jabbed.

Okay, he was one of those alpha-dick hotheads. No reason to rile him up. I kept quiet. The female officer came around the car. "You gonna be able to handle him, Ruiz?" she cackled.

Ruiz scoffed. "Don't start punkin' me, Fowler. Sissy boy like this? I'll keep him in line."

This guy Ruiz was shorter than me, maybe six foot, but he had a small man's complex all the same. Around me, anyway. They usually did. I arched a brow at Ruiz's comment, but dropped it before he could see my casual contempt and pounce on it. Guys like him were always looking for an excuse.

"If he gets uppity, I'll whip out some lightning bolts on his ass." Ruiz gave me the mad-dog crazy eyes, toying with me.

"You mean you'll pull your taser?" Fowler prodded, questioning Ruiz's manhood.

"Hell no! I don't need it. I can *spit* lightning, girl." He grabbed the handcuff chain behind my back and gave it a good yank for effect. "You ain't gonna make me stun you, are you, son?"

I ignored Ruiz and looked at Fowler. She was kind of cute, with her hair bunned up tight. Had that sexy cop thing going. She had penciled-on eyebrows and wore makeup. A woman who cared about her looks. Her uniform looked tailored to fit her flowing curves and her chest pushed out her kevlar vest substantially. I gave her a mischievous smirk, flashing some dimple. I was all about the more honey approach. If I sweetened up Fowler, maybe she'd run defense between me and Hothead. I could tell Ruiz always brought shit to the party, just so he could swarm all over it.

"Leave him alone, Ruiz," Fowler laughed, flashing me a smile, which I reciprocated.

It worked every time.

They led me up to the bulletproof doors and we were buzzed in. The relative quiet outside was shattered by howling, screaming humanity inside. A huge fat guy with no shirt and no shoes flailed on the painted cement floor. Probably tripping on meth. Four officers dog-piled him, broiling with professionally restrained rage. Eventually, they cuffed him and zip-tied his ankles, trussing him up. They picked up the perp and carried him through a steel door.

"We gonna have to do you like that, junior?" Ruiz asked me.

"Not me, sir." I smiled at Fowler when I said it. She liked it. Her duty face went soft, like a teenybopper on a dream date with her favorite heartthrob. I took a moment to silently thank both my parents for good genes.

Ruiz caught my exchange with Fowler. "I hope not, son." He may not have been able to articulate what had just happened, but he sensed it, like a starving wolf. He probably had a secret thing for Fowler. I'm sure most of the squad did, by the looks of her.

Fowler placed her hand gently on my right triceps. Her touch was nearly a caress. "I don't think you have to worry about this one," she said warmly, beaming up at me.

I smiled back. Jedi mind tricks were the most effective form of combat, I'd learned. You can't make my looks go away with threatening insults or manhandling. Ruiz was out of this game, benched on a technical foul.

Fowler's eyes searched mine eagerly. I milked it.

Ruiz scowled while he scrutinized the two of us. Jaw muscles fluttering angrily, he finally cracked. With a grunt, he spun on his heel and stormed up to the desk sergeant, defeated.

I felt bad for Fowler. I'd probably never see her again and she'd be stuck with Ruiz for a partner for who knew how long.

Sometime later, I was led into a white-box interrogation room by two detectives. A round black table with a phone on top sat between us. They'd been drilling me with questions for hours.

I hadn't said shit.

One detective, who had identified himself as Kurt Hewitt, wore a white, too-tight button down shirt. The collar dug into his soft neck and flesh spilled over the sides. He looked ready to pop. He glared at me, "The victim has positively IDed you from the mug book, Christos," he said firmly. "We have witnesses putting you at the scene on the Pacific Coast Highway this morning. We know it was you who beat the guy up then fled."

Beat? I'd hit the guy once. In self defense. I'd even asked him if he needed an ambulance.

"Quit stalling and give us something we can work with," Hewitt finished, "so we can help you help yourself."

That was a riot. He wasn't here to pamper my ass, and we both knew it. All he wanted was for me to slip up and spill some incriminating information, that was it.

"Tell us what happened, in your own words," the other detective, named Andy Vaughn, said calmly, "and maybe we'll let you go home tonight."

I knew that was bullshit.

Vaughn pushed a yellow legal pad and a ball point across the table. He smiled at me like we were best friends.

I leaned back in my chair and folded my arms across my chest. "I need to talk to my lawyer."

Hewitt exchanged a look with Vaughn. Vaughn nodded at him.

"Fine," Hewitt sneered and stood up, jamming his hands in his front pockets. "Call him."

Vaughn slid the phone across the table and handed me the receiver.

I dialed my lawyer's number from memory. I'd used it enough times to know it by heart. He picked up after three rings. "Merriweather."

"Hey, Russell. It's Christos." I'd known Russell since I was sixteen, from the first of many times he'd saved my ass.

"Christos! Sonuvabitch," Russell said cheerily, "whatchoo doing calling me up this late? Better be good news."

I chuckled. "No doubt." Silence lingered.

Vaughn stood up, seemingly to give me some space. Both he and Hewitt remained in the room, leaning against the walls, watching me like hawks, waiting for me to incriminate myself so they could get their talons in me after the call.

"You're in the can again, aren't you?" Russell asked matter-of-factly.

"Yup."

I heard a long sigh on the other end of the phone. "Christos Mother-fucking Manos, when you going to learn to behave like an adult?"

"I'm working on it."

"I oughta whup your ass, son. What is it this time? You roll your Camaro street racing? Wheelies on Garnet to impress the ladies?"

"The charges are assault. And battery. Felony battery."

"Shit."

"Yeah."

"Son, you lucky you locked up, otherwise I'd get in my car and drive down there and break your face myself. When you gonna learn?"

"Like I said, I'm working on it." Russell hadn't had to save my ass in two years. I thought I was doing pretty good.

"You want me to call your grandfather?"

"Don't tell him. He'll be less worried that I don't come home than if he finds out I'm locked up."

"You sure?"

"Yeah. I'll wait until I'm out on bail or ROR, and tell him face to face."

"I'm not a magician, Christos. You may be stuck in there until trial, depending on the evidence, and your record."

"No way. It's total bullshit."

"You're a cocky bitch, aren't you? Shit, maybe I'll tell the judge myself to leave you in, knock some sense in that thick head of yours," Russell said pointedly. His voice softened. "You sure you don't want me to call Spiridon?"

"No, thanks. He'll sleep better tonight not knowing. If I'm not out in the morning, you can call him then."

"Want me to call your father?"

I felt a sharp stab in my gut when Russell mentioned my dad. "He doesn't need to know. He's got enough problems of his own."

"Fine. You need me there tonight?"

"No. I can handle it."

"Remember, Christos. Don't say a word. Not to the detectives, not to the inmates. Nobody. You hear me?"

"Got it."

"I'll call the court house first thing tomorrow and find out when

I need to roll on down and pull your ass out the pokey. For the time being, keep your butt tight, and don't be nobody's bitch," he chuckled.

I knew he wasn't worried about me. Not my immediate safety, anyway. Maybe about my misguided youth and not-so-bright future.

"And no fighting." His words went from warmth to clipped business instantly. "I don't need you stacking more charges on top of the ones you already got. Are we clear?"

"Yes, sir."

"All right. I'll see you tomorrow. And don't say shit about shit to anybody."

"Got it," I nodded to the empty air. I placed the receiver softly in the cradle of the phone.

I smiled sarcastically at the detectives and held my wrists out to them, ready to be cuffed. "Shall we?"

"Book him," Hewitt snarled, and stormed out of the room.

In all the times in the past I'd sat in a room just like this one (shit, I was pretty sure I'd been in *this* room at least once), about to be locked up, I'd never felt like I really gave a shit. Whether I was behind bars or free, I was always incarcerated inside my own prison of pain. So it didn't matter if I was walking the streets or stuck inside a concrete cell.

This time it was different.

This time I had something I was going to miss way more than I wanted to admit to myself or anyone else.

This time I had that kooky angel Samantha Smith wondering where I was and whether or not I was okay.

Guilt slammed me in the face. I was a total douche for getting myself into this mess. I sighed heavily.

Was I ever going to fucking change?

Not if I was locked up.

Fuck me.

Chapter 2

SAMANTHA

PRESENT DAY

Someone knocked on the front door of my apartment.

"It must be them," I said to Christos, and walked out of the bathroom to go answer. I checked the peephole and opened the door with a smile on my face. Christos stood right behind me.

"Hey, guys!" Romeo said cheerfully, standing on the balcony walkway outside. He wore a new steampunk coat I hadn't seen before. Made from tailored black wool, the coat had intricate black-thread embroidery and twin rows of vertical black buttons running down the front and back. As usual, his monocle dangled from one of the coat's buttons. Buckled black boots covered his feet. "Don't I look festive?" he jested while holding his monocle up to one eye.

"Romeo!" I said, holding out my arms.

Romeo wrapped me up in a huge hug. "So good to see you, Sam!"

"What up, man," Christos smiled.

Romeo released me and his eyes roamed all over Christos. "Wow, Sam, I forgot how hot your boyfriend is! Can I lick him from head to toe?"

"No!" I laughed.

"How about just a nipple?"

"No, Romeo!" I insisted.

Christos chuckled, indulging in Romeo's bad behavior.

Someone had to put a stop to it. "Down, Romeo!" I ordered jokingly.

"Easy girl," Romeo faux-frowned. "I was just window shopping,"

"Seriously, dude, I'm flattered," Christos beamed, totally at ease with Romeo's fawning, "but I play for the opposing team."

"Oh! Can I be your water boy?" Romeo pleaded. "Hand you clean towels in the locker room? Bend over and pick up the soap in the shower when you drop it? I'll do whatever you want, Christos. Have your way with me!" He stepped past me, dropped to his knees beside Christos, and wrapped his arms around Christos' legs. Romeo began bawling insincerely, "Please, Sam! Just one sip from his chalice! I want to taste his sweet nectar!" he whined.

"No, Romeo!" I giggled. He was so ridiculous, and I loved him for it.

"Sorry, man," Christos laughed. "I'm sworn to Samantha."

Romeo sneered and rolled his eyes. He stood up and smoothed out his black embroidered steampunk jacket. "You're such a wuss for the puss, Christos," he said dismissively.

"That I am," Christos chuckled.

"Well, we should go," Romeo said, finally over it, "before Kamiko withers away in my car."

"I'm still not dressed!" I blurted. "I can't go out on New Year's in a t-shirt and jeans!"

Romeo frowned. "Have you even picked out an outfit?"

"No," I said guiltily.

Romeo rolled his eyes.. "In that case, I better get Kamiko or she might die of starvation while you do." He winked at Christos.

I stamped my foot and groused, "It doesn't take me that long to pick an outfit!"

Christos and Romeo exchanged a doubtful look.

"You guys suck!" I stormed into my bedroom while Christos and Romeo broke into laughter.

SAMANTHA

Fortunately, I'd finished my hair before Christos had come over earlier. While Christos, Romeo, and Kamiko chatted in my living room, I threw on some eyeliner and lip gloss, and set about picking out an outfit.

My mind drifted as I rifled through my closet.

I still hadn't told my parents about wanting to change my major to Art. I'd wanted to avoid starting World War Smith at my parents' house over Winter Break, so I hadn't brought it up. I'd have to tell them sooner or later. But tonight was New Year's Eve, and I planned on celebrating it with the man I loved. Christos had been amazingly supportive since we'd met. Going forward, I hoped that I could give back to him the devotion he'd shown me.

I finally decided on skinny pants and matching heels, a print shirt, and the new, super-cute pleather coat I'd snagged off of ebay for twenty bucks. I grabbed my favorite clutch purse and came out of my bedroom. "Ta-da!"

"Wow, Sam, you're runway hot!" Kamiko said. She stood up from the couch and gave me a big hug.

"Thanks, Kamiko," I smiled. "How was your Winter Break?"

"Pretty boss," Kamiko said.

I was confused. "You mean you enjoyed it?"

"No," she smirked, "I mean my family bossed me around the whole time. Not just my parents. My older brothers and sisters, too. Since I'm the youngest, it's like having six parents. They ragged on me all break because I got a B+ in O-chem. So I locked myself in my room the whole time and binged on watching episodes of Adventure Time and Bravest Warriors while drawing both show's characters in my sketchbook."

"Did you draw Catbug?" Romeo asked.

"Sugar peas!" Kamiko squealed, flinging her arms wide.

I wasn't sure who or what a Catbug was. I suspected I'd find out over the course of winter quarter while hanging in Kamiko's dorm room between classes.

"Everybody ready?" Christos asked.

"I think so," I said. Romeo and Kamiko nodded at me. "Let's hit it!"

We all piled into Christos' 1968 Camaro downstairs.

"Where are we going, Christos?" Romeo asked from the back seat. "Sam said it was some kind of awesome surprise."

"It should be pretty awesome," Christos replied.

"Are you going to kidnap us, tie us up in some morbid dungeon, then have your way with us?" Romeo mused.

"Only Samantha," Christos joked, rubbing my knee.

"Always a bridesmaid," Romeo sulked.

Christos fired up the Camaro, its engine rumbling in anticipation of the open road as Christos pulled the car onto the street outside my apartment.

SAMANTHA

A short time later, we pulled into a parking lot just south of the airport, right next to the water in the San Diego Bay. The sun rested on the horizon. The sky overhead was a mix of purple and magenta hues dabbed with golden clouds that caught the last of the sun's rays. It was beautiful.

"Welcome to the marina," Christos said as he shifted the Camaro into park.

"What're we doing here?" I asked excitedly.

"Going for a boat ride," he replied.

Romeo leaned forward, both hands on the seat back in front of him, poking his head between me and Christos. "I knew it! You're going to take us to a deserted island and make us your pirate slaves! Christos, please tell me you're going to wear an eyepatch!"

Christos grinned. "Sorry, man. I left it at home. Besides, the closest island is San Clemente. The Navy owns that, so it's not deserted."

"Is San Clemente filled with sex-starved Navy men? If it is, you can drop me off there. I won't complain," Romeo smiled.

I laughed. "OMG, Romeo! Do you ever quit?"

"My apologies, Sam, I'm just so excited to see you all again after break. You know how reunions make me a horny bitch."

Still laughing, I climbed out of the car and flipped the front seat forward so Romeo and Kamiko could get out.

"I can't wait to see this boat," Romeo said excitedly, clambering out of the car.

"Maybe the captain will make you his cabin boy," Kamiko said, following.

"I hope he looks like Gregory Peck as Captain Ahab," Romeo tittered. "I'll walk his gang plank any day, if you know what I mean."

"I remember that movie!" I said. "We watched Moby Dick in high school during AP English."

"I bet Romeo fantasizes about Ahab hunting for *Romeo's* white whale," Kamiko quipped.

"You guys!" I pleaded.

Christos chuckled, totally amused.

"Well, it's more of an olive-colored whale," Romeo snickered like a crazy man, "but yeah, I'd totally let Gregory Peck as Ahab hunt for it all he wants, as long as he harpoons me before the night is over." Romeo wiggled his butt at us.

I clapped my hand to my forehead. "I think Romeo's disease is contagious," I sighed to Christos. "Guys, can we talk about Santa Claus, or something non-sexual for, like, five seconds?"

"You know," Romeo said mischievously, "I always loved it when my parents put me on dirty old Santa's lap as a kid..."

I scowled, "Okay, you just ruined Christmas for me, Romeo. Like, forever."

Romeo cackled with glee as we walked out along the dock toward wherever our boat was moored. We passed dozens of different kinds of boats of every shape and size. Were we getting on a sailboat? Or one of those cool motorboats that went a hundred miles an hour?

As we walked farther and farther, the boats got bigger and bigger.

"Which one is it, Christos?" I asked.

"The one with all the people," he said.

"The huge one at the end?"

"Yup."

"OMG, it looks like a freakin' yacht."

"It *is* a yacht." He grinned.

"Is it yours?" I gasped.

"Hardly," he smiled.

There was a small crowd of a half-dozen people still on the dock and more on board.

"Sam!" Madison stepped out of the crowd and waved. She jogged toward me, gorgeous as ever. "So good to see you, girlfriend!"

"Mads!" We hugged like long-lost BFFs. "I didn't know you were going to be here! You look totally Hollywood tonight, girl! You're all glammed out!"

"Gotta dress up once in awhile," she grinned. "Yeah, Jake made me keep it a secret."

Jake stepped up behind her. "What up, guys." He bumped fists with Christos before they clapped backs. "How was D.C., bro?"

"Cold as witch tits," Christos replied.

"I hear that, bro," Jake said knowingly.

"Why do guys always say things like that?" Madison frowned. "Have either of you ever *been* with a witch?"

Christos and Jake looked back and forth between me and Madison, then back at each other.

I frowned at them. "Don't answer that."

They both burst out laughing.

"Such boys," Madison said, putting her arm around Jake. "Sam, I brought leashes and muzzles for them both, just in case."

"So, Christos," I asked, "whose boat is this?"

He put his arm lovingly around me. "Didn't I tell you?"

Despite the festive atmosphere, I jumped as if someone had driven a dump-truck full of black cats and broken mirrors over my grave. I gasped with trepidation, "Tell me what?"

"Uhhh…" Christos mumbled, caught off guard by my sudden change in tone.

Fearing an unexpectedly ominous turn of events, I peered into Christos' eyes. A quick flash blinked across them, then it was gone.

Why did I have the sudden conviction that with every awesome surprise came an equally earthquaking catch?

What wasn't he telling me?

CHRISTOS

THREE MONTHS EARLIER…

Two uniformed deputies took me out of interrogation and led me to booking.

When the guy behind the camera took my mug shot, I made sure to grin. I figured if I was going to be on the cover of one of those pulp WANTED magazines you could get at 7-Eleven for a buck, I may as well flash my pearlies. Get some lovelorn hunnies writing me on the block. Shit, who was I kidding? I couldn't wait to get processed and get the fuck out of there.

Samantha.

The female officer who led me through fingerprint scanning, DNA swab, cataloging my personals, and fitting me for a prison jumper and paper slippers, was all business. I tried joking with her when I showered and lathered up with the lice shampoo, but Sergeant Stonewall kept her back to me and didn't peek once. She'd probably seen it all before.

Oh well. I was just trying to lighten shit up while I could.

After I toweled off and stepped into my orange jumper, Sergeant Stonewall led me through a series of bulletproof doors. She maintained the social barrier between us the entire time.

I knew from experience to harden my face before I stepped through the final door into the awaiting dormitory. There would be a dozen or more aggressive criminals inside ready to size me up. With my tats, my height, and my impressive muscles, nobody fucked with me, and that was an order.

Sergeant Stonewall signaled the guard at the far end of the hallway. The electric lock buzzed open and Stonewall opened the door for me.

Time to play.

All eyes were on me when I stood in the doorframe. They sniffed for fresh fish. I glared at them.

No dice, fuckers. I'm the bull in this ring.

Psychological intimidation beat out physical violence. There was enough ugliness in this place without me adding to it for real. The men went back to playing cards and doing pushups and wasting away.

I dropped onto an unoccupied bottom bunk, which I preferred because it blocked out the overhead lights. You had to breathe through your mouth, otherwise the smell of human desperation was overpowering. I laced my fingers behind my head and did my best to relax.

The first thing I saw when I closed my eyes was Samantha's smiling face.

God, she was beautiful. Somewhere between Monet's Water Lilies and one of John William Waterhouse's river nymphs.

Memories of Samantha flooded my mind, blotting out the dreariness of my horrible surroundings. Images of her angelic innocence whisked me away to paradise. Something about her open face, the freedom with which her unbridled emotions played across it, touched my heart for the thousandth time that day.

I held in a happy laugh, keeping it safe from the harm that waited to pounce on my joy if I let any out.

I almost felt greedy, as if sharing the good vibes Samantha brought me might actually bring some positive energy to the men in the room around me, but I didn't want any opportunists stomping on my good mood.

Normally, dudes in lock-up would go on and on about fucking countless hot chicks with legendary looks. The stories were about as believable as guys on the outside telling "I caught a fish this big" stories. Trading tall-tales about notching your bedpost was a bonding ritual worth a few laughs when the inmates weren't fighting to survive. But those stories were mostly blustery bullshit.

Samantha, on the other hand, was truth and goodness. At that moment, I needed all the goodness I could get.

I burrowed deeper into my mind. I imagined reaching my hand out to stroke Samantha's cheek and her leaning into it. Not that she had done that today, not even close. I mean, she gave me plenty of green lights, especially after I cleaned her car, but she'd kept me at arm's length most of the day, sizing me up.

Her uncertainty drove me crazy. In a good way. I wasn't used to her kind of behavior from women.

Thing was, usually, when I walked, I swaggered like my dick weighed a ton and hauling it around took gorilla strength. For some reason, Samantha made me want to drop the act. There was a moment earlier, when we'd been walking to the dorms and searching for paper towels for her car, when I'd almost cracked. For a second, all I'd wanted to do was take her hand in mine and skip along together like we were in kindergarten. Just me and her, looking for paper towels. On a mini-adventure.

Me and Samantha.

I suddenly imagined writing "**Christos + Samantha**" on my binder and drawing a heart around it, if I had one. Man, I was nuts. I thought only girls were supposed to do that shit.

I smiled and inhaled deeply, feeling Samantha's energy swirl through me.

I pictured her leaning toward me, lips ready for a tender kiss. Man, was I going through puberty again? I hadn't had thoughts like this since I was chasing chicks in junior high. But it felt wonderful. Like the first day of summer vacation. That's what Samantha was for me, when you get down to it. A vacation from bullshit, from image, from posing, from acting whatever part I felt I needed to play at any given moment.

She was straight-up relaxation.

I must have been trancing, because I could swear I heard soft waves whispering across warm sand and felt a cool breeze kissing my toes as the sun licked my skin. Samantha was right next to me, I could feel her presence.

I almost freaked out, thinking some AC/DC inmate was trying to tongue my toes while I appeared to nap. I peeked out one eye, just to make sure I wasn't losing it. Seeing the coast was clear, I dropped back through whatever astral portal was pulling my heart out of this place and into that distant utopia where Samantha waited for me.

A second later, I was gone from the real world completely.

Samantha and I were lying on loungers on a remote desert island somewhere on the other side of the planet, the fingers of our hands laced together while we sipped cool drinks on the diamond sand. There was not a soul around for hundreds of miles. We inhabited our own private paradise.

I didn't have a clear conception of time, but it must have been right around sunset in the real world. Samantha was probably staring at the sunset at that exact moment, sharing it with me. I don't know how or why I was convinced of this fact, but I knew it to be true.

Was I seeing it through her eyes?

Fuck me if I was. It seemed so goddamned real.

Samantha turned to me and gazed into my eyes. Her face was serenely calm. I could see her complete and total beauty for the first time. It even transcended that moment she'd been in front of my grandfather's painting in the museum. That had been awesome, but this was even better. This time, she was 100% relaxed, completely and totally at peace with herself, her life, the entire world. In this moment, she was fully the woman she *wanted* to become. My heart melted. Holy shit, I'd never felt anything like it. I desperately wanted her to become this woman she was capable of, like her finding herself would somehow complete *me*.

The idea made me shiver with joy and…fear.

Thing was, I lived for taking risks. No matter how fucking frightening they were.

Samantha…

I wanted more. Fuck, I *needed* more.

I needed *us*.

The astral image of Samantha gazed into my soul. Her eyes

narrowed ever so slightly, as if she was struggling with something monumental, then her face relaxed, and all doubt fell away.

"I love you, Christos," she whispered to me, inches away on her beach lounger. We were still on that island paradise together.

What the fuck?! She didn't know my real name, I'd told her my name was Adonis. How did she know to call me Christos?! I started to shake in my swimsuit on my lounger, like something was ripping away the armor around my heart.

I panicked.

"Don't be afraid, *agápi mou*," she whispered, leaning against the armrest of her lounger, caressing my arm with her fingertips as the waves whispered against the shore. "I love you." She reached over to kiss me. Her lips were so close, I could feel their warmth on mine as her sweet breath caressed my soul.

My heart raced.

Suddenly, black storm clouds blanketed the sun. Thunder hammered across the sky.

Samantha was slipping away. I couldn't breathe, couldn't get air. I was scared shitless. I rocketed out of that tropical paradise, all the way across the universe, and shot up in my cramped bunk.

Gasping, I blinked my eyes and shook my head, making sure I was awake. I looked around.

The jail dormitory was totally silent. Nobody was awake. The place was a tomb. They kept the lights on 24/7, but turned off half the fluorescent banks after lights out. It must have been well past midnight.

I rolled over and did my best to go back to sleep.

Sometime later, darkness overtook me.

Horrible darkness.

Something was chasing Samantha. Some *one*. A terrible presence was trying to overcome her, trying to tear away her innocence. She was afraid. I wanted to help her, but I couldn't reach her. She was all alone. There was nothing I could do. She was wounded, unable to escape her tormentor.

I couldn't protect her and it was killing me.

Samantha…

Agápi mou…

Chapter 3

SAMANTHA

PRESENT DAY

Standing on the dock in the Marina, shaking with low-level fear, I did my best to hide my tension as I waited for Christos to clue me in on whatever it was he was hiding from me.

Before he could, Tiffany Kingston-*Whore*house, I mean *White*house, emerged from the center of the small remaining group of people chatting with her on the dock.

The last light of the sunset tinted Tiffany's skin that perfect golden brown you only see on supermodels or swimsuit magazine covers. I'm pretty sure Tiffany had hired a rock video crew to choose just that moment to blow a gust of wind into her shimmering, silken hair. She looked spectacular, and I hated her for it.

Was *she* what Christos had been hiding?

"Hey, Christos!" she squealed, "You came!" She flung her arms around him in total disregard for my existence, nearly slicing my eyeball open with her nails. She kissed Christos' cheek affectionately.

Hello, did she not see me? I glared bullets at Queen Bee-otch.

Christos broke away from Tiffany's embrace before either of them went down in the fully-automatic hail of my jealousy.

I could tell Christos was uncomfortable with Tiffany's flirty come-on, but he played it cool and draped his arm casually around my shoulders, marking a clear boundary between himself and Tiffany.

I smiled triumphantly and reminded myself this was Christos Manos, after all. Not some jerk like Damian Wolfram. I didn't need to worry about Christos having a wandering eye. I trusted him, even if a woman like Tiffany made me nervous.

I took a deep breath. I wasn't going to let Tiffany get in the way of my happiness. I was a changed woman. All that crazy jealousy and self-doubt was behind me.

I hoped.

"Who're your friends, Christos?" Tiffany yawned absently.

Holy Memory Loss, did she not even remember? I sighed. Probably not. All she ever thought about was herself, I'd bet.

Two long-legged hobots walked up behind Tiffany and gave me dirty looks. They were probably Delta Pi Delta worker bees in service to Her Snideness, but I wasn't sure without their bulging sorority sweaters.

"You remember Samantha," Christos offered.

Tiffany narrowed one eye like a nervous ferret before turning her nose up at me. "I didn't recognize her all dressed up."

Her worker bees giggled.

As usual, Tiffany projected the air of having everything you wished you had but didn't. And yet, for once it was the other way around. I knew how badly Tiffany wanted Christos, but he was with me, not her.

I wanted to spin in circles while doing the happy dance, but I wasn't a bitch like Tiffany. So I did the happy dance in my head, and made a mental note to do the real thing later in the privacy of my apartment, with Christos.

We could happy dance together.

Ignoring the fact that Tiffany was such a Queen Bee-otch that she still wouldn't acknowledge me like a polite human being, I offered my hand for her to shake. "Good to see you, Tiffany," I smiled. I wouldn't stoop like she had.

Tiffany shook my hand absently, not even looking me in the eye. Her hand slid free from mine after barely a shake.

Whatever.

Resting her hands on her hips, Tiffany surveyed the boat behind her. "Well, I did say to bring whoever you wanted." She turned back to Christos and smiled. "We can always use more help in the kitchen."

Tiffany's hobot henchwomen giggled.

I really needed to carry a bigger handbag on outings like this. I couldn't fit a bazooka in my little clutch, and you never knew when you needed to blow some bitch's head off on short notice.

"Welcome aboard, Christos," Tiffany said. "Good to see you again, Jake. Make yourselves at home." She smiled at Christos and Jake in turn, but ignored Romeo, Kamiko, Madison, and myself.

How did Tiffany manage to spoil everything with the greatest of ease? It would take an act of heroism for me to enjoy New Year's Eve at this rate.

For a second, I considered asking Christos to take us elsewhere. The six of us could have fun wherever we went. I glanced at Madison, not sure what to do.

Mads lifted a compassionate eyebrow and nodded toward the parking lot with a questioning look. She knew from experience how annoying Tiffany could be.

Sadly, I realized if we left, it would be giving in to Tiffany's aloof bullying. I had done enough of that in my life already.

Emo. Goth. Sorceress. Suicide Watch...

I noticed Romeo and Kamiko marveling at the boat.

"Wow, this thing is huge," Romeo gawked. "I can't wait to see the inside."

"It looks like a frickin' spaceship!" Kamiko whispered enviously.

Neither of them knew how consistently annoying Tiffany could be. They were ready to have fun tonight. No need to disappoint them. I could make this work, if I put my mind to it. Maybe Tiffany would play nice the whole trip and I wouldn't have to worry about anything.

Bitch. Slut. Whore...

I took a deep breath. I wasn't going to let my demons get to me. Screw them!

"Come on, you guys," I said confidently to the gang. This was a New Year's Eve yacht trip after all, and I'd be lying if I said I wasn't curious about what awaited us.

The six of us walked up the ramp together, Jake and Christos trailing at the rear.

When we were out of Tiffany's earshot, Madison leaned into me and whispered in my ear, "Is it just me, or does the perfume Tiff the Quiff is wearing tonight make her smell like mouse farts?"

I belted out laughter so hard, I would've fallen off the ramp and into the water, if not for the handrailing. I grabbed it for support.

I saw Tiffany whip around and give the group of us a dirty look.

Romeo, ever perceptive, had overheard Madison's remark, and

leaned against me while he quietly cackled, "I thought Tiffany smelled a bit musty."

I exchanged a smile with Romeo.

Romeo's eyes twinkled with good humor. "You *know* Tiffany has a poochy cooch."

I was confused. "What, like a pouch?"

"Yes," he said. "It's where she hides the mice. Down *below.* I bet it's a regular mouse sanctuary in there."

I broke into fresh laughter.

Kamiko had overheard too, and stifled her own giggles.

"Sam, ignore Tiffany," Madison encouraged. "Maybe we can knock her over the side when we're in international waters. No one will ever know." She grinned archly.

Kamiko pretended to frown. "Wouldn't that be polluting the environment?"

"I won't tell, if you won't," Romeo winked.

"Thanks, guys," I said. "I needed that." I straightened up and climbed the rest of the ramp, surrounded by the bestest friends a girl could have.

I'd been on rowboats and maybe a few canoes. But nothing like this. There were probably another thirty people on board. The cabin on the main deck literally had a living room, dining room, and kitchen with a full-size stainless-steel refrigerator. A narrow flight of steps led to a second story above and a spiral staircase led to another level below. I'd never been on a three-story boat before. Tiffany hadn't been exaggerating.

"This place is nicer than my parents' house," Madison marveled.

"I know, right?" Romeo said. "I think it's *bigger* than my parents' house."

SAMANTHA

When everyone was on board, two crewmen dressed in fancy black slacks and vests over their white long-sleeve button-down shirts threw some ropes onto the dock. I felt engines rumbling softly beneath my feet as the yacht pulled away from the pier and motored out of the marina.

Christos and Jake knew quite a few of Tiffany's friends and seemed totally in their element. They were sucked into the center of the crowd in the main cabin.

Within seconds, every woman in the room had turned to focus on Christos. His undeniable beauty drew their attention like a magnet. They couldn't look away from his mesmerizing presence. Christos seemed oblivious as he chatted with Jake and the other guys. He'd probably grown numb to this kind of attention after years of it.

From afar, I watched this process unfold for several minutes. The women all primped and preened unconsciously, fluffing their hair, adjusting their dresses to maximum effect, shifting their body language to point their pelvises at Christos, and shoving out their chests.

When Christos chuckled at a random joke, flashing his perfect teeth and panty-dropping smile, several women's eyes goggled and their jaws went slack. When Christos ran his hand through his perfectly mussed hair, other women literally clutched their chests, ready to swoon.

Did they even know they were doing it? Somehow I doubted it. Who wanted to admit that a mere human male, no matter how perfect a specimen he was, could turn them from young women into drooling idiots in heat?

I was torn between embarrassment for all of womankind, and sympathy. Heck, even the men were fawning. Everyone was susceptible. With the exception of Jake, who was almost as handsome as Christos, the other men were smitten, all of them crushing on Christos, in the throes of blatant bromances.

To be fair, I was no more able to resist Christos' physical allure than anyone else. I was hooked. Addicted. Jealousy swam up my throat and threatened to choke me.

Suddenly, Christos glanced at me and cocked his head, throwing his dimpled smile directly at me. He blew me an air kiss.

"That was for me," Romeo joked.

I smirked at Romeo. "Keep your air lips off my man, you horny bitch," I joked, then blew a kiss back to Christos.

He mimed leaning up to catch it before returning to conversation with Jake and some other bitches, I mean, ladies.

I reminded myself that Christos was with me. Not them. Looking at him, at *my* man, I suddenly felt greedy and desperate and horny and proud, all at the same time. Every woman in the room wanted what I had, but Christos was mine, *all* mine.

I think *I* was about to swoon. I shook my head and took a deep breath, trying to clear my head.

"Come on you guys," Madison said excitedly. "Let's watch from the bow!" She grabbed my hand while Romeo and Kamiko followed.

"Check it out," Madison pointed, "that's the naval base on Coronado island."

"Can someone tell the captain to drop me off there?" Romeo asked. "I'm thirsty for seamen."

"Gag!" I said.

"I never gag," Romeo said confidently.

Me, Madison, and Kamiko exchanged a grimace.

A few minutes later, Tiffany's yacht had cleared the San Diego Bay and entered open water. It sure was fast for such a big boat. Wind whipped through our hair as we stood on the front of the boat. Romeo and Kamiko had huge grins on their faces.

Romeo raised his arms and pumped his fists. "I'm the queen of the world! Woo hoo!"

"It's king, Romeo," Kamiko giggled. "*King* of the world."

"Don't ruin my moment," Romeo grinned while basking in the sea breeze, arms wide.

The city lights of San Diego shrank into the distance until they were but twinkling pinpricks against the purple velvet sky. To the west, the last light of the sun faded to pink on the horizon. I traded a smile with Madison.

Eventually, the yacht slowed to a stop in calm waters.

"Dinner is served!" Tiffany called from the dining room while someone clanged a hand bell.

The dining room table on the yacht only seated eight, so dinner was served buffet style. Stainless-steel food warmers covered the surface of the table. One of the crewmen in black and white, now wearing an ankle-length white apron, was pulling the lids off.

We all got in line and grabbed plates. While we waited at the back of the crowd, the other crewman, also in an apron, approached us with a platter brimming with gourmet finger-food.

"What is it?" I asked the crewman.

"Seared sea scallops in a tarragon butter sauce," he said pleasantly.

We all took one while we waited for the buffet. Everyone agreed the scallops were totally yummy. Eventually, Christos and Jake joined us in line. The six of us loaded our plates and climbed up to the top deck together to sit down and eat.

"Wow, this is great food," Jake said.

"Totally," Madison said.

Even if Tiffany was an Olympic bitch, she knew how to pick out a great menu. I doubted she cooked any of it herself, but at least she had good taste, and the food was free.

Was it possible that I could enjoy this evening without Tiffany ruining it? I believed it was. I crossed my fingers.

While I chewed on a mouthful of crab cake, Kamiko leaned into me and whispered, "Don't look now, but here comes the snake charmer."

I looked up, straight into the eyes of Brandon Charboneau. He climbed the ladder onto the top deck, holding a plate of food and glass of wine.

"Greetings, everyone," Brandon said smoothly, holding up his wine glass to toast us.

"What up, Brandon," Christos said with a smile, raising his own glass. "I didn't realize you were on board."

"I was down in the boiler room shoveling coal into the furnaces," Brandon joked.

Romeo smiled hopefully. "Did you have your shirt off and were you all sweaty from the exertion?"

Everyone chuckled.

"I'm afraid not," Brandon said suavely.

Brandon's father owned the gallery that had sold Christos' latest paintings. Brandon was tan, tall, debonair, and very handsome, but there was something slithery about him that always bothered me.

Brandon slid into the end of the booth next to me and set his plate of food on the table. His knee brushed against mine and I jumped.

"Good evening, Samantha," he said charmingly.

I felt trapped. But Christos was sitting on my right, in case of emergency. I glanced at him, worried he'd be irritated by Brandon's proximity, but he merely chewed on a bite of lobster and smiled at Brandon.

I loved that about Christos. He never seemed to get jealous, unlike lame Damian, who always had.

Christos was an inspiration. I leaned into him affectionately and he reached over to caress my forearm. After smiling at me, he wiped his lips with his napkin, and gave me a smoochy kiss.

I was always tickled by how Christos worked the bad boy thing and the gentlemen thing in equal measures.

Brandon smoothed his own napkin on his lap and looked at everyone. "If I remember correctly, you're Kamiko Nishimura, and you're Romeo Fabiano? Did I get that right?" He flashed a warm smile at them.

"Wow, you remembered!" Kamiko smiled.

"Running the gallery requires that I remember a lot of names." Brandon grinned and leaned over the table to shake her hand, then Romeo's. I think Romeo swooned.

"I don't think we've met," Brandon said to Jake and Madison.

"Jake Stratton." He and Brandon shook hands firmly.

"Madison Lockhart."

Brandon shook her hand gently. "Charmed," he smiled. Smooth as always.

"How's the gallery, Mr. Charboneau?" Kamiko asked politely. I think Kamiko still wanted to make a good impression on Brandon, in case she ever wanted to sell her own amazing art through his gallery. And because Brandon was hot, even if he was a serpent in an expensive suit. Plus, I'm pretty sure Kamiko had a crush on him.

"Fabulous," Brandon answered, "Ever since Christos' sold-out show last year, new customers have been pouring through the doors on a daily basis."

"That's awesome!" Kamiko said.

"Christos tells me that you're an artist?" Brandon asked Kamiko. She blushed. "Sort of."

"Kamiko's amazing," I said. "Don't let her bashfulness fool you. Maybe you could sell her work at your gallery, Brandon. She's totally good enough."

"Sam!" Kamiko protested. "I don't even paint in oils!" She blushed crimson, and I half-expected exclamation points to pop out over her head while her face turned cartoony like in one of her Japanese anime shows.

"Sam's right," Romeo said in a normal tone of voice, perhaps for the first time that night. "Kamiko really is hyper-talented."

"Aww, thank you, Romeo," Kamiko said.

"Perhaps you should stop by the gallery, Kamiko," Brandon suggested. "Bring your portfolio. I'd love to see your work."

"Really?" Kamiko beamed. "But all I have is watercolors."

"We have an annual contemporary artists' show that features all types of artistic media."

Kamiko glowed hopefully. "Really?"

"Certainly. Call and make an appointment, anytime."

"Wow! I'll do that!" Kamiko smiled.

I was excited for her. Her art was amazing, and I still thought it would be a shame if she never did anything with it. I suspected that she didn't love the idea of becoming a doctor with the same passion as her parents.

I was in a similar predicament with mine. They wanted me to be Sam Smith, CPA. But the last thing I'd dreamed of as a girl was becoming an accountant. At least Kamiko would help people and save lives. I would just end up pushing numbers around.

"Why don't you submit a piece to the show, Samantha?" Christos encouraged.

"What?" I blushed. "I couldn't! I don't have any paintings!"

"Any type of media is acceptable," Brandon said. "Whenever you're ready, bring something down to the gallery for me to look at. The show is still a few months out."

I looked at Christos, uncertain. I felt like I was getting in over my head.

"Don't worry, Samantha. You can totally whip something up in time." Christos flashed a first-place smile at me like we were both total winners.

He was so confident in me, it was almost impossible for me to doubt myself. My love for him grew every single day. Sometimes, it seemed to get bigger by the hour.

"Okay. I'll do it!" I smiled.

"That's my girl," he said while rubbing my shoulder. "I totally know you'll nail it."

Maybe my New Year's resolution needed to be finally going down to the Registrar's Office in a couple of days to change my major to Art, no matter what my parents said, World War Smith be damned.

Everyone finished eating their dinners over chatty conversation.

The food really was amazing.

"Anyone want to look around the rest of the boat?" I suggested.

"Totally," Madison agreed.

"I can't wait to snoop through Tiffany's medicine cabinets," Romeo said impishly. "She's probably got lots of drugs."

"I've got to hit the head," Jake said, standing up.

"Make sure you don't break it," Madison quipped. "Tiffany's toilet probably costs more than you've earned all year."

Jake smiled at her. "If I win Mavericks this March, then I'll have plenty of extra cash."

"Dude," Christos gawked, "did you finally get invited to surf Mavericks? Why didn't you tell me?!" He flung his arms around Jake, clapping him on the back.

"Cool your jets, bro," Jake laughed. "I'm number seven on the alternates list. Wanna go break some kneecaps, make sure I get on the invite list?" he joked. "We only gotta put seven guys out of commission, and I'm totally in."

"Give me the list of names," Christos smiled, "and I'll make it happen."

Everyone laughed while gravitating toward the staircase leading down to the main deck, except Brandon.

"Christos?" Brandon asked. "Do you mind if I talk to you for a minute?"

"Sure," he said to Brandon. To me he said, "I'll catch up with you in a second."

"All right," I said. "Let's go, you guys."

I followed Madison, Jake, Romeo, and Kamiko down the ladder to the main deck, leaving Christos alone with Brandon.

CHRISTOS

Samantha waved at me as she and everyone else left the upper deck.

It was just me and Brandon.

We walked casually to the railing on the back of the upper deck and looked out at the open water.

As long as I'd known the guy, he was never what I'd call a true friend. My family knew his family and we did business together. I didn't *dis*like the guy. But did I genuinely like him? It changed by the minute, depending on his agenda. He could be a decent ally one second, or that thorny thistle in your sock when you're trying to run a marathon the next.

"Christos," Brandon smiled warmly, holding up his wine glass, "I have to congratulate you, the sales at your first solo show were nothing short of astounding." He clinked wine glasses with me.

"Thanks, man," I said, sipping my wine, wondering where he was going with this. Brandon always had an angle.

"Now I'm getting calls from new buyers almost daily. Celebrity clients, famous collectors, many of them international. You're hot right now, Christos. The influential buyers who dictate the art market want your paintings, and they want them now. How soon do you think you can have a new solo show ready? I'm confident we can double your prices from the last show, and sell everything." Brandon's eyes flickered dollar signs.

There was the angle. Me busting my ass to churn out new work. I had no doubt Brandon was in love with the idea.

I smeared my hand across my stubbled cheeks and sighed heavily.

Reality check.

This was exactly the same shit that had turned my dad from an artist into an alcoholic. He got caught up in catering to a bunch of rich shitheads who didn't give a fuck about him. They just wanted to say they had an original Nikolos Manos hanging in their mansions. Almost like they wanted a piece of him, like his hand or his foot, spiked to the wall over their fireplaces like a human sacrifice.

Look, everybody, they'd all wanted to be able to say to their snooty friends, *here hangs the body of Nikolos Manos, and I own it.*

Shit. I could cut my own head off, have it mounted on a wood plaque, and have Brandon sell it for a hundred million bucks. I'd be the most famous artist in history for a stunt like that. All Van Gogh had to do was lose an ear. Imagine what my whole head would bring.

I sighed heavily.

"Let me know what you need, Christos," Brandon said warmly, like he would do anything for me, like it wasn't about the money, like all he cared about was little old me.

"Supplies?" he continued, "I'll make sure you have whatever

you need delivered directly to Spiridon's house. Art models? I can call some modeling agencies up in L.A. and get you some fresh faces. Fresh faces always sell paintings."

What I needed was a break from his sales pitch. It was making my head spin.

"But there's one face I think you need to paint more than any other," he said deviously.

I knew where this was going. "Yeah, who's that?" I smirked.

"Samantha."

I arched an eyebrow. I hated it when he called her Samantha. He knew I was the only one who called her that.

"I've said it before," he continued, "you need your Mona Lisa, your Girl with a Pearl Earring. Samantha is that girl."

Why did I get a bad feeling all of a sudden?

"I don't think she's going to want to sit for a painting," I said.

Brandon scrutinized me shrewdly. I saw the dollar signs cash-registering behind his eyes.

"No matter," he said calmly. "I'll call L.A. We'll find faces for you to paint. The main thing is that we keep your momentum going."

I chuckled. "Gotta keep the animals fed." Before they chewed my fingers off.

Why did I feel like the golden handcuffs of my art career had become a golden noose around my neck? Oh yeah, because my dad was a famous artist, and it tore my family apart and nearly killed him with drink.

Question was, would I be next?

Amend that. At this rate, with Brandon breathing down my back, the only question was:

When?

Man, I thought I'd had problems when my ass had been hauled to jail three months ago.

Turned out, the shit was just getting started.

I threw back my wine glass and emptied it in one swallow.

I needed another fucking drink.

Chapter 4

SAMANTHA

For the next few hours, everyone had a good time on the boat. The buffet on the dining room table was replaced with an elaborate collection of scrumptious desserts. Me, Madison, and Kamiko had eyes bigger than our stomachs and wanted to munch on each one. Fortunately, Christos and Jake were happy to gulp down what we didn't finish. Romeo avoided the desserts despite his desire, citing the maintenance of his girlish figure.

We circulated amongst the people on board, and it turned out that not all of Tiffany's friends were snooty bitches like she was. I had way more fun than I'd expected.

When the hour approached midnight, everyone gathered in the living room on the main deck.

Gold and silver balloons now decorated the room. Foil-covered letters reading "HAPPY NEW YEAR" hung from the ceiling in several places. People passed around bags of noisemakers containing classic paper blowout whistles, glitter-covered party horns, plastic knockers, and those plastic champagne-bottle confetti poppers.

I snagged one of the confetti poppers. They were always my favorite. Romeo grabbed two golden party horns and put them up to his nostrils.

"You don't sneeze in them!" I joked.

He winked at me. "What do you mean, I thought that's how you worked them!" He gave them a quick snoot-blast and they wheezed weakly. "That was lame. I think I need to blow harder." He sucked in a big breath, ready to blow.

"No don't!" Kamiko pleaded.

"Kidding," Romeo grinned.

Madison and Jake had an arm around each other and were busy

dueling with plastic clackers, laughing hysterically. They were so into each other.

Christos slid his arms around me. "Did you grab me a noisemaker? I totally want one of those air-horn cans."

"You're such a guy," I smiled. "You always have to have the biggest, loudest thing in the room, don't you?"

"That's why I picked you," he joked.

"Are you saying I'm big and loud?" I smiled.

"Loud maybe, but the only thing big about you is your heart, *agápi mou.*"

I gazed into his eyes. So blue, so precious. His exquisite smile widened over his even teeth. My body flushed with heat when he bit his full lower lip. I totally wanted to nibble on that lip myself. He leaned down for a quick kiss.

The two guys dressed in black and white circulated the main deck with trays loaded with champagne flutes.

Tiffany clinked a glass with a fork to get everyone's attention. She was so party appropriate.

"Grab some champagne, everybody!" Tiffany cheered, "it's almost midnight!" I'm pretty sure she'd been captain of the cheerleading squad in high school, based on her tone of voice and delivery. She probably carried pompons in her pockets at all times, in case of a cheer emergency.

Christos had his arm around my waist as the waiters came by and both of us grabbed a glass.

"Do we wait until midnight to drink it?" I asked him.

"Do whatever you want, *agápi mou*. There's no right way to celebrate."

I glanced around the room and saw some people sipping their champagne while others waited patiently. I decided to wait, like Christos was. Somehow, it seemed more special if we drank together at the stroke of midnight.

"Have you figured out what your New Year's resolution is going to be, Sam?" Romeo asked.

"Oh, I don't know, I hadn't thought about it."

"I know what mine is," Christos purred.

"Do tell!" Romeo said. "I'm all ears!"

Christos nodded down at me. "She's right here."

I frowned. "I don't get it."

"I totally do," Romeo said confidently. "He's going to do *you* for the New Year's, riiiiight, Christos?"

"Romeo!" I blurted.

When Christos chuckled, I swatted his arm. "Stop!"

Christos only laughed. "He said it!"

Christos and I still hadn't had sex yet, but geez, did Romeo have to make a national headline out of it? SAMANTHA SMITH, LAST COLLEGE VIRGIN IN AMERICA. I pictured those grainy grocery store gossip magazine photos of me and Christos running shamefully from the paparazzi cameras.

"Don't be bashful, Sam," Madison said. "It's no big deal."

I rolled my eyes. "Easy for you to say, Mads. You and Jake probably—" I stopped myself short.

"What?" Madison giggled.

"You know," I wiggled my head and arched my eyebrows. "Do...it," I said bashfully.

Why did I feel so shy about sex all of a sudden? Maybe because I sensed that in the not too distant future, I would be having it for the first time myself, with the man I loved. I shivered pleasurably at the thought.

"Isn't she cuuute?" Romeo said in a gooshy baby-talk voice. "Widdle Samanfa is going to turn in her V-card for the New Year!"

A group snicker from Madison, Jake, Romeo, and Kamiko ensued at my expense.

Why did the phrase "turning in your V-card" always make me picture an NFL referee in striped black and white, blowing a whistle? *TWEEEEET!!!* Both the ref's arms go up over his head. *"The kick is good! Samantha Smith is no longer a virgin!"* And why was it a kick? Like I laid on the football field, on my back, waiting for the kicker to wind up before ramming his cleated foot home between my legs?

I shuddered to myself.

Wasn't there a better term for it? Like, "Hosting a V-Pageant Celebration?" I mean, "Turning in your V-card" was about as romantic as "Winning the Megafucks V-stakes Sweepstakes Giveaway."

I shook my head, trying to clear that nasty thought. The next thing I knew, I was imagining Christos and I naked in bed together in a more traditionally romantic fashion. My heart accelerated and my entire body flushed with electric heat. I wanted to fan myself, but opted instead for blinking away my steamy fantasy. No need to call more attention to myself.

So why was the gang grinning and staring at me? Were they reading my mind, or what?

Normally, I indulged in my bedroom fantasies about Christos privately. Not with my best friends scrutinizing me with expectant smiles. They may as well have been surrounding my bed while Christos and I finally did the deed.

I suddenly pictured Romeo holding up a scorecard like a figure-skating judge when Christos and I shared our first mutual orgasm. He would say, *"Was it good for you two? Because I know it was good for me!"*

I grimaced.

"What?" Christos asked innocently.

I choked out a laugh. "Oh, you *so* don't want to know."

"Oh, we so do," Romeo chided.

He would. All eyes were still on me. I desperately needed a distraction. Now would've been the opportune moment for our yacht to hit an iceberg. Unfortunately the waters off the coast of San Diego were generally iceberg free, from what I understood.

"It's almost midnight, you guys!" Tiffany cheered. "Get ready for the countdown!"

For the first time since I'd met her, I could honestly say to myself, thank god for Tiffany.

"Ten, nine, eight..." Tiffany started.

The crowd joined in.

"Seven, six,..." everyone chorused.

I glanced up at Christos. The warmth in his eyes wrapped around me as he pulled me into his rock hard chest.

"Five, four..."

Christos leaned down, his lips loose and plump, about to kiss me...

"Three, two, one..."

The universe disappeared as our lips met and we plunged into each other. Heightened by the moment, it was possibly the most intense kiss I'd ever experienced.

"Happy New Year!!!" everyone shouted. The horns and whistles blew, the noisemakers clacked, and the champagne-poppers popped and shot confetti around the room, all while balloons burst and the entire room cheered in 2014.

I was nearly lost to the sounds around me as Christos deepened our kiss, submerging me in an ocean of love. He consumed me, taking my soul into his. I let him devour me entirely with his lips. I gave all of myself to that kiss, and he felt it. His hunger for me was palpable. His tongue teased the tip of mine. My heart raced and my pulse pounded from my head to my toes. I ran a hand down the thin sweater material covering Christos' rippled abs. I grabbed his belt and pulled him toward me. I wanted him. Right now.

His tongue slid deeper into my mouth.

Oh my goodness...

Oh my Christos...

The fact that I felt a bulge in his jeans pressing into my taut stomach may have had something to do with my intense desire. Heedless of the chaotic crowd around me, I was coaxed by sudden lust to release my grip on his belt and slide my fingers down between his washboard abs and his pants while we continued our kiss.

Although our passionate kiss nearly held my full attention, something else tugged at my awareness. My fingers were now officially submerged in uncharted waters. My hands had never been this close to Christos'...

The signals tingling through my fingertips were like sonar messages that sent hazy mental images to my brain. My hand dove deeper and I caressed my fingers along a rigid velvet submersible.

Oh.

I wasn't at all prepared for it.

Apparently, neither was Christos. He spasmed and sucked in a hissing breath, but our lips remained locked.

A distinct visual impression penetrated my brain, igniting my core with desire.

In a word: massive.

Not that I had much experience in this department. Beyond my recent but brief brushes with fate and Christos' manhood, my only frame of reference in the touching department had been picking out mammoth bananas or ripened cucumbers at the grocery store, or maybe squirreling up tree trunks as a little girl, because that was how huge he seemed to me.

I giggled to myself, realizing that sandwiched in the middle of the word cucumber was the word cum. Whoa! I was turning into a female Romeo!

I withdrew my hand from Christos' pants with exquisite slowness, sliding it back up the bottom of his chiseled eight-pack. His feathery hair down there tickled my fingertips. That sensation alone caused my entire body to quiver in Christos' arms.

After my pleasant shudder passed, I peered up into his ravenous eyes. I was so ready for him to devour me…

But we were on Tiffany's yacht, surrounded by revelry and my closest friends. My V-card would have to wait. I reluctantly broke off our kiss and snuggled my cheek into his chest. I slid my hands around his waist and caressed his back. "I love you," I whispered. I was sure my words were lost in the din of everyone's shouts and all the strident noisemakers.

Christos kissed the top of my head. "I love you too," Christos whispered. "Happy New Year, *agápi mou.*"

I stared up into his loving eyes.

"Did you make a New Year's resolution?" he asked.

"Yeah," I said quietly.

"Care to share?"

I squinched up my face timidly. "Not at the moment?"

"Aww, come on. Just a tease? I'm dying to know."

"Let's just say…" I grinned, "…it has something to do with hosting a pageant."

Christos' smile widened and his dimples appeared.

I stood on my tiptoes and licked one dimple, then the other, before pecking him softly on the lips.

I was desperately in love with this man.

I sighed contently. This was the best New Year's Eve I'd ever had. Nothing could ruin it.

My 2014 was going to rock, I was certain of it.

I was so swept away by the moment, I almost completely missed the double-dagger glare Tiffany was giving me.

SAMANTHA

The New Year's celebrations were in full swing.

It turned out there were audio speakers hidden all over Tiffany's yacht, so when someone cranked up the party mix tunes, every flat surface on the ship became an impromptu dance floor.

Christos and I were on the wooden deck on the top floor of the boat, dancing like lunatics, laughing and gyrating under the moon and stars.

Romeo and Kamiko climbed the stairs, drinks in hand, and danced next to us.

"You guys are so cute together," I said to them sarcastically.

"Too bad it feels like dancing with my sister," Kamiko joked.

Romeo planted a big fat sloppy kiss on Kamiko's cheek. "I'm the big sister you wish you had, dearest."

"Gross! You kiss like a fish!" Kamiko cried. "Aren't there any available gentlemen on this boat?"

"Here comes one now," Romeo mumbled as Brandon walked up the stairs. "Where's your date, Brandon?" Romeo asked suggestively.

Brandon chuckled. "I came stag."

Romeo leaned over to me and whispered, "I'd love to bag his stag. It is rutting season, isn't it?"

I giggled into the back of my hand.

"Here," Romeo said, "I'll let you dance with my date." Romeo grabbed Brandon by the hand and practically threw Kamiko into his arms.

"Romeo!" Kamiko blurted, tripping over her heels. Her dress spun as Brandon caught her and twirled her smoothly, swing style.

"Do you mind if I have this dance?" Brandon asked without missing a beat.

"Uhhh…" Kamiko was wide-eyed with embarrassed excitement.

Brandon led while Kamiko fell into step with him. They were actually quite good together, although Brandon towered over her.

Kamiko flashed me and Romeo a look of stark disbelief. She silently mouthed the words, *"I can't believe I'm dancing with Brandon!"*

"Thank me later, darling," Romeo smiled. Turning to me and Christos, he said, "May I have this dance?"

"Huh?" I said. "You want to dance with me?"

"No, you crazy loon! I want to dance with your boyfriend!"

"Why not," Christos chuckled.

Before I could object, Christos grabbed Romeo around the waist and led him in a circle like a ballroom dancer.

"Squueeeeee!" Romeo cried as his eyes fireworked with delight.

Christos laughed and released Romeo after a couple of good-natured twirls.

Romeo literally sagged to a sitting position and pooled on the deck. "I think I've died and gone to heaven, Sam."

Everybody laughed, even Brandon.

"I think I need another drink or six," Romeo said, pushing himself to his feet. "Help me Sam, it's the least you can do after stealing the hottest man on the planet from my greedy grasp."

"We'll be right back," I said to Christos.

"No worries," Christos said. "I may have to cut in on Brandon in a second. He's having a bit too much fun with Kamiko."

Kamiko goggled with girlish glee.

"They're fighting over you, Kamiko," Romeo said. "Enjoy it while it lasts."

I followed Romeo down the steps to the main deck. We walked over to the kitchen where fresh drinks were being poured. I got a refill on my champagne, but Romeo wanted a mixed drink. I think it was an excuse for him to flirt with the guy in black and white tending the bar.

I walked to the back deck on the main floor to enjoy the view.

I didn't know how far we were from shore, but I saw no lights whatsoever, not even the glow of city lights over San Diego. Only the stars above glinted on the vast ocean surrounding us.

After a time, I decided to find everyone inside. I turned around and nearly bumped into Tiffany as she was walking out of the main cabin. "You," she sneered. "Why can't I ever get rid of you?"

My stomach twisted ominously. "Hey, Tiffany," I said, trying to sound friendly, hoping to set her at ease.

She glared in response.

Ooooh-kaaaay. I wasn't sure what to say. "Um, this is such a great party, Tiffany. And you really have a beautiful boat."

"It's a yacht," she corrected.

"Well, it's really nice. And dinner was nice too. Everything was totally yummy." I flashed a nervous smile.

"What is it with you?" she hissed.

"Huh?" I was confused. How did she manage to always make me feel like an insignificant idiot, no matter what happened? I think it was her super power.

"Why did you have to come along and ruin everything?" she snarled.

"What, I didn't—"

"First Christos, then Brandon."

"I'm not with Brandon," I said defensively.

"I see the way he looks at you," she leered.

"I'm not interested in Brandon. I'm with Christ—"

"You think you're all that, you stupid bitch?" she snapped, interrupting me.

Bitch...

She continued her tirade, "Coming into my world and glomming onto Christos? You think it's that easy? You're fucking wrong, you dirty slit." Tiffany had the fangs out now. "I'm sure you gave it up to Christos the day you met him, just like every other slut has."

Slut...

"That's not true—"

She cut me off dismissively. "That's all he wants from you, or any of them," she hissed. "Because that's all you have to give. Just your skeevy, skankish, poorhouse cunt."

I held in my gasp. Tiffany was drunk. I wasn't playing into her torrent of insults.

"I'm the only one good enough for Christos," Tiffany slurred. "He's not going to stay interested in you for long." Tiffany held her glass of champagne in her hand and extended an accusatory finger at me. With each sentence she thrust her hand forward, causing champagne to slosh inside the glass. "As soon as he's had his fun with you, and I can tell you're nothing more than a slimy slutcrack so it won't take long, he's going to move onto the next one, and the next. Until he finally figures it out."

Figures what out? I wondered.

"Sooner or later," she sneered, "the game will get old for Christos, and he'll end up with me, where he belongs. Not. You." She jabbed her glass on her final words and champagne spilled over the rim.

The grim mask of despair on her face was horrid. I'd never seen her so ugly. Her sweaty drunkenness and smudged makeup made her look even worse. She scowled at me, but I detected more than anger brimming beneath her contorted features.

It was obvious that frustrated desire was torturing Tiffany to her soul, but I didn't think the anguish of unfulfilled love was what ate away at her. It was her greed, her lust for the one thing she couldn't have.

Not having Christos was killing her.

Tiffany swayed lazily and a final dribble of champagne splashed onto her shoes. "You ruined my shoes, you boorish whore."

Whore...

I wasn't going to let her get to me. Tiffany wasn't going to take me back to my past.

Bitch. Slut. Whore...

I was stronger than her. Tiffany was pathetic.

She curled her lips and said, "These Louboutins cost more than your car, you asscap. Get off my boat."

"What? We're in the middle of the ocean!"

"You heard me, get off my boat!" She lunged at me.

I sidestepped.

Tiffany stumbled into the handrail. "Oof!" She folded over the metal bar and almost went over edge.

I grabbed for the back of her dress. "Tiffany! Watch out!" If I hadn't caught her, she would've fallen and face-planted on the transom deck at the back of the yacht, eight feet below.

"Let go of me, you cunt!" She spun around and slapped me in the face.

CRACK!

It sounded like a pistol shot. I reeled back, my face stinging. I imagined the red hand-print that would inevitably form on my cheek. I was mortified. Did this yacht have any lifeboats? I needed to abandon ship.

Holding my hand to my cheek, I backed up a step and bumped into Madison. Romeo stood next to her.

Madison gave me a sympathetic look. "I'm so sorry, Sam. You didn't deserve that," she consoled.

"Thanks, Mads," I whispered, still in shock.

Romeo murmured under his breath. "That rabid vagina has no class, no matter how fancy her yacht is, or how much money she has."

Tiffany sagged against the railing. struggling to keep herself on her drunk-ass feet.

Romeo patted my shoulder. "Forget about that uber goober."

Tiffany glared at him, then flexed her fingernails at me. She looked ready to lunge again.

Madison stepped in front of me. "Relax, Tiffany. You've had way too much to drink."

Tiffany ignored Madison. Her sights were still laser-focused on me. She rocked unsteadily on her feet, either weighing the odds, or too drunk to punch.

Madison balled her petite fists and growled, "Back off, Tiffany. I'm warning you." Now she had Tiffany's attention.

"You're no better than she is, stupid whore," Tiffany hissed at Madison.

"Is everything okay?" Christos said as he pedaled down the stairs from the top deck.

Kamiko followed. "What happened, you guys?"

"Uh…" I was speechless.

Tiffany stopped in her tracks. The look of anguish that flashed across her face as she gazed at Christos almost broke my heart. Poor thing. But I was all done being compassionate with her. When someone tries to slice your eyes out, it's time to give up on the goodwill and leave it at polite pity.

Everyone surrounded Tiffany.

I felt like I was witnessing some sort of old-world shunning ceremony where everyone officially scorned the village shrew for taking things a step too far.

Christos walked up to me and I wrapped my arms around his waist, holding onto him. He draped a protective arm over my shoulders.

"What happened, Samantha?" Christos asked, taking in the situation. "I thought I heard a scuffle down here."

I rested my stinging cheek against Christos' chest, hiding the red evidence of Tiffany's ire. "It's nothing," I whispered.

Tiffany's eyes brimmed with tears. A heavy mask of abject panic and profound misery weighed her down. Her head sunk between her shoulders. She barged past the crowd that had formed on the back deck to gawk at the scene. She plowed past, into the living room, then made her way down the narrow staircase beside the kitchen.

You could've heard a pin drop, the crowd was so silent. The sound of a door slamming downstairs shattered the silence momentarily, but it returned as everyone gaped wordlessly at each other.

I hoped Tiffany would stay locked in whatever room she'd retreated to for the remainder of the trip.

Why did I have the sinking feeling that whatever Tiffany did, tonight or in the days to come, she would make sure that *someone's* voyage ended up at the bottom of the sea?

I just prayed it wouldn't be mine.

SAMANTHA

When the commotion died down, and I reassured Christos that I was okay, we all rejoined the crowd inside. Because the alcohol had been flowing for awhile, it didn't take long for everyone to rekindle the party atmosphere. Conversation picked up, and soon the main room filled with celebratory laughter and good cheer.

The dark haze I'd felt after Tiffany's outburst faded from my memory. A few more drinks helped push away the bad vibes. I was in a saucy mood.

"You ready to snoop around the rest of the boat," Romeo asked mischievously, "while the wicked witch is asleep?"

I giggled. "Why not? Maybe we'll find her magic mirror or her bubbling cauldron."

"Or mermen trapped in the cargo hold," Kamiko slurred, then hiccupped. "Mermen are *hot*. I require the services of my own personal merman right now," she said lustily.

"Have you been *drinking*, Kamiko?" Romeo gasped.

Kamiko's eyelids were at half-mast and her cheeks glowed red. Frowning, she said, "So fucking what? It's New Year's Eve, you vag hag, and I'm not the one driving the boat."

Madison and I burst out laughing.

"Goodness gracious!" Romeo feigned offense. "Who knew Kamiko was such a mean drunk?"

We made our way down the cramped spiral staircase beside the kitchen. A number of closed doors encircled the downstairs hallway.

"How many frickin' rooms does this yacht have?" I whispered.

Knowing Tiffany was down below somewhere had me vaguely worried. I suddenly felt like I was in one of those trapped-at-sea monster movies, and some creeping deep-sea Tiffany might burst through one of the cabin doors any second, roaring and raging like a spurned she-shark. We'd all be trapped belowdecks while she rampaged and bit everyone's heads off.

"It's really quiet down here," Kamiko mumbled. "Do you think Tiffany's dead?"

"We can hope," Romeo said.

A doorway at the end of the hall stood open a crack. I peeked inside, expecting to see Tiffany sprawled out on the bed, either dead or sleeping off her drunk. Nope, the room was empty.

The four of us crept inside. I closed the door and fumbled for the light switch. The room was beautiful. It must have been the master suite.

"This is nicer than most of the hotels I've stayed at," Madison said.

Romeo flipped on the lights in the bathroom.

"OMG," Kamiko said. "They have a bidet on their boat."

"That bidet is bigger than my bathtub," Madison said.

"My dorm doesn't even have a bathtub," Kamiko said longingly.

"Tiffany is scary rich," Madison said. "You'd think she'd be less of a bitch with so much money, but I guess it doesn't work that way."

I stuck my head in the bathroom. "We should go, you guys. No one else is down here."

Romeo turned and squeezed out of the bathroom first. "Would you look at that," he said, staring at the large painting over the queen-sized bed. "It's that painting of Tiff the Quiff."

"The one Christos sold at Brandon's gallery!" Kamiko blurted.

I'd totally forgotten about it. She hadn't been kidding when she'd told us it was going in her yacht. The painting depicted Tiffany in a bikini, lounging beside the infinity pool behind her dad's mansion. The night of Christos' show, Tiffany had bragged that her dad had paid $25,000 for it.

Romeo stepped up onto the bed, heedless of the fact he still wore his shoes.

"What are you doing, Romeo?!" I gasped.

The bedspread bunched around his feet. "Whoops!" he said,

giving the covers a wrinkling twist with his shoes.

"You know Tiff's going to make the servants fix the bed," Kamiko said dryly.

Romeo considered. "Maybe it will piss them off enough that they decide to poison her in her sleep." He ran in place several strides, tearing the covers up.

"Get off the bed, Romeo," Madison said.

He ignored her. "I always thought this painting needed a finishing touch. A final flourish, if you will." He pulled a black marker out of his pocket.

"Where'd you get that?" I asked, worried.

"What, the pen? An artist is always prepared." He uncapped the black marker and leaned toward the painting, one arm resting on top of the picture frame.

"Romeo," I warned, "you should stop now."

Kamiko and Madison were both wide-eyed, but no one seemed to be jumping in to save Tiffany's painting. I couldn't blame them.

"Don't, Romeo!" I pleaded half-heartedly. Well, make that quarter-heartedly.

"Worry not, dearest Sam," he said. "It's water-soluble."

"But what if it doesn't come off?" I asked.

Kamiko suddenly went vicious. "Tiffany has been a total bitch to you all night, Sam. She was trying to claw your eyes out and throw you in the ocean. She totally deserves it," Kamiko argued. "Do it Romeo," she goaded, "Unless the meatballs between your legs have turned into cotton balls."

Romeo was never one to be outdone in a comic standoff. "Very funny, Kamiko. I'm sure your gargantuan lady balls swing between your legs like a gorilla's musty nutsack. Anyway, I don't see the pen in your hand, Zorro."

Kamiko parried, "You're the Gay Blade around here, not me."

There was a pregnant pause before Madison, Kamiko, and Romeo snickered their way into boozy belly laughs.

Wow, they were all drunk. This situation was now officially out of hand. I was surrounded by intoxicated idiots.

Romeo was about to resume his penmanship practice when I grabbed for his arm. He dodged clear, almost falling off the bed, but caught himself. "Careful, Sam, the artist is at work." He tilted his head from side to side, examining the painting in preparation.

"That Tiffany is such a total bitch—"

I couldn't disagree with him there.

"—she's like one of those train-track melodrama villains," Romeo continued, "but Christos' painting doesn't quite capture that." He leaned forward and drew a small, twisty black line.

"I don't know Romeo, maybe this is too much," I said nervously, certain we'd be caught. I reached for his arm again, but he shrugged me off.

"Wait," he whined. "I need to get the twirliness just right." Romeo squeezed his monocle into his eye socket. His tongue jutted from the corner of his mouth as he scrawled the other half of a mustache onto the painting of Tiffany's face. "There. Perfect." He stood back to admire his work and let his monocle swing free from its button-string.

"Oh my god, Romeo," I said. I couldn't decide if I was horrified or mortified, or maybe just a bit satisfied.

Tiffany *had* been a Bitch On High to me at every turn since day one. No matter what I did, she hammered me down with obvious delight. A little temporary water-soluble disfigurement of her treasured painting might do her some good. Remind her that she wasn't permitted to walk through life hurting people, free from consequence. Maybe I'd been cutting her too much slack all along, and she needed a wake-up call.

"It captures her inner spirit, don't you think?" Romeo asked joyfully.

I had to agree. Twirly-mustached Tiffany was definitely an improvement. "But it needs one more thing," I said. I stepped onto the bed, took the marker from Romeo, and drew Where's Waldo glasses on Tiffany. Wow, that felt really, really good. I smiled at my handiwork.

"That's more like it!" Romeo cheered.

Madison and Kamiko chuckled.

I handed Romeo his pen and he capped it before shoving it in his pocket. He pulled his smart phone out of his other pocket and snapped a picture. "For posterity," he smiled at me, "And my blog."

He stepped carefully off the bed and helped me down. "I still can't get over how fancy this yacht is," he said. "It's some kind of James Bond boat. I keep expecting Tiffany to strut in wearing a bikini, carrying a loaded harpoon gun like that Octopussy chick."

"What's an octopussy?" Madison giggled.

"Haven't you seen that James Bond movie?" Romeo asked.

"No," Madison answered.

"You mean Octiffany," Kamiko suggested. "She totally has eight arms she uses to snare her unsuspecting prey and eat them alive with her toothy maw."

I think watching Adventure Time *all* the time had finally gone to Kamiko's brain in all the wrong ways.

Madison laughed. "Which maw?"

"Ewwww," Romeo grimaced. "You girls are gah-ROSS! But, what I want to know is," Romeo giggled in anticipation of his own joke, "does she squirt black ink from her pooter or her pooper?" In one motion, he whipped open the cabin door and turned to face us.

Kamiko's mouth dropped open with a clank, totally unhinged.

Madison appeared to suddenly throw up in her mouth, but held it in because she had too good a manners to barf on someone else's boat.

I goggled, fearing imminent execution. I think Madison, Kamiko, and myself were in too much shock to speak.

Tiffany stood in the hallway, a few paces behind Romeo, holding a drink in her hand.

How long had she been outside the door?

Romeo blundered blissfully forward, completely unaware of Tiffany's presence. He stroked his chin thoughtfully, having missed our collective horror. "I'm going with an ink-shooting pooter, because you know that girl has a hollowed out vaj. Plenty of room for extra ink. And mice. Her stench trench has seen so much action, it must be like a wind tunnel in that thing. What do they call that subway tunnel from England to France?"

"The Chunnel," Tiffany said stiffly from behind Romeo.

"That's right, the Chunnel," Romeo chuckled, completely lost in his own mirth. "Tiffany's fun tunnel could accommodate a high-speed train. What the—!"

Tiffany's drink dribbled over Romeo's head.

"You're ruining my hairdo!" Romeo squealed, flicking fingers across his coiffed faux-hawk. "What is wrong with you?"

"What is wrong with *you*, you nasty little man?!" Tiffany seethed victoriously. "You're all wet now, Mr. Funnyman."

Romeo narrowed his eyes at Tiffany. "I would never hit a lady," he said threateningly. "Luckily, you aren't a lady!" Tiffany flinched when he raised his open hand in a quick jerky motion, but he merely smoothed his wet hair against his scalp.

I repressed a disappointed sigh. I hoped sooner or later *somebody* would give Tiffany a good bitch slapping. It would have to wait.

With confident panache, Romeo sucked the dribbles of Tiffany's drink from his fingertips. "Is that a mojito?" he asked thoughtfully. "It could use more mint. This simply won't do." He carefully removed the highball glass from Tiffany's fingers. "Let me get you another."

She was too stunned to object.

Romeo arched his eyebrow suavely. "I'll speak with the bartender and have him mix a proper one for you. Shaken, not stirred." He motioned toward Kamiko, "Miss Moneypenny, help me find Q. He'll know the correct ratio of gassed water to rum, I think." He gave Tiffany a cordial beauty-contest smile and squeezed past her, heading toward the stairs, Kamiko in tow.

Tiffany folded her arms across her chest and stared at me and Madison. "Your friend's an ass."

I grabbed Madison by the hand and we slid around Tiffany. "And that's why we love him," I said to Tiffany with a smile before heading upstairs.

On the main level, Romeo shook his head like a wet dog. Mojito droplets sprayed everywhere.

From downstairs, Tiffany's voice shook the ship, "What did you assholes do to my painting?!!!!!"

"Take that, you twat-waffle," Romeo muttered triumphantly. "Let's go, ladies! Our work is done here!" Romeo said nervously.

But there was no place to go beyond that except the cold ocean.

Tiffany thudded up the staircase in her heels.

"I don't know about you ladies," Romeo whined, "but I'm swimming for shore before Tiffany Scissorhands snips my balls off!"

Chapter 5

CHRISTOS

Tiffany raged like a banshee in the main cabin.

I would've been surprised by her behavior, but I knew her better. Tantrums were par for her course.

Even when you knew it was nothing but theatrics, girl screeching grated on the nerves.

Brandon happened to be standing next to me the moment Tiffany's temper had gone thermonuclear. "What is it this time?" he scoffed.

"She probably found out the bartender is making rum and cokes with generic cola instead of the brand name stuff," I joked.

"Yeah," Brandon chuckled.

"Where is that bitch!" Tiffany screeched. *"She ruined my painting!"*

Brandon stuck his pinky in his ear, wincing. "Did you bring earplugs?"

I laughed. "Sorry, bro."

"Maybe we should find out what's wrong, and try to soothe this savage beast."

"Be my guest," I said. If I'd learned one thing over the years, it was that Tiffany was never worth the trouble.

"Hey, I'm thinking of everyone else," Brandon said, patting me on the shoulder. "This is hardly what I'd call a joyous atmosphere. Care to give me a hand?"

"If you insist." I followed Brandon over to where Tiffany stood surrounded by her sorority entourage.

"I can't believe what she did!" Tiffany whined.

Her sorority girlfriends hovered around her protectively and nodded mechanically.

Brandon gave me a hesitant look. We both knew I had always been better at talking Tiffany off the ledge.

"What's wrong this time, Tiffany?" I asked with a blend of friendly compassion and parental amusement. I wanted to send her a signal that her childish behavior was off the scale.

"Your *girlfriend* ruined my painting!"

"What are you talking about?" That didn't sound even close to possible.

"You don't believe me," she accused. "Fine, I'll show you." She took a step forward and stumbled over one of her friends. "Move it!" Tiffany snarled, kicking past her.

The young woman slunk away, eyes bulging in terror.

Tiffany marched downstairs, surprisingly steady on her feet for how much I knew she'd drunk since the New Year's countdown earlier.

I followed, Brandon behind me. We ended up in the master suite of her yacht. It was her dad's cabin. I'd hung my portrait of her in this very room myself, several weeks ago, when she'd told me about tonight's New Year's Cruise. I'd taken the opportunity to invite myself and some "friends" without telling Tiffany who I planned to bring. I'm sure it irritated the shit out of her to no end that I'd brought Samantha.

Good.

I believed Tiffany would mature as a person if she were forced to deal with more obstacles in her life than she had thus far. Especially recently. She'd become dangerously entitled in the last couple years.

"Look at it!" Tiffany screeched at the painting. "It's ruined!"

"What?" I wasn't getting it.

"My painting!"

I always cringed when she called it her painting, like she'd done the work herself. "Am I missing something?"

Brandon chuckled, but covered his flashy smile by stroking his mouth with his hand.

"Shut *up*, Brandon!" Tiffany roared.

Then I saw it.

I had to hold my breath and clamp my jaw shut. If I tried to breathe, I was going to bust a gut laughing. I'm pretty sure I'd turned red.

"It's not funny, Christos," Tiffany pouted.

I snickered, "It kind of is."

A wheezy chuckle broke from Brandon.

Tiffany glared at him.

"Sorry," he laughed, "sorry." He turned away politely, trying to get a grip on himself.

I was grinning ear to ear. "The technique is flawless. I didn't even notice it at first. Blends in perfectly with my oils." Had Samantha done this? Man, I sure hoped so. Someone needed to knock Tiff down a notch.

Tiffany gave me a pouting, pleading look. The momentum had turned against her. She knew she'd dulled her Angry Sword from overuse, so she switched weapons. That girl could drum up tears faster than a baby. It was amazing to watch her in action, but I knew better.

"It's ruined," she sobbed. "My painting is *ruined!*"

I gave her a gimme-a-break eye roll that I'd used on her a thousand times over the years.

It didn't help.

Nothing would, until Tiffany somehow got her way.

"Hey," Samantha said from the doorway.

Romeo, Kamiko, Madison, and just about everyone else on board stood behind them.

Great, now Tiffany had an audience. I couldn't escape the feeling she'd orchestrated this entire scene. Maybe *she* had defaced the painting herself, just to get my attention.

I gave Samantha a look and silently mouthed the words, *"Did you do this?"*

A guilty looked strained Samantha's face. I smiled a big grin at her and nodded approval behind Tiffany's back.

Then I noticed Romeo biting his lower lip. He looked guilty as fuck, too. I liked the guy better and better.

"I'm sorry," Romeo apologized. "It was my fault."

Tiffany snarled at him, but I detected a hint of disappointment in her eyes. Like she wanted it to be Samantha.

Romeo pulled a marker out of his pocket and held it up.

Yeah, Tiffany's disappointment was obvious. She was such a drama queen.

"I did it too," Samantha said.

Tiffany's eyes shot wide. "You *what?!*" She lunged at Samantha, but I grabbed her, holding her back.

"It's water-based ink!" Romeo hollered defensively. "It should come right off!"

Tiffany lunged again, but I had a good grip on her. "Easy, Tiff. Don't get ahead of yourself." To Romeo, I said, "Let me see that pen."

He handed it to me. I read the label. I'd used these pens before. They totally came off.

Tiffany was shaking with fury. I still had one hand clamped around her arm.

"Calm down, Tiffany," I encouraged. "The painting is sealed with varnish. It'll be fine." To Brandon, "Hold her for me, would you?" I said, referring to Tiffany.

He put a comforting hand on her shoulder, but that was it. With any luck, she wouldn't pounce at Samantha like a jungle cat the moment I turned my back.

I slid my boots off and carefully stepped onto the bed. I licked my thumb and rubbed at the mustache. The water soluble ink instantly smeared. "See? It totally comes off. Someone get some tissues and a glass of water. I'll clean it up right now."

"I'll get it," Romeo said, guilt tinging his voice. He squeezed past several people into the cabin's bathroom and returned a minute later with a glass of water and toilet tissue.

"Thanks, man," I said.

For whatever reason, maybe because all eyes were *not* on her, Tiffany started bawling again. One of her leggy minions ran to her. "It's okay, Tiffany." She wrapped her arms around Tiffany.

Tiffany fell into the embrace and wept like an alligator. I knew she was still totally pissed at Samantha, but I also sensed she had other plans brewing behind her false bawling. Tiffany *always* had other plans.

Romeo flashed a nervous smile and stepped away while I went to work. I dipped, dabbed, and wiped with the wet tissue. In a minute, the painting was spotless. "See, Tiffany? It's fine."

She pursed her lips while she removed her heels. She climbed onto the bed and huffed. Hands on hips, she leaned toward the painting, her nose inches from the canvas. "I can still see black ink."

"Where?" I asked skeptically. I hadn't missed any.

"Here!" She stabbed her finger toward the painting.

I leaned forward, and wiped at it, just in case.

"It's still there!" she cried, pointing dramatically, as if identifying a suspected murderer in the courtroom.

"What?" I peered closely. "That's nothing, Tiffany. It's just a shadow from the brushwork, beneath the varnish."

"No, it's not!" She had no idea what she was talking about.

"Yes. It is. I remember painting it." I stepped calmly off the bed and stood with my hands resting casually on my hips.

Tiffany looked around at everyone.

Nobody seemed very sympathetic, from what I could tell.

Tiffany knew she was losing her audience. "It's not okay!" she stomped once, still on top of the bed like it was her own personal pulpit, then folded her arms across her chest defiantly. "And I want my money back!"

Brandon flashed me a worried look.

"This simply won't do!" Tiffany huffed. "I'm telling Daddy first thing in the morning! How do you think he'll react, *Brandon*, when he finds out there's graffiti all over my painting? Hmmm? It's ruined!" Barefoot, she stomped off the bed and out of the cabin.

I sat down on the mattress and slid my boots on, one at a time. Time for a fight. Too bad it wasn't the easy kind, with knuckles and knees.

This was turning into a royal pain in my ass.

CHRISTOS

"We should deal with this," Brandon said in front of everybody, "before it gets any worse."

"You sure you don't want to let her cool off," I suggested. "She's still loaded. Maybe you can smooth-talk her tomorrow."

"I'd like to spend my New Year's day doing something other than handling fallout from Tiffany's asinine antics."

"Yeah, you're right."

"Excuse me, everyone," Brandon said as he squirmed through the gawking crowd.

He followed Tiffany up the stairs. "Tiffany, wait!"

I raised my eyebrows at Samantha. "Sorry. Duty calls."

Samantha gave a compassionate sigh. "I'm so sorry Christos. I shouldn't have done that."

"Me too," Romeo moped. "I'm totally sorry, C-Man."

"Doesn't bother me," I smiled. "The painting is fine. Tiffany needs a reality check now and then. Too bad she gets less than one a decade. I owe *you* guys."

"You sure?" Samantha asked plaintively.

I could tell she felt terrible. "Don't worry, *agápi mou*," I reassured. "No sense letting the drama llama ruin your evening any more than she already has."

"She does kind of look like a llama," Romeo said thoughtfully.

Samantha struggled not to smile too widely in front of Tiffany's remaining sorority friends.

"All right," I said, "I'll be upstairs with Brandon, tending to Bitching Beauty."

When I went upstairs and saw Tiffany talking to Brandon in the living room portion of the main cabin, she took one look at me and bee-lined out to the back deck.

Brandon followed her.

I sighed. I knew this game. She played it all the time. The "follow me" game. I trudged out to the back deck, but she left Brandon and continued around the walkway to the bow of the ship.

"I think it's yours from here," Brandon said sympathetically. "My attempts to placate her were met with resolute pouting."

"Great. Fine, I'll see what I can do."

I strolled around to the front of the ship.

Tiffany stood with her back to me, arms folded. I could tell she was fuming because she hadn't gotten her way.

I paused for a moment, shaking my head. This girl was a woman-sized baby. Her dad had made her into so much of a princess, demanding things was the only way she knew how to operate.

"Tiffany, the painting's fine."

She whipped around to face me. "No it's not Christos. Nothing's fine. Your girlfriend is ruining everything."

What the hell was she talking about? "Nothing's ruined, Tiffany."

She looked up at me, her eyes soft, her lips full. Her hair fluttered in the ocean breeze. On an objective level, Tiffany was truly gorgeous. Anyone who said otherwise was in denial.

I knew from years of experience that her beauty was a dangerous lure. She loved to use it on me more than anyone else in her life. She'd almost reeled me in a hundred times over the years with that same angelic look, but I knew well the devil that waited in her darkness. Because of that, no matter how much of a wreck my life had been at any given point, I'd always managed to break free of her grasp just in time, right before she could swallow me whole and no doubt shit me out the other end when she got bored.

Luckily for me, I'd become permanently immune to her gamesmanship the second Samantha had walked into my life.

"Tiffany…"

"Yes, Christos?" she asked hopefully.

"…don't."

"Don't what?" she played innocent ignorance perfectly. Gazing up at me from beneath her delicate brow and flawlessly shaped eyebrows, she coquettishly caressed my arm with her fingertip.

"Don't play me." I yanked my arm away.

The beauty on her face was replaced by pragmatic frustration. "Can't blame a girl for trying."

I waited her out.

"I don't care about the painting, Christos. I never have. It's you I want."

I sighed. "I'm off the table, Tiffany. If you want, I can take the painting back to my studio and go over it with a microscope."

She cocked her hip to one side and planted a defiant fist on it. Her nose tilted up commandingly. "Not good enough. Either you get rid of that Floozy Footstool you're dating, or I want a new painting."

I cocked an eyebrow at her. "Leave Samantha out of this. Your painting will be fine, Tiffany. You're over-reacting."

"No!" she pouted. "The painting is worthless! I won't accept it!"

Now I was irritated. "You want me to redo it? Whatever. I'll take this one home and knock out a copy in a few days. Then you can have two. Put one in your private jet, or where the fuck ever."

Changing tactics, she smiled hopefully, "But we had so much fun doing that painting together."

"*You* had fun, Tiff."

"I thought you had fun too," Tiffany mused.

"You're kidding, right? I let you micro-manage that painting as a favor to you and your dad. Remember how many times you changed your swimsuit?"

"I wanted to pick the perfect suit. Can you blame a girl for wanting to look her best?"

"Uh-huh," I said sarcastically. "Remember how many comments you made like, 'Don't make my thighs look fat,' and 'Show more cleavage,' and 'My waist is slimmer than that.' Remember all that?"

She looked guilty as hell. "Maybe." Denial.

"Don't play dumb, Tiff. You may as well have painted it yourself, for all the artistic input I had. I'll do a copy for you, from the original, if you really want it. But I won't pose you again."

She looked slightly chastised, a rare thing. For a moment, she chewed on her lip, unsure what to do. Then, in a little girl voice, she said, "Christos, I really just want you to paint me nude again. Then we won't have to worry about the swimsuit," she murmured sensually.

I didn't like the way she said "we."

The previous nude of her was the one I'd been finishing up when I'd started mentoring Samantha. I remembered working on it clearly. Every time I'd give Tiffany a break from posing, she'd flirt like crazy, giving me the come-hither bedroom eyes, leaning her exposed breasts into me fifty times a minute. Normally, artists' models would put on a robe between poses and take some time to themselves. Not Tiffany. She was naked the entire time, and followed me all over my studio, hanging off me like an out-of-work prostitute.

"And I promise," she said breathily, "no micro-managing. I'll do whatever you say," she winked suggestively. "Just you and me in your studio, like last time. I'll pay for it. Fifty thousand cash, up front. Straight to you, no gallery commission to Brandon."

She wasn't trying to buy a painting, she was trying to buy me. "You're nuts, woman," I scoffed.

"But it was so romantic. You and me in your studio, the artist and his muse."

"You're not my muse, Tiff."

"But I could be, again. If you let me," she said demurely.

"You never were. Sorry."

"Please, Christos?" she begged, reaching out to me again.

"No, Tiffany."

"No, what?" Brandon asked. Where the fuck had he come from? It didn't matter. I was happy for the reinforcement.

"Christos refuses to paint me again," Tiffany whined.

"No," I corrected, "I'm happy to do a copy of the poolside portrait for her."

"So what's the problem?" Brandon asked.

Sensing defeat, Tiffany struggled with herself. Her face contorted angrily. "The pool painting is ruined!" She stomped her feet on the deck of the yacht.

Welcome to Tantrum Town, population one.

"Okay," Brandon soothed. "Christos already said he'd paint another one."

"That's not good enough!" she shouted.

Brandon suddenly looked squeamish, and for a second, slightly sniveling. He was unsure how to proceed.

I stifled a chuckle. Yes, Tiffany could ruffle even Brandon's unshakable feathers.

"So what would you like, Tiffany?" Brandon asked calmly, having regained his composure.

"I want Christos to pose me for a new poolside painting."

I'd had it with her manipulations. "Has she paid you yet, Brandon?" I asked. I still didn't have all of the money from my show, which meant not every buyer had cut a check to the gallery, which was normal.

Brandon chuckled.

"What's so funny?" Tiffany hissed.

"Why no, Tiffany's father still hasn't issued a payment," Brandon said, a bemused grin stretching over his perfect teeth.

That was news to me. I'd hoped the Kingston-Whitehouse check might be one of the first to come in, considering how long my family had known theirs. Why wasn't I surprised? Oh yeah, it was the Kingston-Whitehouses.

"Slow pay, huh?" I grunted, looking at Brandon. "It's been almost two months, Tiffany. You took possession of the painting, and your dad still hasn't cut a check? Come on. At this point, it's not even yours. Your dad having money troubles?" I jabbed.

Tiffany frowned.

"No deal," I said, a tinge of irritation breaking through my voice. "Keep the painting, Tiff. It's on the house." I glanced at Brandon.

He nodded, smiling furtively at me. We both knew with all the recent interest in my art, we had far bigger fish to fry than the Kingston-Whitehouses.

"But it's ruined!" Tiffany shouted.

"Throw it over the side of the boat, for all I care," I growled. I'd always hated that painting anyway. It was nothing more than hackwork for the all-time, ultimate, pain-in-my-ass client.

I'd already wasted enough time on Tiffany. I turned on my heel and went looking for Samantha.

I just hoped that Tiffany and her family wouldn't bite me in the ass in the coming weeks, because they were sharks and always struck the second you weren't looking.

Fucking Tiffany.

My New Year was already looking like a disaster, and I was less than three hours into it.

Could it get any worse?

CHRISTOS

The yacht arrived back in the harbor several hours after midnight.

Everyone on board was tired, buzzed, or completely asleep on one of the yacht's many cushioned surfaces when the crewmen moored the boat to the docks.

Tiffany hid in her cabin while people disembarked. I think she wanted to avoid me after our discussion.

Samantha and Madison had their arms around Kamiko as they led her along the docks. She was still somewhat hammered. Brandon joined them to help with Kamiko.

Romeo walked over to me and Jake as the seven of us ambled toward the parking lot.

"Christos," Romeo pleaded earnestly, "I'm so sorry about Tiffany's painting. None of it was Sam's idea, it was all mine. I drank too much and Tiffany was being a class-A bitch to Sam. I couldn't help myself."

"Dude, no worries." I clapped him on the shoulder. "You were standing up for my girlfriend. How can I hold that against you?"

"Thanks, C-man," Romeo said, but he still sounded distraught. "You got all the ink off, right?"

"Yeah. I covered that painting with some old-school Renaissance varnish before I sold it. That shit is bulletproof. It's as good as new."

"Are you sure?" Romeo obviously felt terrible.

I didn't feel like explaining that the painting was now a total write-off because Tiffany was insane and her dad had never paid. I really didn't care, but it probably would've bummed Romeo out to know. "Seriously, dude. It's fine."

"Thank you, C-man." Romeo gave me a fist bump.

"Whoa!" Samantha cried.

Me and Romeo turned around to see what the fuss was.

Kamiko was having difficulty walking, even with Madison and Samantha helping.

I immediately went to help, but before I got there, Brandon swept Kamiko up into his arms and carried her. Compared to him, she looked like a small child.

"Don't puke on him, Kamiko," Romeo warned.

"It's okay," Brandon said confidently. "I think she'll be fine."

"Okay, puke away!" Romeo joked tiredly. It had been a long night for everyone.

When we got to my car, Samantha offered to sit in the back so Kamiko could have easy access to the window in an emergency.

"You don't have a barf-bag in the glove box, do you?" Samantha asked.

"No," I smiled.

After we all climbed in, Brandon gently lowered Kamiko into the front seat.

"Look at her love eyes," Romeo snickered.

Brandon looked slightly embarrassed. I couldn't tell if he was into Kamiko or not. He was usually inscrutable when it came to the ladies, with the exception of Samantha, where he'd made himself crystal clear from the start. Who knows, maybe Kamiko would grow on him. She was pretty damn cute.

"Good night, everybody," Brandon said. "And happy New Year!" He slapped the roof of my Camaro as we drove off.

I smirked to myself.

If this year was going to be a happy one, I was going to need all the help I could get.

Chapter 6

SAMANTHA

We made it back to my apartment shortly before sunrise. Kamiko was passed out. Christos picked her up out of the car.

"Where do you want her?" he asked.

"Oh, I don't know," I said. "Romeo? Are you okay to drive?"

"Uhh," Romeo said nervously.

"You guys better sleep here," I said.

"Okay," Romeo said reluctantly as we all walked up the stairs to my apartment. "But only if I get to sleep with Christos."

"As if," I said while unlocking my door. "He's sleeping in my bed."

"Perfect!" Romeo said, "you can share the couch with Kamiko while Christos shares your bed with me!"

"Down, Romeo!" I said. "It's my apartment, and I decide who sleeps where."

Romeo rolled his eyes. "Fine. Party pooper."

While Romeo and Christos took turns in the bathroom, I changed into a t-shirt and boxers.

"Christos," I asked, "can you pull out the bed in my sofa while I help Kamiko use the bathroom? I've got extra sheets in my closet."

"Sure," he answered warmly.

"Gaaaah," Kamiko moaned as I walked her into the bathroom.

Kamiko managed to pee on her own, but I stood watch in case she accidentally slipped into the bowl while flushing and we never heard from her again.

The sofa bed was all made up when I led her out of the bathroom. I sat her on the end of the mattress. Romeo took her shoes off while I pulled her dress over her head. Since it was Romeo, I never thought twice about him seeing her in her underwear. Christos, on the other hand, waited in my bedroom, I think out of politeness.

I removed Kamiko's bra and slid one of my t-shirts over her head before putting her to bed.

"Nnnnn," she said when her head landed on the pillow.

I put the wastebasket I kept beside my desk for paper trash next to Kamiko's side of the bed.

"You're on puke patrol," I said to Romeo. "If Kamiko needs to hurl, you need to help."

"It would be my honor," he said, tucking in one arm while bowing in a courtly manner. He hung his jacket and pants over the back of my desk chair. While standing and bouncing on one leg, he pulled his skinny jeans off one leg at a time, turning each one inside out. "I forgot how tight these are." He rolled his eyes. "The things I do for fashion."

As he lifted up the corner of the covers, he gave me a serious look. "Are you sure it's okay for me to sleep with Kamiko?"

"What do you mean?"

"I might try to take advantage of her in the middle of the night. Maybe it's safer if the boys sleep with the boys, and the girls sleep with the girls."

I folded my arms. "No, Romeo," I smiled.

He crawled into bed and I shut out the lights.

"Fine, Sam. But don't blame me if you're torn from your slumber by Kamiko's plaintive cries for help."

"I think Kamiko will be fine," I said. "But I better lock my bedroom door, for Christos' sake. You better not try anything," I warned.

"How about a three-way?" he whispered hopefully. "You won't even know I'm there. I'll be in the back, if you know what I mean."

"No, Romeo! You're crazy! Now go to sleep," I pleaded before closing the bedroom door behind me.

Christos was already lying on my bed, stripped to his boxers. His tattooed arms were folded casually behind his head. My bedside lamp shone on him invitingly, casting dramatic shadows over his ripped muscles in the near-darkness of my bedroom. His abs suggested that now was a good time to lick them, no matter how late it was.

"Hello," I purred.

He chuckled. "Don't you think you're being a little hard on

Romeo? I mean, can you blame him for lusting after me?"

I smirked. "I'm going to be hard on you, if you don't stop talking about Romeo." Seized by newfound confidence, I crawled onto the bed on all fours and dipped my head, licking my way around his abs, loitering around his navel for awhile, which made him moan. I licked my way up his chest, then stopped at a nipple and nipped it with my teeth.

"Mmmm," Christos moaned.

I suppressed my giggles as my hair pooled over his chest. I reminded myself Romeo and Kamiko were in the next room.

"I heard that," Romeo said in a low voice from the living room.

I froze in place, the tip of my tongue touching Christos' nipple.

"Please, Sam?" Romeo begged. "Can I at least watch?"

Christos and I burst out laughing.

"Quiet, you guys," Romeo said sternly, "I can't sleep with all that racket."

I rested my head on Christos' chest. "We're going to sleep now. I promise, Romeo."

"Awesome. I'll wait until you're snoring, then I'll sneak in like a butt bandit. I'll even be wearing one of those little black bandit-masks with the eyeholes."

"Good NIGHT, Romeo!" I said.

"Uuuuugh," Romeo sighed. "Fine. See you guys in the morning."

"Sorry, no New Year's nookie for you, *agápi mou*," Christos whispered sarcastically.

"That goes for the both of us," I taunted before kissing him on the lips, turning off my lamp, and snuggling up against him. "I'm sure we'll have ample opportunity later."

"You mean for that pageant you talked about hosting?" I heard a smile in his voice.

"Yes," I said. "It will be a very exclusive event. Only the two of us are invited."

"Mmmm," he said, "I like the sound of that. If you hear me moaning in my sleep, you'll know that's me dreaming about it. Good night, *agápi mou*."

"Hey, no fair! How am I supposed to sleep now that you put that idea in my head?"

"You'll figure it out." He kissed my cheek and stroked my

shoulder. "I'll be right here. Wake me if you need anything."

Christos commenced softly fake-snoring.

"You *so* suck, Christos."

"I've been known to suck things," he murmured suggestively.

I immediately remembered the universe-shattering oral sex he'd given me only a few weeks ago. I was instantly wet. Great. I was never going to sleep like this. Because I felt his hardness pressing against one of my butt cheeks.

"Is that a steel pipe in your boxers, or what?" I whispered.

"I like to think of it as a lamp post," he snickered.

Romeo's voice drifted in from the living room, "I'm writing all this down, you guys."

My breath froze mid-inhale. Caught.

"I'll be referring to it later," Romeo said slyly, "for educational purposes only, of course."

I winced as Christos blew out a guilty chuckle.

Surprising all three of us, Kamiko roared, "Would you three either get on with your menage a *twat*, or *SHUT THE FUCK UP!!!*"

Romeo, Christos, and I all erupted with laughter.

Thankfully, everyone drifted off to sleep not long after.

SAMANTHA

Kamiko was disastrously hung over the next morning.

We had to practically drag her out of the apartment to get brunch. The four of us drove to my favorite breakfast place, The Broken Yolk Café in Pacific Beach.

We parked on the street and had to walk a couple of blocks to get there. I couldn't believe San Diego was having a heat wave in January. And by heat wave, I mean it was like, sixty-eight degrees. The weather was absolutely perfect.

Kamiko trudged far behind, head hanging between her shoulders. She wore a pair of movie-star glasses that I'd loaned her to block out the sun, and her rumpled dress from last night.

"Poor thing," Romeo said compassionately. "She looks like she's been run over by a garbage truck. I gave her two glasses of water at some point during the night, but I don't think it made much difference."

"Somebody carry me," Kamiko begged. "I'm not going to make

it."

It was one more block to the Broken Yolk, but we all stopped to wait for her. Kamiko's response, rather than hurrying up, was to sit down on a bus bench. "I'll meet you guys there, but I'm taking the bus." She laid down on the bench with her head hanging over the side of the armrest.

"I'll get her," Christos said. He literally picked Kamiko up and put her on his shoulders like a little kid.

"Hey! Goliath!" Kamiko groaned. "You better not drop me!"

Romeo and I both chuckled.

When the four of us made it through the café doors, Christos set Kamiko down on one of the padded benches in a sitting position. She immediately fell over onto the cushions and curled into a ball.

The line inside wasn't too bad, but there was a short wait. Christos gave his name to the hostess, who was none other than Skylar, the girl who'd chatted Christos up at the Student Center the first day of classes last quarter. I vaguely remembered her saying something to Christos about some club named Onyx downtown, kitchen-table sex after, and her unbridled whorish desire for more furniture sex with my boyfriend.

Well, to be fair, Christos wasn't my boyfriend at the time. I was still calling him Adonis at that point. But still, wasn't my current BF-GF status with Christos retroactive? Which made the way Skylar was ogling him right now totally inappropriate?

And why was it that practically everywhere we went, we ran into some hot hobot who'd slept with my boyfriend?!

"Hey, Adonis," Skylar said flirtatiously, thrusting her inflatable pool toys out at him scandalously. Based on the way they strained at her shirt, I'm pretty sure she'd had them pumped up another 40 P.S.I. since the last time I'd seen her.

Christos smiled at her casually, "What up, Skylar."

Was he smiling too much, or was that an appropriate amount? I wanted to consult my Guidebook to Proper Ex-etiquette, but I'd left it at home.

Skylar bounced around the hostess podium, arms wide for a hug, leading with her buddy-bumpers. For an agonizing moment, elongated beyond reasonable proportion, I worried what kind of hug Christos would give. Would it be full-frontal? As in, pelvis to pelvis? Or a one-armed side-hug with hips at least twelve inches apart? Or would he spin and dodge out of her reach like a respectful boyfriend, and merely shake hands?

Moment of truth.

Christos leaned sideways toward her, clearly intending to give her the one-armed hug with a full twenty inches of lower-torso clearance. He even had the appropriately indulgent half-smile straining his face.

Skylar was undeterred. She thrust forward with her hips, limboing under Christos' arm, determined to hump him like a puppy. Her body tilted so far back, Christos had no option but to catch her before she fell to the ground.

"Whoa, careful!" he said, concern on his face. She hung in one of his muscular arms. "You okay?"

"I am now," she smiled, eyes glassy with desire, her luxurious auburn hair draping over his arms like a hair-care commercial. She looped her arms around the back of his neck like some kind of choreographed Tango dance pose.

That bitch! She was master of feminine wiles. Not to worry, I had a few ninja skills of my own. I grit my teeth, ready to pounce and tear some hair out.

Before I could attack, Christos stood Skylar up and bodily set her down two feet away, then shifted his body language away from her while folding his arms protectively across his chest.

I could deal with that. His body language was clear. I retracted my poison-tipped ninja claws back into my fingers and tried to breathe evenly while my adrenalin wore off.

"Be careful, you almost cracked your head open," Christos said to Skylar.

"Oh, it's my heels," she giggled. "I'm always tripping on them. Clumsy me."

Tee-hee, you bitch. I was ready to trip my heels all over her face. Too bad I was wearing flats. I took a deep breath. Was I being jealous? It seemed highly unlikely, but there was a minuscule possibility. I tried reasoning with myself.

Christos had already proven himself to be the most devoted man I'd ever known. He'd done numerous crazy-stupid things to hold onto me. Why would he suddenly throw that all away for some random girl he'd had, *ahem*, table sex with, and if I recall, barely remembered banging?

Okay, that thought just derailed my happy train and crashed it into a kitten farm, killing everyone on board and all the kittens frolicking in the fields.

My panic level skyrocketed out of control. Did somebody have a bottle of Xanax? Or a case? Or a truckload? Screw it. Somebody call FEMA. I was about to have a natural disaster. Rev up those rescue helicopters, boys. I needed to be flown out of here.

"Skylar, you remember my girlfriend Samantha?" Christos said while wrapping his arm possessively around my waist.

Cancel emergency. Phew.

"Not really," Skylar said, flustered.

"Skylar, Samantha. Samantha, Skylar," Christos said.

Were we supposed to shake? I hoped not. I gave Skylar a little wave. She made a cat-pee face. Served her right. Not that she was a bitch or anything.

"Yeah, me and Samantha are totally in love," Christos said, gazing into my eyes.

Out of the corner of my eye, I could tell Skylar was now making a cat-poop face. It looked just right on her.

While I wrapped my arms around Christos' waist and swooned into his side, Skylar returned to her podium and asked Christos blandly, "How many are in your party?"

"Four," Christos said, his confident dimpled smile having returned.

"Your table should be ready in about fifteen or twenty minutes," Skylar said while jotting down the information. "Next!"

With his hand on the small of my back, Christos led me through the growing crowd in the lobby to where Romeo sat next to Kamiko, who was still curled into a ball on the cushioned bench.

I was smiling over the fact that Christos had so decisively referred to me as his girlfriend in front of Skylar. I gazed up at him and fell into the intense desire pouring out of his sapphire eyes. He lowered his lashes and his dimples deepened as he smiled at me. "Have I told you how unbelievably gorgeous you are today?"

"Um, not since my apartment?" I giggled.

"Are you serious? That was like thirty minutes ago," Christos said, feigning shock. "I must be the worst boyfriend ever. We'll have to work on that," he smirked.

I wondered what that meant. I saw the wheels turning behind

his eyes as he worked over some mysterious thought in his head. My heart suddenly fluttered.

"Samantha," he said softly, "to me, your beauty is the most treasured gift Mother Nature has ever given. Like the petals of a rose, your face reminds all mankind that in a harsh world, impossible beauty is still possible. To gaze upon you is a blessing to all men, but I am the luckiest of all, for each morning I am reborn as I drink from the golden cup of your grace, and find that my deepest dreams and desires have all come true."

Oh. My. Fuck me now, God.

The lump in my throat was the size of a basketball. My mouth hung open. I suspected drool ran down my chin, but I was distracted by the fact my body was on fire, raging with desire. All I could think about was the nuclear blast mushroom-clouding out from my core.

Would it be impolite for Christos to lay me down on one of the cushioned benches in the lobby of The Broken Yolk and take my virginity in front of everyone while we waited for our table? Unfortunately, a foggy corner of my brain suggested it would.

Drat.

Not that I wanted an audience, but I was feeling slightly impatient to get my panties off at the moment. Maybe someone could yell "Fire!" and clear the room?

No, that wouldn't work either. The fire department would show up way too quick, which would again put a damper on things. On second thought, I'd probably need them to douse me and Christos to keep us from spontaneously combusting while we went at it.

Okay, this wasn't getting me anywhere. I tried to snap myself out of my sultry fantasy. So I focused on Christos' grinning lips, which were an inch from mine. Not helping. I wanted to devour them.

Luckily, out of the corner of my eye, I slowly became aware of Romeo gawking at us like we were a three-dollar peep show. That broke the spell.

I glanced over at Romeo. He looked hypnotized. His eyes seemed to spiral randomly. His head lolled in lazy circles. I think he was in rapture.

"Are you okay, Romeo?" I giggled.

"I think I just witnessed the second coming," he moaned.

Kamiko groaned from the bench, "Yours or Samantha's?"

Romeo burst out laughing.

While snickering at Kamiko's punchline, Christos pecked me on the cheek. "How was that?"

I blinked at him several times. "Huh?" I was still transfixed.

"My love sonnet?" he grinned.

"Oh, yeah. Did you make that up just now, or did you read it somewhere?" His answer had to be no, because no man could possibly be this perfect.

"No," he smiled.

I felt a sudden pinch of disappointment. Oh well. No one was *perfect* perfect. Not even Christos.

He flashed a cocky smile. "I worked it out in my head this morning after I woke up, while you nuzzled against me. I kept looking at you, feeling this overwhelming sense of gratitude and love for having you in my life. I didn't have a paint brush handy, and I didn't want to wake you up to grab a sketchbook, so I did my best to capture the moment in words."

THUMP!

Romeo had slid from the bench and fallen to his knees. He wrapped his arms around my leg and wailed, *"Please, Sam! Let me have just one night with him! I'll do anything! Please!!!"*

Yes, everyone in the lobby was gawking at Romeo while he sobbed. He didn't care.

Between Romeo's emotional flood and my full body flush, I needed a moment away from the staring eyes of the customers in the lobby.

"Hey, Kamiko," I hissed while tugging at her shoulder, "do you need to go to the bathroom?"

"Baaaaah," she moaned, still balled up on the couch.

I was on my own. "I'll be in the restroom," I said to Christos. I skulked into the Ladies Room and locked myself in a stall, fanning my face while my heart rate returned to normal.

After splashing water in my face at the restroom sink and toweling off, I returned to the lobby.

SAMANTHA

The waiting crowd at the Broken Yolk had thinned. Romeo sat

beside Kamiko on the couch.

"Hey, Kamiko," Romeo said, trying to shake her awake. "I know Cartoon Hangover is your favorite channel on Youtube, because they have all the episodes of Bravest Warriors for free. But how do you like having a real hangover? Are you going to officially 'Like' it and click the thumbs-UP icon?"

"Leave her alone, Romeo," I smiled. "She's dying."

Without looking up, Kamiko raised her hand and gave Romeo a thumb's DOWN gesture.

Romeo cackled with laughter. He leaned over and massaged her shoulder affectionately. "Don't worry, Kamiko, we'll kick your hangover by dinner. Even if it means more drinks."

Kamiko groaned.

One of the things I loved about The Broken Yolk was that they were locally notorious for serving a dozen-egg omelet and biscuits called the Challenge. Madison had told me all about it the first time she'd taken me here.

The Challenge omelet was free if you finished it in less than an hour, and you even got a plaque on the wall of fame, but one person had to eat the whole thing by themselves. The idea made me want to barf, but I still thought it was totally cool that they made it free for the winners. I never dared. I was totally down with their human-sized portions.

"You know, Christos," I said, "they serve a gigantic dozen-egg omelet here."

He raised an eyebrow thoughtfully. "Really?"

"Yeah, it's, like, thirty bucks, but if you finish it in an hour, it's free."

"Wow, that's amazing," he smiled.

I grinned coyly. "I bet you couldn't eat the whole thing."

"Probably not today."

"You're not chicken, are you?" I prodded.

"Who, me? No way," he scoffed.

"Then you should totally order it."

"Naw, I think I'll be good with a three-egger. Maybe four, if I'm feeling dangerous."

I cackled, "Chicken! Bock, bock!"

Christos smirked, glancing at Romeo. "Look at this crazy girl, trying to goad me into a gut-bomb."

Romeo put his hands on his hips and did a head roll. "I don't know, C-man. A real man never backs down from a challenge."

"You calling me out, Romeo?" Christos asked confidently. "You ready to go head-to-head?"

Fear pinched Romeo's face. "Oh, um," he giggled nervously, "I'm not a real man." He shrugged his shoulders.

Christos smirked. "That's what I thought."

"Come on, Christos," I jabbed, "you don't get off that easily. I'm still issuing the challenge, for the Challenge," I winked at him, "no pun intended."

Christos sighed indulgently. "Give it a rest, Samantha."

"I knew it!" I squealed. "You're just chicken! I'm totally not buying your whole 'I'm too cool for gruel' routine. Be a man, Christos. Show us what you've got. Order the Challenge."

Christos tilted his head at me with a mildly annoyed look on his face, then held his hand up and tipped it behind him, pointing at a wall covered in row upon row of little brass plaques. His finger pointed decisively at one specific plaque.

Not getting it, I frowned. "What?"

"Go ahead and look, big mouth," he said confidently.

I squinted.

"Do you need me to pick you up so you can read it?"

"No," I said dismissively, "I can do it myself." I stood on my tiptoes to read it.

"Christos "The Man" Manos

7-21-2010

17 MIN."

"What!" I gasped. "No way!" I scanned the other plaques. Most seemed to be in the 30, 40, and 50 minute category. "Seventeen minutes has to be the record!"

"Last I heard," Christos said casually, "the record was seven-fifteen. Guy had a hollow leg."

Beside me, Romeo scrutinized the plaque. "Wow, C-man, you sure have a manly appetite."

"Thanks, bro," he grinned.

"I'm pretty manly too," Romeo fawned, "does that mean you'll eat me?"

Christos chuckled, "You just said you weren't a real man a minute ago. I'd probably starve." He gave Romeo a good natured back-smack.

"He's right," Romeo said to me, unashamed. "I'll have to start hitting the gym if I ever want Christos to take a bite out of me."

"You are so totally dick sick, Romeo," I laughed.

Skylar the hostess called our name apathetically and took us to our table. Hungover Kamiko managed to make the daunting trek under her own power. Romeo offered to help her, but she pushed him away and said, "I'm man enough."

We all sat down and Kamiko whooshed a sigh. "Do they have Bloody Marys? I so need one," she said while flipping through her menu.

"I don't remember you ever liking Bloody Marys," Romeo said, concerned.

Kamiko glared at him over her movie-star sunglasses, "And?"

"Maybe you should stick to OJ?" Romeo suggested tentatively.

"You're right. Why didn't I think of that before? I can't stand tomato juice first thing in the morning." She licked her lips. "I'm totally going to have a Screwdriver instead."

Romeo goggled at me. "What did we do to her last night?"

"I think maybe champagne is her kryptonite," I suggested, somewhat worried myself. "It must be her one weakness. She drank so much on the yacht, it's tipped her over the edge."

"That's right!" Kamiko beamed. "Thank you guys! I don't know what I was thinking. I wanted a Mimosa all along!"

I wanted to glare at Kamiko and steer her back on the straight and narrow with some tough love. But frankly, I was afraid that if I said anything she would bite my face. So I glared at Romeo instead, because I needed to glare at *somebody*.

"Don't look at me, Sam!" Romeo pleaded. "The yacht trip was Christos' idea!"

I glared at Christos and folded my arms across my chest. "That's right! It *was* your idea, Christos. What have you got to say for yourself?"

"It's not like I was handing her drinks all night," Christos said calmly. "She's a big girl. But if this keeps up, I'll be happy to stage an intervention."

"Calm down, you guys," Kamiko said forcefully. "I think I had maybe five glasses all night. I would've stuck to my limit of two if *Romeo* hadn't thrown me in Brandsome's arms on the dance floor. I got all nervous and couldn't stop thinking about him after that. Champagne was my only recourse. So if I want to have a Mimosa for breakfast, you all can shut the fuck up."

Christos chuckled.

"Brandsome?" Romeo chuffed. "You mean *Brandon?*"

Kamiko smiled bashfully.

"You're crushing on Brandon?" I blurted.

"So?" Kamiko blushed, "he's hot, isn't he? Is that okay with you guys?"

The waitress arrived to take our drink orders. At the last second, Kamiko ordered straight orange juice instead of a Mimosa. My mounting guilt over corrupting her innocence subsided instantly.

When the waitress was gone, Romeo asked, "Who's ready for classes to start tomorrow?"

"I think I need a week's vacation after last night," Kamiko groaned. She folded her arms on the table and rested her head on top of them.

"What classes are you guys taking this quarter?" Christos asked.

"I think Kamiko's taking Napping 101," Romeo joked.

"Grrrr," Kamiko mumbled.

I totally didn't want to think about college right now. It reminded me that I had another Accounting class to look forward to for ten more weeks, plus more Sociology and History. I did have Oil Painting, and I was happy about that. I'd signed up for it at the last minute, a fact which my parents didn't know. But the thought of accounting turned my stomach. Meh.

"I can't wait to start the term," Romeo beamed. "I'm taking Intro to Acting, Intro to Playwriting, Figurative Sculpting, and last but not least, Oil Painting 10, with Sam and Kamiko."

I goggled. "What? Those are all classes? Like, actual college classes?"

"Yeah," Romeo said quizzically. "I am double-majoring in Art and Theater, remember?"

"But your schedule sounds like…fun," I sighed.

"You're taking Oil Painting with me," he said encouragingly, having sensed my distress. "That's going to be a ton of fun."

Maybe it really was time for me to change my major to Art. I couldn't let Romeo have all the fun. But the mere thought of it made me nauseous. What would my parents say? Maybe I didn't have to tell them. Not right away, anyway. I could wait a few days before giving them reason to kill me. Groan!

Our breakfast arrived shortly thereafter.

Kamiko snored through hers, Christos had a conservative four egg omelet, and I pretended that my future wasn't a Bill & Linda Smith-shaped time-bomb waiting to blow up in my face. Sigh.

Fake smile!!

Chapter 7

SAMANTHA

We drove back to my apartment after breakfast. Romeo and Kamiko hung around for a few hours until Kamiko was finally up for the drive back to her dorm on campus.

When they were gone, I suggested Christos and I go for a stroll on the boardwalk.

"Do you wanna do some crayon paintings?" he asked.

"That's a great idea! There's a new café I've been meaning to try."

We grabbed paper and my box of crayons and headed down to the boardwalk. At the café, I found a table outside while Christos ordered our drinks. I was so tickled to be sitting outdoors on January 1st. In the sun, no less. Not even remotely possible in D.C. this time of year.

Christos arrived with an Italian soda for me and an iced tea for him.

"You remembered!"

"What?" he scoffed.

"That I love Italian soda!"

"How could I forget? It's been less than a month since the last one you had," he smiled.

No matter how much he dismissed it, I loved that he knew what I liked to drink. "What flavor did you get me this time?" It was a green one I didn't recognize.

"Celery."

I grimaced. "Celery? You're not serious, are you?"

He grinned. "No. It's kiwi."

I took a sip. "Mmmm, I love it! Thank you!"

"You're welcome." Christos opened the box of crayons for us and we both went to work on our own crayon paintings for a time

"So," he asked, pausing to peel back the paper on his lemon yellow crayon, "you still planning on changing your major?"

"I'm thinking about it," I sighed while selecting a crimson crayon from the box.

"You sound like you're not sure."

"Maybe I'm not."

"What's worrying you?" Christos asked.

I leaned back in my chair and looked around the café while collecting my thoughts. I noticed an older couple sitting next to us stealing glances at our crayon pictures.

I don't know what it was, but whenever I was out drawing in public with Christos, people wanted to watch. It wasn't just because of hot-bodied Christos either. Sure, women were always checking him out, but when we were drawing, the people seemed genuinely interested in what we were doing. I guess it wasn't every day that you saw people over the age of eight or nine drawing with crayons in a public place.

"Lost in thought?" Christos asked.

"Oh, sorry. What was the question?"

"Changing your major to Art?"

"Oh yeah. Hmmm. I'm worried my parents will freak when I tell them I'm changing my major to Art. They'll probably threaten to send me away to a convent or make me get electro-shock therapy."

"That's crazy," he said dismissively while sipping his iced tea. "Don't they see how talented you are?"

"Don't you remember what they were like over Winter Break?"

Christos nodded thoughtfully. "Yeah, they did seem somewhat uncertain about the whole idea."

I choked out laughter while shading purple shapes on my drawing. "Somewhat? You literally told my dad you made over six figures in one night of selling paintings at Charboneau, and he acted like that was something that only happened to other people, like you were a myth or something."

Setting his crayon down, he grinned. "Just because your parents don't realize that an art career is an actual possibility for you *now*, doesn't mean they won't come around eventually. Maybe you have to prove how serious you are. Show them all the steps you're taking."

"I feel like the only way they're ever going to believe Art is a valid career choice is if I show them the mansion I bought with my as-of-yet unearned art earnings, and a hefty art-funded retirement portfolio."

Christos smirked. "I get it. It's just not real to them. So put a piece in the Contemporary Artists show at Charboneau Gallery. When you sell it, you can show the check to your parents. Take a photo of you standing in front of your painting during the show."

"Wait, you're talking like I've already sold the painting! I haven't even *painted* a painting! Aren't you jumping ahead?"

"Not in my book. You've got to set the intention."

"Yeah, but who's going to buy *my* painting? You?"

"I could," he smiled, "if you wanted."

"Thank you, Christos," I said, picking up a tangerine crayon to draw some squiggly lines. "I totally appreciate the offer, but if this crazy idea of yours is going to make any kind of sense, some stranger would actually have to buy it. And that's never going to happen." I glanced at the older couple, who were still sitting next to us. They looked like they were eavesdropping. For some reason, I felt like they were going to report everything I was saying to my parents. Whatever.

Christos said, "Don't start doubting everyone else in the world. You already doubt yourself, and that's more than enough of a struggle. Your job is to put your work out there, and hope for the best." He winked at me, flashing his sexy dimples.

"Thanks, Christos," I sighed, doubt dragging me down. I completely appreciated his confidence in me, but it all seemed like a distant fantasy.

"Excuse me," the eavesdropping man sitting next to us said. He had salt-and-pepper hair and wore reading glasses. The woman with him wore her hair in a short silver bob. She set down her eReader and smiled at me warmly.

"I'm sorry to interrupt," the man continued, "but I couldn't help overhearing your conversation with your friend here."

I was right. Eavesdroppers! And there weren't any eaves for miles around. At least this guy was with his wife, so he *probably* wasn't a creepy stalker.

The man continued, "My wife and I have been watching both of you drawing this whole time, and we were wondering, are you Christos Manos?"

"That I am," Christos nodded at the man and they shook hands. "How do you know my name?" Christos asked casually.

"We're both fans of your grandfather's work," the man said.

"You know my grandfather?" Christos smiled.

"No," the woman grinned, "but we've met him."

"Really," Christos smiled.

"Yeah," the man said, "my wife and I used to go to the gallery openings here in town quite a bit. We've chatted with Spiridon more than once. In fact, I seem to recall seeing you as a young man at one of the openings. Isn't that right, dear?"

"Oh yes," his wife beamed, then said to Christos. "But you wouldn't remember us boring old farts—"

I giggled when she said "farts".

"—but you must've been twelve or so at the time."

"That's great," Christos smiled. "So, are you guys collectors?"

"We are," the man said. "We bought several of Spiridon's smaller seascapes back in the day."

"That's terrific," Christos said smoothly. I could tell he was used to conversations like this. I was in awe of how comfortable he was.

"Speaking of which," the man said, "my wife and I were looking at the work you two were doing, and thought we'd like to buy it."

"Oh," Christos said, somewhat surprised. "I don't think I've ever sold one of these crayon paintings before. I usually just sell my oils at Charboneau Gallery in La Jolla."

Wow. Christos wasn't even trying and people were approaching him to buy his work. I was both amazed at the power of his family's reputation and bummed that I was at least a decade or ten behind him in my own embryonic art career. Oh well. Maybe when I turned sixty it would be like this for me too. Assuming I didn't throw in the towel and carry the torch of *my* family's legacy. I could imagine forty years from now, silver-haired couples in coffee shops asking me if I was Sam Smith, CPA, and would I be willing to do their taxes this year? Sigh.

"Actually," the man said sheepishly, "we were hoping to buy your friend's piece."

Christos' eyes lit up and he grinned. "You mean Samantha's?"

"Yes," the man smiled. He offered his hand to me to shake. "Pleased to meet you, Samantha."

His wife shook my hand and said, "We heard you two talking

about trying to sell Samantha's work. We've always tried to support the arts any way we can."

I was blown away. "Are you guys serious?"

"Yes, we're serious," the man smiled. "And we're not just doing you a favor, young lady. I can tell from here your work is good."

"Oh, Ted," his wife said, "Stop. You're embarrassing the poor girl."

"I'm serious, Victoria. I think her work is excellent."

I blushed from head to toe and smiled wide. I think my teeth were blushing too.

"Do you mind if I take a closer look?" Ted asked, reaching toward my crayon painting.

"Sure," I smiled.

He picked it up and held it so his wife could get a better look.

"Isn't that beautiful," Victoria said to her husband, then turned to me. "You have a terrific sense of color. And I can't believe you did this with kids' crayons!"

Ted peered through his reading glasses at my art. "It really is good. Excellent composition." He looked at me over his reading glasses. "How much do you want for it?"

"Uhhh," I was stunned. "I don't know?"

Christos chuckled. "Samantha's new at this, as you may have guessed. Why don't you guys make an offer."

I was glad Christos stepped in. I was going to say they could have it for free.

"How about a hundred bucks?" the man said, pulling out his wallet.

"A hundred bucks!" I clapped my hand over my mouth.

Victoria smiled at me and giggled.

"Okay, how about one fifty?" Ted said.

"Oh my god!" I slapped my other hand over my mouth, totally surprised and slightly embarrassed, like I was manipulating them somehow.

Ted looked at Christos shrewdly. "I think your lady friend is an expert negotiator. One fifty it is. But she has to sign it." Ted winked at me.

"I, no! I mean, I didn't—" I looked at Christos for help. He merely smiled. "I can't take your money! You guys can have it. I can't believe you actually want it."

Ted and Victoria exchanged a laugh while Ted counted the money out of his wallet and laid it on the table.

"Go ahead and sign it, Samantha" Christos encouraged.

"What? How?"

"You know how to sign your name, don't you? Pick a color and sign the thing on the front or the back."

"Oh, on the front, please," Ted said. "We want people who come to our house to know who the artist is."

I selected a gold crayon from the box. It seemed appropriate for the occasion. I signed my name on the front corner. When I was finished, I handed my crayon drawing to Ted. "I've never sold a painting before," I squeaked.

He read my signature. "Now we can tell people that we have Samantha Smith's first sold work in our collection." He turned to his wife. "This oughta be worth something in a few years." He handed me the money.

"Thank you so much!" I said to Ted, then reached over the table and hugged Christos. "I sold my first painting!"

Ted and Victoria chuckled.

"Here's my business card," Ted said, pulling one from his wallet. "Be sure to let us know if you have any work in the Contemporary Artists show you guys were talking about."

"Ted, we should go get this framed," Victoria beamed. "Thank you guys so much. Good luck!"

When they were gone I gaped at Christos. "Did you like, plan that or something?"

He laughed. "No. But I did help set the intention for you."

"I really can't believe that just happened!" I said, still gaping.

"I've seen crazier shit a hundred times in my own life. This is just the beginning, Samantha. I promise, *agápi mou*."

I wrapped my arms around him gave him a huge smooch. "I love you so much, Christos!"

SAMANTHA

When Christos and I left the boardwalk café we both were getting hungry for dinner. We walked past the strip mall where Thai Doughnut was located. They were still open.

"Hey," I joked, "want an Apple Fritter for dinner?"

"Tempting," Christos said thoughtfully. "Maybe dessert?"

"Okay, let's get regular Thai food."

Back at my apartment, we hopped in my VW and drove to Bangkok Bay as the sun went down. Christos ordered Roasted Duck Curry and a side of Drunken Noodles.

"How much do you eat a day, really?" I asked.

"Same as a regular horse," he joked.

I ordered yellow curry, and we drove back to my apartment. We ate sitting on the floor with our backs against my couch, our food on the coffee table.

"Congrats on selling that crayon painting today," Christos said before forking noodles into his mouth.

"Are you sure that wasn't a setup? That woman Victoria said she remembered meeting you."

"That was ten years ago. Probably my grandfather's last gallery show. There were tons of people there. If I met them, I don't remember."

"Are you *sure* sure?" I prodded.

"Accept it, Samantha. Someone bought your artwork today."

"I know!" I shook my hands in a seated happy dance. "I made a hundred fifty bucks!"

"Now you're on your way. I think this deserves a celebration. Maybe even a pageant," he winked.

"Uhhhh...." I squirted a gush of Sriracha hot sauce on my yellow curry.

"Whoa! You got enough hot sauce?" Christos laughed.

"Whoops! Guess I like it hot," I protested.

"Me too," Christos winked.

Gulp. I took a bite of my curry. "Woo, hot!"

I was reminded again of the intense oral sexcapades I'd shared with Christos right on this floor, beside this couch and table, less than two months prior. We had been eating Thai food then, too.

As I chewed my curry, the spicy Sriracha sauce must have kicked in because my whole body was hot-flashing. That was the only rational explanation. I was also sure that my equally sudden horniness had nothing to do with the fact that the hottest man on the planet was grinning at me with his sexy dimples from less than a foot away.

"Are you sweating?" he asked.

"No!" I said, fanning my face. I gulped a swallow of water from my glass.

Christos grinned. "You look all hot and bothered to me."

"It's the hot sauce!" I choked, pointing at my mouth. "Totally spicy!"

"It's not that bad, is it?"

I nodded.

"Let me see…" He leaned toward me and slid his tongue across my lips. "You're right. It is pretty hot. But I don't think it's the Sriracha." He sat back down. "I can think of a few good ways to cool off," he murmured.

"Ice cream!" I jumped up and went to my freezer. I still had several pints of that sweet salve remaining. I grabbed three and carried them back to the coffee table. "This should keep us busy for awhile. Oh! Forgot spoons." I jumped up and got two spoons from the kitchen. "Dig in!" I said, handing one to Christos.

"I haven't even finished my duck."

"Better hurry up, before I eat all the ice cream." I popped the lid on Double Mint Chocolate Chip and shoveled out a bite.

"You okay, Samantha?" Christos asked shrewdly.

"Mime fine," I mumbled over a mouthful of ice cream.

"You sure, *agápi mou*?"

I gazed into his amazingly soulful blue eyes. I felt his intense yet endlessly comforting love wrap itself around my heart. I was instantly calm. What *was* I doing? Running away again? From what? From Christos? Was I crazy? Yes. But for once, I finally felt like I had a choice *not* to be. I set my spoon down and took a deep breath.

"Christos, ever since we got back from D.C.," I said, "I can't stop thinking about how lucky I am to have you in my life. You're the most amazing guy I've ever met, but I keep thinking I'm going to wake up back in high school in D.C., with everyone calling me Whore and Suicide Watch and laughing in my face in the hallways."

"I'm not a dream, *agápi mou*. I'm real." He leaned into me and pinched my forearm gently. "You're awake."

"For the first time ever."

"What do you mean?"

"I mean," I sighed, "maybe this is the first time I've ever been awake in my whole life. Like I'd been walking through a haze until I met you. I sold a fricking painting today!" I wrapped my arms around him and kissed him. "Thank you, Christos. I love you so much."

"I love you too, *agápi mou*." He kissed me again, passionately. Our lips slipped across each other's mouths as mutual desire kindled between us.

"I want you, Christos," I said, feeling suddenly bold, "Now."

He pulled back. "Are you sure?" he asked, his face serious. "Have you thought this through?"

"No."

"Then maybe we should wait. Until the time is right."

I sighed and considered for a moment. "That's what I did with lame Damian. I waited and waited, and everything turned out terrible."

"I'm not Lamian," Christos smirked.

"Did you say *Lame*-ian?"

"I did," he grinned. "Samantha, I can wait as long as you want. I'm not going to rush you or throw a tantrum because you're not ready."

I collapsed into him. "I'm *soooo* ready."

Christos slowly stood up, leaving me on the carpet.

"Where are you going?" My heart clamped up.

"To put the ice cream away. So it doesn't melt." He picked up all three pints and carried them into the kitchen.

Silly me.

When he returned, he said, "Are you ready to host your pageant?"

"Yes," I smiled.

"What does that mean, anyway?"

"Don't you know? It's my V-Pageant Celebration tonight," I smiled coyly.

He chuckled. "Is that the same as turning in your V-card?"

I grimaced. "No. This is way more upscale."

He squatted down next to me and pulled me into his arms. I instinctively wrapped mine around his neck as he stood up and carried me to my bedroom. My heart raced. My toes tingled. This was it. It was really going to happen.

With the man I loved.

"Shouldn't we brush our teeth first, or something?" I asked nervously.

"If you want."

We stood in front of my bathroom mirror, brushing our teeth together. We'd done it before, but it still felt like we were two little kids having a sleep-over, getting ready for bed together.

He grinned. "What?"

"Nothing," I said shyly.

When we finished brushing, he stood by the bathroom door, gesturing back into my bedroom. "After you."

"Oh my god, I'm so nervous."

"Relax. It's going to be fine."

Somehow, I knew it was. Because I was with Christos. Then panic seized me. I slapped my forehead. "Wait!"

"What?"

"I don't have any condoms! Do you have any condoms? I'm not on the pill."

He opened his mouth, then closed it. "I don't."

"Don't you carry a condom in your wallet like most guys?"

"I used them."

"*Them*? As in, plural?"

He raised his eyebrows and shrugged his shoulders. He was about to say something.

"Stop! I don't want to know." I sighed. "So what do we do now?"

"We go buy some."

"We?" I said nervously. The idea of walking into a store and buying condoms seemed like something you were supposed to do while wearing a trench coat, a wide-brimmed hat, and dark glasses to hide your face. "Can't we order some online? Rush delivery?"

"What, from 24HourCondoms.com?"

"They deliver, don't they?"

He smirked, "I don't think they even exist."

My shoulders slumped in disappointment.

"Don't worry, Samantha. Everyone has sex. No one's going to judge you for buying condoms. Last time I checked, safe sex is cool."

"Yeah, but the cashier will be looking at me thinking about how I'm going to be having sex with you later. Maybe we could ask the cashier to join us? Maybe film it?" I joked nervously.

"Isn't there some slogan like, 'If you're afraid to buy condoms, you shouldn't be having sex'?"

"I think it's, 'If you need condoms, ask your boyfriend to buy them while you wait in the car.'"

"Mmmm...no." He smiled compassionately. "Let's go."

"All right," I sighed. "But I'm wearing a ski mask."

"They'll think you're going to rob the place if you do that."

"That's a great idea!" I beamed. "They'll never know who we are! And we can steal them! Do you have a gun? We'll need it for the stick up."

He shook his head. "Uh, no."

"You don't have a gun? Okay. Maybe Walmart is still open?"

"No."

"Are they closed?" I asked, worried. "It's not *that* late."

Christos rolled his eyes. "No, we're not buying a gun. Let's go."

"We're just going to shoplift them? Five-finger the condoms, one for each finger?"

"No, Samantha. We're going to pay for them. Like adults."

"Fiiiiiine," I groaned. I grabbed my purse and we went out the door together.

SAMANTHA

I drove us in my VW to the grocery store. Holding hands, Christos and I walked down an aisle until we stopped at the condom display.

"Which ones should we get?" I asked bashfully.

He scanned the packages hooked to the display. "I'm looking for my favorites."

"You have a favorite?" I grimaced

"Yeah, why?"

"That's so weird!"

"Do you have a favorite tampon?" he said cockily.

"Yeah?"

"Exactly," he grinned.

"That's different!"

"Really?" he said thoughtfully. "How?"

"Because I go through a dozen tampons a month!"

"I go through more than that."

Confused, I said, "you don't wear tampons!"

"Nope." he smiled that stupid cocky smile again.

"Oh," I grimaced, "…are you talking about rubbers?"

"Yep."

"That you use when you're—!!"

"Yep."

"Christos!"

"Samantha!" he mocked.

"How much sex do you have?! Wait! Don't answer that!" I jammed my fingers in my ears.

He pulled my fingers out of my ears. "Since I decided I wanted to be more than your mentor? None."

Phew. That definitely made me feel better. But there was still the issue of quantity to consider.

"Let me get this straight." I started ticking off on my fingers the number of times he…you know…per month. I gave up. I didn't have enough fingers. "You have sex, what, every day?"

"Usually. Until I knew you were the woman I'd been waiting for my entire life."

Swoon. Wait, he was getting me off track. "So, since you started dating me, you've gone from doing the deed daily to *never*? For *months*? Isn't that like, physically impossible for men? To go so long without, you know?"

He hung his head pathetically. "It's been a rough two months."

"Oh, Christos," I placed my palm on his cheek consolingly, "you must be like a parched man in the desert begging for a glass of water."

His cocky grin spiraled into a dimple. "More like a guy with two hand grenades between his legs with their pins pulled out, or two swollen balloons filled with—"

"I get the idea!" I said, jamming my palm against his chest. "If the pressure isn't released soon, your boilers are gonna explode or your volcano is going to erupt," I mocked.

He grinned. "It isn't *that* bad. I do have a hand," he said calmly.

"You are such a perv!"

He chuckled some more.

Despite my semi-disgust at this topic of conversation, I couldn't stop myself from imagining his now-defunct harem of harlots parading around the site of where his manly edifice jutted up mightily from God's green earth. I pictured a large circle of cavorting concubines with flowers in their hair and wearing short Grecian dresses while they held hands and danced around King Christos' fleshy obelisk, preparing to sacrifice their virginity to the God of Love. All while a sweltering sun illuminated the ritual from the sky above.

Yeah, I was ready to change this subject.

Heedless of the fact we were in the middle of a grocery store, I said, "So, we came here to grab condoms so we could have sex. But now I'm feeling like I'm at the back of the unemployment line, waiting to pick up my check, and I'm the girl who gets to the counter last thing before closing, after five hundred other women who've already received payment from you have come and gone. Is that supposed to be romantic?"

"No payment ever changed hands, I swear," he smirked confidently. "But I do accept tips."

"It's not funny, Christos," I sulked.

He sighed. "Samantha, if you want to wait, that's okay with me. But my history is never going to go away."

I simmered.

"I'm sorry, Samantha. But that's the facts. It's who I am. Had you come into my life sooner, things would've been different. What can I say? I dropped all the women in my life the second I decided I was so deeply in love with you that I couldn't live without you."

I liked that last bit about him not being able to live without me, but I didn't want to tell him that the phrase "dropping all the women in his life" made me imagine him coming home from the grocery store cradling paper grocery bags in his arms, the bags overflowing with dozens of miniature naked women, each with a label that read:

Step 1: Add water to create a full-sized floozy.

Step 2: Insert tab A into slot B.

Step 3: Repeat step 2 until desired result is achieved.

Step 4: Have fun!

I took a deep breath and let it out. I knew Christos was right. I had to accept him as-is. He was used goods. Or pre-owned, as the luxury car dealerships liked to say.

Hold on. What was I thinking? Christos wasn't an object. He

was a person. And people were messy things. I was a recovering hot mess myself. I leaned into him. "You're right, Christos. I'm sorry. I'm being totally lame."

"It's okay. I understand, *agápi mou*. But I want you to know that the last thing I thought about when I realized I was crazy in love with you was how we were going to work out the sex thing. I just thought about the fact that I desperately loved you and needed you in my life, no matter what. I figured everything else would work itself out if we loved each other. You love me, don't you?"

I gazed into his mesmerizing blue eyes. They swallowed my heart every time. I also realized that this man standing in front of me had heard my darkest secrets, yet he still accepted me unconditionally. How could I give him any less of myself than everything?

"I do love you, Christos. I love you more than I ever thought I could love another human being."

"You two are so darling together," an old woman standing behind a grocery cart loaded with cheap wine said to both of us, her eyes twinkling.

OMG, How long had she been listening? She pushed her cart past us.

"Mmm, mmm," she hummed, "young love gets me every time. You better hold onto this one," she said to me as she squeezed my arm gently. "They broke the mold when they made him, I can tell you. I've been around the block once or twice in my time, and they don't usually look like him. Mmmm, mmmm," she shook her head. "And I suggest you buy the extra large," she nodded toward the condoms.

I gasped. How the hell would she know that?

"It's the hands," she whispered surreptitiously, "I can always tell." She nodded confidently as she walked away. "*The hands*," she mouthed silently before turning the corner.

Christos did have ginormous hands.

"What she said," Christos said with a pussy-eating grin on his face.

I say pussy-eating, because, based on the look in his eyes, that's probably what he was thinking about right at that moment.

I'm only slightly ashamed to admit I was sort of thinking about it too.

And other things.

Christos finally grabbed a box from the display.

"That's a big box!" I goggled. "How big are those extra large condoms?"

Gulp!

"The box is big because it has a lot of condoms," he said.

"How many do we need?! Isn't one enough?"

Christos smirked. "No."

Double gulp!

"How many are in that box?" I asked.

"Thirty-six," he said matter-of-factly.

Triple gulp!

"Should I get two boxes?" he asked casually, "so we can have more for tomorrow?"

"Uhhhh…." Part of me wanted to run screaming from the grocery store with my knees clamped together. I wouldn't be running per se, it would be more of a potato-sack race-hop, but it would be effective. Instead of bolting for the door, I took a good look at Christos.

He was tall. Like, mythically tall. His face was model hot. He was extremely well-built. His chiseled, muscled arms, covered in sexy tattoos, danced hypnotically every time he moved them. I knew from first-hand experience that his eight pack was ribbed and rock hard. I would be lying if I denied that I wanted to learn everything I could about his hard things.

Oh yeah, and I loved him.

I think I was drooling.

Shiver.

Waiter! Check, please!

Oh wait, where was I again?

I think I'd just lost my mind.

Chapter 8

SAMANTHA

When we brought the box of condoms to the cashier, I decided to woman-up and proudly pay for them myself.

The cashier looked sort of like my dad, but had a mustache. Although this made me fidgety and uncomfortable, I was determined to go through with it. I almost blurted, "I'm buying condoms because my boyfriend and I are going to have sex right now." Instead, I said, "We're going to fill these up and have a water balloon fight."

I grimaced because I half expected the guy to ask what we were going to fill them with. Eww.

Christos rubbed the small of my back while we walked to my car. "Well done, Samantha. That wasn't so bad, was it?"

"Except for the fact the cashier reminded me of my dad."

"I noticed that."

"Now it's like my dad knows I'm about to have sex."

"I'm pretty sure that guy doesn't know your dad, but I can run back inside and give him your parents' number, if you want," Christos joked. "He can call them and let them know."

"No, don't!"

"Totally kidding," he smiled.

I huffed a sigh, "Is it possible to have my anxiety surgically removed?" I asked.

"I don't think so. But my bet is that you're going to forget your own name in about an hour. An hour after that, you won't even know what planet you're on. And then…"

"Whoa, how long does sex take? I thought it was like ten or fifteen minutes, tops."

"Maybe with an ordinary mortal," he winked. "You might want to consider clearing you calendar for the rest of the week."

"Get in the car!" I ordered. "Now!"

"Yes, ma'am," he grinned, and casually swung himself into the passenger seat of my VW.

If there were any stops signs or red lights between the grocery store and my apartment, I may have skipped one or two of them.

I was burning up when I pulled into my parking space and turned off the car. My nipples were tight against the cups of my bra. My panties were noticeably damp. I squirmed in my seat while my heart raced. I looked over at Christos.

"So, um, from this point forward," I said nervously, "you're pretty much in charge, because I have no idea how this is supposed to work."

He leveled a penetrating gaze at me. "You're sure?"

"Yes."

"Well, you still have the safe word, just in case."

"You mean grapes?" I asked.

"Yeah."

"I don't think I'm going to need any fruit tonight. I've got you," I winked.

"You going to peel my banana?"

"What?" I was confused. "Oh! No! Gross!"

He chuckled as we got out of the car. I held the bag with the condoms in my hand.

"Stay right there."

"Okay."

Christos came around to my side and picked me up. I wrapped my legs around his waist and we instantly started kissing. His tongue probed deeply into my mouth. I welcomed it. Our tongues danced and explored as our lips twisted wetly together.

We continued kissing while he carried me up the stairs to my apartment.

"I have to warn you," he cautioned, "once we walk through this door, you may never want to come out."

"I'm okay with that."

Christos carried me inside and with a soft click, closed the door behind us.

I don't know how long we made out in the living room with Christos holding me in his arms. My legs got tired at some point, but the way his strong hands cupped my ass made me want to stay right where I was. Not because I was scared to go further, but because he was kneading my ass, which sent pleasurable jolts rocketing throughout my entire body.

I was vaguely aware of the fact that his rock hard arms were like steel, and he never seemed to tire, like he could hold me up forever. His unshakable strength made me even hotter.

Eventually, I did drop the bag of condoms on the floor.

Christos gave a throaty chuckle. "Maybe we should use those."

"I'm ready when you are," I smiled.

He squatted down, still holding me with one arm, picked up the bag, and carried me into my bedroom.

He set me down on the bed and looked at me. He was so impressively tall. From this angle, he looked like a mountain towering above me.

"Are you nervous?" he asked softly.

"A little," I said in a quavering voice. By a little, I meant more nervous than I've ever been in my entire life.

He sat down on the bed beside me. He no longer felt imposing. He felt protective. His hand stroked my cheek, brushing my hair aside. "It's okay, *agápi mou*. Right now, I bet your head is telling your heart to be careful. It's trying to protect it the best way it knows how. But I think if you look into your heart, you will realize how much I love you."

I gazed up into his eyes. "I do love you, Christos. More than I know how to say. I love you...but I'm still nervous." I was afraid my reluctance would break the fledgling magical enchantment that surrounded us and ruin the mood before we could go all the way. At the same time, I was frightened of what was supposed to come next between a man and woman in love.

"You know what?" he asked.

I suddenly feared the worst.

"You just need to relax. You're never going to enjoy this if you don't."

"That's what I'm afraid of," I murmured while my eyes teared. I covered my face with my hands. I didn't want him to see my fear.

I felt gentle fingers on my wrists, pulling my hands away.

"Don't worry, *agápi mou*. I'll show you how. Lie down."

My heart seized, afraid of what came next. Old memories of Damian punched my heart.

Bitch. Slut. Whore…

I wanted to sob, but I did my best to hold it back.

Christos looked at me with ultimate concern in his eyes. "What is it, *agápi mou*?"

"It's Damian," I hitched, "I can't stop thinking about that night. Like it's happening right now. Like, any second, I might change my mind, and if I do, you'll get angry and yell at me and throw me out."

He smiled. "I can't throw you out of your own apartment." His grin was so friendly, so comforting, it calmed me. "Besides, Lamian isn't in this room. It's just the two of us."

I giggled when he said "Lamian." He was right. I didn't want phantoms from my past invading my present. I steeled myself and did my best to prepare. "Okay, I'm ready."

"You're not relaxing."

"I…*I don't know how!*" I pleaded, about to shed tears.

"You will in a second. Turn over."

"What?" I was scared to death, convinced my nervousness was going to ruin all of this.

SAMANTHA

"I'm going to give you a massage," Christos said. He stood up and pulled his boots off, then slid my shoes off my feet before climbing back onto the bed.

"Oh." I rolled onto my stomach. His weight shifted then I felt warm, powerful hands squeeze the muscles around my neck and shoulder blades through my t-shirt in a pulsating rhythm. "Oh!"

"You like that?" I heard him grinning.

"Yes. It's…exquisite."

"Good."

He continued massaging, pressing, releasing, squeezing, relaxing. It was so soothing. Then his hands slid down my back, sending a jolt through my body. They changed direction at my pelvis and pushed back up toward my neck. He did this repeatedly, like he was forcing the bad energy out the top of my head. I sighed about a hundred times. It felt really, really good.

His hands continued their pattern, but he added another piece. When his palms reach my shoulder blades, they circled out and down my arms. His skin touched mine and I shivered. I felt goose bumps prickling up the backs of my arms. I shivered from head to toe.

After awhile, he changed things up again, and pressed his thumbs deeply into the knots between my shoulder blades.

"Oh, god," I blurted.

"Right there?" he chuckled.

"How did I get so tense?"

He laughed. "You're probably like this all the time and never notice."

"What?"

"This is your normal state. Or at least, it's what you've become accustomed to. I'm trying to work you down to a more relaxed state. One you probably haven't experienced since you were a little kid."

I scoffed. "I doubt I was relaxed, even as a kid. You've met my parents."

"You might be right. I guess that means you're in for a treat. I'm going to knead all these knots out of your body until you're a heap of floppy flesh."

"Eww!" I giggled.

"You're going to love it," he purred as he slid his hands down and firmly clenched my ass.

I jerked as jolty pleasure sizzled in my hips.

He slid his hands down the sides of my legs, then pressed firmly as he slid his palms up the backs of them. His thumbs dug into the bottom of my butt, pressing up around my tail bone and finally curving across the crests of my pelvis. Lightning bolts coursed out from his fingertips, or my tense muscles, I wasn't sure which.

"Oh, wow. Keep doing that."

"You like having an ass massage?"

"Am I a slut if I say yes?"

"Only if you want to be," he joked.

I giggled. "Can we do this every day?" I asked hopefully.

"Yes."

There was such finality to the way he said it, I knew I could have this any time I wanted it. Which would be daily. Well, maybe only three times a week. He was doing such a good job, I doubted I'd need it more often than that.

Wow.

Christos continued his firm hand-motions around my ass. Every time he did, he went harder, causing my pelvis to tip forward with each thrust, then tip back as he released. I almost felt like I was being taken from behind, in the conventional sense of the term. Yet I was still fully clothed, and I'm pretty sure my panties were going to be soaked before the massage was over, or in the next two seconds, whichever came first.

Christos shifted his weight around on the bed again as he stood up.

"Where are you going?" I begged. "Are we done?"

"Just getting started. Your feet need some love to."

"Oh," I said, relieved.

His weight pressed down on the bed near the bottom and he took one of my feet in his hands and laid it on his thigh. Thumbs slid across the sole of my foot, fingers caressed the sides, pressure, then release, pulsing motions toward my toes, electricity swirling to life then exiting in every direction.

"Uhhhh." It was all I could manage to say.

After all the muscles in my foot felt creamy and relaxed, he repeated the process on the other side. Then he pressed down on the backs of my calves with considerable weight and rolled his hands toward my ankles several times.

When he was done, he shifted again and sat down on the backs of my legs while he forcefully pressed what I think were his forearms up my lower back, on either side of my spine. It was delicious.

Every time he pressed down and slid upward I moaned, "Oooohhhh," like he was squeezing the sounds out of my body.

Slowly, I realized that his pelvis was now pressing against the ass of my jeans with every forward thrust. My immediate response was to arch my back, thrusting my butt into him.

"Mmmm, I think you're starting to get warmed up," he purred.

"Starting to? I've already melted. I'm a puddle of butter. I don't think I've ever been so relaxed." I pushed back with my hips, trying to somehow bridge the distance between his flesh and mine, but our clothes still blocked passage.

"Do me a favor, agápi mou?"

"Anything, love."

"For now, keep relaxing. Lie still. I want to squeeze every drop of tension out of you."

"But, Christos, I want you to feel good too."

"You have no idea how much I'm enjoying this."

"Really? But you're doing all the work."

"It's simple The more relaxed you get, the bigger the smile on my face gets."

"And other things" I asked. "Are they getting bigger too?"

"We're talking sperm whale back here," he chuckled.

"Thar she blows, Cap'n Ahab! 'Tis Moby Dork!" I laughed.

"Exactly."

I eased my hips back down to the bed and he continued to knead the tension out of my back. He paused from his big motions to gently rub my neck with one hand. Oddly, I felt my throat suddenly relax. I didn't know your throat could relax. "How did you do that?" I asked. My voice came out uncharacteristically breathy. I didn't know I could *sound* like that. *I had bedroom voice!* Oh, wait. Getting excited. *Stay relaxed.*

"Do what?" he mused.

"Relax my voice?"

"Your neck and throat are one big unit. It's all connected. Now it's time to turn over." He went up on all fours.

I spiraled beneath him and stared into his eyes. In the faint glow of my nightstand lamp, they were a deep ocean blue. Bottomless. Like his devotion. "Hi," I said huskily. "Do you like my sexy voice?"

He grinned. "The sexiest ever." He slid his palms down my cheeks, across the sides of my neck, down my chest and across my breasts. Oh, my. Fireworks ignited in them and my nipples popped, straining tightly inside my bra.

"I should take my bra off, don't you think?"

"Do we dare?" he winked.

I grinned. "Yes."

He slid his hand expertly under my shirt and up my back. I arched and he unhooked it in a single motion.

I narrowed my eyes and said, "You're way too good at that."

"Practice makes perfect, just like my massaging skills."

"Is that a good thing?" I asked doubtfully.

"Have you ever had a *bad* massage?"

"I've never even had a massage, until now."

"A bad massage either feels like the masseuse isn't doing anything, or like they're cranking down on your muscles with pliers while trying to peel your skin off with sandpaper. I can recreate both, if you want to test it out."

"No, I'll opt for the good massage."

"You sure?" He began tickling my ribs with feather fingers.

"Stop! Good massage! The kind only experience brings!" I giggled.

He smiled and slid his hands down my flat stomach.

"I think I want to take my bra off," I said nervously. "Do you mind?"

"Not at all," he said warmly. "Whatever makes you most comfortable, *agápi mou*."

I wiggled out of my bra and pulled it through my sleeve before tossing it on the floor.

"Better?" he asked.

I nodded.

The heels of his hands pressed gently down the center of my rib cage and fanned gently outward as he reached my pelvis.

"Mmmmm," I moaned.

Then his hands slid up my sides, again tickling my ribs, but not nearly as intensely as a moment ago. It was electric. His palms circled my breasts and squeezed them softly through my shirt, then slid back down my stomach, his thumbs tracing down my center line and dancing over my navel.

Christos moved his body down toward my feet as his hands slid across the tops of my thighs, his thumbs prying between my inner thighs. He did this repeatedly and I felt an ember begin to glow between my legs. I slowly lost track of time as that ember ignited into a fire. He kept going, his thumbs now rubbing across my womanhood through my jeans, stroking mesmerizingly in longer and harder semi-circles until the fire in my pelvis was a roaring blaze.

My thighs had completely relaxed and opened to allow him free access. I was so ready.

"Christos?" I moaned.

"Yes, *agápi mou*?"

"I need you. Inside me. Now."

"Your wish is my command," he smiled cockily.

Cocky was good. I was all about the cock at that moment.

I had no idea what I was even talking about!

COCK!!!!!

SAMANTHA

Christos sat up and slid his shirt over his head. His abs were the first thing I saw. Evenly spaced, rigid, hard. Like armor. I stroked my fingers across them. I couldn't wait for his shirt to come off.

"Mmmm," he moaned. "Like those?"

"*Love* those," I whispered. "Yummy to the millionth power."

Now his shirt was up over his head, revealing his amazing chest with its soft, downy hair. My hands slid up, following the shirt, and I traced the script of his "Fearless" tattoo as he pulled the shirt all the way over his head. He tossed it to the floor and lowered his hands to his thighs.

I reached up to touch his massive shoulders and arms. I marveled at the intricate tattoos on both. He was so damn hot.

I grinned, "Christos, do you ever notice how hot you are?"

"I—"

I pressed my finger to his lips. "Of course you do." I smiled.

He slid his hands under my ass, pulled my hips toward his. One hand supporting my back, he sat me up on his lap. I wrapped my legs around his waist, our chests inches apart.

I didn't resist when he lifted my shirt over my head. It joined Christos' shirt on the floor. I looked at our two shirts in a tangle on my rug. Somehow, they were sordidly symbolic. Christos and I were about to be similarly tangled.

My breasts were now fully exposed, my nipples tight with need. I leaned forward until they pressed against Christos.

Christos tipped his head back enough to gaze at my breasts. "Fuck, you are so totally fine, Samantha. You are perfect. Damn, you are unbelievable. Do *you* realize how hot *you* are?" he asked, biting his lower lip and wrinkling his nose with animalistic desire.

I was too shy to respond.

"When Mattel was making the Barbie doll," he smiled, "they called God and asked him for your measurements."

I rolled my eyes. "I think Mattel should file a cease and desist order against that joke."

We laughed together.

"Let me put it another way," Christos said, "every time I look at you, Samantha, I'm reminded of how perfect you are in every respect. Every last bit of you, inside and out. Your flawless skin, your tender heart. Your perfect curves and your unbridled joy. Your alluring eyes and your gorgeous laughter. You are the epitome of beauty, you are the ideal to which all women aspire. Your physical beauty makes Aphrodite weep with envy. She doesn't have what you have. No other woman on this planet, or goddess above, does." He let his words linger.

I was speechless, to say the least. My mouth hung open and I clamped it shut before a moth or whatever flew into it.

"So, should we take our pants off now?" he smiled cockily.

"Uh, yeah!" I joked.

"You wanna go first?"

"No, I'll let you." I lifted my legs and he slid his feet onto the floor.

He unbuckled his belt and pushed his pants down, then pulled them off. He was now down to socks and boxers. He stood up and faced me.

I savored every inch of him with my eyes. He was unbelievably constructed from top to bottom. His powerfully muscled legs were the pillars that supported his sleek, narrow hips. Wedging out from his pelvis were his rugged abs, the foundation for his massive chest and shoulders. His muscled arms hung at his sides like steel girders. And those god damn tattoos! Why were they so unbelievably sexy?!? On top of it all, like a golden monument, was that perfect face, angelic and devilish at the same time.

His eyes shone into me and I felt the heat between my legs intensify.

My eyes gravitated back toward the rod of iron hidden beneath his boxers, which were tented out comically. I stifled a laugh. Was I ruining the mood again? I couldn't help myself. One step at a time.

"How many rings do you have in that circus tent of yours?" I giggled.

"Three," he grinned. "Dancing elephants in one, lion taming in another, and a tiny car with a bunch of clowns hanging out in the last. Take your pick."

"Are the clowns blowing bugles?" I smiled.

"No," he frowned, "they're girl clowns, and they're blowing skin flutes." He shook his head, smirking. "Come on, you were supposed to pick lion-taming. How is a crowded clown car sexy?"

"I can't help it! I like clowns!" I laughed.

"You are so wrong," he smiled his dimpled smile. "Now, quit stalling."

It didn't take long for my laughter to fade as I continued to take in his amazing body. His nearly naked, aroused, throbbing…BODY! His body! I was only looking at his body!

He stood in front of me smiling, enjoying the way my eyes were devouring him. "Your turn, *agápi mou*."

I wrinkled my nose. "Um…you're still wearing your socks."

He peeled each one off.

All that was left between me and his clown bugle…were his boxers. My nerves rattled again, although not nearly as loudly as before my massage. I stalled anyway, looking for the most obvious distraction. "What about your boxers? You haven't taken them off!" Suddenly, I realized this strategy was not going to help my nerves.

He slid his boxers down and stepped out of them casually.

Holy shit.

I mean, I'd seen it. I'd touched it, I'd shared a bed with it and Christos. Yes, it seemed sort of like a third person that snuggled between us at night. Because it was so very, very large. And it was pointing right at me. Like a cruise missile, laser sights targeting my…oh, my.

He smirked, and chuckled. Obviously, he was reading my mind. Or his guided missile had sonar, radar, and ESP-ar.

"Your turn," he grinned. "Do you need help?"

"I'm pretty sure I can't even move." My eyes were glued to his Member's Only *Member*, a club to which I was about to gain admittance. "I'm going to need some help, I think."

I sat up on the edge of the bed, topless, braless, my breasts inches from his Holy Manhood, Batman.

I unsnapped my jeans and leaned back on the bed, propped on my elbows. "Care to help a damsel in distress?"

"I'm about to steal your virtue, young lady. Is this the sort of assistance you require?" he winked. "Or should we stop off at the vineyard for some…"

I shook my head.

He leaned over and tugged at the sides of my jeans, pulling them slowly down, leaving my panties behind, thank goodness. My jeans passed over my thighs...oh my god...over my knees. No going back. He stopped when they were bunched around my ankles.

Then he knelt down and raised one of my feet a few inches off the carpet, holding the sole in his hand almost like he was about to do the glass slipper routine. Instead, he carefully peeled my jeans off one foot, then the other. Prince Charming.

My panties were my only protection. Suddenly shy, I plopped back on the bed and crossed my arms over my breasts as my most pressing issue came up once again. And I didn't mean the pink torpedo shooting out from between Christos' legs.

"You know, Christos," I said, my sexy bedroom voice replaced by a trembling one. "I'm still a virgin."

"I know," he whispered, still kneeling at my feet. He rested a comforting hand on my knee.

"And you're not." I winced when I said it, dropping my head onto the bed and staring at the ceiling. I teared instantly. Why did this bother me so much? I had no explanation. But I was tremendously sad, as if I'd lost something before ever finding it.

Christos crawled onto the bed and laid beside me. He propped himself on one elbow and gazed at me.

He stroked my hair out of my face and smiled at me in a small, private, intimate way. There was a sudden softness to his face that was new to me. It was perhaps the most beautiful expression I'd ever seen on another human being. I took several deep breaths, and really took in the look of loving compassion in his eyes. It was tremendously comforting. He was completely vulnerable and open to me in that moment.

As he opened his mouth to speak, my heart raced out of control. I think I feared what came next, simply because it was the unknown.

"I've never given my heart to anyone, *agápi mou*. You are my first. And you will be my last. You are my forever."

My heart stopped. I couldn't believe my ears.

The universe collapsed in on itself.

Somehow, on an atomic level, I knew his words were the truth.

He was truth.

Oh my god.

I knew then that he could take my virginity. I was ready to let him.

I reached up to caress his cheek. My hand trembled. I could barely speak as my tears flowed freely. I whispered, "Christos, I, I love you, so much, I…"

He gazed into my soul, his eyes alight with brilliant, abundant love. His lips curled into a dimpled smile, but the customary cockiness was not there. Only warmth, acceptance, certainty, and love.

Love.

My heart slowed and my breath returned. I realized that I was not about to let Christos *take* my virginity. I was willingly giving it to him, giving my gift to the one man to whom it truly belonged, for him to treasure and protect forever.

I was filled with a warm, soothing confidence that this gift I was about to give to Christos was unique, and this moment would never be repeated in my entire life. Or his. It only happened once. For either of us.

This was it.

This was true love.

Christos lowered his lips to mine and began kissing me.

Interlude

SAMANTHA

We kissed passionately for a long time. Our lips were joined, our tongues entwined, our hearts united. His hands stroked my face, his murmurs caressed my soul. We kissed increasingly deeply, our passion growing and expanding to encircle both of us, blocking out the outside world.

All that existed was Christos and myself.

I was scared, but I had never felt safer. Worried, but confident that Christos was the only man on Earth who could protect my tender heart. I was fearful, but the connection I felt with Christos gave me courage. My heart had been empty for so long, but now I felt it filled to completion. With Christos.

At last.

His hand slid down my naked chest and his fingers brushed across my nipples, stopping on one, gently plucking and twisting. My nipple ached with succulent hardness. I moaned softly, our lips still together, and he swallowed my passion.

His powerful hand kneaded the entirety of my full breast. Swirls of pleasure whirlpooled around it before dissolving throughout my body.

It felt so incredibly good.

Without breaking our kiss, he slid his knee over my legs and was hovering above me, sitting astride his heels. He massaged both my breasts simultaneously. I was consumed by his mouth. His tongue fought with mine, filling me.

I felt my other nipple pinched. I gave into electric sensation as another maelstrom of energy erupted out from the center of this breast, and the two currents of energy now swirling in each co-mingled and pulsed down to my core. My sudden awareness of my own heat between my legs alerted me to a foreign, throbbing presence. His immense length was laying across my panties, a thin filament of cotton between his manhood and my womanhood.

I wanted it. I needed it.

"Are you ready?" he asked.

"Yes."

He reached over to the nightstand and opened the box of condoms. He pulled one out, tore the package, and squeezed the tip while rolling it onto the length of his erection.

His smile curled up mischievously as he hooked his fingers through the waistband of my panties. "It's your last chance to abandon ship before this submarine submerges."

I blurted laughter. It rolled out long and loud. Soon, Christos was laughing with me. He hovered over me on all fours, his arms two stout columns on either side of my face. I inhaled the scent of him on the breeze of his laughter. He was so sweet, in every way, to all of my senses. Sight, sound, taste…touch. I was finally ready for the ultimate touch. Christos was the perfect man, perfectly erect, right between my legs.

"Dive, Captain, Dive! Pull those panties off!" I said in my version of a soldier's voice, "before they catch fire!" I giggled again.

He made "Wee-Ooh, wee-ooh" noises as he slid my panties down.

As corny as the moment was, I honestly didn't think I could possibly have crossed that final line of allowing myself to be exposed so fully to him if I hadn't been laughing the entire time. Wasn't humor supposed to be an aphrodisiac? I could testify to its seductive effects.

Christos sat up and dangled my panties over the side of the bed and gave me a questioning look, my final opportunity for reprieve.

I nodded.

He dropped my panties to the floor. I half expected them to explode like a bomb when they hit the carpet, but they merely shushed into a heap on top of our other castoff clothes.

Christos looked into my eyes for a long time. His were so infinitely blue, endless, limitless. They slowly darkened, all lightness gone as naked desire lowered his lashes over their smoky, shadowy depths.

He inhaled and exhaled heavily.

"I want you more than I have ever wanted *anything*, Samantha.

You are the woman I have dreamed about all my life, but never found. You are the peace I have longed for. You are the home I've never had. You are the reassurance that life is beautiful, that life has purpose, that my time on this earth with you is the most precious gift in existence."

My heart exploded with love.

I held my arms out to him and he lowered himself on top of me. I opened my heart to him completely. My legs parted freely. He lay back down at my side, his knee draped over my thigh. I wasn't sure what was going to happen next until his hand reached over and began caressing my wet cleft. His index finger slid up and down my entrance, teasing it open, spreading my slickness around as his finger pushed and explored.

We weren't kissing, but we stared into each other's eyes while his finger probed deeper and deeper. I wasn't aware of how deeply he'd gone until I felt his knuckles brush against my wetness. Then he withdrew his finger slowly. No! I wanted his finger back!

Then two fingers slid inside me and I shuddered and moaned, "Oh, it's so good, Christos…"

He began an easy rhythm with his hand. Pleasure wound up inside my pelvis at an alarming speed. I was going to come. There was no stopping it. I tried to hold his gaze, but my body bucked as my head lifted from the pillow and my eyelids fluttered. I couldn't, it was so, the pleasure, so intense, oh god, it was…

I moaned. "Cah, cah, cah, Christos…"

"Let it out, agápi mou. Let it all out."

I groaned and writhed and squirmed on the bed as his fingers plunged in and out, over and over again.

"Huh, huh, huh," I breathed as pleasure pounded throughout my body, my orgasm humming through my very bones.

Then his thumb circled my clitoris and a firestorm hailed through my body in electric ecstasy. The sensations intensified as his thumb persisted, pleasure ricocheting throughout my body, tickling my teeth, my toes, even my fucking fingernails, with fluttery sweetness.

His fingers continued their unrelenting slip and slide, in and out.

I was coming again. Another wave of overwhelming orgasm rippled up and down my body. I was gone. Lost. Stolen away to the most incredible destination a man and a woman could know together.

The crashing waves continued for I don't know how long, or for how many orgasms. I lost count.

I had never had anything remotely approaching this kind of sexual experience.

And this was only the beginning.

His fingers slid slowly out of me.

I tingled and my head spun and I was dizzy and lightheaded and didn't know up from down or left from right.

But I was aware of Christos lowering his weight on top of me. My legs were wide open.

Welcome home.

His arms pillared around my shoulders, he was a massive Grecian temple erected around me, and I was his place of worship. Consecrated ground. The sacredness of this moment silenced all fears with a sense of eternal love, support, protection, comfort, and peace. Eternal peace. In that moment, I felt I'd unwittingly discovered the meaning of life.

Love.

Christos. Samantha.

Together.

As one.

Forever.

"I love you, Christos."

"I love you, Samantha."

His chest was hot and heavy against my electrified breasts. I felt his hardness press against the entrance to my core. I was drenched with wetness. The tip of him tingled against my folds. I shivered with expectation. He reached down and held himself in one fist while he slid his hot head up and down against my lips.

Then he eased himself into me a fraction of an inch.

My mental fog burned away instantly.

He pulled back without pulling out completely, then eased further in. He was stretching me, but I wanted it. I think I was so relaxed from the massaging, the foreplay, the love, that I felt my muscles relax, inviting him deeper inside, all the way. His hardness eased into my softness, completely and perfectly filling me up.

"Now."

That was all he said.

That was all it took.

I felt the muscles in my core tingle and seize in a vibrating release of yet another orgasm.

I couldn't believe it.

I was coming again. Christos was inside me.

I was coming.

"Christos," I cried. "It's so good…"

"I know," he whispered.

Euphoria swept through me. It wasn't the fiery orgasm of before. It was a consistent throbbing that just wouldn't stop.

The amount of pleasure flowing through me was impossible. But it was real. It was the greatest pleasure I'd ever experienced.

He started to move, withdrawing with exquisite slowness, then plunging back into me.

Oh my god, I thought he had somehow finished a moment ago when he'd said "now."

No, he was just getting started.

He thrust slowly into me, all the way. To the hilt. For a second, I'd expected it to hurt, but it didn't. Instead, he was so gentle, so tender, so conscious, so aware of my needs and my limits, it was perfect. He paused and I felt his fullness pressing into me, deep down inside, as the jewels of his manhood rested warmly against my slick entrance.

Our heat combined.

I was so at ease, I spontaneously wrapped my legs around his waist and squeezed, allowing him even deeper access as my core consumed the most intimate part of him.

After a moment, he retracted slowly, then began sliding rhythmically in and out of me in perfect communication, the essence of one body co-mingling with the other.

His pace increased. Every thrust pushed me toward the edge of oblivion, but I remained balanced on that thin line of awareness, knowing only infinite ecstasy. I was trapped in a delight so sweet that it blotted out my consciousness of all things save the plunging of Christos' cock into my core, over and over again, as he planted seeds of pleasure in my center that blossomed inside my pelvis and grew throughout my body. He was the root and I the flower. My wet petals spread wide as our souls were bound together with every intimate stroke.

I clasped his ass with my fingers and whispered into his ear, "harder, Christos, harder."

He accelerated like a steam engine. Slowly, but so massive, turning and spinning and pounding into me again and again and again.

Hammering, driving, filling me to straining excess.

I floated in clouds of ecstasy as he thundered into me. I was a rainstorm of pleasure quenching his insatiable fire.

He grunted, he groaned, he moaned with his own volcanic release.

"Samantha," his words were rugged, rocky with naked desire, "I need you, I need…"

"You have me, Christos, we have each other…"

"Oooh," he sighed, "it's too much, it's too good, it's never been like this…"

I knew exactly what he was talking about.

Thoughts ceased as my pleasure mingled with his.

His moans blended with my own, our cries combining harmoniously with our sighs.

I was dying as I awoke to overwhelming rhapsody for the first time in my life, and I never wanted it to stop. Christos kept pounding and pounding in and out, each thrust squeezing more and more pleasure into me, filling me up with an impossible amount of intense sensation. I couldn't handle it, it was too much, I was overwhelmed but I needed more, ever more. I would do anything for *more*…

"Don't stop," I moaned breathily, "don't ever stop…"

"Never, *agapi mou*…" *thrust*, "This is for us," *thrust*, "always for us," *thrust*, "*only* for us…" he grunted and moaned, thrusting and thrusting and thrusting.

I was being consumed by love and pleasure in equal measure. While his words healed my heart, his heavy thrusts destroyed my core with sweet fire. I burned with need for more, for all…

For us…

I sobbed, barely able to speak. "I…I'm coming… again… Christos…" Lightning shattered my body with release. Yet another orgasm boomed through my soul as Christos' body crashed into mine. My tears flowed freely.

I circled my arms around his neck. He leaned down and kissed me passionately, locking us together as he thrust and thrust and thrust. My legs gripped his waist more tightly as my core locked onto him, my entire body begging him not to retreat. My heart didn't want to let go.

My heart would never let go...

"Ahhh!!!!" he shouted. "Fuck! It's too much! I can't stop!"

I didn't want him to.

My mind spun out of control as another electrical storm took my body into the stratosphere. I had lost all control of my world and I didn't care.

Christos had taken me. Taken me to a place no one had ever been.

To *us*...

I was lost inside...

Trapped in a hot, wet, maze of pleasure. A maze I never wanted to leave. My mind was confused at every turn, uncertain which way to go other than inward. So I went deeper into the moment, leaving the world around me behind, seeking the center, seeking the freedom of imprisoning myself inside the infinite pleasure of...

Us...

...for what I prayed would be eternity...

I lost all track of time. I spiraled down into my core, to my center. I found Christos waiting there for me, his eyes ablaze with lust and love and desire for...

Us.

Agápi mou...

I found freedom.

Christos was now bound to me for eternity.

His manhood thrust relentlessly into my soaking womanhood, his arms columned around my head as his eyes drilled into my soul and my legs knotted around his waist. We left the universe behind.

Together.

"I love you, Samantha, I love you!" He cried with total vulnerability, as if he had bared his most precious secrets to me and only me.

"Christos," I sighed breathlessly, then began mumbling nearly unintelligibly as he pounded himself into me, "oh, Christos, I'm yours, my love is yours, for you, only for you..." I could barely form the words. But I knew he needed them, needed my reassurance and love in that moment. He needed me.

He needed us.

My heart swelled with love and empowerment. I held this man's heart in my hands and I was determined to protect it forever, and heal all his wounds.

"Oh god," Christos whispered, "I'm going to come, *agápi mou,* I'm going to come!!!!"

"Do it, Christos, come inside me. Now. Do it."

Violent, building, mounting. Growing, swollen, expanding. Contracting, tight, wet ecstasy took us both.

I was afraid he was going to break something, but then he sunk himself into me all the way to the bottom and roared. But he didn't stop. His body rocked and shook traumatically even though he was all the way in. He was trying to drill deeper and deeper, as if his entire being was rocketing into mine through his manhood.

That sense of completion finally shattered me over the edge and quaked my world.

I screamed release.

I was falling from an infinite height, every cell in my body crying out as the acceleration overtook my mind for the last time, blinding my senses, blanking out my awareness of all things beyond the boundaries of his body and mine.

My soul ignited, and I was gone.

Christos went with me.

We went together.

To us.

Chapter 9

SAMANTHA

We laid together on my bed, cradled in each other's arms.

"I think I lost my virginity," I snickered.

"Yep. After that, no one's ever going to find it," he chuckled. "So, was your pageant a success?"

"You mean my V-Card pageant?"

"Yeah."

"The Queen of England has never attended such a sensational soirée."

As I laid in Christos' arms, basking in the afterglow of our love-making, my wonderful mood sank into dark waters. Was it a hormonal thing? I didn't know. Maybe it was normal to worry about losing something great after it came into your life. Either way, I couldn't explain it. But the feelings were there.

Slowly, my amorphous worry solidified into tangible panic. I knew the sensation well.

Bitch. Slut. Whore…

Not that again.

Emo. Goth. Suicide Watch…

Where was all this coming from? Wasn't all that crap behind me now? I'd finally come clean to the whole world about Taylor Lamberth. Why was it still bothering me? Was it residual guilt, or something more ominous?

I shivered with sadness and uncertainty.

"Is something wrong, *agápi mou*?" Christos asked softly.

"I don't know…" I cried.

Go, you dumb broad…

Christos kissed the top of my head and pulled me more tightly against his warm body. "I'm here, Samantha. You're safe. Nothing can hurt you. I love you," he murmured.

"I love you too. But I have this bad feeling like, like nothing has changed since I left D.C. Like I'm still the same lonely girl with no place to turn for love and support."

You made me miss the light, stupid bitch...

Christos smiled. "I'm right here, *agápi mou*. I am your love and support."

"But, I'm afraid it's all going to come crashing down around my head. Like college is going to somehow go away, and I'm going to lose Madison, Romeo, and Kamiko. Worst of all, I feel like I'm going to lose you."

Get off the road, slut...

Christos shook his head. "That's crazy, *agápi mou*. I would never let that happen. I love you more than anything in life."

"I know, but...I don't know. I just feel worried." Silent tears were flowing now. I sniffled and smeared them from my face. I began sobbing softly.

Don't back talk me, whore...

Christos stroked my temple, gently smoothing my hair while kissing the crown of my head. "Shhh, *agápi mou*. I'm right here."

"Promise me you're not going anywhere?" I pleaded.

Move it, skank...

"I promise," Christos said solemnly.

I eased further into his loving embrace, my back warmed by his solid front. Enfolded against him like this, I felt shielded from all the terrible things the world might throw at both of us, like his powerful arms would defend me from all forces that might try to tear us apart. Nothing could come between us.

So why was I still worried?

I'm talking to you, pinhead...

No answer came as I drifted off into deep, dreamless sleep.

CHRISTOS

THREE MONTHS EARLIER...

In the morning, a couple of deputies led me out of the crowded inmate dorms at the downtown jail and shackled me in the hallway while I leaned my face against the cold cement wall. When I was chained, the deputies walked me through a bunch of security doors and hallways that slowly transformed from bulletproof and cement to painted sheetrock and carpeting.

At the end of a new hallway, a third deputy opened a door into the side of a dark, oak-paneled court room.

Russell Merriweather stood ramrod straight, waiting for me behind the defendant's table. He was a dark-skinned African-American man in his mid-40s wearing a perfectly fitted athletic-cut suit. He was even taller than I was, although not quite as built. He struck an imposing figure anywhere he went.

The deputies hovered on either side of me like I was Public Enemy Number One.

"Give the young man some breathing room, if you please, deputies," Russell commanded.

Both deputies stood stoically behind me. Neither of them moved an inch.

Ignoring them ignoring him, Russell reached forward and pulled me into his chest. He embraced me affectionately and clapped me on the back. Whispering in my ear, he said, "What kind of trouble you got your ass in this time, boy?"

I couldn't stop a huge grin from drawing out my dimples.

Russell pulled away and looked me in the eye. "Stow it," he murmured. "Game face from here on out. Got it?"

I nodded solemnly, and reeled my smile back in.

"Keep your mouth shut, and I'll do the talking, feel me?" he ordered quietly.

Russell pulled out a chair for me. I would've done it myself, but it was embarrassingly awkward with my wrists chained to the belt around my waist.

I leaned toward him and said quietly, "Such a gentleman."

"I know how to treat a bitch," he whispered in my ear before sitting down next to me. His face remained blank and rock calm. Only his words belied his good humor and confidence. "If you're lucky, I'll buy you dessert. Now shut the fuck up."

The judge had not yet entered the courtroom, but the judge's assistant was already sitting at one of the tiered sub-desks surrounding the judge's palatial bench.

A moment later, a door opened at the back of the courtroom.

"The Court will now come to order," the uniformed bailiff said. "All rise for the Honorable Geraldine Moody, presiding."

The judge walked in, her black robes billowing around her like a dark ghost. She was not what I expected. Normally, when it came to judges, I imagined some kind of stern, cranky Judge Judy grandmother-type, or an aging tough guy who fancies himself the law of the land, Old West style with six guns holstered beneath his robes. The woman in front of me was a graceful beauty. Older, but still radiant. Long blonde hair fell to her shoulders and careful makeup enhanced her features. She sat down primly on the edge of her chair, scooting up to the desk, looking like the fucking Pope on high.

Had this been any other situation, I would've flirted things to my advantage. One look at Mizz Moody, and I decided to hold my charm in check.

She surveyed me with a single top-to-bottom glance. A savage scowl flashed across her features, but was quickly quashed by her professionalism. Somehow, I felt like I was the guy who'd run out on her after cheating on her, leaving her with a hefty mortgage and stranding her children high-and-dry without a father. Not that I knew the first thing about Geraldine's personal life. But her expression told the story.

I wished my prison jumpsuit had long sleeves to cover my ink. My confrontational tats were incriminating me without me opening my mouth.

"The State of California versus Christos Manos, felony arraignment," the judge's assistant read from the paperwork in front of her.

"Mr. Manos," Judge Moody intoned, "There's been a complaint filed in case SD-2013-K-071183A against you that alleges count one, charging the defendant with felony Aggravated Assault, which occurred on September 22nd, on or around 8:30 a.m., in violation of section 240 of the penal code, Christos Manos did willfully and unlawfully attempt, coupled with a present ability to commit, a violent injury on the person of Horst Grossman."

Horst Grossman? You've gotta be fucking kidding me. *That* was the name of that fat fuck who'd tried to bite Samantha's face off on her way to SDU yesterday? It suited him well.

"Count two," Geraldine continued formally, "Christos Manos did willfully and unlawfully use force and violence on the person of Horst Grossman. An enhancement is alleged, in violation of section 243 D of the penal code, Christos Manos did willfully and unlawfully use force resulting in the infliction of Serious Bodily Injury on Horst Grossman."

In other words, I punched that fucking lunatic when he tried to jump me because I was helping out Samantha, and he got hurt.

"How does your client plead?" Geraldine asked Russell without once looking me in the eye. Business as usual for her, I'm sure. If she had any kids, she probably never looked them in the eye either, unless she was sending them to bedroom lock-up for leaving dishes in the sink.

"We are entering a plea of not guilty, your honor, on all counts," Russell said smoothly.

"Shall we discuss the matter of bail, Mr. Schlosser?" Geraldine asked the Deputy District Attorney.

"Due to the seriousness of the charges, the State asks that bail for the defendant be set in the amount of $25,000."

"Your honor," Russell said calmly, "Christos Manos has significant ties to the community. His family is here, and he is a graduate student at San Diego University. He's not at risk of flight. If it pleases the court, we ask that he is released on his own recognizance, your honor."

Judge Moody flicked her eyes at me, then flipped through the paperwork on her desk. "Due to the defendant's prior record of ongoing offenses for reckless driving, numerous speed contests and exhibition of speed, multiple counts of misdemeanor assault *and* multiple counts of misdemeanor battery," she paused to jot down a note, "bail will be set in the amount of $150,000."

"If your honor would please note," Russell said gently, "my client has not committed any crimes in the past two years. I would ask for bail to be set to a more reasonable amount."

The judge lowered her head and glared at Russell from beneath her brows. "I can set bail at $175,000 if you would prefer, counselor."

"No thank you, your honor," Russell said confidently, showing no sign of reproach.

"$150,000 it is," Judge Moody said flatly. "The defendant is not to have any contact with the victim and shall be restricted to the state of California until trial." She consulted her calendar. "At this time, I will set a trial date of February 14th, 2014, at 10:00 a.m., and a pre-trial date of February 12th, 2014."

A trial on Valentine's Day? The universe was having a laugh at my expense on that one.

"Anything further from the State, Mr. Schlosser?" Judge Moody asked.

"No, your honor," the Deputy Distract Attorney answered.

"Anything further from the defendant, Mr. Merriweather?"

"No, thank you, your honor," Russell smiled curtly.

The deputies led me out of the courtroom. Russell followed.

In the carpeted hallway, Russell asked one of the deputies, "May I speak with my client in private for a moment, gentlemen?"

"I'll give you two minutes," the guy with the buzz-cut replied.

"Thank you, deputy." Turning our backs to the officers, Russell walked me several paces away. "You need me to call your grandfather for bail money?"

"Yeah," I sighed. "I don't have any choice."

"You could call your dad."

"No way."

"Thought I'd ask," Russell smiled. "You really oughta cut the man some slack, Christos. He is your father."

I ground my jaw.

"Anyway, I'll call Spiridon and have you out by this afternoon. You heard what the judge said. Keep your ass in town. And don't get in any trouble. In other words, keep it under the speed limit and keep your hands to yourself. I advise you to garage that crotch rocket of yours and take the bus. If I find out you get in any more fights? I'll bust your ass myself. Feel me?"

"Like a sandpaper massage," I said.

"Don't get smart with me, young man." Russell squeezed my neck with one large hand and shook me affectionately. "This is the last time I save your ass. Hear me? I don't want to do this again. You're better than this, Christos."

"I promise you, Russell, this was self-defense."

"You got any witnesses?"

I thought about Samantha. She'd seen the whole thing up close and personal. Maybe too personal. That scumbag Horst Grossman had put her through enough already. Did I want to drag her into my mess too? Make her take the stand while Horst fucking Grossman gave her dirty looks and the whole courtroom stared her down? Hell no. I'd known her for all of one day. She deserved better. Besides, I didn't want her to see how much of a fuck up I really was underneath my carefully constructed yet fragile facade. I wanted her to believe I was the man I *wanted* to become, not the punk I'd been for most of the last six years.

"No witnesses," I said.

"None?"

I shook my head.

Russell's lips pursed in a flat smirk. He slapped my shoulder vigorously. "Don't worry. I'm glue. I'll make the self-defense claim stick. They'll have that guy brought up on battery charges for hitting *your* fist with *his* face by the time I'm through." He grinned wide.

"I hope so."

Agápi mou...

What have I done?

Chapter 10

SAMANTHA

PRESENT DAY

In the morning, I awoke feeling rejuvenated and excited for the first day of Winter Quarter classes, and with the pleasantly certain conviction that my year was off to a great start. Losing my virginity to Christos the night before had swept away any remaining ill feelings I'd had after Tiffany's bitchery on her yacht.

With any luck, my entire 2014 would be as fabulous as the last twelve hours.

Christos and I had a quick breakfast of toast, eggs, and orange juice at my apartment, before heading out the door.

Christos drove his Camaro home. He said he had some work to do in his studio, but he might drop by campus later.

I imagined us carpooling to SDU together, like a happy and contented married couple. I was so looking forward to that day when our matching cups of coffee sat in the cup-holders as we held hands the entire drive. My mental image was so sweet, I wondered if I might induce my own diabetic coma thinking about it.

I snickered to myself as I drove along the Pacific Coast Highway and gazed out at the Pacific Ocean.

My commute this morning was a brilliant contrast compared to my first day of classes three months prior. I knew to get an early start to avoid traffic. No spilling my coffee causing the screaming fat guy to chew me out afterward. Parking was a snap, no shoehorn necessary, and I made it to class with time to spare.

My first class was Sociology 2, another one of my General Ed classes. The professor was ancient and looked ready for the grave, or else she was *back* from the grave. Either way, she had a distinctly mummified appearance that matched the tone of her lecture delivery.

I think every sentence she uttered slowly suffocated my will to live. I pictured each one of her drowsy utterances fluttering out of her mouth like mummy bandaging that wrapped me up from toe to top, slowly mummifying me as she droned on and on and on. And on.

And on.

Groan.

I imagined by the end of class, I too would be completely mummified. Perhaps the entire class would be similarly swaddled. And you wouldn't even hear crickets chirping in the tomb-silent room because the crickets would be mummified as well, laid to rest for eternity inside their little cricket sarcophagi.

Sigh.

Last quarter, I'd sort of enjoyed Sociology 1. I don't know what had changed. This time around I could barely keep my eyes open for the entire hour, and I'd gotten plenty of sleep, and other wonderful things, the night before.

Maybe I couldn't focus because images from last night with Christos kept flashing through my mind. The tingling between my legs wasn't helping either.

I willed my memories to take a breather while I tried to concentrate. But Professor Tutan-yawn-yawn's droning delivery was putting me to sleep.

I did the only thing I could think of. I pulled out my sketchbook and started doodling. The next thing I knew, I had drawn a picture of Christos in a sexy pose, wearing a Pharaoh hat and mummy bandages for pants, showing off his awesome eight-pack. That wasn't helping any.

Determined to pay attention to the lecture, I closed my sketchbook and put it away like a good girl...and realized class was over. Not only that, the text document on my laptop intended for note-taking was blank. Great. But I did have a great drawing of Christos the Pharaoh in my sketchbook. Why did I feel like I was in the wrong class?

Groan!

I swear, I'd tried hard to listen to the lecture about the structure of society and how it impacts the people who are a part of it, but it wasn't doing it for me anymore. I scooped up my laptop and my bag and headed to my next class.

Hopefully, Managerial Accounting would be better.

I cringed at the thought.

Oh, joy.

At least Madison was in accounting with me.

SAMANTHA

The lecture hall for Accounting was on the other side of campus from my Sociology 2. I had to hoof it not to be late, but I knew exactly where I was going. The perks of experience! I would be on time to class so I wouldn't have to miss a single riveting Accounting fact!

Can I get a fist pump?!

Yeah!!!

Sigh.

At least I was getting better at this college thing and didn't feel like a newbie anymore. That was something, right?

Yeah.

:-(

I opened one of the double doors at the back of the hall and was greeted by a packed theater-style room with plunging rows of seats that brimmed over with chatty coeds. You'd think from the energy in the room that it was a nightclub before some hot new band hit the stage.

Was I missing something?

I was in Managerial Accounting, right?

I scanned the room for Madison. I'm sure she'd saved me a seat. There was no sign of her that I could see. I texted her.

I'm here. Where r u?

A minute later I spotted Madison waving at me. She sat in the middle of the room, amongst a crowded row of students.

I trotted down the stairs and squeezed into her row. I nearly tripped on a half-dozen people as I made my way toward her. At one point I stepped on some girl wearing a purple hoodie and Converses.

"Hey!" she snarled.

"Sorry," I mumbled as I stumbled to avoid landing in her lap. This move caused me to sway back toward the row below, but I righted myself by flailing my arms. I swung forward and almost landed palms-first in the lap of the guy next to Purple Hoodie.

He of course smirked and nodded. "My lap is free," he said suggestively, "if you need a place to put your hands."

I scowled at him. "Uh, no?" I blundered past and scrunched my way through more knees and backpacks until I plopped down next to Madison. "What up, Mads," I sighed, sinking into my seat. "Do I have, like, huge flipper feet or elephant ankles? I barely made it through that gauntlet," I said sarcastically, nodding back the way I'd come.

"No, Sam," Madison smiled. "Your feet and ankles are normal. Sorry about the crowd. It was totally empty when I got here."

"Fundamentals wasn't nearly this packed. What's the rage with Managerial Accounting?"

"Easy A? I have no idea," Madison confessed. "So, have you recovered yet from our New Year's cruise?"

"You mean from Tiffany bombarding me with her all-night Bitchkrieg?" I rolled my eyes, then thought about last night with Christos, and smiled. "Pretty much."

"I can't get over that she slapped you."

I'd almost forgotten. "Yeah, Tiffany is over the top. She should be locked up in a padded cell. With any luck, we'll never see her again. At least she's not in any of our classes."

Madison laughed sarcastically, "Probably because she's a Cosmetology major."

I grinned, "Does SDU even have a Cosmetology major?"

"If they don't, maybe Tiffany's dad can donate a Mani-Pedi Building or a Salon Wing to the university."

"Would they call it the Kingston-Whitehouse Whore College for Women?" I said snidely. Something suddenly smashed into the side of my head. I whipped around. "Hey!"

Tiffany Kingston-Whitehouse's book bag had just clipped me in the back of the skull, nearly beheading me.

"WTF!" I growled while ducking in case of another sneak attack. "Watch where you're going, Tiffany!"

"You got it wrong, *Scum*antha," Tiffany sneered, "they'd call it the Poor House College for Campus Pumps like you, and I'm not talking about shoes, you cum-dumpster."

Madison rolled her eyes. "Shut your barking vagina, Tiffany, I can smell your dog breath from here."

I giggled.

"Twat did you say?" Tiffany snarled at Madison.

Madison stood up in her seat. "I said, how would you like me to shove your designer book bag up your ass, buckles and all?"

Had Tiffany just called me "Scumantha?" Wow, that meant Tiffany theoretically remembered my name. Not that I was flattered, just surprised.

Tiffany scowled. "I don't know *what* Christos was thinking when he invited you ho's on my yacht," she hissed. "I had to have it fumigated after your skanky asses left." She flipped me and Madison off before turning and walking away.

"Shouldn't you be in Intro to Arithmetic or something?" I growled at Tiffany's back.

She stopped in her tracks and turned around. "Just because I'm richer and prettier than you doesn't mean I'm stupid, you butt plug," she spat, then continued toward the far side of the lecture hall. She must have made a special trip behind our row just to whack me on the head.

"Wow, I didn't think she had it in her," Madison said gravely.

"What, to be such a terrific bitch?" I said, rubbing my head.

"No, to be clever. That means she's a *dangerous* bitch."

Tiffany sat down and flipped up the collapsible desktop hinged to her chair and slammed her book bag on top of it.

Boy, she really didn't like me, did she? I don't know how I'd gotten so far under her skin without even trying. Served her right for blindsiding me like that.

Madison shook her head, "That girl is trippin' monkey nuts. I thought she'd gone over the edge on her yacht, but now I'm worried we've only seen her at stage-one crazy."

I didn't want to consider the morbid lengths to which Tiffany might go when pushed to her limits. She'd demonstrated her penchant for violence toward me twice already. For all I knew, she was planning on making me the first tragic victim in her very own true-crime documentary about girl murderers gone wild. "What's she doing here anyway?" I sneered. "She wasn't in Accounting last term, was she?"

"I don't remember," Madison said thoughtfully. "You think we would've noticed her throne and her attending hobots parading in and out of class every time."

"She's such an amaze-douche." I rubbed the back of my head again. A knotty lump was already forming. "Maybe we can have her assassinated after class."

"Let me know if you need to hire a hit man," Madison said cagily.

"Why, do you know one?" I asked skeptically.

"No, I'll do it for you." Madison smacked her little fist into the palm of her hand. "Just give me a reason." She glared at Tiffany.

"Are you mad-dogging her?"

"Yeah," Madison smiled. "That's why they call me Mads."

I giggled, glad to have Madison on my side. Not that Tiffany seemed worried. Now that she was settled into her desk, she wasn't paying any attention to us at all. Probably for the best.

"If push comes to shove, I *will* cut a bitch," Madison said.

"Well, she pretty much pushed *and* shoved me with her book bag a minute ago," I suggested.

Madison narrowed her eyes and snarled. "All right, fine. I'm cutting the bitch's guts out after class. Don't try and stop me," she said menacingly.

"I won't," I smiled. "Promise."

Me and Madison broke into giggles.

SAMANTHA

A few minutes later, the professor walked through a pair of double doors at the bottom of the lecture hall. He wore a white button-down shirt with a conservative tie. He was cue-bald with a thick ring of head-warmer hair.

I was totally stumped.

Why the heck was Managerial Accounting so packed? For this guy? Based on the crowd, I'd expected some gorgeous supermodel (male or female) or maybe a dancing bear.

Perhaps Madison's easy-A theory was accurate? It was all I could think of.

The professor set his shoulder bag down on the table at the bottom of the lecture hall, and pulled out the contents. I was expecting stacks of free money and booze for all the students, but all the professor pulled out was a laptop and a stack of syllabi.

I was perplexed.

He walked up to one of the wall-to-wall chalkboards behind him, grabbed a fresh stick of yellow chalk, and starting spelling out his name.

"All right class," he quacked, and I mean *quacked*, "My name is Doctor Dorkman—"

What?! He couldn't be serious. Did he just say Dorkman? My jaw practically banged against my desktop as he spelled out his name on the board in all caps, like so:

DR. D O R Q U E M A N N

"—and I will be instructing you on the topic of Managerial Accounting for the duration of the quarter. Shall we begin?"

When I said quacked, I literally meant quacked. Like, I was expecting a flock of mallards to come flapping in and settle down at the bottom of the lecture hall by the side of their great king.

Because Dorquemann had the nasaliest voice I'd ever heard in my entire life.

Madison and I exchanged a horrified look. There was no way we were going to make it through the hour without getting ejected for interrupting the lecture with our hysterical laughter.

I gave us five minutes, tops.

Our only option was to focus on the material.

We did our best to take notes.

Unlike in Sociology 2, where I'd easily tuned out the droning Professor Tutan-yawn-yawn, listening to Dr. Dorquemann forced me to dig deep and find reserves of concentration I didn't know I had. I teetered on the precipitous ledge of silence while staring down at a pit of insanely inappropriate laughter. The only thing preventing my fall from grace was my ingrained sense of politeness. At least my parental upbringing had been good for something.

Despite my best efforts, I knew my silence wouldn't last much longer. Within minutes, snickers issued from around the lecture hall. I was certain the professor—I couldn't even *think* his name without wanting to laugh—would notice his anonymous hecklers, but he didn't seem to care. Was he ignoring everyone?

Maybe he was used to this.

I, on the other hand, was about to lose it. I did the only thing I could. I pulled out my sketchbook, ready to start drawing. I had learned over the last several months that drawing consumed my attention like nothing else. It sucked me right in.

But I needed to find a subject to draw, quick.

I glanced around the room, looking anywhere except at the professor. It only took a second before my eyes landed on Tiffany, and I had my subject.

I went to work in my sketchbook doodling out the gory cartoon murder of Tiffany Meanston-Lightsout.

Madison, bless her stone-cold focus, was busy typing notes into her laptop. "Shouldn't you be taking notes, Sam?" she whispered seriously.

"I can't!" I whisper-whined, "not without losing my shit. This guy is going to be the end of me if I listen to one more word, I swear."

"I hear you, girlfriend. I'll share my notes with you later."

"Thanks, Mads," I whispered, still drawing.

Madison periodically peeked over at what I was doing.

"Don't look!" I whispered, a big smile lighting up my face. "Wait till I'm done."

The drawing had been the perfect protection against Dorquemann's quacky voice. I don't think I heard a word he said for twenty minutes.

During that time, I scrawled a cartoon of Tiffany lying on a big table with her tongue hanging out, her head haloed by a pool of blue ballpoint blood, her torso cut in half by a giant circular saw operated by what was supposed to be Madison wearing a magician's tuxedo and a top hat with her blonde hair flowing out below the brim. I made Madison's eyebrows a stark, angry V and gave her snarling fangs. I drew a word balloon over cartoon Madison's head that read:

"WHEN I SAY **I'LL CUT A BITCH**, I MEAN IN **HALF**."

When I leaned back in my seat, finished, with a satisfied smile stretched across my face, Madison glanced over. I allowed her a good look at my handiwork.

Madison erupted like a laughing klaxon, snorting bellows of belly-laughter, drowning out the professor.

Everyone in the entire lecture hall stopped and slowly turned to stare at us.

Unsure whether I should be proud of my comic accomplishment or horrified, I sank down in my seat, trying to slide to the floor. But the seat-back in front of me was too close. I was stuck in plain view.

Madison clapped her hand to her mouth in mid-bellow.

The room was pin-drop silent.

The sensation of nuclear embarrassment continued unabated for what seemed like an hour. Or four. I don't think I breathed the entire time.

"Should I call for an ambulance, miss?" Professor Dorquemann quacked at last. He had a good-natured smile on his face, as if nothing was wrong. "Or is Managerial Accounting inherently funny?" He paused in thought for several moments as a smile of his own appeared, then he honked, "I always thought so, anyway."

I couldn't help myself, I had to say it, even if everyone was still staring. In the smallest squeaky whisper I could manage, I said to Madison, *"How does he not realize it's his voice?"*

"Shut up!" she whispered from the corner of her mouth through clenched teeth, then kicked my ankle.

Although my ankle smarted, I couldn't hold it against Madison. I'd triggered her laughter by showing her the Tiffany cartoon, and she was the one in the hot seat.

Dr. Dorquemann raised his eyebrows at Madison expectantly.

"Uhhhh," Madison croaked. She glowed tomato red, her eyes darting around for the nearest hole to hide in. *"Sam! I'm going to pee my pants!"* she hissed.

"Please don't, Mads," I whispered pathetically. *"Otherwise they'll never stop staring."*

Four hundred pairs of eyes were pinned on me and Madison.

I wasn't any better with crowds than she was. With no place to go in my cramped desk, I held my sketchbook up to my face, trying to hide behind it. Too bad it was so small. It barely covered my face. I tried to think like a toddler. If I can't see them, they're not there, right? I peaked over the top of my sketchbook a moment later, in case it had worked.

Nope. Everyone was still there, all of them still staring. I sunk back behind my sketchbook.

"Ladies," the professor honked in an amused tone, "as much as I'd like to issue you both detention slips and send you to the office, this is a university where we are beyond such things, wouldn't you two agree? If my lecture isn't properly stimulating, perhaps you both can sign up for a drama class instead."

I happened to peak over at Tiffany who sneered with ample superiority at both me and Madison, resting her chin casually on her hand, her middle-finger extended against her cheek in a stealth flip-off.

Bitch.

There were several random chuckles from some of the students, but the professor resumed lecturing as if nothing was amiss. To say that he was unruffled by our antics would be an understatement.

I was impressed.

Did Dr. Dorquemann's bizarre demeanor belie the most laid-back professor of all time? He had my vote for the Cool Cat of the Year award.

No wonder everyone liked his class.

Amazingly, I actually managed to take notes for the remainder of class.

SAMANTHA

Madison and I made our way to the Student Center. It was crowded as always. We got in line for coffee at the Toasted Roast.

"What the hell happened back in Accounting just now?" I asked.

"Oh, Sam, I almost died in there. Dorquemann? Really? I think we were in the Twilight Zone or a Saturday Night Live skit."

"I know, right?"

"I think Managerial Accounting is going to be way better than Fundamentals was last quarter," Madison said. "That class was a snooze-fest by comparison."

I smiled. "Yeah, but how can you *not* laugh at Dr. Dorquemann's voice for ten whole weeks?"

"If you keep drawing cartoons of murdered Tiffany, I don't stand a chance," she chuckled.

We made it to the front of the line and ordered our coffee, then sat down outside. The sun peeked between cloud banks intermittently, and the weather was slightly chilly, but not cold. My unzipped hoodie and jeans were more than enough to keep me warm.

Madison wore an SDU sweatshirt and shorts. She was always trying to catch as many rays from the sun as she could, even in winter.

I inhaled the aroma of my brew before taking a sip. "So, Mads, I was thinking about changing my major."

"To what?"

"Art?" I said with a tinge more reluctance in my voice than I wanted.

"You should totally do it," Madison said confidently. "Christos was telling me on Tiffany's yacht the other night how far your drawings had come in a few short months. And based on your murdered Tiffany cartoon, I can see what he's talking about."

"You really think so?"

"Totally," she reassured.

"Thanks, Mads." Sharing that moment of comedy gold in Accounting with her was exactly why I was reluctant to change majors. "Would you be bummed if it meant no more accounting classes with you?"

Madison smiled. "Why would I be bummed? You've got to do what's right for you."

"But it's our only class together."

"It's not like we won't see each other all the time. Don't worry about it, Sam. I'm not going anywhere."

"You're sure?"

She squeezed my wrist. "Totally, girlfriend. Besides, my stay in Dorquemann's Domain will be more productive if you aren't there busting my guts with your newfound cartoon genius."

"But aren't shared experiences like that an important part of the college experience? What if we never see each other?"

"Don't worry, Sam. We'll hang plenty outside of class."

"Promise, Mads?"

"Totally," she smiled.

I was suddenly on the verge of tearing up because I was so grateful to call Madison my friend. She was so understanding. After my outcast status for the last two years in D.C., being welcomed, valued, and accepted at every turn by my new friends was still a noteworthy experience for me. I still wanted to pinch myself every five minutes to make sure my friends and boyfriend weren't all just a dream.

"And speaking of classes," Madison said, "I've got Spanish in ten minutes." She stood up and slung her book bag over her shoulder.

"Oh crap! My history class is on the other end of campus! How do I manage to have classes so fricking far apart?" I grabbed my book bag and we walked out of the Student Center's outdoor seating area.

"Try taking the campus shuttle," she suggested as we walked up the steps beside the zig-zag fountain.

"I hate waiting for them. I'd rather walk."

"So take the underground riot tunnels," she winked.

We paused at the top of the stairs, on the Central Walkway.

"What are those?" I asked.

"There's some rumor about tunnels that run under the entire SDU campus like catacombs. Supposedly, they were used in the sixties by the cops when everyone was protesting all the time. But I think Morlocks live down in them now."

"What are Morlocks?" I asked.

"Didn't you have to read The Time Machine by H.G. Wells in high school?"

"No, we read A Brave New World."

"Oh. Well, Morlocks are these horrid troglodyte things. Anyway, have you ever noticed all that steam pumping out through the tall vents near the music building? The ones that look like obelisks?"

"Yeah, I always wondered about that."

"I'm telling you," Madison looked around cagily, "it's the Morlock machines. And they'll kidnap any unsuspecting young maidens they find and enslave them to work in the bowels of the earth below campus until you die young from hard labor."

I grimaced. "Who wants to work in a bowel?"

"I know I don't," Madison chuckled.

"I think I'll skip the tunnels. Well, I better run, or I'm going to be late."

"Bye," Madison waved as I ran off. "Watch out for Morlocks!"

As I ran, I was on my guard for Morlocks *and* Tiffany Kingston-Whitehouse, because based on Madison's description, they were pretty much the same thing. And I always seemed to stumble over Tiffany when I was in a hurry. I'm convinced she was bitch-stalking me. Was she the Morlock Queen? It made sense.

But I was in luck today. I made it to the other end of campus to my history class on time. It wasn't nearly as packed as Managerial Accounting. But then again, the legendary Dr. Dorquemann wouldn't be presiding.

I found a seat and pulled out my laptop, determined to do nothing but take notes about fascinating historical topics. I pictured myself recounting the highlights later to my friends while they all listened attentively.

Yeah, right.

Despite my best intentions, history class went over like a Roofinated sleeping potion. I could barely keep my eyes open.

I swear I had no intention of doodling during class yet again. But some alien pod creature must have suckered into my brain through my ear canal while I was carefully avoiding the Morlock tunnels. You were damned if you did, and damned if you didn't.

When the professor finished his lecture, I realized that not only had I not taken notes, but my laptop was asleep. On the plus side, I had drawn more cartoon doodles in my sketchbook.

I did the math:

One sketchbook full of doodles
- One empty laptop

= Time to change my major.

At least my Accounting skills were good for something.

I stuffed my laptop in my book bag and marched up the steps of the lecture hall, determined to change my major.

It was time.

Ten minutes later, I was smiling as I walked through the doors of the Registrar's Office. Despite its DMV vibe and long lines, everything moved quickly and efficiently. I filled out the paper work to officially change my major to Bachelor of Fine Arts. And I dropped Managerial Accounting. My condolences to the great Dr. Dorquemann. I was going to miss him.

When I walked outside, the sun had broken through the overcast clouds that had hung over campus for much of the morning. Brilliant sun rays slid around the clouds, illuminating the cloudscape in shimmering bronze and gold.

Looked like a good omen to me.

Bye-bye, Sam Smith, CPA. Hello, Samantha Smith, world-renowned crayon craftswoman.

Nothing was going to stop me from following through to becoming an artist.

Now I just had to figure out how to break the news to my parents.

Chapter 11

SAMANTHA

Christos met me at my apartment that evening for dinner. His '68 Camaro rumbled downstairs as he pulled into a visitor's parking space. When I glanced out the curtains, it was already dark due to the winter hours. I think the evening hour made me feel like we were any other married couple, like I should have a drink waiting for him, or dinner cooking, or whatever.

When he rang my doorbell, I had a fantasy of a little boy and a little girl running up behind me, so the whole family could greet Christos together, the kids shouting "Daddy!" in unison. My heart accelerated at the thought. I took a deep breath and reminded myself it was only a fantasy.

I opened the door and was greeted by a face full of flowers. Not the real kind, but a big oil painting of a bouquet of them. It was gorgeous.

I tried to peek around the picture frame. "Christos? You back there somewhere?"

Christos leaned over the top of the giant painting, his even white teeth gleaming back at me as he grinned.

"What's this?"

His dimples flashed. "Most English speakers refer to this as a painting."

"Duh, I know what it's called. But what's it for?"

"It's for you, *agápi mou*," he smiled. "I painted it."

I was flabbergasted. "What? When? Today?"

"No," he chuckled. "Between Thanksgiving and Winter Break, when you were avoiding me. I wanted to do something special for you. Show you how important you were to me. Anyone can buy flowers, but I figured a painting of them would be twice as nice, and it lasts forever."

"Oh my God, Christos, you shouldn't have done this," I was tearing up already.

"Why not?"

"I don't know, shouldn't you save this for a special occasion? Like an anniversary or whatever?"

"Every day is a special occasion with you, *agápi mou*. That seems reason enough to me."

My heart hammered again. It seemed like this evening was going to be rich with fantasy fulfillment.

Christos walked through the doorway, careful not to bump the painting into the doorframe. "Where should I hang it?"

I had a chance to better appreciate the painting as he held it up for me to inspect. It was intricate and breathtakingly beautiful.

"How long did this take you to paint?" I gaped.

"Does it matter?" he smiled.

"Yes, it matters! It looks like it must have taken forever!"

"For you, *agápi mou*, forever is the right amount of time," he grinned.

"Oh, Christos," I smiled. Yes, tears were imminent.

"How about I hang it on this wall?"

"That would be perfect," I sniffed.

He pulled a hammer out of his back pocket, and some small nails. After eye-balling the wall, he tapped several nails into the plaster, then hung the painting. "How's that?"

"It's perfect."

"Remember, don't over-water them. That's a common mistake," he winked.

"I won't," I laughed. "It's beautiful, Christos." I wrapped my arms around him and hugged him fiercely. "This is the best bouquet ever."

"Anything for you, *agápi mou*." He kissed the top of my head softly. "You ready for some dinner?"

"I'm getting sort of hungry."

"I don't know about you, but I'm getting a bit tired of takeout. We're going to have to either start spending more time over at my place so I can cook for you myself, or I'm going to have to stock up your fridge so I can cook for you here."

"Wait, both of those options are you cooking for me. Isn't that only one option?"

"That I cook for you is a given," he smiled, "it's only a question of where."

I frowned. "Are you saying I can't cook?"

He grinned. "Samantha, I have no doubt you make a mean ice cream sundae. But a man requires sustenance. So what'll it be?"

"An ice cream sundae sounds pretty good right about now," I winked.

"I've got a better idea. Grab your purse."

Five minutes later, Christos parked his Camaro on the Pacific Coast Highway and we walked toward a restaurant with big blue awning. He held the door for me as we entered Pizza Port.

"I've never been here before," I said.

"What? How can you not have discovered Pizza Port? You practically live right on top of it!"

The interior was covered in crisscrossed bare wood, surfboards hanging from the ceiling, and photos of surfers all over the walls. Picnic tables with the attached benches were laid out on the floor. A bunch of kids in soccer uniforms and their parents occupied most of the seats in the room.

"Wow, it's packed," I said. "My parents would never go to a rowdy place like this."

"Do you want to go someplace else?"

"No, I kind of like it," I smiled. "It's perfect."

While we waited in line to order, I noticed they had these huge metal tanks behind the counter. "What are those tanks?"

"They brew their own beer," Christos said. "It's good stuff. I can buy some for you, if you want."

"Oh, I'm good."

At Christos' suggestion, we ordered a Pizza Carlsbad, which had pesto, grilled chicken, sun-dried tomatoes, artichoke hearts, and feta. Then we found a place on the benches to sit, squeezed between what looked like two opposing soccer teams, green uniforms on one side of the divide, orange on the other.

"You sure you want to sit here?" Christos asked.

"It should be okay, right?" I said cautiously, not sure what he meant.

"These kids seem sort of surly. Like a drunken brawl could erupt any second."

The kids were all about eight years old. I giggled. "If you need me to protect you, Christos, just say the word."

He smiled and extended his hand toward the bench. "I'd pull the bench out for you, but it's bolted down."

"Always the gentlemen," I smiled.

He held my hand as I lifted one leg, then the other, over the bench. "Thank you, sir."

As he was about to slide in next to me, two boys in green soccer jerseys who had just finished playing a video game at the back of the restaurant came barreling toward Christos, shouting, "We need more quarters!"

The second boy wasn't watching where he was going. He was distracted by Christos' lifting his leg over the bench.

"Be careful, Jordan!" a woman hollered at the boy.

Jordan pivoted to avoid running into Christos' knee but stumbled headlong in the direction of a floor-to-ceiling post. I grit my teeth as I imagined the certain concussion the boy was about to suffer.

Christos reacted instantly. His knee still in the air, he spun on his planted foot and swept Jordan up in his arms, pulling him off his trajectory. Christos planted his elevated foot and swung the boy high into the air.

"Airplane ride!" Christos sang as he held Jordan aloft.

The boy was surprised for a second, but all smiles.

Christos continued to hold him up. "Jordan, can you touch the ceiling while you're up there?"

The boy giggled and slapped the beam overhead.

"Got it!" Christos said before lowering him to the floor.

The woman who had hollered at Jordan was already walking over to claim him. She was smiling nervously. "Thank you so much. I think you saved my son a trip to the Emergency Room."

"No problem," Christos smiled.

"Say thank you to the nice man, Jordan," the woman said.

"Thanks," the boy said bashfully.

"Any time, little man," Christos winked. "Let me know if you need another airplane ride."

"I think he's had enough action for the evening," the woman said.

"But, mom!" he begged. "Me and James weren't done playing Galaga! We need more quarters!"

"You need to finish your pizza, young man. Then we'll see about more Galaga."

"Mom!" Jordan pleaded as his mom led him back to their bench.

"Thank you so much," the woman said to Christos.

"Any time," he smiled at her before sitting next to me.

I pulled at Christos' collar and looked down his shirt.

"What are you doing?" he laughed.

"Are you wearing blue pajamas under this shirt? With a big red S?"

Christos chuckled. "Sorry, my tights are at the cleaners with my cape."

A short time later our pizza arrived. I'd never had a pizza like this, and definitely not one with artichoke hearts. It was amazing. "This is like, the best pizza ever," I said before taking another bite.

"Wait'll you try their beers."

"Really?" I mumbled as a string of cheese stretched from the slice in my hand to my mouth. It kept getting longer and longer and didn't seem to want to break. "I think I need scissors!" The cheese finally broke and stuck to my chin in a wiggly string.

"That's a good look for you," Christos laughed before leaning over to lick it off.

I couldn't decide if that was gross or hot. Maybe both. I grimaced while he did it. I hoped no one was watching.

"Daddy," a little girl sitting two seats over said, "that man is eating pizza off that girl's face!"

Nope, no audience.

"Kids are the best," Christos said.

After my public humiliation subsided, I said, "Do you ever think about having kids?"

"When I'm older. But you have to find the right person to do it with first." He gave me a knowing look. "Emphasis on the 'do it' part, and the 'right person' part," he winked.

"Stop!" I giggled excitedly, a flash of that earlier family fantasy I'd had warming my heart once again. Could it be true? Me and Christos, and babies? Some day? I pushed the thoughts quickly away, afraid of jinxing myself if I thought about it too hard.

"What," he looked confused. "You don't want to do *it* anymore? Was *it* that bad?"

I blushed thinking about how unbelievably good "it" had been.

"Eat your pizza, Christos!"

"That's not all I'm going to be eating," He said suggestively.

Yes, my thighs quivered expectantly beneath the picnic table for the remainder of dinner. In a good way.

SAMANTHA

After dinner we went back to my apartment.

"Oh, I almost forgot!" I said as I raced up the stairs. "You've got to see what I drew in my sketchbook today!"

"You mean the little traveling one I gave you for Christmas?"

"Yeah!"

I opened my apartment door and we went inside. I pulled the sketchbook out of my book bag and opened it to the page with the drawing of Madison sawing Tiffany in half.

Christos barked laughter instantly. "That's awesome! Is that Madison slicing Tiffany to pieces?"

"Yeah!" I was kind of surprised he could tell. "How did you know it was them?"

He studied my drawing thoughtfully. "This is obviously Tiffany. I think it's the hair. Besides, what other bitch could the caption be referring to?" He winked at me. "With Madison, I don't know, you just captured that smile of hers."

"But it's just cartoon drawings," I said. "Not like your oil paintings that look like photos of people. Anyone could tell your painting of Tiffany was her."

"I see what you're saying, but cartoons have their own weird kind of magic. I can't articulate why, probably one of those mysteries of how the mind works. But have you ever noticed how with political cartoons you can always tell it's a drawing of the president?"

"Yeah?"

"That's what you did with Tiffany and Madison. You captured the essence of them in your drawing. That's pretty amazing, Samantha. I've been telling you that you have talent from the beginning. This is further proof. Who knows, maybe you'll be a famous cartoonist someday."

I was bashful again. Would I ever be able to accept all the compliments that Christos showered on me?

"Speaking of which," Christos said, "did you change your major?"

"I did," I smiled, proud of myself.

"That's awesome, *agápi mou*. You totally did the right thing."

My stomach somersaulted. "But I haven't told my parents yet," I winced.

"Ah. I imagine that'll be tough."

"Do you want anything to drink?" I asked, needing to change the subject.

"Sure. Water's good."

I walked into the kitchen and pulled a pitcher out of the fridge and poured a glass. When I put it back, I couldn't help staring at the freezer. "Want some ice cream?" I hollered.

"I could go either way," he said, now standing in the kitchen. "You're freaking about telling your parents, aren't you?"

"Stop reading my mind!" I whined. I couldn't help my sudden poutiness. The idea of finally telling my parents about changing my major made me want to eat too much ice cream, vomit it up, get drunk, vomit *that* up, then go for a jog so I could eat more ice cream.

"You want to talk about it?" he asked softly. He walked toward me and clasped my arms in his warm hands. He leveled his super-powered blue eyes at me.

Why did I feel so at ease every time I gazed into those eyes of his? Was it their color? Because they were impossibly beautiful? Or was it the man behind them, and his love for me? I'm sure it was both. But it was also the fact that I'd never felt this kind of love in my entire life. Unconditional, supportive, understanding, compassionate love. I was tearing up again. It was starting to become a bad habit.

Is that what love did to you? Made you cry all the time?

Christos pulled me into his arms. "You don't need ice cream, *agápi mou*. You need to talk, I can tell." He grabbed his water and led us to my couch. "What's eating you?"

I sniffled and giggled. "My need for ice cream."

He chuckled. "We can have some later. But right now, I want to know what's bothering you so much about telling your parents, if you want to talk about it. If you want to wait, that's fine too. But it needs to come out, or it's going to keep eating away at you."

I wasn't sure where to begin. I held my hands up plaintively, then dropped them in my lap. But I knew Christos was right. This was just like the Taylor Lamberth situation. I knew I needed to get it out. I took a deep breath, and began.

"I never told you this before," I started.

"Sounds like a familiar opening," he smiled.

I shook my head and leaned into him. We were thigh to thigh on the couch. He put his arm around my shoulder and I rested my head on his chest. It was so firm and supportive, just like he was.

"When I was applying for colleges in high school, I got the idea into my head that maybe I could go to an art college. But I never told my parents. I went online and found a bunch of different schools, all of them in California."

"Which ones?"

"Mainly CalArts and Art Center College of Design."

"Those are the big gun schools in Southern Cal."

"I know. Anyway, I read about portfolio submissions, and realized I needed to do some drawings of my own. Some serious drawings. So every day after school, I would draw all kinds of different things at home. Since I'd lost all my friends after the Damian thing, I had plenty of spare time. But every day, I'd make sure to put away my drawings before my parents got home. Somehow, I intuitively sensed they would say something to knock me down if they ever found out."

"Serious?" Christos frowned.

"I guess it wasn't like that in your house growing up."

"Heck no. My dad and my grandad were always wanting to see what I was working on, always trying to help me make my work better."

"You have no idea how lucky you are," I said, my voice quavering. "Because, one time, I was so wrapped up in one of my drawings, I never heard the garage door when my mom came home from work. I was trying to copy a photograph of a horse, and I remember how amazed I was that my drawing looked good. I was drawing the entire horse, legs and all, and for once, it didn't look like a kid's drawing. To me, anyway.

"The next thing I knew, my mom was over my shoulder saying, 'What are you doing?' I covered my drawing instinctively, fear instantly knotting my guts."

I looked up at Christos. "How lame is that? I was afraid of my mom looking at my drawing."

Christos cupped my cheek with his palm and stroked my face with his thumb, wiping away my tears.

I continued. "I told my mom it was nothing. I remember her eyes narrowing as she searched my face, almost like she knew I was up to something...I don't know, like I was up to something *dangerous*..."

SAMANTHA

PAST...

"What is this?" my mom asked.

"Nothing," I said.

"It's not nothing. It's a drawing." She reached over my shoulder and pulled it off my desk to examine it.

I watched her face, trying to figure out where this was going to go. She knew I didn't socialize much anymore. I'd thought maybe she would've said something about how it was nice I had a hobby or whatever.

"Why were you hiding this, young lady?" she demanded, like it was a crack pipe or a handgun.

"I don't know," I said.

Then she rifled through the other drawings I had laying out on my desk. I'm sure a normal girl would pin her best work to her bedroom wall. I kept mine in a stack under my books when I wasn't working on them so my parents wouldn't notice them.

"What have you been up to, Sam?" my mom asked, eyes narrow.

"Drawing," I said.

"Why?"

"I don't know, because I like it?"

"You sure have a lot of drawings here. You're not sacrificing your study time to do these drawings, are you?"

"I—"

"You need to be focusing on keeping your grades up, studying for the SATs, and college applications, Sam. Not on goofing off drawing all these worthless drawings."

"I'm not goofing off! I have to do these drawings for the art schools!"

"Art schools?" my mom sneered. "We never talked about any art schools."

"So?"

"So? You're not going to any art schools."

"Why not?"

"Because we already discussed this with your father. We're looking at business schools."

I folded my arms across my chest. *"You're* looking at business schools."

My mom's brows knit together. "Don't take that tone with me, young lady."

"Yes, ma'am." I sighed. I almost gave up. I was about to stack my drawings up and set them aside to make room for my school books. But I couldn't. I *had* to say something. "Mom, I really want to go to art school. I've been looking at a bunch of different programs online, and I think maybe I could get in. I read the different portfolio requirements, and you can't get into an art school without submitting artwork. It's not just grades and SATs."

My mom looked at me, assessing me. "Is that so. How long have you been thinking about this?"

"A few months?" I was so unsure of myself.

"Have you looked at tuition?"

A felt a glimmer of hope. "Yeah."

"How much is it?"

It always came down to the bottom line with both my parents. I sighed heavily. "It's almost double."

"Double?!" my mom blurted. "You're kidding," she laughed.

"No."

"It's out of the question, Sam," she said with finality.

"But what if I can get a scholarship or something?"

My mom put her hands on her hips and her lips welded together sternly. She picked up my drawings and flipped through them so heatedly I thought she was going to tear them up. But I kept my mouth shut, hopeful.

She nodded with increasing intensity as she flipped. "Mmm-hmm. Hmm. Mmm-hmm." She dropped them on my desk dismissively. "I don't think you're good enough for a scholarship."

My jaw dropped. "Who are you to say that?"

"I'm your mother, Sam," she growled.

"Mom, you don't know anything about art!" My face was hot with anger.

"I know enough to know you're probably not going to get a scholarship."

"But shouldn't I try?" I struggled to hold back my tears.

"Not when it means taking time away from your studies and your other applications."

"But I'm getting A's in all my classes! And I have time left over. How do you think I've been able to draw all these drawings and still keep my grades up?"

"Yes, but you have SATs coming up. You need to be focusing on your SAT study guides."

"I have been!" I protested. "And I still have time for drawing!"

"I don't want to hear it. No more drawing, Sam. We're not paying double for some fancy art college. Your father and I simply can't afford it. And that's final." She marched out of my bedroom.

When my father came home, I didn't even bother to mention it. I didn't want to have him look at my drawings and tell me I wasn't good enough, too.

Over dinner that night, my mom just *had* to bring it up. Dinner with my parents was never actually fun.

"Do you know what crazy scheme your daughter has been cooking up?" my mom orated as she scooped a spoonful of carrots onto her plate before passing them to Dad.

"What's that, dear?" my dad asked, spooning carrots.

"Sam has the crazy idea she can go to art college. And get a scholarship, no less."

I felt like the literal translation of my mom's words would be *"Our daughter is insane, isn't that a laugh riot? What an idiot."*

"Art college?" my Dad frowned. "We've never talked about art college. A good business college is the proper place for her."

They were talking like I wasn't in the room.

"That's what I said," Mom said, chuckling.

Was it okay to think your mom was a total bitch? I mean, not every second of the day. But more often than not?

My dad turned and addressed me directly. "Sam, art colleges are generally private universities, and therefore, significantly more expensive."

"I already knew that," I sniveled. Demonstrating that I wasn't a completely ignorant idiot was my only remaining defense. Sadly, I didn't think it was going to get me anywhere.

"Knowing doesn't pay for anything," my mom laughed.

Called it.

"Your mother is right, Sam," Dad said. "We don't have the money."

Called it again.

"But I could get loans, maybe even a scholarship!" I protested.

"That's all well and good, Sam, but how do you plan to pay off those loans? Have you thought about what kind of a job an artist can get? Do you intend to draw caricatures at the county fair? Sell watercolors on the boardwalk in Atlantic City? How could you possibly support yourself making twenty dollars here and there?"

"I wasn't talking about that kind of an artist!" I argued. "There's other kinds of artists everywhere. What about that painting you guys bought, the one of the waves that hangs in your office?"

I was grasping at straws, and my parents knew it.

"Sam," my dad said condescendingly, "I paid one hundred dollars for that painting. How long do you think it would take you to paint such a painting?"

I didn't want to say that I didn't know how to paint an oil painting. I'm pretty sure if I had, my dad would've said *"Check and mate, game over."*

"Your daughter doesn't know how to paint in oils," my mom said. "She just draws in pencil."

Thanks, mom. I rolled my eyes. They were both playing with me like cats before the kill.

My dad was smiling now, always happy to run the numbers. "Now hold on a second, Linda. Let's think this through. Sam, how long does it take you to finish a drawing? And I mean a *good* one?"

Why did I feel like I was walking into a trap? "Um, all day?"

"Okay. Let's call that eight hours. So, for eight hours of work, you make one hundred dollars. That's $12.50 an hour."

My dad was a human calculator, and quite proud of it.

"That's pretty good, isn't it?" I knew minimum wage was $8.25 in D.C. $12.50 sounded pretty damn good to me.

"Hah!" my mom bellowed. Her eyes twinkled as if she enjoyed the way my dad was shredding my artistic dreams with practiced ease.

Groan.

"Let's not get ahead of ourselves," Dad said. "You have to assume the cost of supplies. Conservatively, let's say ten percent for paint and whatever other materials artists use, another ten for the frame. I'm sure the gallery gets some kind of commission, so another, oh, fifteen for that. Now we're down to $65.00 for that painting of yours. That comes out to $8.13 an hour, Sam. You'd make more pouring coffee at Starbucks. And I hear some of the big corporate coffee chains have decent health insurance plans these days, which aren't cheap. Working as a barista would put you significantly ahead of the guy who painted that painting in my office."

My mom smiled at me with a mixture of superiority and, I hate to say it, glee. "Your father's right, Sam. Being an artist is a bad idea."

I felt something close inside me at that moment, like my parents had somehow proved with total certainty that it was impossible to be an artist.

I remember trying to swallow a bite of mashed potatoes, and it knotting in my throat like a ball of lead. When I went to my room that night, I buried all the drawings I'd been working on in the bottom of my closet.

SAMANTHA

PRESENT DAY

Christos said, "That's rough."

I wrapped my free arm around his chest and hugged him while I sobbed weakly. "Now you know why I don't want to tell my parents."

"I don't know if you realize this, Samantha, but your parents are ignorant."

"What do you mean?"

"I mean, there's thousands of different jobs out there for artists. Your dad, as smart as he may be with numbers, doesn't know shit about the art business. He is literally ignorant of the options that exist for artists."

"But I still have to convince them of that. I don't know what you know, so I feel like they'd try to change my mind over the phone, and who knows, maybe by the end of the call, I'd be agreeing with everything they said all over again."

"That's not true," Christos said encouragingly. "Didn't you tell me you took Life Drawing last quarter, even though they wanted you to take Economics instead?"

"That was an elective class. I had to take one anyway. Actually changing my major is a whole 'nother level."

"If you want, call them while I'm here. I can cheer from the sidelines. I'll get some pom-poms and do those goofy clapping high kicks. Then you'll be able to see my underwear," he chuckled. "Not that I'm wearing any."

The idea of Christos, in a skirt, with no underwear, kicking his legs high while his jewels jiggled made me wrinkle my nose.

"Okay, maybe I'd wear underwear for the high kicks," he grinned. "But seriously, I'll totally back you up. I'll talk to your parents if I have to. Whatever you need, I'm here for you, *agápi mou*."

"Thank you, Christos. That means so much, I can't even tell you."

"You want to call them now?"

I almost said no, but then I felt something I'd never felt before. Anger. I was suddenly mad at my parents. No matter what I'd tried to do to shape my own future, they'd always pushed back, steering me away from where I wanted to go. I *could* let this go on forever, always caving into them, but I was tired of being bullied by everyone, and that included my parents.

I'd chosen San Diego University for college because it would put me far away from their constant control, and I would be free to make my own choices for myself. And I had stood up to Damian when I'd broken my silence about Taylor Lamberth.

Back then, Damian had threatened to kill me. Now, my parents were threatening to kill my dreams. It almost amounted to the same thing, in my book. One just took longer.

Screw it.

I was going to call them.

It wasn't quite 10:00pm on the east coast, and my parents were usually awake until eleven. I dialed the house and put my phone on speaker. My nerves went nuts before the phone even rang. I stood up from the couch and started pacing my living room. I held my finger up to my lips and made a shhh face to Christos.

He nodded understanding.

"Hello?" my dad said.

"Hey, dad," I sighed.

"What a pleasant surprise. It's so good to hear from you, Sam. Your mother and I thought you wouldn't call for a few more weeks. How is Micro Economics?"

Jesus. A *"How are you?"* would've been nice. In general, I felt like my father was more of a manager to me than a father. His relationship with me was something he calculated, weighed, considered. The feelings and love parts were glaringly absent.

"Sam?" he prompted.

I steeled myself. This was it. "I'm not taking Econ."

"What?" My dad was shocked. "Sam, we *talked* about this."

I rolled my eyes to Christos.

He made a compassionate sort of wince. At least he understood.

"*You* talked about this, Dad. I mostly listened. I don't want to take economics."

My dad pushed out a hard sigh on the other end of the phone. "Fine. But you can't keep putting it off if you plan to graduate in four years. What about accounting? How is Managerial Accounting? I always enjoyed that topic."

OMG. "I'm not taking it. I dropped the class."

"What?!" my dad panicked. "Sam, what are you doing? You can't take the upper division classes for an Accounting major if you don't finish the lower division foundation courses first!"

"That's okay."

"No, it's not."

"It is, because I changed my major."

"What?!" My dad was going to explode at this rate. "To what?"

"Art." I expected him to explode. A hot flush bounced through my body, and not in a good way. I fanned my face. This was about to get ugly.

"Hold on, Sam. I'm going to have your mother join us on the extension."

Like I said.

While I waited for doomsday, I glanced at Christos. He took the cue and walked over to me. He placed a comforting hand on the small of my back and rubbed it gently.

A moment later, I heard my mom pick up the other line. "What is going on, Sam?" she demanded sternly.

"I'm changing my major to Art."

"You can't do that!" my mom said.

"I meant, I already changed my major."

"Then change it back," she said stridently.

I'm pretty sure my apartment was shrinking around me. Was I sweating? My arm pits felt like furnaces. I took a deep breath.

"Sam? You will change your major back. Immediately," my mom commanded.

This was it. "No."

I think I had expected the ground to open beneath my feet or maybe a giant asteroid to crash into San Diego at that moment. But all I heard was silence.

I had never stood up to my parents like this. Could it be this easy?

"Bill?" my mom asked. "Did you hear what your daughter just said?"

I'd always loved how my mom disowned me the second I disobeyed.

"I'm nonplussed," my dad said. I don't think I'd ever heard him sound so exasperated before. "Aaaah…" he mumbled. "Linda?"

I had the distinct sense that the phone in my hand had started to heat up to like two hundred degrees. I know that was silly, but I knew something was about to go thermonuclear.

"If you insist on disobeying your father and I, then you—"

I cut her off. "Disobey? This is *my* life, mom. I don't want to be an Accountant. I want to make my own decisions about what I'm going to do for the rest of my life. I'm nineteen, for god's sake!"

"Watch your mouth, young lady!" my mom barked. "And don't use that tone with me! You will march down to the Registrar's Office first thing tomorrow morning, and you *will* change your major back to Accounting. And that's final!"

"Do what your mother says, Sam," my dad grumbled.

I sighed petulantly. Did my parents still believe I was in junior high? "No, mom," I said softly. "I'm not changing my major."

"Do *not* disobey me!" my mother shouted.

"I'm not doing it, mom."

"Bill! Talk to her," my mom said, flustered.

There was a moment of silence.

"Bill? Say something."

"Hold your horses, Linda. I'm thinking."

I didn't know if that was good or bad. I looked at Christos. He shrugged his shoulders. There was nothing he could do.

"We have an opportunity here, Linda," my dad said calmly. That always worried me. "I think it's time Sam learns the true value of a dollar and an education. I suggest we terminate the subsidization of Sam's living expenses."

"What?" my mom and I asked in unison, although the tone of our voices was quite different.

"Yes, I think that is a terrific idea," my dad continued. "Sam, your mother and I will no longer pay for your apartment. In addition, any incidentals that we have been funding will be your responsibility. Linda, does that make sense to you?"

"Perfect sense," Mom said victoriously.

"Wait," I said, "You guys can't—"

My mom cut in. "Oh yes, we certainly can, young lady."

I goggled at Christos, unsure what to do. "How am I going to pay my rent? I don't have any money!"

"I'm sure there are ample opportunities for work-study programs on campus," Dad said. "Failing that, there is a myriad of unskilled jobs available in the labor market. I suggest you try the shopping mall or fast food restaurants. Either will be more likely to hire a young, able-bodied person with no work experience. You are intelligent, and if you are enthusiastic and ready to work hard, you will find a job in short order."

"I can't argue with that," my mom said, a smile in her voice. "This will be good for you, Sam. I promise, when you look back at this experience, you will thank your father and I."

I glanced at Christos. The expression on his face was what I would imagine a normal person would look like if they arrived at the scene of a terrible traffic accident and discovered all their children had been crushed under an over-turned delivery truck. I kind of felt bad for Christos. I was used to this sort of behavior from my parents. He wasn't.

I sighed.

I had always suspected my parents were insane. Now I had proof. They were trying to blackmail me, or maybe bribe me, into following their abhorrent order to become an accountant no matter how much the idea sickened me.

How had my life managed to take a nose dive in less than twenty minutes?

Oh yeah.

My parents.

CHRISTOS

I was grinding my jaw the entire time Samantha talked with her parents. For all the shit I'd dealt with after my parents split, I'd never gone through something like this. My parents never forced me to do something I hated. Sam's parents didn't even seem like human beings to me. More like robots.

After Samantha said goodbye to her parents, she stared at me with watery eyes.

"*Agápi mou*," I said. "I'm so sorry."

She reached out to hug me.

I wrapped my arms around her and squeezed her tight. "That was total bullshit."

"What am I gonna do?" she said, panicked.

"It's okay, *agápi mou*. We'll figure it out."

"I need to look for a job. Right now." She looked up at me, her eyes wide with fear.

It was the saddest thing I'd ever seen, like her whole world was gone. My heart was breaking as her fear escalated. I don't think I'd seen this much fear on her face even on the day we'd met, the day I'd punched out that fat dude screaming at her.

Right now, she looked scared to death.

Samantha pulled free from my arms, like I wasn't able to protect her or comfort her. She rushed over to her book bag and yanked on her laptop. The computer was caught inside the bag. She panicked and pulled harder, but what she needed to do was relax. The laptop didn't budge. "I can't get it out!"

I kneeled down and put a hand on hers. "Relax, *agápi mou*."

She looked at me, a mixture of hope and doubt in her eyes.

"You know that saying 'easy does it'? It applies in situations like this most of all."

"Huh?"

"Stop pulling so hard."

She relaxed her grip on the computer.

I peeled back the corner of the book bag gently. "Now try it."

She slid the laptop free. Her hands shook. She sat down on the couch, flipped the computer open, and fired it up. "I have to look for a job. Right now. I've only got enough money to last till the end of the month. Then I'm out." Her hands clenched into fists over and over. You'd think she'd just been told her world was ending.

Maybe she had.

My guts twisted as I watched the growing horror on her face. She was freaking out. I couldn't deal with it. "Samantha, you don't need to worry about this. I've got money. How much do you need?"

"Oh, I couldn't take your money, Christos."

"Why not?"

"It wouldn't be right."

"You took your parents money, why can't you take mine?"

She paused, eyes darting around the room uncertainly. "That's different. They're my parents."

"And I'm your boyfriend. I've got more than enough money to help you out."

"No, Christos, I just couldn't."

"Samantha, please try to understand my side of things. I'm sitting here watching you freak out because your parents suddenly fucked you over. You're feeling betrayed. Right?"

"I don't know what the word is for what I'm feeling right now, Christos. But it's terrible. It's like they're trying to control me. They're not listening to me, to what I want. They never ask, they just issue orders."

I had to clamp down because I really wanted to go off on her parents right now. I wanted to snag her phone, dial her parents, and tell them they were fucked up bungholes. But I didn't think that would help the situation any.

"Samantha, I'm listening to you. I can bail you out of this situation." I winced when I said the word bail. That was my problem, not hers. Samantha's seemed manageable. All she needed was some extra cash. That, I had.

What I didn't have was a bottle with a genie waiting to grant me three wishes, one of which would be to make my trial go away. Not gonna happen. But I *could* fix Samantha's money situation. I could be her genie, even if I didn't have one of my own. I smiled at her. "Samantha, my money is your money. Just say the word, and poof! Your problems are solved."

"Oh, Christos. I can't tell you how much that means to me. But I feel like I need to do this myself. Otherwise, I'll feel beholden to you. I can't take your money."

"What do you mean, beholden?"

"I don't know. I just have to do this myself." Her eyes glazed over.

She wasn't getting it. You could lead a horse to water, but you couldn't make it drink. And you weren't supposed to look a gift horse in the mouth, either. Sam was doing both. I couldn't blame her. She had too many horses and too many problems all at once.

All because Samantha wasn't thinking rationally. Her fear was driving all her thoughts like wild horses. See? Too many fucking horses.

I shook my head and sighed while she searched online job websites.

"My parents didn't say they'd stop helping with tuition," she said to herself. "Just rent. I can figure that out. There's jobs. I'll go to career services tomorrow and see what I can find. I'm sure I can figure this out."

Yeah, she wasn't talking to me. She was just thinking out loud.

I tried to catch her gaze, but her eyes were wild, like those god damn horses again. She didn't even realize I was in the room with her, willing and able to help her through this.

She was oblivious to my presence.

There was nothing more I could do but give her time, enough space, and be there if she fell.

I heaved another sigh.

It hurt that she didn't want my help, like I was somehow a bad person waiting to take advantage of her. But I couldn't force my help on her, no matter how easily I could solve her money problems.

Man, that sucked.

"Samantha, if it gets to be too much," I reassured, "let me know. I'm here for you, *agápi mou*. No matter what."

I don't think she'd heard me.

I needed a drink.

Chapter 12

SAMANTHA

Needless to say, I slept like crap that night. I couldn't stop thinking about finding a job. Christos had left after an hour. I only had the one computer, so there wasn't much he could do in the way of helping me job hunt.

I had searched around the internet for hours, trying to find something, but had no luck. I would look on campus for a work-study job today between classes, but feared there'd be none left this late in the academic year. If that happened, I'd try looking in my neighborhood for a restaurant job, a coffee shop, anything.

I did my best not to think about it.

My only class that morning was Oil Painting with Romeo and Kamiko. I had to buy supplies at the campus bookstore before class. I picked out the paints, brushes, palette, canvases, and other supplies and took them to the register.

The total was $147.38.

My money was going to be gone in two weeks at this rate.

I walked toward the Visual Arts building with my bag of supplies. When I'd walked this route to Life Drawing for the first time three months ago, I'd been full of hope. Now I was full of dread. I had to find a job. That was all I could think about. My lack of money.

How was I going to concentrate on painting? Or my other classes?

"There goes Poor House," Tiffany Kingston-Whitehouse giggled.

Great. That was all I needed.

Two hobots stood next to her on the pathway. All three of them held cups of designer coffee from Toasted Roast. I'd already cut daily coffee from my budget.

I ignored her and kept walking.

"She lowers thrift-store chic to a whole new low, don't you guys think?" Tiffany asked her minions.

"Totally," they chorused.

"She makes bargain-basement look bad," one said.

I had a moment to think about how Tiffany's yacht probably cost more than four years of college tuition for fifty kids. Whatever. Envying her wealth wouldn't help me find a job. I didn't have time for her childish insults anymore.

"Grow up, Tiffany," I said, never looking back.

I made it to the painting studio shortly after.

People were already setting up at the easels. I found a space next to Romeo and Kamiko.

"Hey guys," I said. I was so happy to see them. "What are we going to paint this quarter to top all the nude models in Life Drawing last term? A live sex show?" I joked, trying to force myself into a better mood.

"I wish," Romeo said. He gestured toward the center of the room. A waist-high pedestal had a square of black cloth draped diagonally over it. A wooden bowl of fruit sat on top.

"A still life," Kamiko said. "Fruit is way easier than people."

"But not nearly as interesting," I said.

"Wait and see. Dealing with mixing paint and working with brushes will offer a bunch of new challenges. You'll be glad you're just painting apples and grapes."

"I agree with Sam," Romeo said thoughtfully. "I preferred painting people. Especially fully-nude Christos. But there *is* a huge banana in the fruit bowl. It's about the right size, wouldn't you say, Sam?"

My cheeks glowed red. "Romeo!"

"Relax, Sam," Romeo said dismissively. "We've *all* seen what's in Christos' fruit basket more than once. But we have no expertise in the fully erect department. For that, I turn to you for corroborative evidence. Can you describe his manana to us?" He arched an eyebrow while pretending to hold a microphone in front of me like he was a news reporter.

Kamiko gawked at both of us.

"No!" I blurted.

"No, you won't describe it," Romeo said, "or no, you haven't peeled it?"

"Uhhhh…" Why did I feel guilty all of a sudden?

Kamiko snorted laughter. "Romeo, even *I* know you don't *peel* them."

"If they have a foreskin, you do," Romeo said plainly.

"It's not the same kind of peeling," Kamiko corrected. "It's more like pulling down the wrapper on a freezer pop."

I grimaced. "This conversation has officially become uber disgusting."

Romeo frowned. "Wait a second, Kamiko, how do you know so much about mansicle wrappers?"

"I am pre-med, in case you forgot. I know what a foreskin is."

"Yes, but you seem to have intimate knowledge of their function. First-hand experience, perhaps? Are you hiding a boyfriend, Kamiko? I mean, other than Finn the Human? Like, a real live boy, boyfriend?"

"No, Romeo," Kamiko insisted.

"Whoa!" Romeo chided. "Down, girl! Strident denial is a sure sign you're hiding something!"

"Do you think she's secretly dating Brandsome?" I suggested coyly, happy to have the heat off of me.

Kamiko's cheeks flushed red. "I don't know what you guys are talking about!"

"Hmmm," Romeo considered shrewdly. "This bears further investigation. I do believe the plot has thickened. Unless that's just me thinking about Christos' manana again." He shifted his belt around and wiggled his pants while jiggling his hips. "Yes, my plot has definitely thickened."

"Oh, gross," Kamiko grimaced.

"Anyway," Romeo dismissed her, "back on topic. Sam, is Christos' peeled manana curved or straight? I need to know." He held the imaginary microphone up to my face again.

"Romeo!" I pleaded, pushing his hand away.

"I hear the curved ones hit a lady's G-spot the best. Although, I think when it comes to my B-spot, straight is my preference."

"What's a B-spot?" Kamiko asked, confused.

"It's in your bu—"

"Okay, class," the professor said, clapping loudly several times right behind Romeo's head, "enough chatter. We have a lot to cover today. Shall we begin?" The professor was a middle-aged guy with unruly hair and a permanent frown which reminded me of pictures I'd seen of Ludwig van Beethoven.

Romeo's lips curled into a sneer and he frowned at the professor's back.

Me and Kamiko both choked down our respective giggle fits.

The professor wore a button-down shirt with the sleeves rolled up, and jeans. Despite his casual appearance, he seemed a bit too serious for my taste. "My name is Professor Cogdill," he said. "I will be your Oil Painting professor this term. Today we'll be painting a simple still life. I'll do a brief demonstration before you begin your paintings. I will show you how to prepare your palette. I will show you how to block in the basic composition. I will show you how to contrast warm colors against cool. I will show you how to…"

I glanced over at Romeo, who was frowning at the professor like they were lifelong enemies.

"Professor Cogdildo needs someone to peel his manana immediately," Romeo whispered while rolling his eyes. "Maybe then he wouldn't be such a stick in the butt. Because I'm telling you, he's so not my type. I'm going to be stuck squeezing my butt cheeks together all term long."

I stifled another giggle while the professor droned on.

Despite the professor's stiff demeanor, no pun intended, he was extremely knowledgable and logical in the way he explained everything. I was amazed that he was able to paint an awesome picture of the fruit bowl in about twenty minutes. I'd never seen someone paint so fast before. It was amazing to watch him work. Afterward, while he rinsed his brush in a can of Turpenoid, he said, "All right, everyone, please take your places and go to work."

At my easel, I squeezed out paint like the professor had shown. He had used some burnt sienna paint to lay in sketchy lines on his canvas. I did the same, blocking in the basic shapes with a medium-sized brush.

"Remember, class," the professor intoned, "your block-in can be loose. You will correct things as you go."

I glanced over at Romeo, who was already laying in the shapes with his brush. He was focused on getting the shape of the banana just right, by Romeo standards.

"Um, Romeo?" I whispered. "Why does your banana look like

it's going to have a mushroom tip?"

"I'm just painting what I see, Sam," he said, somewhat offended.

Kamiko leaned over to look at Romeo's painting. She grimaced, then looked at the fruit bowl. "I don't see a mushroom tip on that banana, Romeo," she jabbed.

"I see dicks everywhere I look, darling," Romeo said dismissively.

"You are such a Peen Queen, Romeo," Kamiko smirked.

"I admit it," Romeo said, hand held dramatically over his heart. "I am cock royalty. Although I like to think of myself more as the Princess of Penis."

"Am I the only one throwing up in my mouth right now?" I grimaced.

Kamiko puffed out her cheeks and her eyes went wide. She held two fingers to her lips while she made fake gagging noises.

I was giggling as I returned my focus to mixing colors on my palette.

Between Romeo's antics and the painting itself, I had a blast. By the end of class, I also had a pretty good oil painting of the fruit bowl, banana included, but no mushroom tip.

"Wow, Sam," Kamiko said. "You did a great job with your lights and darks. Your lighting and shading is so realistic."

I couldn't believe it either. "Thanks, Kamiko!" I looked at Kamiko and Romeo's work, and theirs were really good too. "Yours looks great, Kamiko."

"Thanks," she smiled. "I was worried working with the oil paint would screw me up."

"Yours is awesome, Kamiko. Even Romeo's looks great, now that his banana doesn't look like a manana anymore. I think we all owe Professor Cogdill some thanks."

"Because his last name is so phallic?" Romeo asked.

I had to laugh at that.

Maybe my life wasn't about to blow up in my face. Maybe things were looking up.

CHRISTOS

When Russell Merriweather had called personally that morning to tell me to meet him at his law offices downtown, I knew it was not going to be good news.

I parked my Camaro in the downstairs garage and took the elevator up to the twentieth floor of the building. Russell had spared no expense when he'd leased the place.

"Hey, Rhonda. I'm here to see Russell," I said to the receptionist. I'd met Rhonda the first time I'd come in six years back. I'd always been impressed with her professional attitude. Russell only hired the best. She was also hot, but she was all business and great at her job.

"Mr. Merriweather is expecting you, Christos. He will be with you in a minute. Can I get you anything to drink while you wait?"

"I'm good, thanks, Rhonda." I strolled over to the picture window and gazed out at the stunning view of San Diego bay. An aircraft carrier was parked at the naval base, covered with F-18s. What I wouldn't do to hop in one of those jets and Mach 2 the fuck out of here.

"There he is!" Russell beamed, smiling wide, striding into the waiting room a short time later. Even when he wasn't in court, Russell wore immaculate, tailored suits that enhanced his already towering silhouette, making him basketball-tall. His exuberant personality added another three inches at least. "Christos Manos, in the flesh!"

I hadn't seen him face-to-face in a couple months.

We clasped fists and slapped a man hug on each other.

"Did Rhonda offer you a beverage?" he asked.

I winked at Rhonda. "Twice."

She returned a curt smile.

"Hold my calls, Rhonda. I've got Christos Manos up in here." Russell chuckled heartily. "Come on, son, let's talk in my office."

The offices of six other attorneys and several paralegals opened off the long hallway that led to Russell's office. He had done quite well for himself.

"Have a seat," he said while motioning to a leather chair in front of his desk. The corner view in his office was more impressive than the one in the lobby. You could see up and down the coast of San Diego. The Pacific Ocean seemed to go on forever.

"Did you come here on that crotch-rocket of yours?" he asked, raising his eyebrows parentally.

"Nope. Garaged it, like you said. My Camaro's downstairs."

Russell nodded approvingly. "Good boy. There may be hope for you yet." He smiled reluctantly, but I could tell it was genuine. He patted my shoulder firmly several times. "Very good."

He closed his office door and lowered himself into the executive chair behind his desk. His jovial demeanor dimmed about a hundred watts as he laced his fingers together on the blotter in front of him.

"I'm not going to sugar-coat it, son. My private detectives have failed to turn up a single clue that can be of use. We can keep throwing money at them, but I highly doubt they'll turn anything up at this point."

I'd been doing my best not to think about any of this for the last several months. I trusted Russell, and knew he hired only the best. I'd seen the invoices. "Where does that put us?"

"I don't know if you're aware of this, Christos, but if the jury finds you guilty on all charges, you could face up to four years in the state penitentiary."

"Prison," I said.

"Yes."

"What are the chances of clearing that extra charge, the one that means prison time?"

"You're talking about the secondary charge? Serious Bodily Injury, correct?"

"Yeah, that. What's the status on that?

"The State is claiming that the man you assaulted has endured all manner of ongoing health-related issues because of the incident. I have my team investigating the facts, and I intend to call the man's personal physician to the stand during trial. I will also be calling a physician friend of mine as an expert witness. Then it will be up to me to prove in court that the man's medical conditions either preceded the incident, or came about wholly separate from it. But it will ultimately be up to the jury to decide whether his injuries qualify as Serious Bodily Injury, or not, as per the judge's instructions at trial."

"In English?" I asked.

"From what I've seen, that crybaby Horst Grossman wants to blame you for everything from his hangnail to his hair-piece. My task will be to convince the jury that Horst Grossman, is in fact, a cry baby."

I chuckled. "That sounds like good news. What about the rest of the charges? I mean, I actually hit the guy."

"Yes, and for that, even if we knock it down to a misdemeanor, you could still face up to a year in jail."

"Are we going to be able to say it was self-defense?"

"We can say it all we want, but we still have to convince the jury."

"Can we do that?"

"At this point in time, that part of your case does not look nearly as good. We're up against the issue of reasonableness. In your case, we're going to have a very difficult time proving to the jury that you were in fear for your life when Horst Grossman lunged at you. The state will argue that you could've easily dodged out of the way without striking him."

"I didn't even have time to think about it. I just reacted."

"Unfortunately, the Deputy D.A. is going to ask why you even walked up to the man in the first place."

"Because I was trying to help that girl," I said. I still hadn't told him "that girl" was Samantha. I really wanted to keep her out of the case entirely. Because if I told her about *this* trial, that would lead to her inevitable questions about all my *other* trials. The trials where I'd been found guilty, and rightfully so. I'm sure Samantha would be ecstatic when she found out all about my criminal past.

I'm sure her parents would be happy about that. They'd jump for joy when they found out their daughter was dating an ex-con. They'd want to know when I was going to pressure Samantha into changing her major from Art to Assault.

"And there's the rub," Russell said without humor. "If we could find that girl, she may very well convince the jury that *she* was in fear for her life, and your actions constitute self-defense of another. Then your actions suddenly become more reasonable, both objectively and subjectively." Russell searched my eyes. "Christos, is there anything you can remember about her? What kind of car was she driving? What color was it? Have you ever seen the girl since the incident, perhaps on the same route? Maybe she commutes to work that way every day. Is it possible she's a student at SDU? Think hard, son. We're running out of options."

Samantha.

Agápi mou.

I couldn't do it. I couldn't tell her. I couldn't bring her into my mess. It was mine to deal with. Time to suck it up.

With any luck, Russell and his crack team would get me off. Then Samantha and her controlling parents wouldn't have to worry about my past.

Everything would be perfect.

SAMANTHA

Romeo, Kamiko, and I walked out of Oil Painting class together.

"Do you guys want to get lunch?" Romeo asked.

"I have to go look for a job," I sighed.

"Why? What happened?" Kamiko asked.

"I changed my major to Art."

"That's awesome, Sam!" Romeo said. "You should take Figurative Sculpture with me! There's still a couple of spots open."

"Really? I thought it would be full by now,"

"Nope, but you should sign up ASAP."

"So how come you need the job?" Kamiko asked.

"Oh," I sighed again, "because I told my parents I changed my major. They flipped and told me they wouldn't pay for my apartment anymore."

"That sucks," Kamiko said. "Do you want to live in my dorm room?"

Kamiko had a double room, which she shared with a roommate. "Thanks, Kamiko. I don't think there's room. Well, guys, you should go get lunch. I better take care of things."

"Do you want us to wait for you?" Romeo asked.

"We totally can," Kamiko said.

"Thanks, guys. You're the best. But you should eat."

We said our goodbyes and I trotted over to the Registrar's Office first. I was in luck. Figurative Sculpting still had one space left. And class was today. I stopped at the Campus Bookstore to buy supplies.

The clay and sculpting tools were another $139.85. Now it looked like I'd be broke by Friday. Maybe I needed to start skipping lunches. Groan.

I walked back to Career Services in the middle of campus and took a number. I was finally called and sat down at a desk facing a cute guy. He wore a polo shirt with an embroidered SDU logo over the heart.

"How can I help you today?" he asked charmingly.

"I need to find a work-study job."

"Do you have your student ID?"

I pulled it out of my purse and handed it to him. He punched my info into the computer, then clicked through a few screens.

"It's a little late in the school year," he said. "Most of the jobs are usually taken at this point."

"Oh." I had been right. Crap.

He smiled at me. "Don't worry, I'll find you something. Let me see here...I see that you recently changed your major to Art?"

"I did!" I couldn't hide my excitement.

"Maybe there are some internships with the professors." He clicked several more keys and moused around, reading intently.

My stomach knotted tighter and tighter as I waited hopefully.

"Hmmm," he frowned. "I'm not seeing anything."

"Oh." My heart sank.

"Let me try one more thing." He searched around for another minute. His face broke into a smile and he turned to me. "How about working in the Eleanor M. Westbrook art museum?"

"Really? That sounds awesome!"

"They need someone to work the front counter. Do you think you could handle that?"

"Of course! How much does it pay?"

"Ten bucks an hour. Will that work?"

"Totally!" $10.00 an hour was more than my dad had calculated that artist had made on the hundred dollar oil painting in Dad's office! I smiled smugly to myself. Christos was right. I was already going to make more money doing art things than my parents believed possible. I was determined to prove to myself, and to them, that I could do this. That art wasn't a pipe dream career.

"I'll shoot an email over to the head curator at the museum to let them know you want to apply for the position, but you'll have to go over there and fill out the application and do an interview. Is that okay?"

"I can totally do that! Thank you!" I was elated.

I left Career Services and headed straight over to the museum, smiling the whole way there.

When I walked inside, I told the girl sitting at the cash register that I needed an application.

"Are you applying for the cashier job?" she asked.

"Yeah," I said.

"Would you like to speak to Mr. Selfridge? He's in his office."

"Sure," I said. I had an hour until Sculpting class with Romeo. My stomach grumbled, but I'm sure I would have time to grab a snack on the way to class. I just hoped I could afford it.

The girl at the counter made a call on a phone behind the counter. "He'll be out in a second. You can wait here."

"Okay," I smiled. I stood at the entryway to the main gallery. I had loved the museum the first time I'd been in it last quarter. It was big and quiet and calming. The paintings were amazing. I couldn't imagine a better place to work.

Not long after, a tall, handsome man in a tweed sport coat came walking out of the main entrance to the gallery.

"Hi, I'm Samantha Smith," I extended my hand.

He shook it. "I'm Mr. Selfridge."

"Did you get the email from Career Services?"

"I did. Do you want to apply for the counter position?"

"Definitely. Do you need a résumé or something?"

"No. You're a student here, correct?"

"I'm an Art major," I said proudly.

He smiled. "You don't say. That's terrific. Then you'll be right at home at the museum." He folded his hands together. "I can only offer you ten hours per week. Is that acceptable?"

Oh. I hadn't been expecting that. Ten hours meant about $400.00 a month, less after taxes, a fact I knew from growing up in the Smith household. Thanks, Dad. I would need to find a second job. But in the mean time, I needed to take whatever I could get. "Uh, yeah, that would be great," I smiled.

"Excellent. Here's the application," he said, handing me a pre-printed form. "Bring it back on Monday. You can start then."

"Okay, thank you," I smiled.

"I look forward to working with you, Samantha," he nodded pleasantly.

"I'll see you Monday!" I walked out and jogged to the Food Court at the Student Center.

My phone jangled. A text from Madison.

Where u at?

I replied, *Running to Student Center.*
Wanna get lunch?
Don't have time. Late for class.
Ok. Tomorrow.

As I jogged, I had a moment to wonder how I had ended up right where I'd started at the beginning of the school year last quarter, late and running from one place to the other.

I really needed to figure out the campus shuttle. This was getting ridiculous.

I considered fish tacos, but didn't want to spend the extra money. I grabbed a protein bar and a bottled smoothie from the convenience store beside the campus bookstore and saved $1.38. It wasn't much, but every bit helped.

I trotted back toward the Visual Arts building.

"She's late, she's late! For a very important date!" Tiffany mocked as I ran by.

"Don't you have class?" I sneered.

"More than you, you genital sore!" she shouted at my back. Her minions cackled. They were all in league with Satan.

But seriously, didn't she have anything to do other than stand in the same place all day long and mock me? Or was she just working this campus street corner, waiting for rich upperclassmen to come along and buy things for her?

Probably.

SAMANTHA

I ran into the Visual Arts building and blundered down the hallway to the sculpting studio. Inside, I heard an echoey voice. The door was locked, so I knocked furiously. After a minute, the voice stopped, and I heard heels clicking closer and closer to the door. Someone opened the door.

"Perhaps if you were on time, you wouldn't have to interrupt the entire class," the woman holding the door said snidely. Despite her casual clothes, she had big hair and carefully applied makeup. Her hair was a work of art unto itself. She didn't strike me as the sort of woman who would be teaching a sculpting class. Maybe fashion design or even a cosmetology class.

I was breathless from running. "I, uh, had, an, on, campus, job, interview."

Despite her striking lips gloss, her lips thinned out of existence when she frowned at me. "Next time, be on time." She held the door for me, still irritated.

I cringed as I skulked past her. The sculpting studio was a high-ceiling room with exposed pipes painted black hanging overhead, and a concrete floor beneath. A wall of windows mounted on high-tech steel frames allowed ample light. It was not nearly as warm and comfy as Professor Childress' inviting Life Drawing room had been last quarter, but it was better than another boring lecture hall.

I searched the room for Romeo. He waved, but the positions next to him were taken by other students. I grabbed the only remaining spot.

Like drawing and painting, the students surrounded the center of the room in a circle. But instead of easels, everyone had their own elevated square table on wheels. The table was not much bigger than a barstool. I set my stuff down on the floor next to mine.

I noticed that everyone's table was adjusted to a different height. I realized there was a twisty handle on the side of the lone post supporting the table top. I twisted it and...*BLAM!!* My table top crashed down to the lowest height. The noise boomed throughout the room.

I think the echoes lasted for three or four minutes. The room had a cement floor, after all.

Everyone stared at me. Of course.

"Sorry," I mumbled. Undeterred, I twisted the handle slightly to add some friction, so the table wouldn't slam down again and maybe slice my fingers off. I lifted it up slowly. Somebody had forgot to oil my table.

!!SQUUUUEEEE!!—

I had to put my foot on the base to hold the stand down while I lifted. It was really sticking now. I put my back into it. Needed to adjust it sooner or later.

—*!!EEEEEEEE!!*—

Everyone was staring again. I shrugged my shoulders sheepishly, still lifting. May as well get it over with now that I'd started.

—*!!EEEEEEEE!!*—

Several students were wincing like they were getting their teeth drilled.

—*!!EEEEEEEE!!*—

Almost got it…

—*!!EEEEAAAK!!*

There! All finished! I smiled at everyone. Why did I feel like I was in the gas chamber and all the people around me were about to witness my execution?

Whatever. Smile!

:-)

The woman who had opened the door for me shot me a bow-and-arrow glare before rolling her eyes dramatically and huffing, "As I was saying before I was so rudely interrupted, my name is Marjorie Bittinger and I am the sculptor in residence here at SDU. I will be teaching you the basics of figurative sculpting. I hope you all came prepared." She singled me out again, "Miss, did you forget your supplies in addition to being late?"

Wow, what a bitch. "No, I have them right here," I said confidently, holding up my bag of sculpting supplies from the bookstore.

"I don't see a proportional caliper sticking out of your bag," Professor Bittinger gloated.

I was confused. "What's a proportional caliper?"

"Exactly," she sneered. "Would someone care to show our late arrival what a caliper is?"

A couple of students pulled these giant metal things out of their own bags and held them up. They looked like giant metal earwigs with those freaky pincer tails on one end, and a smaller matching pincer mouth on the other.

Oh. How had I missed those? I must have been in too much of a hurry at the bookstore.

Marjorie raised her eyebrows triumphantly. "I hope you will come prepared next time, Miss…what is your name?"

"Samantha Smith."

"Miss…*Smith.*" The look on her face made me think that Major *Bitch*inger had spent her childhood torturing squirrels and kittens, doing their hair and makeup after strangling them. I refused to be her next victim. "Did you at least remember to bring your armature wire, Miss Smith?"

Why was she singling me out? Whatever. I reached into my bag and pulled out the ring of wire. I didn't know what it was for, but I held it up proudly. "Right here," I smiled my fakest smile.

The professor nodded while smiling smugly.

Had I made a mistake signing up for this class? I didn't want to think about it.

"Do you have any further interruptions before we begin, Miss Smith?" she glared at me. She was expecting an answer.

After a minute, I cracked. "No." Did I sound like I was thirteen after being scolded by my mom? I hoped not.

Professor *Bitch*inger gave me a curling smile, "Very good." She turned to address the entire room. "Today, class, we're going to craft a simple armature and start doing quick sculpts of the model. Please get out your armature wire."

The professor, who was sadly a total bitch, was also a total professional. She quickly demonstrated how to make a twelve-inch tall stick figure out of the armature wire by bending the wire into the proper shape and twisting the wire around itself to add rigidity. She walked the room as students repeated the process from her demonstration. When necessary, she made corrections and improvements to the students' efforts. She was not kind, but she was very informative and knowledgable.

Luckily, she circled in such a way that she came to me next to last, so I had time to build my armature.

"Let's see what kind of mess you've made, Miss Smith," she snarked.

I held up my completed armature and smirked.

The look of superiority on her face did not falter as she scanned my armature. "Well, it looks like we have an over-achiever in our midst," she said, loud enough for the entire room to hear.

Okay, she was lame. She hated me, whether I was a screw up or top of the class. Whatever.

The professor abruptly yanked the armature from my hand and turned it over and around, wiggling it in several places before slapping it back into my hand. "Good job, Miss Smith," she said dismissively, turning her back to me as she walked to the final student and inspected their work.

"Okay, class," she said in a clear voice, "everyone place your purchased clay into the bin next to the clay warmer. After you've done that, take a few blocks of warm clay out of the warmer."

The clay warmer turned out to be a refrigerator that had been converted into a re-warmerator. Inside it, something circulated hot air, and on the shelves were dozens and dozens of warm chunks of green clay.

I grabbed a few and returned to my sculpting table.

Miss Bittinger turned to a cute guy in a bathrobe who sat casually on a chair in the corner of the room reading something on his smart phone. His bare feet were casually crossed and laid out in front of him.

"Hunter," the professor said, "would you please take the stand?"

Hunter walked onto the dais in the center of the room and threw his robe open dramatically. Whoops. He was hot. No tattoos like Christos, but definitely chiseled and manly, with flawless tan skin. None of the other male models in Life Drawing had been remotely attractive. This Hunter guy was quite handsome. He had a mess of blond hair, striking amber eyes, and the requisite six pack, heavy pectorals, and bulging shoulders. He clearly worked hard to maintain his impressively rock-hard physique.

Well, I was here to sculpt, not gawk.

Romeo took care of the gawking for me. His eyes popped and his mouth was a big O. He was in heaven.

I smiled at him and waved my finger in an "uh-uh-uh" gesture.

He stuck his tongue out at me.

"Is something funny, Miss Smith?" the professor asked.

I frowned. "No."

"If you can't maintain a professional attitude, perhaps you're not ready for this class?"

I opened my mouth to protest. I was here to work. Whatever. She'd decided I was the flake student. I'd have to prove her wrong.

"Hunter," the professor said, "please take a relaxed standing pose."

Hunter settled his weight on one leg and cocked his hip. He was the California surfer version of a perfect marble statue.

It turned out that a "quick sculpt" took a lot longer than a quick sketch. At first, I wasn't sure what to do. Everyone around the room started slapping clay on their wire armature. I did the same, noticing how warm the clay was. It was really squishy and buttery, sort of like lard in terms of firmness, but not greasy at all. I could squish this stuff around all day long. Warm clay. Who knew?

It didn't take long for me to get the hang of the actual sculpting. It was like playing with Play-Doh, but easier because the armature helped keep the clay in the right places.

Soon, people pulled out a variety of wooden tools from their own bags. They used the tools, which looked like a variety of wooden letter-openers or butter knives, to further shape the clay. Some people just used their fingers. I was a hands-on kind of girl. Fingers seemed to be easiest.

At one point, I glanced over at Romeo. He was hard at work, but when he saw me looking at him, he held up his rough sculpture, which resembled nothing more than a rudimentary clay voodoo doll at this point, and pulled the legs apart with his fists. Then he jammed one finger up into the sculptures' crotch while running his tongue around his own lips and giving me bedroom eyes before blowing me a kiss.

I winced, and tried to focus on the sculpture in my hand, but Romeo was still trying to get my attention from across the room. I glanced up and he bent his sculpture at the waist, then jabbed his finger into the sculpture's butt.

I grimaced and giggled reflexively.

"I didn't realize this was your own personal comedy club, Miss Smith," the professor barked behind me. "Are you here to work, or goof off?"

"I'm working," I said, sounding thirteen again. I held up my sculpture.

She looked down her nose at it, then glared at me for what seemed like an hour. She jammed her fists defiantly on her hips. "Well, keep working! Do you need an invitation?" She stalked over to the next student, her heels click-clacking.

Oh boy. What had I gotten myself into?

Chapter 13

SAMANTHA

"All right, class, now we're going to find out why our tables have wheels," Professor Bittinger said. "Please shift your table two positions to your right. If your bags are in the way, you can set them against the walls."

Everyone moved their tables in the circle, but Hunter remained in his same position and pose. As soon as I looked at Hunter from my new vantage point, I saw all kinds of problems with my sculpture, so I went about fixing them, until we moved positions again. More problems. Sculpting was a whole different animal from drawing, but I kind of liked it. In some ways it was easier, because you could squish the clay around to fix things without using an eraser and then redrawing everything.

We shifted positions two more times in the next twenty minutes, then took a break.

The students circulated the room, chatting and looking at each other's work.

"How'd it go?"

I looked up, right into the amber eyes of Hunter. "I'm sorry, what?"

He haphazardly strapped the belt of his robe around his waist, almost as if he'd just gotten dressed in the privacy of his own bedroom first thing in the morning, as if covering his wing-wang in public was a formality for him. "How is your sculpture so far?"

I was blushing, I think from embarrassment. Was I the only person in the room? Couldn't he talk to someone else? "Oh, uh, pretty good, I guess. I've never sculpted before. It's a lot different than drawing."

"That's what they tell me," he smiled. His teeth were white and even, as perfect as his physique.

"What, you don't draw, I mean sculpt?" I stammered.

"Nope. I leave it to the professionals." He winked at me and flashed his smile.

Was it just me, or had he not belted his robe tightly enough? It looked like it was going to fall open if he wasn't careful. I considered telling him as much, but couldn't think of the right way to say it. Was he doing it on purpose? Setting me up for a stealth flashing? Probably.

"What's your name?" he asked, holding out his hand to shake. This caused the top of his robe to billow out, revealing his chest and abs as he leaned forward.

"Oh, uh, Sam." I reluctantly shook his hand.

The shaking made his robe ripple, and I saw the belt sliding apart. When we finished shaking hands, he straightened up and I swear the only thing stopping the robe flaps from sliding completely away to reveal his full splendor was that they had caught on the, um, prominence, between his legs. Not that he was sporting wood, but it, well, it was *uncommonly* obtrusive. Not that I was looking. Sure, I'd seen it five minutes ago, but not from two feet away.

He needed a harness for that thing.

The second I realized what Hunter was doing, because the look on his face made it obvious he was orchestrating this imminent yet "unintentional" unharnessing, I appropriately bolted my eyes on his.

"I thought you said your name was Samantha," he said, giving me a cocky smile.

Ever since Christos had started calling me Samantha all the time, I'd decided to stop introducing myself as Sam to everyone. But this Hunter guy was dangerous, and needed to be kept at arm's length. "Oh, uh, yeah," I grimaced, "my, ah, friends, call me Sam."

I was regretting locking my eyes on his because their amber color was trying to hypnotize me. Was he making them shine and glimmer on purpose? Or was that their natural state?

"Sam it is. My name's Hunter Blakeley." he said casually, hands on hips.

Out of the corner of my eye, I noticed old man gravity was further working his dirty magic on Hunter's robe. Full disclosure was nearly upon me. Ew.

"You seem pretty good at sculpting," Hunter grinned.

A few months ago, I would've blurted out words of nervous self-doubt. But that was a few months ago. I'd made steady progress since then, and after my parents' bombshell the night before, I wasn't in this class to mess around. I was here to work, not flirt. I knew what Hunter was doing. Besides, I totally wasn't interested, and I'm pretty sure my artistic advancement wasn't his top priority. "Thanks," I said flatly.

Hunter gazed at me. His robe shifted another inch. I'm pretty sure there were no more inches left on his robe before his...*inches* were unveiled. In my head, I shouted at him,

FIX IT!!!!!!

He smirked confidently, probably reading my mind. Yeah, he knew what he was doing. He probably did this to women every day. Practiced on street corners as old ladies walked by. Helped them across the street while his robe accidentally fell open, just to see if they had heart attacks.

I needed to remove myself from this situation, because he was clearly indulging his desires to the hilt. Hilt was the wrong word, because we all know a sword and its hilt can be a euphemism for the male genitalia, just like a scabbard can refer to a woman's—

STOP!!!

That was me shouting at me.

Get a grip, girl!

No!! Don't GRIP anything!!!!

Yes, I was going insane. I was only human. And Hunter was hot. I took a deep breath and said to him, "Well, I need to get more clay, er, ah..."

"Hunter!" Professor Bittinger said, standing right behind me, "so good to see you posing again!"

Jesus Christ! She almost gave *me* a heart attack. Maybe that was her plan. But seriously, how the hell was it that most of the time her noisemaker heels machine-gunned across the cement floor when she was on the way over to chew me out, but now all of a sudden she managed to sneak up on me like she wore ninja slippers?

My operative theory was Magical Shoes. That was the only plausible explanation.

"Heeeyyyy, Marjorie," Hunter drawled to the professor, giving her a cocky head nod.

He called her *Marjorie*? Were they pals?

"What have you been up to?" the professor asked Hunter. "I haven't seen you since Spring quarter last year." Her eyes gleamed at him.

"This and that," he smiled.

She giggled girlishly.

How was "this and that" worthy of laughter? I guess the comedy bar for horny older women was set pretty low. Because she was obviously acting like a lovesick teenager around this Hunter guy. I also noticed that Marjorie had no problem gawking at his groin every two seconds. Between stares, she preened and flipped her hair saucily with her hand.

Harlot.

Wait a second! Maybe this new development could take the heat from Hunter off of me! I just needed to leave him alone with Marjorie and they could go at it like rabbits on the sculpting studio floor!

Problem solved. All I had to do was get Hunter off *my* back by getting Marjorie on *her* back, and maybe she wouldn't be such an uptight bitch to me anymore!

Perfect!

Just give them a little privacy and let nature take its course.

Unfortunately, I was stuck where I stood between them and my sculpting table. Worse, Marjorie was going to drip on me any second while drooling over Hunter.

Crap. I'd forgotten to wear my rain slicker.

"Sam here seems pretty good at sculpting," Hunter said, nodding toward me.

Marjorie blinked free of Hunter's love enchantment and looked over at me. Her lovesick face soured into hatesick.

Not what I needed. Where was my escape hatch?

Shit!

The professor looked me up and down, her nostrils flaring, as if deciding someone had just farted, and it had to have been me. "I see you've met Miss Smith," she sneered.

Great.

"You should've told me you had such a cutey in your class," Hunter said.

WTF was he doing?! Red alert! Abandon ship! It was so obvious

Marjorie Bittinger wanted Hunter Blakeley all to herself.

Marjorie's eyes narrowed at me. I'm confident she was thinking carnivorous thoughts, imagining skinning me alive and roasting my flesh on a stick while I begged for mercy. The new white meat: Boneless, skinless Samantha Breast. And not in a sexy way. Because I wouldn't put it past Marjorie to believe that if she ate my flesh, she would consume my power over Hunter, making it her own. No wonder she taught sculpture. She was a Voodoo Priestess all along, I was sure of it.

Marjorie snarled directly at me, "My only concern is whether or not Miss Smith's sculpting skills warrant her presence in my studio."

My eyes goggled. I wanted to duck under both of them and bolt for the door. Instead, I mentally rolled up my sleeves and lilted, "I'm sure they will."

"We'll see about that," Marjorie said before turning and walking away.

Great. The Wicked Witch of the West was my sculpting teacher and I was fresh out of water buckets, otherwise I would've poured one over her head right then.

"Take your positions, class," the professor barked. Her voice thundered around the room. An omen of things to come? I'm sure she was already formulating a surprise lightning strike on my ass sometime this quarter, and I feared her particular version of a lightning strike would include a squadron of flying monkeys soldiers flying out of her butt and setting their sights on me, something I hoped to avoid because I was fresh out of monkey repellent. Because you *know* her butt-monkeys didn't shower, or at the very least *rinse*, upon ejecting from Marjorie's rear end. Maybe she could install one of those drive-thru car-wash machines in her rectum? It *could* work. I would have to sketch up plans later.

"Don't worry about her," Hunter mumbled to me after the professor had walked out of earshot, startling me out of my reverie, "She's always like this."

"And that's supposed to be a good thing?" I scoffed.

He chuckled. "You're cute when you get all intense like this."

I rolled my eyes and turned around.

He was still standing behind me.

"Shouldn't you be modeling or something?" I said over my

shoulder.

"Oh, did you want a better look? Let me take my robe off…"

"Can you wait until you're on the stand?" I pleaded. "Then the professor can have you all to herself."

He chuckled and walked back to the dais, taking his robe off halfway to it like he owned the place. But we both knew this was Marjorie's boudoir, not mine.

Luckily, for the remainder of class, Professor Bitch left me alone. I was able to focus strictly on improving my sculpture.

Much to my surprise, sculpting class, which was supposed to be a welcome relief from Managerial Accounting, was making me increasingly uncomfortable. I was irritated that Hunter had forced me into a suicidal love triangle between him and Professor Voodoo, and I wasn't even interested in him.

I had Christos.

My feelings for Christos were unbreakable. So why did Hunter have to force himself on me? His eyes were always on me, no matter where I was in the room, with the exceptions of the times that I was behind him. I was glad he was stuck in his pose and couldn't turn around. If the professor hadn't been there, I'm sure he would have, and blown off the entire class just to hit on me.

Whatever.

I was thankful when Hunter finally put his robe on at the end of class. I was so done.

With any luck, I'd be able to squeeze out the door without Hunter or the professor jumping all over me.

SAMANTHA

While quickly packing my supplies, Romeo came over to my sculpting station. We walked out together.

Luckily, Hunter was busy talking to Professor Bittinger, but that didn't stop him from staring at me as I passed them by.

"Laters, Sam," Hunter said over his shoulder.

Professor Bittinger frowned at me.

I'm surprised she didn't hiss at me and bare her teeth. With any luck, maybe Marjorie would have an affair with Hunter and get herself thrown out of SDU for sexual harassment. I wouldn't be the one to say anything if they did. With my new financial predicament, I had too many problems of my own to worry about, but maybe some of the other students might get uncomfortable enough with Hunter's blatant behavior to file a complaint against both of them.

Romeo and I walked out of the Visual Arts building into the Eucalyptus grove outside.

"That guy was *hot!*" Romeo moaned.

"I guess," I replied reluctantly.

"Oh, come on, Sam. You were drooling too."

"I was not!" I protested. I really wasn't. Why did I feel guilty all of a sudden? Looking at the model was part of class. So what if class consisted of staring at a naked guy. Who was hot.

Was I a bad girlfriend because I could see that Hunter was attractive? I didn't think so. It was just an observation. It didn't mean I was attracted *to* him.

Romeo narrowed his eyes. "But you have to admit he was a Grade-A Meat Monster."

"What's a meat monster?"

"Didn't you see his package?"

"Not really," I smirked.

"You're such a bullshitter, Sam. He was hanging out like an elephant trunk the entire time. I would totally be that guy's dick sharpener."

I giggled. "Dick sharpener?"

Romeo nodded coyly.

"Who was hanging out?" Hunter asked, jogging up behind us, all smiles. He wore a black collarless polo shirt with white detailing around the throat. It was unbuttoned, revealing the muscles of his neck and the defined ridges of his chest. The sleeves were bunched up, showing off his rippled forearms and several different gold and silver bracelets. Dark jeans and expensive dark suede shoes completed his look. Hunter dressed to impress as purposefully as he undressed to impress.

Romeo gulped. "Ahhh…" He was swooning.

"Hey, Sam," Hunter said. "What're you guys up to?" He was looking right at me.

"Ahh, I'm heading home. I've got tons of homework to do," I said apologetically.

"Do you need a ride?" Hunter asked.

"No, thanks. I drove myself."

"Well, what're you doing later, for dinner?"

"More homework," I said.

"I'm free," Romeo tittered.

Hunter was thrown off by Romeo's comment. His smile dimmed, but then he shook it off. "When *are* you free, Sam?" Hunter asked.

"Probably never?" I said reluctantly.

"I doubt that," he smiled.

I stopped in my tracks and looked Hunter in the eyes. "I have a boyfriend, Hunter." That should do the trick, right? Lay it all out on the table so there's no confusion.

"So?"

I frowned. "Hunter, I'm in a relationship."

"I'm not," Romeo said.

Hunter frowned at Romeo again before looking back at me. "Are you serious about this guy?"

"Of course I'm serious!" I protested. "That's why he's my boyfriend."

Hunter cocked a thumb at Romeo. "You don't mean him, do you?"

That was actually funny. I chuckled. "I mean my *other* boyfriend."

"You have more than one?" Hunter asked. "Because I can be number three. Third time's the charm, right?" he flashed his swoon-worthy smile.

He was charming, all right. And by the looks of him, he could have any woman he wanted. So why me? He was wasting his time. I was in love with Christos, and that was that.

I decided my best strategy with Hunter was to remain silent.

Hunter followed me and Romeo out of the Eucalyptus grove.

Minutes later, we were passing Tiffany, who was still camped on the side of the main pathway. Did she even have any classes? She was holding court with her two satanic hobot minions as I passed. No matter. She was the perfect distraction. Her smile faded when she saw me.

I stopped suddenly in my tracks. Romeo nearly knocked me down as he stumbled to a stop.

Hunter swerved, but kept his balance. "I see you changed your mind," he smiled cockily.

"Tiffany," I said, smiling merrily, "meet Hunter Blakeley."

She took one look at him and her frown was gone. But then it was back. She looked between me and Hunter. "Is this some kind of a joke?" she scoffed.

"No," I smiled, "Hunter is totally in need of a date, and I thought you two might hit it off. Hunter, this is Tiffany Kingston-Whitehouse. She's a great girl—" yes, I almost gagged when I said it, "—and I think you two ought to get to know each other."

"Did she put you up to this?" Tiffany glared at me suspiciously.

Hunter was thrown off his game. He was obviously checking Tiffany out. I couldn't blame him. Tiffany was very good looking. On the outside. Her insides looked like a sewer, based on my experiences with her. And I wasn't talking about her colon. I meant her personality. Tiffany was one of those girls who wanted the world to believe that when she went number two, rose petals sifted out. Well, what really came out and fell into the toilet bowl was her personality. You know what I mean.

"No," Hunter said to Tiffany, "I, we just met. Samantha and I."

"Who?" Tiffany said.

"I thought you guys knew each other?" Hunter asked, confused.

"Her?" Tiffany sneered. "I think she scrubs toilets around campus. Yeah, that's where I've seen her."

I was right. Tiffany and toilet bowls went hand-in-hand. Maybe I needed to start thinking of her as Tiffany Kingcolon-Shithouse.

"Enjoy!" I waved to Tiffany and Hunter before hurrying off, pulling Romeo behind me.

"Wait, Sam!" Romeo said. "He's totally staring at us!"

"I don't care, let's just go."

"But what if he's staring at *me*?!" Romeo whined.

"I doubt it."

"You think he wants *both* of us?" he gasped hopefully.

"No, I think he just wants to add another notch to his belt."

"I'll be his notch!" Romeo pleaded.

"Shut up, Romeo!"

With any luck, Tiffany and Hunter would tear each other to shreds like ravenous predators. Because that's what they both were.

I shuddered as I wondered what kind of babies they might make. Velociraptors and Sabertooth Tigers, look out! The Kingston-

Whitehouse-Blakeley Boys are in the house!

Somehow, I thought if Tiffany and Hunter *did* hit it off, it would be the end of the human race. What had I done?

Romeo had section to go to for one of his theater classes, so we parted ways for the afternoon.

As I walked to my car, I half-expected Hunter to pop up out of nowhere and pressure me to go out with him again. Thankfully, he wasn't around.

Unless he was watching me from the bushes with some of those infrared goggles that serial killers liked to use when stalking innocent college coeds.

Okay, wrong train of thought.

I walked across the gigantic parking lot.

Alone.

SAMANTHA

On the way to my car, my phone rang. It was Christos. "Hey, you!"

"*Agápi mou!* So good to hear your voice. I've been thinking about you all day."

"You have?" I beamed.

"Of course. You are my everything. What else would I be thinking about?"

I sighed, "I love you, Christos."

"I love you too. Hey, guess what?"

"You're even more beautiful this evening than the last time I laid my eyes on your perfection?" He sounded like he was smiling, "No, I don't think that's possible."

"I found a job today!" I said.

"Sweet! I knew you would, Samantha. Doing what?"

"Working at the campus art museum at the cash register."

"Congratulations! You're diving right into the art world, *and* getting paid. Remember what I said about your parents not knowing about all the opportunities out there?"

"You were right," I smiled.

"I think we should celebrate."

"What did you have in mind?"

"You coming over to my grandfather's house. I'll make you

dinner. All you'll have to do is sit back and relax while you keep me company."

"I think I can manage that."

"Perfect. Get your fine ass over here."

I dropped my cell phone in my purse and walked down the aisle in the parking lot toward where my VW was parked.

I sensed a car approaching me slowly from behind. I angled toward the side, giving the car plenty of room to pass. The driver honked the horn twice. What the hell? There was plenty of room for them to drive around me. Whatever. I kept walking.

The car pulled along beside.

"Hey, beautiful," the driver said.

I'd spoken too soon.

Hunter Blakeley grinned from his convertible Porsche Boxster. He wore aviator sunglasses that looked like they were used in conjunction with his car to stalk innocent college coeds and coerce them into his clutches.

He wasn't fooling me. I smirked at him.

"Aren't you going to say hello?"

I raised my eyebrows skeptically. I was so not playing into his flirtatious game.

His arm rested casually on the steering wheel as his car rolled along beside me at two miles an hour. "I'm hurt, Sam. I thought we were friends."

"I barely know you, Hunter."

"That's how friendships start. But we have to get past the barely stage before we get to the Blakeley stage."

I rolled my eyes. "Please tell me you just made that up, because if you've used that line on women in the past, there's zero chance we can be friends."

He chuckled. "Then I'm in luck. I did in fact just make it up."

I said nothing and kept walking. Where had I parked my car? Was it like ten miles from here? I sensed Hunter might even follow me all the way home, trying to wear me down the entire way.

Two could play at this game. I turned between two cars and crossed over to another aisle. I smiled at myself. The aisles were so long, it would take him forever to drive around.

Unless he floored it, whipped around the far end of the aisle, and drove down mine.

I sighed and kept walking as his car drove toward me.

When his car reached me, he stopped and smiled. "There you are. I've been looking for you all day." He said it like it was no big deal. He was totally at ease. This was his sport, and Hunter Blakeley was a total player. I'm sure he'd Gold Medaled in it in London in 2012.

I kept walking.

He put the car in reverse and caught up with me, his car keeping pace with me going backward. "There you are," he smiled, "almost lost you."

"You're going to hit something," I said dryly.

"Nah, I've got my eye on the road." He stared right at me.

"Not from where I'm standing." I'd had enough of this. I crossed back over to the aisle I'd just left. I expected him to speed back down the way he'd came.

No, he simply put his car in park and left it idling where it stopped in the parking lot. He hopped over the door and trotted after me. He caught up quickly.

"Hunter, your car is still running, aren't you worried someone's going to take it?" I asked.

"Why? The most desirable thing in this parking lot is right here in front of me. I'd rather someone snatch my car instead of you."

Groan. Was it time to shout rape? He was never going to quit.

Fortunately, I saw my VW a short distance away.

Hunter kept pace with me. "I'll just walk you to your car. Keep an eye on you."

I stopped and faced him. "Hunter, I don't want you to walk me to my car. Can you please just go get your car before you get a ticket or something?"

"I don't care about getting a ticket. I only care about you."

Why did that nauseate me? "Hunter, please leave."

He smiled, completely undeterred. I had a moment to notice that he was amazingly handsome. But I didn't really care. He would find someone else, I was sure. I turned on my heel and continued to my VW.

"All right," he said casually as he caught up to me again. "No worries. I'll see you in class next time."

I was so surprised, I almost stopped, but managed to keep moving. "Huh? We have a different model every time."

"Not in Bittinger's class. She hired me to work the entire term."

My eyes goggled. I made a vomit face as I thought about how the next ten weeks with Hunter and Marjorie going at me in sculpting class were going to drive me nuts.

Thankfully, I made it to my VW. I slipped inside before Hunter could propose marriage.

In my rearview mirror, I watched him wave at me as I drove off.

At least he didn't sprint to his Porsche and stalk me all the way to Christos' place.

As far as I knew, that was.

Double groan!

SAMANTHA

Christos made me dinner, as promised. We sat at his kitchen table chatting long after we finished eating dinner. I didn't notice the time until it was late, and made my way home. Christos couldn't come with me because he had plenty of extra work to do around the studio with all the new demand for his paintings. That was okay because I still had homework and a job search to contend with.

I guessed our Honeymoon was over.

Whatever. I still loved Christos with all my heart.

I hit the books the minute I got in the door at my apartment. When my eyes were swimming from pouring over my History and Sociology readings two hours later, I decided it was time to close my books and take a break. I needed a moment to regroup, but I immediately felt the lurching pull of my crumbling financial situation.

With a pathetic groan, I opened my web browser and checked some of the job websites. Doing a search based on location, I discovered that, surprise, the very first jobs on the list were for accounting positions.

My lips curled as I imagined both my parents clasping their hands together while smiling innocently at me with "we told you so" looks all over their faces.

Screw them. I wasn't giving up. I tried searching by job type rather than location. Maybe I'd find something that way. When the list came up, I scrolled down it further and further. And further.

Almost every single job was somehow related to moving money around or computers. I took a moment to lean back, raise both my middle fingers, and launched both birds at my monitor.

But I still wasn't giving up. I did notice several jobs for long-haul truckers. Maybe I could do that? Wasn't there something sexy about a woman who drove a big rig and had dinner at truck stops nation wide? Some of those truck stops even had showers for the truckers. How awesome was that?

Uhhhh, no.

Besides, I needed something part time. And it turned out, most of the jobs were full time.

I did find one company that wanted to hire tutors for high school students. The subject they most needed, and for which I was best qualified, was math. Groan.

"We told you so," rang through my mind.

I dropped my head back against my couch, grabbed the nearest pillow, squished my face into it, and screamed.

That felt good.

I did it again.

I lowered my pillow and sighed.

As much as I hated to do it, I filled out the online application for math tutors. Couldn't the tutoring company have been seeking art tutors instead? Not that I was qualified, but why did it have to be math?

We told you so!

:-)

SHUT UP!!!!!!

I filled in the fields asking for my ACT and SAT scores were. Thanks to my parents, I'd taken both, and scored well on both.

After filling out all the remaining information, I clicked SUBMIT and prayed that my age and inexperience would put me at the bottom of the application pile.

I spent another hour combing through job listings. There were absolutely zero jobs related to art.

We told you so!

:-D

A knot had formed in my stomach over the course of the hour. I started to wonder if my parents *were* right. Based on the jobs I'd found online, it sure seemed that way. But I reminded myself that I did have the museum job. That was art. And Christos' whole family made money selling art. Heck, I'd made $150 on my crayon painting.

Was it possible to sell ten crayon paintings a month? That would be $1,500, which combined with the $400 from working at the museum, would probably be enough for *all* my bills. I certainly had time to draw that many.

But would I be able to sell all of my crayon paintings, month after month? Or would I end up sitting down on the boardwalk with stacks of crayon paintings laid out on one of those knitted blankets from Tijuana, and a sign that said "Prices reduced!" and the number "$150" would be Xed out, along with the numbers $125, $100, $75, $50, $25, $10, $5, $1.99, etc., all the way down to "FREE! Please take one!"

It seemed all too likely.

I needed to find a job with a paycheck while I still had a roof over my head.

I ended up submitting a few other applications that I doubted would turn into anything because the jobs actually sounded cool and paid well.

Was it time for me to hit the bricks tomorrow and follow in the time-honored American tradition of working for a fast-food chain restaurant?

We told you so!

Shudder.

I texted Madison to see if she was awake. When I didn't hear back from her, I called Christos. No answer from him, either.

I did have ice cream in the freezer.

I walked into my kitchen and opened the door. It was like a winter wonderland inside. Icicles everywhere, surrounding creamy, sugary escape. I could spare the calories. I'd been good. I'd barely had any ice cream in weeks. And I didn't think I'd had a single spoonful over Winter Break with Christos.

I opened up the container of Chocolate Chip Cookie Dough. There was hardly any ice cream left inside. I mean, it was almost half gone. Or some amount less than half-gone, but nowhere near a full pint. Because two good spoonfuls already gone was at least a half pint, according to my math. Anyway, it was going to get freezer burn sooner or later, then it would go to waste, and I was not one to waste food. Not when there were children in third world countries who never got to eat ice cream. Ever.

I would eat it for their sake.

I swear I would've shared, had any of those children been present in my apartment. I sort of wished they were, because I think the joy on their faces would've filled me up better than the ice cream. But I was all alone, and had no choice.

No ice cream would *ever* go to waste on my watch.

Chapter 14

SAMANTHA

My same pattern of school, homework, job hunt, and no Christos continued for the next several days.

Lame!

I managed to actually hook up with Madison on campus a few days later. It was the first time I'd seen her since I'd dropped Managerial Accounting.

We met for lunch in the Student Center.

"Mads! So good to see you!" I said.

Madison wrapped her arms around me. "I totally missed you, girl!"

"Me too. You wanna get fish tacos?"

"Hells yeah," Madison said.

We walked into the food court and got in the long line. I worried about spending the extra money, but I couldn't ask Madison to have protein bars for lunch with me. Meh.

"So, how's Dorquemann?" I asked.

"Doctor Dorquemann is the greatest sleep aid known to man. I think the medical school on campus has researchers in the lecture hall recording the sound of his voice every day, trying to pin down the exact pattern of frequencies that Dorquemann uses when he lectures. I hear they're trying to get FDA approval already."

"That good, huh?" I smiled sympathetically.

"No biggie. If I'm ever going to run my own company, I have to learn this stuff sooner or later."

"You want to run a company?"

"Yeah," Madison said, "Jake and I have been talking about it. He wants to start his own line of surf clothes, maybe even open a shop here in San Diego. If he wins a few more competitions and gets some good endorsements, he'll have enough of a name and enough extra cash that we might be able to do it."

"Look at you," I smiled, "Miss Go-Getter. That's awesome, Mads. I totally think you could pull it off."

"I just wish I was taking more of the upper division Marketing classes for my major. I need to learn all that stuff, like, yesterday!"

We finally made it to the front of the line and ordered our fish tacos. I tried to pay, but I'd already told Madison about my job hunt, and she refused.

"It's on me," Madison said. "When you're a world-famous artist, you can pay."

"Thanks, Mads." I went and filled up salsa containers for both of us. I'd grown increasingly accustomed to hot sauce, and couldn't seem to get enough. Plus, extra hot sauce was free, unlike extra guacamole. Sigh.

We took our trays outside to eat. It actually started to sprinkle, so we found an inside table.

"So, how's the new major coming along?" Madison asked.

"Other than my sculpting professor hates my ass, and my looming financial ruin, I couldn't be happier."

"Do you want to move in with me?" she asked seriously.

"Is one of your roommates moving out?"

"No, but I have a big room. We could share."

I smiled at her, almost in disbelief. I couldn't get over how supportive she was. I'd never had friends like Madison in high school. I didn't realize friends could be so generous. My eyes watered, but I did my best to keep my tears to myself.

"What about Jake?" I asked, trying to hide behind my napkin. "I don't want to cramp your style."

"Oh," Madison groaned, "my cramps have been cramping my style since Wednesday." She folded over and clutched her belly. "I've been having a bad case of the Monthlies all day today."

"See," I giggle-sniffed, "you don't need me adding more blockage to your hoo-ha than you've already got."

She shook her head. "I'm serious, Sam. If it becomes a problem, and you need a place, you're welcome to my apartment. Jake and I can always go to his house."

"Wow, Mads, I totally appreciate it. Based on the way my job search has been going, you may have more than one monthly visitor in February." I hoped my joking would disguise my imminent tears of gratitude.

"As long as you don't make my cramps any worse, I will consider it a blessing," she groaned. "I feel like I'm going to give birth to a tampon baby." She grunted. "I think it's going to be a redhead."

Grimacing, I set the remaining half of my fish taco on my plate. "Well, I'm done eating."

Madison cackled with laughter, "Sorry!"

SAMANTHA

Christos and I had dinner on Sunday night, but that was it. Groan. Had my predictions been right all along? Was he going to always be too busy with his burgeoning career to find time for a relationship with me? I hoped I was wrong.

On Monday, I went to the campus art museum after History class to report for my first day of work.

Mr. Selfridge turned out to be totally cool. He showed me how to operate the cash register and explained the ground rules. This job was going to be cake.

"We don't get a lot of traffic during the week," he said, "mainly art students like yourself. They come in to study the paintings and sculpture, and they get in free with a valid Student ID. But you do have to punch them in." He showed me how on the cashier's computer. "When it's slow, feel free to do your homework behind the counter. Just make sure that you set your work aside for any customers."

"Got it," I smiled.

"Well, that about covers it. I'm going back to my office. If you need anything, ring my phone. But I'm sure you'll be fine."

"Thanks, Mr. Selfridge," I smiled as he walked back into the museum.

The museum didn't have a gift shop, but there were a number of books behind the counter for sale. Since no one was coming in, I perused the shelves. One of the books was 'Retrospective: A life outdoors, the art of Spiridon Manos.' I picked it up and flipped through it. So much beautiful work. I'd seen a few of these paintings in Spiridon's home, but most were new to me. He was truly an amazing landscape painter. I flipped to the back of the book and saw that most of his paintings were on display in major museums around the country, even a number in Europe. Wow, Spiridon was a total art rockstar.

And his grandson was on the way to being one too.

Over the next several hours, three people came into the museum. All of them were art students, two I recognized from Life Drawing and Oil Painting class.

This job was super easy, which was perfect because I had homework to catch up on.

During a lull, I texted Christos.

Thinking about you. <3

I hoped for an instant reply. Nope. It took about ten minutes before he texted, *I'm always thinking about you, agápi mou. Miss you.*

I replied, *I miss you more ;-) What are you doing right now?*

I didn't receive a response. Sigh.

I opened up my Sociology reading and did my best to read through the assignments I'd fallen behind on. I kept checking my phone, making sure I hadn't missed an incoming text. After half an hour with no response, I made sure my alert volume hadn't somehow been turned off, or that my battery hadn't died, or that aliens or hackers hadn't hijacked my phone and changed my phone number.

Nope, everything was fine.

Except Christos was too busy to text me back. Should that have bothered me? I don't know, but it did. Was I being too needy?

Eye roll.

When it came to being needy, what was the official demarcation between "too" and "the right amount" of needy?

Groan. I didn't want to be the pathetic desperate girl who clung to her boyfriend's knees everywhere they went.

Maybe I needed to conduct a poll and figure out a hard number regarding appropriate levels of neediness. Whatever that number turned out to be, I was pretty sure with all of my time apart from Christos, I fell on "the right amount" side of the needy line.

My phone bleeped.

Christos: *Sorry, agápi mou. In the middle of things. Ran out of painting medium, had to run to art store. Miss you love you need you. :^**

I sighed contently. Not because I was "too" needy and needed to hear from my boyfriend right at that moment to set me at ease, because I had already established that in all likelihood I fell into "the right amount" category when it came to neediness at all times; no, my contented sigh was appropriate for any woman with the "right amount" of neediness. Because I knew it was "right" that I should be pleased to receive such a text from my boyfriend.

Telling me he needed me.

I wasn't needy at all.

Nope.

I was normal.

I texted Christos back, *I miss you too, my love. Can't wait to see you tonight! <3 <3 <3*

Was three text-hearts too needy? No. Four text-hears would *definitely* have been too needy, but I'd only used three, so I was good.

Too bad I ended up alone in my apartment that night and fell asleep cuddling my history textbook because Christos had too much work to do and told me it was best I not come over.

Was I disappointed? Of course.

Was I being "too" needy?

NO!!

It was "the right amount."

No more, no less.

Sigh.

SAMANTHA

On Saturday morning, a knock at my front door woke me up from my lonely bed. I dragged myself out from under my snuggly covers and trudged to the living room. Wow, my week must have been harder than I'd thought! I needed coffee badly.

I opened the door.

Christos held up a big cup of coffee for me. "Morning, sunshine!"

"Christos!" I was so glad to see him. It seemed like forever since we'd been together.

"I thought you could use some TLC this weekend, *agápi mou.*" He leaned in and kissed me before walking inside my apartment.

"Venti Americano, half coffee, half half-and-half, right?"

"Perfect," I smiled, taking the cup in both hands and inhaling the wonderful aroma before sipping some.

"I brought appetizers," he said, holding up a bag of apple fritters. It turned out, Christos had known all about Thai Doughnut and their awesome apple fritters long before I did. "I also brought breakfast," he said, holding up a bag from the grocery store.

I grabbed a plate from the kitchen and set one of the apple fritters on it. Christos and I pulled pieces off and nibbled on them while we sat at my little round dining room table and sipped our coffees.

"You ready for an omelet?" he asked.

"Sure!"

"Okay, you sit, and I'll cook." Christos went about dicing onions, tomatoes, and mushrooms, chopping up a bell pepper, and heating up some butter in one of my skillets on the stove. He cracked eggs into the pan and put some bread in the toaster. When the eggs were solidified into a spongy yellow disc, he sprinkled cheese and vegetables on top, then folded it over before serving it up with buttered toast and strawberry jam.

"Wow, Christos. You cook better than I do. You got everything ready all at the same time. That's an art form."

"Practice," he smiled as he set the plate in front of me. "Dig in, before it gets cold." He poured me a glass of orange juice, then he cooked an omelet for himself.

"Are you going to make yours with a dozen eggs? Like at The Broken Yolk?"

He smirked. "No, I'm good with six today."

"What's the plan for our mentor date?" I asked.

"You want to hit up the library? Show the kids your newfound crayon skills?"

"Oh yeah, Crayons with Christos!" I smiled.

He smiled back. "Why didn't I think of calling it that? It was 'Drawing with Christos,' but I like your name better." He held his hands up and spread them apart, like he was picturing a huge sign, the kind with the changeable movie-theater marquee letters. "We should call it 'Crayons with Christos and World-Renowned Master Crayon Artist Samantha Smith'."

"Would it be up in lights?" I pondered. "Our sign, I mean?"

"Totally. Like forty feet tall and two hundred feet wide. Right over the library. You'd be able to see your name from space."

I giggled at the thought.

"Don't laugh, you're going to be famous one day."

"*You're* going to be famous," I parried.

"Don't doubt yourself, Samantha. In twenty years, people will be calling me Mr. Samantha Smith."

My brows knit together while I smiled. "Wait, what? That was like a hundred things all rolled into one."

"I was suggesting that as your skills develop and you make a name for yourself, people will forgot about my work, and I'll just be along for the ride while your career goes into outer-space."

"That's crazy," I said dismissively.

Christos poured himself a large glass of OJ and took several swallows. "Not at all," he said, grinning wide. "You have the raw talent, which you're going to develop in the coming years. Then you're going to take over the art world like wildfire. Everyone will want to buy your work. By then, I'll have retired because we'll be able to live off your earnings alone. I'll be kicking back at home playing Mr. Mom while you're busy schmoozing with clients and creating masterworks in oil on canvas. Or, who knows, maybe you'll revolutionize the art world by resurrecting the medium of crayon. Anyway, my job will be to make sure our house is clean, diapers are changed, and dinner is waiting for you every night when you get home from being famous. You'll walk in the door and our kids will dog pile all over you while I kiss you on the cheek and ask you how your day was."

I smiled, picturing it. "That sounds pretty good. Will you be wearing an apron?" I sipped on my orange juice.

"Well, before the kids are born, I will *only* be wearing an apron when you come home. You know where that kind of behavior will get us…at least three kids. After they come along, I'll be wearing daddy clothes with spit-up on them, and the apron."

I was really getting into this fantasy of his!

"After we spend each evening playing with the kids and put them down for the night, we'll sit on the couch together and I'll give you neck, back, and foot rubs until you fall asleep. Will that work for you?"

"What if I miss you and the kids?" I asked. "I mean, maybe I don't want to be gone all the time."

"No problem. You can work in your home studio, sort of like I do now at my grandpa's house. While you're painting away, I'll be home-schooling the kids, either in the next room, or in the studio. Me and the kids'll be around as much as you desire," he grinned. "However you want it, *agápi mou*, we'll make it happen. We can build the perfect life together."

I smiled. I was about to open my mouth when sudden panic lanced through my belly. He was practically proposing marriage to me, living together, having kids, everything. It all seemed so perfect. But would it be perfect? Would it really happen like that? If it did, OMG, I couldn't imagine a better life.

Christos sat down at the table with his own giant omelet and toast. He gazed into my eyes with his impossible blues, casting a spell of love and fulfillment I'd never known before.

In moments like this, Christos' eyes made me believe that the impossible came true for him every day. And today, he was sweeping me into his fantasy life with him.

Was it possible that the impossible fantasy Christos was proposing would come true for me too? I dove into his gaze and let the magical feeling of certain joyful bliss fill me up.

Life with Christos. A family and a successful art career with the most amazingly beautiful, thoughtful, kind man in the world. I shivered thinking about it, barely conscious of my breakfast as I indulged in our loving daydream.

After finishing our food, we drove to the library for Crayons with Christos and World-Renowned Master Crayon Artist Samantha Smith. Christos must have called it that twenty times on the way over. I was starting to like it quite a bit.

Mrs. Elders greeted us when we walked through the main doors. "Good morning, Christos! You too, Samantha! What a pleasure to see you both. Some of the kids have been asking about you two since Christmas."

"Hey, Mrs. Elders," Christos said, hugging her. "I missed you, too."

"Oh!" Mrs. Elders said, patting his back. To me, she said, "Isn't Christos such a nice boy?"

"The nicest," I said.

"Well, the children are waiting for you," Mrs. Elders smiled.

Christos and I walked into the room where the kids waited. As always, they erupted with excitement when they saw us.

Some of them chorused, "Christos!" while others hollered, "Samantha!"

Christos winked at me. "See, you're already famous."

One of the little girls, named Abby, ran up to both of us in a frilly pink dress. "Did you go on a honeymoon together?"

I knelt down beside her, smiling. "What do you mean, Abby?"

"When I didn't see you and Christos since forever, I told my mommy you got married. She said when a daddy and a mommy got married, they go on a honeymoon."

I smiled at her while thinking about everything that had happened since my trip to D.C. with Christos. Despite both our crazy schedules and all the ups and downs, the last several weeks of my life had felt like a honeymoon to me. Especially when I compared them to the last few years of my life.

Bitch. Slut. Whore...

Emo. Goth. Suicide Watch...

Yeah, compared to my past, my present was most definitely a paradise. I repressed a shudder and closed the lid on my old demons before they could pull any tears from my eyes today. As much as I wanted to sweep away my past forever, it still haunted me.

Looking into Abby's beaming, joyful eyes made it easy to focus on the present. I smiled my biggest smile at her, "That's so sweet, Abby," I sniffed, "but Christos and I aren't married."

"Why not?" she asked innocently.

I looked up at Christos, surprised by the huge grin on his face. My eyes were watering.

"That's a good question, Abby" he smiled.

Gulp.

I totally needed a tissue.

"All right!" Christos bellowed to the roomful of kids. "Who wants to draw today?!"

"We do!!!" the kids chorused.

Oh well. Tissues later, kids and crayons now!

SAMANTHA

The drawing lesson with the kids was a blast. Afterward, we said goodbye to the children and walked outside.

"That was so much fun!" I said. "I'd forgotten how much I enjoyed those kids."

"Yeah," Christos smiled, "I never get tired of them."

"So, what's next?"

Christos suddenly looked nervous, and ran his hand through his hair. I think this was the first time I'd *ever* seen Christos nervous. "Would you be bummed if I had to work today?"

Of course I would be, but I didn't want to say it and sound like a complaining baby. So I half-smiled and shrugged my shoulders.

"I really have a lot to do at the studio today," he said regretfully. "I've got a model coming in half an hour."

"Oh." I think my disappointment bled through into my voice. I couldn't help it. I knew what "a model" meant. It meant a nude woman sitting in front of Christos while he stared at her for hours. I wanted to be the only nude woman he ever stared at. But I knew he couldn't make a career out of painting portraits of me in the nude, over and over again. Who would buy them? Probably no one. Lame.

Besides, I didn't want to be painted in the nude anyway. It would almost be like I was getting lumped into the same category as all his other trophy nudes. I felt special because he had *not* painted me nude. Best to keep it that way.

"*Agápi mou*, I know last year we had mentor dates every Saturday, but with all the work coming in from Brandon, I don't think I can swing it today. Maybe next weekend? I promise I'll make it up to you."

I sighed. We hadn't seen much of each other since classes had started. All I wanted to do was spend the day with Christos, but we both had lives and commitments to attend to. I really was determined not to be "too" needy. "It's okay," I said softly. "I really need to look for a job today anyway."

"That's right," he said, sounding relieved.

I hoped not *too* relieved. Stupid nude models.

"I wish I could help with the job search," he said with genuine regret, "but I don't have time."

"It's fine," I said, wishing he could too, but I knew his work was important right now. Just like my job search. It had to get done.

Meh. "At least Romeo is coming with me."

"Awesome. He should liven things up."

"Yeah," I said apathetically. Romeo would add some spice, but why did I feel like something was ending between me and Christos? Maybe little Abby was right. Maybe my honeymoon with Christos was behind us, and it was back to the usual daily grind from here on out. Maybe Christos' rosy fantasy was nothing more than that. A fantasy.

"I should drive you home," Christos said, "or I'm going to be late for my model."

"Yeah," I sighed. Wow, this sucked. I was going to hunt for a job at the first fast-food joint that would have me and my boyfriend was going to hang out with a hot nude model the whole time. Was there something wrong with this picture, I mean, other than the fact that my boyfriend's portion of it sounded like a double-page spread in a nudie magazine?

Christos dropped me off at my apartment and kissed me goodbye.

I clomped upstairs and called Romeo. Time to start looking for work as a fry cook or burger flipper. I was not looking forward to it.

"Sam!!!!!" Romeo answered. "Are you ready to hunt for a job?"

"If I must," I groaned.

"It's going to be so exciting. We'll be like jungle explorers, beating through the bush looking for the Lost City of Gold!"

"Totally," I grimaced to myself. The only gold I could imagine we'd find were Golden Arches. But at this point, working at McDonald's sounded better than going back to Accounting.

"I'll be over at your place in twenty minutes," Romeo said.

"Okay. See you then."

When Romeo arrived we walked westward, toward the downtown area a few blocks from my apartment. We hit up every possible place we could find. Coffee shops, a dry cleaners, a used bookstore, a furniture store, a chocolate shoppe, a bicycle store. Half of them told me to fill out an application or bring back a résumé for future reference.

We even tried a head shop, err, I meant, "An establishment that sells tobacco accessories and smoking paraphernalia." And black-light posters of Bob Marley smoking a huge joint. Did they think they were fooling anybody with their convoluted tagline? I knew it was for legal reasons, but seriously, did anybody buy a tobacco pipe from a head shop and use it for tobacco?

Maybe I could find out when I went door-to-door conducting my "needy" survey. I bet I could even get paid to do it! Didn't the Census collect information like that every ten years?

I could totally picture myself holding a clipboard and asking a house-wife with curlers in her hair and a baby on her hip, "Ma'am, do you consider yourself:

A) 'too' needy or

B) 'the right amount' of needy?

"And, do you use your tobacco pipe for:

A) tobacco or

B) marijuana?"

It was genius. I needed to call the Census Bureau and tell them to add those two questions. They'd hire me on the spot because I wasn't afraid to address the important issues John and Jane Q. Public were dying to know.

Or not.

Back to my job search.

The restaurants Romeo and I visited needed wait-persons, but they wanted people with experience. Did putting Mom's cooking on the dining room table and clearing it after dinner count? No? Oh well. Next.

I tried a bar with a HELP WANTED sign out front, but they only hired people over 21.

Two hours later, we were back where we started. I had a thin bundle of worthless applications under one arm.

"We didn't find the buried treasure," I sighed. I wasn't ready to bite the fast-food bullet yet.

"I swear that golden city is around here somewhere," Romeo said. Even his spirits had sunk. "What do we do now?"

"Drive to the mall?"

We went to the UTC shopping center, just east of the SDU campus. We went from store to store to store. Nothing. The restaurants in the food court were no better.

"You still haven't tried Hot Dog On A Stick," Romeo suggested. "They have those awesome primary-colored uniforms. You'd totally look cute in one."

"You're kidding, right? I don't want to wear one of those corny uniforms," I quipped.

Romeo chuckled at my pun. "I wish I was, but beggars don't get to choose their uniforms," he winked.

"Okay, let's try them. I think I'm *that* desperate."

Both girls behind the counter wore those red and white and blue and white and yellow and white and red and white and blue and etc., etc., etc., striped uniforms. While I talked to one of the girls, Romeo ordered a fresh lemonade from the other. She filled him a glass from one of the giant square lemonade jugs.

"Do you guys have any job openings?" I asked the other girl, sounding as enthusiastic about the prospect as I felt.

"Sorry," she wince-smiled.

"No worries," I said, glad to be spared the opportunity.

Romeo and I found a table in the middle of the mall's food court and plopped down.

"Want some?" Romeo asked, proffering his lemonade.

"No, thanks," I sighed.

Romeo took a long sip on his lemonade.

"I think we tried every single store within a five-mile radius of my apartment," I said.

"You could be a bootblack," Romeo offered.

"What the hell is a bootblack?" I scoffed.

"A shoe shiner."

"Do people even do that anymore?"

"I have no idea," Romeo grinned. "How about street walking? I hear pimps are *always* hiring."

"Tempting. But I wouldn't work for just any pimp. I'd need one who offers medical *and* dental," I grinned. "Can you recommend any good ones?"

"No, but I've always wanted to be a pimp myself. Drive a Cadillac, wear cool Zoot suits, and smack my bitches around."

I chuckled. "You'd be the best pimp ever. I can totally picture you in a pink chiffon Zoot suit. But you'd have to be willing to hire me without sampling my merchandise."

Romeo frowned, leaned over to me and whispered conspiratorially, "In case you haven't heard, Samantha, girls are gross."

"Cool! I'll start work on Monday!" I laughed. "I just have to buy some six-inch hooker heels first."

Romeo chuckled and took another sip of his lemonade. "So, how are things with Christos?"

I sighed. "Good."

"Hmmm. That didn't sound good."

I rolled my eyes. "He's busy. I was hoping to spend the day with him today, but he has to paint some nude model or other. I feel like I've barely seen him since New Year's Eve."

"You're not worried about him, are you?" Romeo said uncertainly. "I mean, you don't think he's sampling his merchandise, do you?"

My stomach knotted at the thought. "Christos isn't like that. He's totally in love with me."

Romeo had an apologetic look on his face as he sipped more lemonade. "You're probably right," he said. "I guess I just worry because gorgeous women are always throwing themselves at him. Heck, I throw myself at Christos every chance I get."

I smiled. "I'm not worried about you, Romeo." But I was worried about all the other women. Especially the nude one in his studio right now. I'm sure she looked like a super model and was thrusting her breasts at Christos this very moment.

I sighed and looked around the food court. "Is there any place around here that sells ice cream? I think I need a sundae. Extra fudge, extra whipped-cream, extra ice cream."

"Let's go find out," Romeo offered. "You look like you could use an ice cream pick-me-up."

He had no idea.

CHRISTOS

"Can you arch your back just a bit more," I asked the model.

"Anything for you, Christos," Isabella said breathily. She tossed her hair back and smiled at me seductively through her alluring lashes. She was naked from head to toe and reclined on a divan a few feet in front of my painting easel.

"Perfect," I said. "Hold that pose." When it came to Isabella, perfect was an understatement. She was a gorgeous Brazilian girl from L.A. Brandon had found her for me at one of the big modeling agencies in Hollywood. He wasn't kidding about finding fresh faces.

She winked at me right before I turned my attention to my palette.

They didn't get any fresher than Isabella.

Facing my palette, I dabbed my brush into the pile of burnt sienna, then mixed it into the smear of flesh tone I had on my palette. I needed to richen up my mixture if I was going to capture Isabella's caramel skin tone.

My mind wandered as I mixed.

Brandon hadn't been blowing smoke when he'd said everybody wanted a piece of me. I had a list of commissions as long as my arm. It was good to be loved.

Too bad the checks only came after I delivered the paintings. I had lawyer's fees to pay. Russell Merriweather was far from cheap, but he was worth every penny if he kept me out of the big house. Maybe I needed to talk to Brandon about pre-sales, get some cash flowing.

The only down side to the influx of business was finding time to fit everything in: Samantha, painting, school, working out, eating, sleeping. Something had to go, so I took the term off from SDU. No surprise. Who needed a graduate degree when people were throwing money at you?

Besides, canning my class schedule was the only way I could make any time for Samantha. As it was, I had what seemed like thirty minutes a day for her. Not my preference.

Not even close.

But the iron was hot, as Brandon had said. Six-figure hot. Which meant the painting had to be my main focus for now.

Samantha was totally busy herself with her classes and work schedule, so it worked out. Sort of. I don't think either of us were truly happy with our schedules.

But there was work to do.

I had several canvases of various L.A. models in progress. Different women came in throughout the week. Jacqueline on Mondays and Thursdays. Becca on Tuesdays and Fridays. Isabella on Wednesdays and Saturdays. I never had a break.

I'd only finished one painting so far. The model's name was Avery. She was an actress in L.A. struggling to get work. I don't know why her face wasn't plastered on magazine covers already. The painting of her was drying in the rack against the back wall.

The in-progress paintings of Jacqueline and Becca sat on smaller easels in the studio.

These next few months were going to be insane. The good thing about the hectic pace was that it kept my mind off my fucking trial.

I did my best not to think about it.

The current painting of Isabella sitting on my main work easel was life-sized, which meant the canvas was huge. One thing was a constant in the art world: bigger work meant bigger money. I was up for it.

Time to turn the money crank.

I turned to look at Isabella, assessing her lines and forms, the lights and darks, and the overall composition of her pose. She was so beautiful, you'd think painting her would be a slam-dunk. Just paint what you see, and you had a masterpiece, right?

Nope.

Portraits didn't work that way.

I didn't know a thing about Isabella, other than she was hot, which ironically served only as a distraction. Her flirtatious behavior wasn't helping either, because I knew she was repressing her authentic personality when she was coming onto me.

The obvious solution would be to paint the come-hither look that was on her face at the moment, right? Nail her sultry hot-and-bothered-babe expression and I'd sell it for a million, right?

Maybe in porn, but not in fine art.

I could never figure out why it worked this way, but the proof was in the end result.

When I painted strangers, people would say shit like, "That's a great painting," or "Amazing composition, Christos," or "Beautiful brush work," or "I love the colors."

But when I painted people I knew, the comments would be things like, "Wow, she seems so sincere, so kind, the sort of person I'd want as a friend" or "Do you know that crazy guy? He looks like a real bastard!" or "I feel like I'm looking at the ghost of my grandmother."

Yeah, some of the comments were totally freaky.

The weird thing was, most people didn't actually know which of my paintings were which. I never told them, never made it obvious from the titles. Yet the responses were consistent. Viewers always preferred the paintings of people I knew, spent far more time looking at them, and paid higher prices for them than they did for the ones of strangers.

I couldn't figure out why.

One time, I'd asked my grandfather what he thought the reason might be. He'd said it was the spiritual component, the ineffable connection that existed between two people who knew each other that no camera could ever capture. He'd said that the more you knew a person, the more your relationship with them worked its way into the painting, and the more that such a painting would captivate any viewer, even if they didn't know why.

I guess this mysterious element was what made art so captivating for me.

For the rest of the afternoon, I continued to paint Isabella, giving her intermittent breaks. I tried to find something about her personality to work with, something to draw out her true nature, but all she did was flirt. Her gamesmanship was exhausting. I tried telling her to be herself, but I don't think she knew what I meant because of the language barrier. She had a fairly thick Portuguese accent that was sexy as hell, but English was definitely her second language.

When I finally set my brushes down, I was wiped.

At the very least, I was doing a decent job of capturing Isabella's exterior beauty on canvas. Not every art collector was a connoisseur. Somebody with money would buy it.

"We're all done for today," I said.

"I finished?" she pouted in her thick accent, still flirting.

"Yeah. Why don't you go get dressed."

Isabella stood before me fully naked. Challenging me.

I smiled at her, but stood my ground. I'd been staring at her for the last four hours. Whatever.

She winked at me and turned seductively before sashaying into the studio bathroom to get dressed.

I went about cleaning my brushes.

The bathroom door opened and Isabella strutted out on heels, buttoning her blouse from the top down. I caught a flash of her flat stomach in the A of her blouse's two billowing panels. She really had an amazing body. Even in clothes, she was stunning. Again, whatever.

She stopped in front of the canvas, her top now completely

buttoned, and smoothed her tightly-fitted skirt. She examined the painting. "Christos, is beautiful!"

"Thanks," I smiled. "You make the work easy," I lied.

She raised an eyebrow. "You call me easy girl?" she flirted. When I didn't respond, she leaned into me. Every guy I'd ever met would've been pitching a tent with a beauty like Isabella coming onto them this blatantly.

I wasn't every guy.

Undeterred, Isabella gave me one of those purring laughs that few men will ever hear in their lifetimes. Not a trashy stripper laugh. I'm talking about the kind of laugh you only heard from the world's sexiest women, the kind they saved for the special men in their lives.

Isabella was holding her door open for me, telling me to come inside. Emphasis on "come" and "inside." And I'm not talking about any literal door. I'm talking about *her* door. Yeah, *that* one.

But I'd heard it a hundred times before. On several memorable occasions, I'd heard it from women hotter than Isabella.

But none of that mattered to me. What mattered was that I had Samantha, and there was only one of her in the entire fucking universe.

I really didn't care what Isabella had in mind.

Unrelenting, she cocked her own crazy-sexy dimpled grin at me. It didn't have the desired effect on me.

I sighed and stepped away from her, trying not to be rude. I walked over to the table where I kept my receipt book in a drawer. "Did you want cash? Or am I supposed to pay the agency directly?"

"Is all taken care of," she smiled.

That meant Brandon. I'm sure he'd send me the invoice later. Or maybe not. When you're slinging six-figure canvases out the door one after the other, a few grand here and there doesn't make anyone blink anymore. At least, that was the plan.

"Do you need anything for the road?" I asked Isabella. "You want some water to take with you?"

She walked over to where I stood at the desk and placed her palm on my painter's smock.

"Please," she flashed her wide-mouthed smile.

Please was right. I gently skirted around her and headed toward the kitchen. "Come on, I'll grab you a cold bottle from the fridge."

I heard her clacky heels following behind me.

I'd already grabbed a water from the fridge by the time she made it to the kitchen. I leaned against the doorframe when she came in.

"We drink together?" she pouted her lips in that way women who know how to use their looks always pouted. The way that makes most guys drop to their knees, tongues hanging out, and start begging and promising the world and anything else they can think of. She wasn't getting it.

"Sorry, Isabella. I've got a ton of work to do before the sun goes down."

"Is good, having so much work, no?"

"Yes." I said flatly. I could tell she had no intention of moving from where she stood, hand on her cocked hip.

Fine. If she wanted to play games, I knew my way around the board. I raised an eyebrow and waited her out. My guess was her next move would be a hair flip.

She raised an eyebrow.

That was her tell. The hair flip was seconds away.

Wait...wait...

Oh! There it goes!

She tossed her lustrous main around with spectacular grace.

Hair flip!

I'm sure she'd practiced that move for photo shoots a hundred times. She finished by tilting her chin down, another camera-ready pose. She really had nice eyes.

I didn't care. It was Game Over time.

I turned and walked into the entryway and opened the front door.

I heard her pout again. This time, it was the real pout. The frustrated kind that sounded like a little girl not getting her way. When she walked out of the kitchen, she looked a bit sulky. I felt sort of bad, but she *was* throwing herself at me. She'd get over me. Someday.

What could I say? Old habits died hard. This shit was regular as breathing to me.

Isabella stopped on the runner in the entryway and eyeballed me again. Was she not getting the hint? She had it bad.

I motioned outside with my arm. "After you."

"Your tattoos are very sexy."

I already knew that. "Thanks."

Finally, she walked outside.

I would be a completely rude dick if I didn't open her car door for her. We walked to her shiny Jetta together. When she clicked the alarm, I opened the door.

"You are very gentleman," she said in her lusciously accented broken English.

"Always," I smiled.

"Maybe next time, we eat lunch, yes?"

"Maybe." How many more sessions did I have with her? I'm thinking one too many. I sighed. At least she was easy on the eyes, and her painting would sell for a bundle to some shallow rich schmuck who didn't look beyond the surface. Business was business.

Isabella stuck her hand out her window as she drove off and waved at me with her $400 nails. "*Até logo*, Christos!" She actually blew me a kiss.

I shook my head when she was gone. Poor thing. I'd have to ugly myself down for her next sitting, keep her in line. Maybe I could wear a pair of those classic novelty glasses with the big nose, bushy eyebrows, and Hitler mustache. Maybe that would tone her flirting down.

Mental note: buy novelty glasses ASAP.

I chuckled, because I was seriously considering doing it. Sure, she'd see right through the disguise, but I'd be willing to bet she'd think I was two handshakes away from being a serial killer after that. It *could* work as a deterrent.

Samantha, on the other hand, would probably think it was hilarious. Maybe Brandon was right. Maybe I did need to paint Samantha.

But I didn't think I'd get her to sit nude.

Then again, the Mona Lisa wasn't a nude. Neither was the Girl with the Pearl Earring.

It could work.

I walked back into the house. In the living room, I opened the liquor cabinet and poured myself an inch of bourbon, straight up. After my long day in the studio, I needed to unwind.

I threw back the entire glass in one long swallow. I poured

myself another inch and walked into the studio.

The painting of Isabella was coming along faster than I'd expected. Most of it was still rough, but the face was finished and was as flawless as Isabella's. My technical mastery of oil paint was clearly evident.

The only problem?

It wasn't doing anything for me. Sure, her face looked photo-real, but it was lifeless. I'd captured her pouty, full lips, her sultry eyes, her delicate jawline. She looked textbook sexy, which meant boring sexy. Cardboard. Cookie-cutter.

There was no spirit to the painting.

I'm sure I could sell it to some pin-up art collector for ten grand. But that would be taking five steps backward with my pricing. The painting of Isabella needed to go for at least $80,000 if I was going to build my name. Not $10,000, of which I'd get $5,000, meaning $3,000 after taxes, another $500 for supplies, leaving me with $2,500, which was not worth the weeks I would end up putting into it by the time I was done.

I gulped down the rest of the bourbon in my glass.

Maybe the painting would come together when I finished her body.

I went into the living room to pour myself more bourbon.

Chapter 15

SAMANTHA

Romeo and I walked into Professor Bittinger's class extra early. I wanted to get there long before the woman had reason to give my grief.

The room was empty when we arrived, so Romeo and I set up on sculpting tables next to each other, pulling out our sculpting tools and armature wires from the previous class.

"Do you think Hunter will be back today?" Romeo asked as he peeled clay off of his armature.

I did the same with my clay, preparing my wire stick-figure for today's sculpting. "Yeah, he told me he's going to be here all quarter."

Romeo frowned. "When did he tell you that?"

"When he followed me to my car after the first day of class."

Romeo's face lit up. "Hunter is stalking you? You lucky bitch!"

I rolled my eyes. "You can have him."

"I think I'd need to get breast implants first." Romeo pushed his chest muscles together with the palms of his hands. "I'd have awesome cleavage, don't you think?"

"Are you saying you would go girl, just to get Hunter? I mean, have a sex change operation?"

Romeo rolled his eyes dismissively. "I may be gay, Sam, but I'm not crazy. I would never behead my Little Romeo." He patted his crotch affectionately. "Poor little guy, Sam here would have you sliced off with one of those little cigar-cutter guillotines. But she totally didn't mean it," he looked at me pointedly, "did you Sam? Tell him you're sorry," he demanded.

"I'm not apologizing to your pants, Romeo!"

Romeo looked heartbroken. Then he cupped his hand to his ear. "What did you say, Little Romeo? Uh-huh. Mmm-hmm. Oh, Little

Romeo, how rude! Don't talk like that about Sam!" Romeo's face turned sad. In a grave voice he said, "You really hurt his feelings, Sam. You really ought to apologize." Romeo raised his eyebrows expectantly.

I was so swept up in Romeo's genuine outpouring of emotion, I actually whispered, "I didn't mean it, Little Romeo." I giggled, and looked Romeo in the eyes. "How was that?"

"Excellent, now just give Little Romeo a hug and a kiss, and everything will be fine."

"I'm not hugging and kissing your Little Romeo!" I blurted, perhaps louder than I'd intended now that the room was full of students.

"I'm kidding, Sam," he smiled. "Little Romeo only likes boys. Just like his old man."

Chuckling, I shook my head.

"Good afternoon, class!" Marjorie Bittinger said as she walked in the door. "Sorry I'm late. Traffic was terrible due to an accident on the Five."

I guess it was okay for *her* to be late and full of weak excuses.

"I'm sure the only accident she had on the freeway was in her pants," Romeo said. He wrinkled his nose.

I giggled, but, ew. "I think that's her perfume."

"Smells like pewfume to me," he winced. "Did somebody let a skunk in?" he whispered.

"Are you through?" Professor Bittinger asked, suddenly standing behind Romeo. How the hell did she always do that? Did she have a teleportation device in her pocket, or just trapdoors scattered throughout the room for her to pop up through?

"All done," Romeo said casually while holding up his cleaned armature wire, purposefully misunderstanding her.

Marjorie scowled at him. "I'm glad to see that you have paid such fastidious attention to your 1/12th scale armature, because you won't be needing it today," she said victoriously. Marching to the center of the room, she said, "Today we'll start on our 1/3rd scale sculpture of the model. We will be using the large armature wire you purchased at the beginning of the term." She turned to me whip-fast. "Did you remember to purchase the large wire, Miss *Smith*?"

I struggled to not stick my tongue out at her. "Yes I did,

Professor—" I almost said Bitchinger, "…Bittinger."

She glared at me like she'd known what I'd been thinking. Then she closed her eyes dismissively before turning away, as if merely closing her eyes would magically banish me to Hell or Hades, or wherever she hoped I'd rot for eternity.

For the next hour, we built a much larger wire stick-figure man.

When I was finished, I noticed Hunter Blakeley walk into the room. He was preppie-sexy and had the aviator sunglasses on again. He walked directly to the professor and they chatted for awhile.

Marjorie Bittinger transformed into her usual preening, flirty self when Hunter was in close proximity. The way Hunter acted, you'd think they were dating.

"Do you think those two are hooking up?" Romeo whispered.

"It seems that way."

Hunter walked into the corner and changed into his robe behind a hanging curtain. Marjorie stole glances at him the whole time.

"She's peeping at him!" Romeo whispered, faux-offended. "You think she'd wait until he was standing naked in front of the entire room. She's totally desperate."

I could relate to that feeling of desperately wanting something you couldn't have. I felt like I'd been seeing as much of Christos lately as Marjorie was getting to see of Hunter at the moment. Glimpses.

With any luck, that would change this evening when I had dinner with Christos. I crossed my fingers. And my toes.

Hunter walked out from behind the curtain and onto the dais wearing his robe. He flung it off with a flourish.

Sigh, yeah, he was totally hot.

I noticed a gleam in Marjorie's eyes as she pretended to give Hunter's naked body a cursory inspection. She tried to play it off like no big deal. But her hunger was obvious.

"Hunter," the professor said, "please take your pose. Class, grab some clay from the warmer, and go to it."

It turned out the bigger sculpture needed way more clay. I had to go back to the warmerator three times before I had enough. I slapped clay onto my armature, and went to work with a wooden paddle smoothing out the planes. I was getting the hang of this sculpting thing, and had my voodoo man blocked in pretty quickly.

Minutes later, I discovered that working larger was more difficult. There was a lot more room to screw things up. I was getting hung up on one of the legs. The knee looked wrong and the calf was three sizes too big.

"Your paddle," Marjorie demanded.

"Huh? Oh." I handed her the wooden tool, which looked like a small spatula.

Despite Professor Bittinger's lack of interpersonal pleasantries when it came to anyone other than Hunter, she was amazingly skilled at sculpting. She plucked off a hunk of clay from the calf muscle on my sculpt. Then, with three quick swipes of my paddle, she transformed my wonky clay leg into a work of art.

"Wow, Professor. That looks amazing."

She handed me the paddle unceremoniously and walked away.

I rolled my eyes behind her back. Was that supposed to be teaching, or just showing off? Despite her clinical beauty, she was a robot in the social arena. She was totally hotistic.

During the break, Hunter robed himself and bee-lined right over to me. I couldn't help but notice Marjorie's glaring eyes glued on him. I felt like running out of the room, just to get away from Hunter. Either he didn't realize or didn't care that he was souring my relationship with my professor, which would probably have an impact on my grade.

"Hey, beautiful," he smiled. "Been thinking about you."

I almost said, "That's funny, because I haven't," but realized such a brush-off might sound like flirtation. I didn't want to be a rude Bitchinger either, so I opted for bland, "Hey, Hunter."

"You remembered my name?" He grinned. "That's a start."

"If you say so."

"I do," he smiled.

I swear, everything with Hunter was a come on.

"Hiiii, Hunter," Romeo smiled longingly. I think he batted his eyelashes. At least, he may as well have based on his fawning tone.

Hunter glanced at him dismissively. "Hey, dude."

"You remember Romeo, don't you, Hunter?" I shifted positions so Romeo was between me and him. "I need to, ah, get some more clay." I didn't, but it was a worthy excuse.

Too bad Hunter followed me to the warmerator. I opened the door and pretended to scan for what I needed.

"How was your weekend?" he asked.

"Fine."

"Aren't you going to ask me about mine?"

"No."

"It was pretty awesome."

"I'm sure."

"Me and some buddies went skiing at Mountain High. Powder was insane. Do you ski?"

"No," I lied.

"I could teach you. I bet you'd be great, with some expert instruction."

How the hell did he manage to turn everything I said into an opportunity to hit on me harder? He was a genius. Maybe if I led him toward Marjorie, she could take over for me. But she was on the far side of the room, talking to a couple of students. Weren't there any other available females for him to honey badger?

Hunter chatted me up for the remainder of the break. Luckily, it lasted only five minutes. It seemed like five-hundred and five. Sigh.

Who would've thought a hot guy hitting on you could be so tiresome?

The class resumed sculpting when Hunter returned to his pose in the dais.

At one point, I glanced beside me at Romeo's sculpture and noticed his had a huge erect dick.

I clapped my clay-covered hand over my mouth before I guffawed.

"What are you doing!" I whispered.

He looked confused. "What do you mean?" he asked innocently

"His thing!" I whisper-squealed. "It's not that big!"

"You sure?" Romeo asked doubtfully. He lifted his monocle to his eye, squinched it into place, and glanced repeatedly between Hunter and his sculpture. "Looks right to me," he said seriously, then lowered his monocle, allowing it to pendulum from its string.

"Yours is like twenty sizes too big. And his isn't at attention."

Confused, he said, "It was earlier, wasn't it?"

"No!"

Romeo shrugged sheepishly. "Silly me. I must have been day-dreaming." He pressed the clay penis down with two fingers, causing it to break off and topple to the floor. "Oops!" He bent over and picked it up, holding it in front of me. "You ever hear that song 'Detachable Penis' by the band King Missile?"

"What?! There's no such song!"

"There totally is. Look it up."

"Having fun?" Professor Bittinger asked, fists on hips. The toe of one of her shoes machine-gunned on the cement with restrained irritation.

"Definitely," Romeo smiled at the professor. "Have you ever heard that song—"

I clapped my hand over Romeo's mouth.

Through my fingers, he said, "Defafaffle Fefis?"

Marjorie frowned at me. "Is your friend all right?"

"No, I need to get him to a doctor or something. He's sick."

"Perhaps you should escort him to Student Health. That way, neither of you will waste anymore class time with your obtrusive Tom Foolery. While you're there," she said to me directly, "perhaps you should see a doctor as well." She stalked off on her firecracker heels.

"Shut up!" I hissed at Romeo. "You're going to get us kicked out."

"Do you think Marjorie has a detachable vagina?" he whispered. "I think she does, and she lost it at a party, like, ten years ago. She hasn't been laid since then. That's why she's so irritable."

SAMANTHA

After sculpting class, Romeo walked me to my job at the campus art museum and we said our goodbyes. He had section for acting class again.

When I was behind the counter, I pulled out my notes from History and started reviewing them.

Not long after, Hunter walked through the doors of the museum.

I tried to duck behind the counter, but he'd already spotted me.

"There you are," he smiled, striding over to the counter. "I thought I saw you walk in here."

"Hey," I said morosely. Maybe he'd pick up on my zombie tone and take the hint?

Nope.

"You looked like you were having fun in class with your buddy today," he smiled. "I saw Bittinger giving both of you guys dirty looks. What was that all about?"

"I think she hates me," I groused.

"Why? What's to hate?"

I smirked and rolled my eyes. "I've been asking myself that since class started." Wait. I just realized Hunter was tricking me into a conversation. I wasn't going to say anything else. I officially zipped my lips.

Hunter grinned. "She's probably jealous, like all the other women on campus. Speaking of which, I went out with your friend Tiffany."

Okay, that was worthy of de-zipping. "You what?!"

"Yeah. I took her out for sushi at Japengo. It's a fancy sushi place on the other side of the freeway. A workout buddy of mine is a waiter there. He always cuts me deals."

"Okay, wait. Back up. You went out with Tiffany? Like, on a date?"

"Yeah," he smiled.

I was in shock. I hadn't actually seen or heard of such a thing. All I knew was that Tiffany was always trying to steal Christos from me. "Well, how'd it go?" I was dying to know.

"I don't kiss and tell," he said suggestively.

Bastard! But I wouldn't let on. The last thing I wanted Hunter thinking was that he had *anything* I wanted, even if it was merely gossip. I stared at him, waiting him out.

I scrutinized his face. I couldn't decide if he had really gone out with Tiffany, or if he was lying to make conversation. Sure, I could picture Tiffany going out with a guy like Hunter, but I needed proof.

Then, inspiration struck. "Well, if things went well, she probably wouldn't be happy seeing you here with me." That was an understatement. If Tiffany *had* gone out with Hunter, and the date had gone well, she'd tear me apart if she caught Hunter with me.

Hunter chuckled cagily. "Why, does Tiffany hang out at the art museum a lot?"

"No."

"Then we don't have to worry about her, do we? It's just the two of us."

Like I suspected, Hunter was a player or a liar, which basically amounted to the same thing. "Hunter, I'd love to chat, but I have homework to do." I motioned toward my books.

"I can come back later."

"Please, no," I pleaded.

He chuckled and waved as he walked out. "Until next time, beautiful."

I didn't wave back. The last thing I needed in my life was more Hunter, no matter how hot he was.

Where was Christos when I needed him?

Sigh.

If Hunter were to take one look at my hot, tattooed boyfriend and see how totally in love we were with each other, I believed Hunter would finally give up on me and go away.

I truly knew my love for Christos was *that* strong.

But I needed Christos in my arms for our enchantment to work and shoo Hunter off.

At the rate things had been going, that might not happen for days or even weeks.

Sigh.

SAMANTHA

The drive north from campus took awhile in traffic. I knew the Pacific Ocean was somewhere to my left, but it was blacked out by the glare of oncoming headlights.

My relationship with Christos was starting to feel as inconsistent as my view of the ocean. We never had enough time for each other, just brief moments that lacked in both quantity and quality.

Between my classes, my homework, my museum job, my never-ending job search, and Christos' crazy round-the-clock work schedule, I feared we were slipping apart.

I started weeping at the wheel of my VW.

Yes, I had met the perfect man and we had fallen in love, all in the span of a few short months. But in the span of a few short weeks, I felt like our relationship was crumbling to dust. I knew our love was strong, but if we never saw each other, how could it grow? Love wasn't a static thing. It required effort, commitment, and constant attention. It needed tending and care for it to grow, otherwise it was bound to wither and die.

I knew, because I felt Christos slowly slipping away from me.

Worse, despite our increasingly tenuous connection, my feelings for Christos had grown immensely, and I feared what would happen to me if our connection were to break completely.

I wasn't sure I could handle it.

Whatever heartache and betrayal I'd gone through with Damian would be nothing compared to what I'd go through if I lost Christos.

I wiped my eyes on the back of my hand, probably smearing my eyeliner. I didn't care. I drove to my apartment, looking forward to another evening alone.

Where Is Your Heart by Kelly Clarkson was the next tune to play on my car's MP3 player. Half way through the song, I punched the OFF button.

Stupid Kelly Clarkson. Why did you have to be so right all the time?

I hated her.

I tried to think constructively. What could I do to help my relationship with Christos? No matter where my mind went, I always smacked up against the same wall: we needed more time together.

But we didn't have more time in the day. Maybe I needed to sleep less?

I parked my VW at home and trudged upstairs to my apartment. I dropped my book bag on my coffee table and sank into my couch.

I texted Christos, expecting no reply.

I miss you, Christos. My heart is aching for you. We never see each other. I need you. I love you. When can I see you again? <3 <3 <3 <3 <3

Yes, I used *five* hearts, which was *two* more than I'd decided was officially "too" needy. Screw it. I didn't care. I set my phone down and waited. I stared at it, willing it to beep. What was that old saying? A watched phone never bleeps?

I opened my book bag and dug out my books and laptop. It was time to pick my poison.

History, Sociology, or job search.

Where was my ice cream?

I jumped when my phone bleeped.

A text from Christos, *Want dinner? Got some cooking right now. And a surprise...*

I was right. The two extra text-hearts I'd used had done the trick. I texted him right away. *I LOVE surprises! Be right over! <3 <3 <3 :- D*

I only used three hearts this time. I didn't want to ruin my good luck.

I washed my face in my bathroom and hurried to my car, wondering what the surprise might be. I never knew with Christos. It didn't matter. Having dinner with him was more than enough.

A few minutes later, I pulled into his driveway and parked. Christos walked outside before I climbed out of my car. He opened and held my door for me.

"Your feast awaits, madam," he said, bowing and offering his hand.

I took it and he helped me out of my car. "Thank you, kind sir," I said, sounding ten times more buoyant and happy than I would've thought myself capable twenty minutes prior. I tiptoed up and kissed him.

Without warning, our simple kissed turned passionate and our tongues danced together. I'd forgotten how much I missed his touch. How many days had it been? I didn't know for sure, but it seemed an eternity. I wrapped my arms around his neck and fell into the kiss.

"Samantha," he murmured. "I missed you so much, *agápi mou*."

Our lips continued to press and throb against each other as I mumbled, "I missed you too, my love."

He reached down and hooked his arm under my knees and carried me toward the front walkway.

I continued kissing him as he carried me into the house. Would I ever get tired of being carried over thresholds?

Probably not.

Christos kicked the door closed with his boot and immediately crushed his mouth into mine once again.

My heart thumped in my chest as he held me in his tattooed arms. He was ravenous, and his need awoke mine. My body was on fire. All I could think about was getting my clothes off...except. I pulled away from his luscious mouth and muttered, "Is Spiridon home?"

"My grandfather's out back reading on the deck. He won't notice."

I suddenly felt like a fumbling teenager and couldn't decide if the tension of getting caught by his grandfather was thrilling or a turn-off.

Christos gazed at me with his blazing blue eyes.

I forgot about everything else.

My eyelids fluttered and I lunged for Christos' mouth. I needed more of him. Memories of having sex with Christos flowed through me, spinning my body in a maelstrom of remembered sensation. Passionate, overwhelming ecstasy.

I was ready to fall over and go at it right there in the entryway. Or have Christos smash me up against a wall while I straddled him and he entered me.

The next thing I knew, my mind-reading man repositioned me so I was straddling his waist. His powerful hands gripped my ass firmly. I hooked my arms around his neck and pulled myself close.

"I need you. Right now," I murmured in his ear.

Christos carried me upstairs. I noticed art hanging along the walls in the upstairs hallway. Spiridon's home was truly an artist's paradise. I loved this place.

But I was even more in love with Christos.

My awareness of anything beyond him faded from my mind as we turned through a doorway. He kicked the door closed behind us, and he lowered me onto a large bed.

Chapter 16

SAMANTHA

The clicking of my zipper being pulled down swept me away.

To my pleasant surprise, having Christos pull my pants off without asking was perfectly acceptable. He was welcome to do whatever he wanted to me. The dirtier, the harder, the wetter the better.

I was smiling from ear to ear as his hands slid up my naked thighs. My pants, shoes, and socks were piled on the floor a second later. I was down to my panties, my shirt, and my sweater.

Nope, now my panties were off.

Oh, my.

Christos gently parted my legs, revealing my hot, wet center.

"You have no idea how often I've thought about this moment in the last several days," Christos moaned. "I've been missing you like crazy."

"Me too," I whimpered.

He stood up and ripped his shirt off. He was totally, certifiably sexy. His muscles were worthy of a magazine cover. His tattoos made me quiver with anticipation. He had a face that captained a thousand ships. I could picture him standing at the front of an ancient warship, wearing Roman armor, one sandaled foot planted commandingly on the railing as he pointed his sword forward and led his men to victory. Christos was some kind of mythically sexy hero of legend, and he was all mine.

He stared down at me. "You have the most beautiful pussy I've ever seen, *agápi mou*."

"Christos!" I blurted, throwing my forearm over my eyes. He'd torn me right out of my romance novel book-cover fantasy moment by using *that* word. I'd never had anyone call my lady bits *that* before, and I wasn't sure what to make of it. Christos was always throwing me off balance.

"What?" he smiled his cocky grin. "Do you want me to tell you your pussy is average looking? Or maybe a bit hideous?"

"Christos!!" He was making this worse.

He chuckled. "Then tell me how I'm supposed to describe it."

"I don't know!" I whined. "Are you even supposed to actually talk about it at all?" I wasn't sure of the answer to that myself.

"Fuck the rules. I make my own. Your pussy is smokin' hot. It tastes like cinnamon or I don't know what, but I can't get enough of it. It's like dessert, but it never spoils my dinner." He winked.

Suddenly, I was extremely nervous as I gazed up at this impossibly handsome and uninhibited man. He looked at me like I was a plate of food, so I asked, "What's for dinner, anyway?"

"After I have dessert?" he stared between my legs as he said it, "then we're having the main course, which will be my pig in your blanket," he grinned that stupid, smirking, dimpled grin of his. "Oh wait, Pigs In Blankets is breakfast. Duh."

I paused and took in the ridiculous look on his face. How did he always manage to set me at ease so damn easily? There I was, naked from the waist down with a handsome cavemen hovering above me, drooling over his dinner, and I burst out laughing.

He chuckled as he pulled his pants off one leg at a time like a normal mortal.

"Come here," I said, holding my arms out to him.

He stood at the foot of the bed. "Boxers on or off?"

"What happened to going commando?" I dropped my arms to the bed, feigning surprise.

"Like I said before, when it's winter, I need insulation for my jewelry."

"Your *jewelry*?" I sneered.

"Gotta keep my 24-carat boys warm," he snickered.

"Are they diamond studded too?"

"For *her* pleasure," he said suggestively.

I shook my head. "Take your pants off, funny man."

"Your wish is my command." He pushed his boxers down, revealing his rigid length. He was completely naked and completely flawless.

Oh, yeah. There was a reason why we were in his bedroom with the door closed and my pants and panties off. I fanned my face, suddenly struck by a 103-degree fever.

"Is it just me," he asked, "or is your hotness turning my bedroom into a fucking sauna?"

"What, you mean like one of those bathhouses were people go to have sex?" I asked, still fanning myself.

"No," he chuckled at me," I meant *your* hotness."

I frowned. "*You* were the one who said, 'Fucking Sauna,' so I thought that's what you meant," I sniveled.

He smirked and shook his head, gawking at my crotch as he crawled between my legs. "You're crazy," he grinned.

Before I could object, his arms were under my legs and his mouth was on my lips. My oh-so-very-wet lips.

My head fell back on the bed and I moaned long and low, then suddenly stopped short. "Are there any windows open? Can your grandfather hear us?"

Christos lifted his head and gazed up at me from between my legs with his mesmerizing eyes. "No, the deck is on the other side of the house. He can't hear a thing."

That feeling of sneaking around returned, but this time, with myself completely bared to Christos, his breath warming my core as he locked eyes with me, I was ready to indulge in some illicit love-making. Even if he had used *that* word to describe my, uh, female porthole. Or whatever it's supposed to be called.

Christos' head sunk back down and his tongue spiraled across the tight bud of nerves above my cleft. The intense ecstasy was instantaneous.

"Oh, Christos," I moaned.

His tongue slid up and down my entrance before his fingers entered me.

"Ohhhh…" I moaned again.

He plunged and licked and loved my core until I orgasmed in his face, my back arching, his mouth pushing deeper into me, his tongue circling my pleasure center as my legs trembled and pressed against him.

When I had released the last breaths of my orgasm, I sank into the bed. He climbed up to my face and kissed me passionately while massaging my breasts through my sweater. I felt so kinky being clothed from the waist up and naked from the waist down.

"Cinnamon or nutmeg?" he asked.

"What?"

"How do you taste?"

"Christos," I giggled.

"It's like dining at a doughnut shop down there," he laughed as our lips pressed together.

"You're terrible!"

"Hey, what can I say?" He pulled away. "You're the sweetest glazed doughnut I've ever had!" He hopped away before I could slap his arm.

He was laughing as he landed several feet from the bed, watching me. I had crawled to the edge of the mattress, ready to chase him, when I realized, once again, I was not wearing pants or panties.

I vaguely remembered seeing a Porky Pig cartoon as a little girl and being entirely disturbed that he wore a dinner-jacket and bow-tie, but no pants! And nobody ever said anything! Oh, and white gloves! Porky never forgot his gloves! Nobody went out of the house without *gloves*. He was shameless, that pig.

"Did you happen to notice the wall of mirrors behind you?" Christos asked mischievously.

"What?"

"It offers a truly tantalizing view from where I'm standing," he grinned through lowered lashes.

I twisted my head around, and was greeted by a view of my naked backside. I was down on all fours, which provided a perfect view of my privates.

Horrified, I dropped my bottom to the bed, hiding it from prying eyes. I swore I'd heard someone shout, *"Put your pants on, Porky!"*

I glanced around, but it was only my imagination. However, I was *not* imagining Christos leering at the mirror.

I whined, "Stop staring!"

"Why?"

"Because I'm embarrassed!" I shrieked.

"Don't be."

There was such a finality to the way he said it, I had to pause.

"Agápi mou, you are the most beautiful woman ever created. You are a child of Mother Nature. Your beauty as a woman is your birthright. You should be proud of yourself. Own your

womanhood. Own your femininity."

I stared at Christos. He was completely naked, all muscled chest and rock-hard abs. His manhood was fully, proudly erect. He looked at me lovingly. If he could be confident, why couldn't I?

I pulled my sweater over my head, then my shirt. I calmly reached behind myself and unhooked my bra. I tossed it at Christos. It landed right on his...

Leaning Tower of Pisa.

Where it dangled and swung.

I pointed and said, "*It landed on your*—!!!" That was all I could get out before I fell face first on the bed, bellowing laughter, clutching my sides.

"*Gooooaaaallll!!!!*" he shouted, then burst out laughing.

I buried my face in my arms and laughed so hard I couldn't breathe. After a minute, I looked up and saw Christos still standing and laughing heartily, but bent over at the waist, resting his hands on the tops of his thighs.

"*It's shaking!!*" I screamed, pointing at my bra. "*Every time you laugh, it shakes!!*"

He broke into another round of laughter and finally dropped to one knee. I expected my bra to finally fall off, but it didn't.

Somehow, that was even funnier than everything else.

"*It's stuck!!*" I squealed. "*I lassoed your man-steer!!!!*"

He laughed harder, but stood up slowly. Then he began to twirl his hips, and my bra twirled too. So did his man pole. Why did I imagine a rodeo cowboy swinging his cowboy hat in the air?

My bra spun faster and faster—

"*Meat spin!!!!*" he cackled breathlessly.

—until it flew off and landed on top of my...

Head.

I fell onto my back and couldn't stop laughing. My bra was still stuck to my head.

"Nice hat," Christos laughed.

I didn't care. I was laughing too hard.

Christos stumbled over to the bed and plopped onto the mattress next to me. He rolled over until we were laying side-to-side.

He laced his fingers through mine and we held hands while we laughed and laughed for a long time. Slowly it faded into chuckles, then just breathy sighs.

"Was it good for you?" I gasped.

"Best ever," he chuckled.

I glanced down and noticed he was still erect.

"How can you stay hard for so long?" I marveled.

He sighed while pulling my bra off my head and tossing it to the floor. "That's easy, *agápi mou*. Everything about you turns me on. You're my own personal Viagra. When I'm seventy-two and can't get it up anymore, all you'll have to do is throw your bra on my cock and I'll be hard as a rock."

"I can't imagine you not being able to get it up, no matter how old you are."

"Me neither," he said with cocksure confidence.

"Tell me that part again about being together when we're seventy?" I prompted.

"Oh, you mean when we're old and gray and have been together for fifty years?"

"You mean when I'm like, 69?"

"I like 69," he smirked.

"Christos!" I sighed. Why did I like the sound of that so much? I'm not talking about the 69 part, not that there was anything wrong with that, but I meant the being together fifty years part. And why was that making me horny again?

He rolled on top of me and I felt the length of his shaft pressing against my cleft.

"Condom!" I gulped.

"I bought a box on the way home." He reached over and opened the drawer mounted to the wall and pulled out a new box. He sat up and opened the package with both hands while flexing all his muscles and snarling, as if the box were made of steel. "Roar!" he joked. Condoms flew everywhere.

"What are you doing?!" I asked.

He grinned. "You know that moment when pro-wrestlers rip their t-shirts off in front of the roaring crowd?"

"I guess?" I frowned.

"I've always wanted to do that. This seemed like the closest I was going to get. Roar!" he said again as he tore the flimsy condom box to shreds.

"You are *such* a dork," I giggled.

"I *have* such a dork, but I assure you, I am not one myself."

"Oh, that's terrible. Don't quit your day job. Comedy is *not* your calling."

He smiled at me and licked his lips lasciviously while rolling the condom on, which for some reason was absurd. I couldn't help but laugh again.

Then he leaned down between my legs and yodeled at my crotch, "Here, pussy pussy! Here, pussy, pussy!" He held his hand to his mouth as if he were trying to make his voice carry farther.

I propped up on my elbows and gaped at him. "What the hell's balls are *you doing?!*"

"Don't you like my catcalls?"

"That makes zero sense."

"I'm catcalling your pussy." He was totally amused with himself. "Here, pussy, pussy!"

"Stop!" I chuckled then dropped back down on the bed, shaking my head, but smiling wide. I loved his dorkiness more than I would ever admit to him. It somehow humanized him. It took him from being the finest man on the planet to a regular guy I could relate to. No matter how ridiculous his jokes were.

"You sure?" he asked. "Maybe I didn't make myself clear."

"What?"

He slid his tongue between my folds and I quivered. My legs lifted off the bed and my feet shook as his tongue swirled around my wetness. Then I jolted as the tip of his tongue stroked the center of my pleasure. I tingled and trembled to my toes as an orgasm rushed through my body almost instantly.

He lifted his head and gave me a curious look. "Yeah, that didn't do it. I still haven't made my case. I need to inspect this situation more carefully…"

"What?" I said breathlessly, still coming down from my orgasm. "I'm confused."

He climbed up the bed and mounted me, lowering himself into my waiting heat. His rigidity entered my wetness.

"Ohhh my g-g-god-d-d-d," I moaned as he filled me up with his massive fullness.

"Ahhh…" he groaned, all sense of comedy gone. "Every time I'm inside of you," he hissed harshly, "I feel like it's the first time I've ever had sex in my life."

"Me too," I murmured, "me too."

He began a rhythmic thrusting that sent waves of pleasure cascading out from between my legs. I opened my legs farther, letting him in all the way. Within seconds, I tipped back head-first over the edge of ecstasy as another orgasm surged through me.

He sat up, repositioning himself so that his knees were now forward and his weight rested on his shins. My thighs draped over his as his hands cupped my hips and his thumbs caressed the crests of my pelvis. "Fuck, Samantha, your hips are a work of art. Fucking perfect, I've never seen anything like them," he grunted as he worked his body repeatedly into mine.

My pleasure was building again. "Christos," I moaned.

"Fuck..." he responded.

I felt a powerful orgasm about to peak as he plunged and plunged.

I was surprised when he started stroking my ribs with his fingers. "Christos!" I shrieked, kicking my heels up. I hadn't expected his tickling touch and it distracted from my orgasm.

"Relax," he said as he continued more gently, still stroking my ribs.

Strangely, the tickling sensation transformed into fluttery pleasure that danced in my chest like icy fireflies. I shivered instantly as waves of electric sex pulsed between my abdomen and my throat.

"Ohhh," I moaned. My orgasm began to build again, but the sensation between my legs joined with the intensity in my ribs as he slid in and out of me. "Oh my god, what are you doing?" I moaned. "It feels so good..."

As the pleasure in my body built to maximum, his hands slid around my breasts and massaged them, heightening the fireflies in my chest ever further. It felt so unbelievably good. As if sensing my need, his palms brushed over the tips of my hardened nipples. He stroked them with the lightest circular touch, my pebbled flesh catching and scratching beneath his rugged palms. I shivered feverishly every time he completed a circle.

"Don't stop," I whispered. "Whatever you're doing, don't stop."

A waterfall of sensation poured down my taut stomach as his hands slid downward and his fingers resumed their gentle feather strokes over my ribs. I was quivering and shivering as my entire body covered in goose bumps. I mean my *entire* body. I was freezing as pleasure wind-stormed through me.

I felt my orgasm building toward infinity as he pushed deeper and deeper. He arched his head back. "Fuck me... Samantha, you're like fucking crack cocaine, woman. I'm addicted to you, *agápi mou...*"

Then he slid one hand around between my legs and his fingers found my clitoris. He rubbed and caressed, causing a firestorm to erupt from it. "Uhhhh," I moaned as wet pleasure flooded out from my center and another orgasm took me.

I floated high on a cloud of pleasure far above the world, as everything slipped away, far, far below.

SAMANTHA

I heaved and sighed breathlessly for a long time. What an unbelievable release that had been.

When I calmed, Christos reached his arms behind my shoulders, sat me up with my legs still looped around his waist, then suddenly spun onto his back.

The next thing I knew, I was on top of him. He was still inside me.

"Was that some kind of Cirque du Soleil move?" I asked breathlessly.

He chuckled. "No, nothing that gymnastic. But if you want, we can try some things. Let me know if you want to play Pommel Horse or Parallel Bars," he grinned.

"No! All fine here!" I was freaked out as it was being on top, I didn't think I needed to be his human pommel horse.

I looked down at him. The view from here was quite different from what I was used to.

Whoa.

Guy candy alert! I ran my hands all over his muscled chest and tattooed shoulders. I think my mouth was watering. Time to unwrap my very own piece of gourmet man candy!

"Now it's your turn," he smirked.

Gulp. That's when I realized he was *my* human pommel horse. "To what?" I squeaked.

"To move. However *you* want, *agápi mou...*"

Fear smacked me in the chest. I folded my arms across my breasts and collapsed against him. I was no gymnast! Gulp, gulp!! "No way! I can't do that!"

"Why not?" he murmured, wrapping his arms around me in a warm hug.

My cheek laid against his chest. "I don't know," I said shyly. "I guess I'm just nervous. I've never done this before."

"I know," he said, kissing the top of my head gently, "and that's okay. We can stop if you want. Or..." he murmured.

That was my Christos. Always pushing my boundaries, making me try new things, but always giving me the choice to wait, to try again when I was ready. He either believed in me like no one else and was the most nurturing man ever born, or he was a complete sadist. Maybe he was both. Oh! I wasn't sure how I felt about that. I'd have to table that discussion for another time, maybe in ten years? Grin. Yeah, that would be perfect.

"Or what?" I asked coyly.

"Or you might discover you like it. A lot."

Oh, yeah. He was talking about me being on top. Um... Er... Ah... Uh... Hmmm.

Yeah, that.

"But I don't know how," I whined. Yes, I sounded like a baby. But I forgave myself on the grounds that an angelically beautiful man who was perfect in every respect, especially when it came to his performance in the bedroom, was asking *me* to pleasure *him*.

Gulp, gulp, gulp!

I was ready to bite my nails typewriter-style. Bite-bite-bite-bite-*ching!* Bite-bite-bite-bite-*ching!*

"All you have to do, *agápi mou*," he whispered, "is move. Whatever you do will be perfect."

"You sure?"

"Just being inside you makes me want to come. I'm amazed I haven't already." He kissed the top of my head several times. "Whatever you want, *agápi mou*..."

I sat up slowly and planted my hands on his muscled, pommel horse chest. I hoped he would be satisfied with a beginner's routine.

Distracted by his beauty, and only slightly stalling, I started sliding my hands up and down his smooth skin, luxuriating in the feel of his manly chest. Damn it, he was totally hot! And the next thing I knew, I was too.

His cock throbbed inside me, growing impossibly larger, filling me up. I don't know how that happened, but he really did feel even bigger than before. I rocked tentatively forward, then back.

"Like this?" I asked.

"Yes."

I began rocking in a steady rhythm.

"Yeah..." he moaned. "That's epic," he sighed. He wrapped his hands around my pelvis gently and caressed the exposed ridges of my hips again.

He really liked doing that. Okay by me. For whatever reason, it made me feel very womanly. Not overly hippy, like I'd always felt in the past.

"Aaaaah," he moaned. "Keep going, you have no idea what you're doing..."

"I knew it, I'm doing it wrong!" I sighed, almost stopping.

"No-o-o-o," he moaned, "don't stop. You're doing it *perfectly...*"

"You really like it?" I asked, sliding up and down his hard length.

"I fuh—*fucking love* it, *agápi mou.*"

I realized in this position my clitoris was tickling across the bottom wedge of his pelvis, right above his manhood. If I tilted my hips forward while thrusting backward onto him, the motion lit my bud of nerves up with a buzzing billow of pleasure. Oh, wow. This felt really good.

"Oh, *hells* yeah," he groaned. "That's unbelievable... You are *so* fucking tight, *agápi mou...*"

For a moment, I was amazed I was pleasuring *him*. It had always been the other way around, or so I'd thought. I was so taken by my revelation and Christos' repeated moaning, I almost forgot to enjoy myself.

Almost.

Heat expanded inside my core and poured down my legs. Ecstasy was building, thrust by thrust. I ground my pelvis down harder and harder, my clitoris tingling, sizzling, burning with intense pleasure.

"Oh, Christos," I moaned.

"*Agápi mou...*"

I could tell he was lost to the pleasure I was giving him. Knowing this increased my own tenfold. I was so wet, my desire for him was pouring out of me and onto his skin as I slid against his rigid root with every frantic thrust.

My orgasm was building, filling past my belly, up my chest and spine, my throat, up to the top of my head. I was about to launch into space as the energy swelling inside my body expanded to maximum.

He responded by pressing himself repeatedly deeper into my core from below as his hands clamped onto my pelvis.

"I can feel you tightening up around me, Samantha," he hissed, "Fuck, you're coming. You're *coming…*"

I was. It was so amazingly good. The energy in my body built to a heightened pitch as my orgasm shot upward and quaked my entire body. My knees clamped together as every muscle in my body locked up with intense release. I moaned long and low as he strained into me.

Suddenly, his whole body bowed beneath me, lifting me up off the bed as he came inside me, every muscle of his beautiful body flexing as his face screwed tightly into ecstasy. I felt him jolting inside me, pressed all the way in, his cock spasming with hammering release deep in my core. "*Agápi mou!* Aaahhh!!! Fuck! *Samantha!!!*"

I arched my back and bore down with my pelvis, quivering as all my weight pressed down on his thick length.

"Christos!!!!" I screamed.

"*Agápi MOU!!!!*" he shouted.

His body relaxed finally and he fell back to the bed. I collapsed onto his chest, spent, wet, exhilarated, relaxed, released, at peace.

I sighed heavily. "Oh. My. God. What did you do?"

"What did *I* do?" he asked. "That was *all* you, *agápi mou.*"

It was. I couldn't believe it.

I smiled silently.

Yay, me!

I didn't suck in bed!

He wrapped his arms around me and I lifted my head to kiss him affectionately. "Mmmmm," was all I said.

"Mmmm-hmmm," he replied.

I lowered my head back to rest against his chest as echoes of our mutual orgasm subsided.

I laid on top of him for a long time, silent, my legs wrapped around him. I didn't ever want to let go.

"I gotta deal with the condom," he muttered.

"Okay," I whispered, afraid he was going to leave.

"You should roll off," he whispered.

I didn't want to, but I supposed I had to. I felt him pulling out of me.

He reached down and pressed two fingers against the base of the condom until he was withdrawn. He dropped it in a small waste basket beside his bed.

He laid back next to me and took me in his arms.

Thank goodness he didn't go.

I draped my knee over his hips as he pulled me to his chest and kissed me passionately. We continued kissing for a long time, softly, quietly, intimately.

SAMANTHA

Eventually Christos gently broke our kiss and stroked a lock of hair behind my ear. He gazed into my heart with his healing blue eyes for a long time before murmuring, "Samantha, you are the most amazing woman in the history of women. Every time I'm with you, whether it's in bed together, or drawing with crayons on a coffee table, or even just sitting in silence, I marvel at how lucky I am to have found you."

"I thought I was the lucky one," I whispered shyly as I ran my fingers through the hair on his chest.

He chuckled. "Yes indeed, you are. But I'm luckier."

"What are you saying, Christos? Are you saying I'm more awesome than you?" I grinned.

"Yup."

I gasped. "No way! Can your ego allow such an admission?"

"It can, when it's the truth. You're even more awesome than I am."

"Does that mean you'll stare at me more than you stare at yourself from now on?"

He frowned while smiling. "I don't stare at myself."

"You are such a liar! I've seen you in my bathroom. You're so in love with yourself, I'm surprised you don't jerk off every time you see yourself in the mirror!" I giggled.

"If I was gay, I'd do me in a second," he smirked.

I squeezed one of his cheeks, and in mocking baby-talk said, "There's that ego I so wuv." I gave him a twinkling smile.

"I don't know about you," he smiled back, "but I'm getting pretty hungry."

"Is it time for dinner?"

"Yeah, I need to clean you up first," he said. "Would you like the shower or my tongue?"

"I'm pretty sure if you use your tongue, we'll never get out of your bedroom."

"Shower it is." He stood and picked me up and carried me into the bathroom attached to his bedroom.

Nope, getting carried never got old. "If you keep carrying me everywhere, my muscles are going to atrophy and I won't be able to walk," I joked.

"Then you'll be stuck in bed and I'll be forced to ravish you all day long."

"Do I get time off for sleeping?"

"No, but I will fuck you until you're unconscious."

I blurted a laugh. Because I believed he could.

Christos set me down on the bathroom floor while he filled the round jacuzzi bathtub and added bubble-bath soap. When it was full, he picked me up, stepped into the tub, then set me on my feet in the water. He gently washed me from top to bottom while I stood in foamy suds up to my waist. He caressed my body with a sopping natural sponge then rinsed me with the ceramic pitcher kept on the edge of the tub.

I felt like Cleopatra or some other high queen who was bathed by handmaidens, except Christos was much better than a handmaiden. I had a moment to wonder what sort of funny business Cleopatra must have gotten up to with her hot handmaidens. It seemed a likely outcome. I imagined most empresses did whatever the hell they wanted.

When Christos slid his soapy fingers between this empress's legs, I quivered and moaned. "Bathtub sex, my king?"

He chuckled mischievously and kissed me on the cheek. "Dinner first."

He finished bathing me and toweled me dry.

"So, was that my present?" I asked.

"What, the hot sex or the bathing?"

"Yeah," I smiled.

"Nope. I've got a couple more downstairs. One is dinner."

"Awesome!" I couldn't wait to eat.

While getting dressed in the bedroom, I finally noticed the decor. Not the man-cave I'd expected.

I had imagined Christos either lived in an actual subterranean cave surround by the bones and antlers of the animals he'd hunted and killed with his bare hands, or maybe some kind of mechanic's race garage with motorcycles and muscle cars surrounding a red satin bed with a chromed tread-plate bedframe.

Instead, the room was stylish in an art-deco sort of way. Lines and abstract shapes in the form of inset bookcases and earth tones led the eye to a massive abstract painting over the straight-edged king-sized bed stand. A bizarrely delicate light fixture with dozens of tiny white bulbs that resembled a starburst hung from the recessed ceiling.

"I was beginning to wonder if you actually lived here with your grandfather," I said as I took in the decor.

"Yeah, he likes having me around. He says it keeps the energy in the house young."

"I'll say," I smiled and winked at Christos.

My eyes were drawn to the huge abstract painting hanging over Christos' bed.

"Tell me about this beautiful painting," I said. "It doesn't look like one of Spiridon's."

"It's my dad's. Well, mostly. I helped him paint it."

"Really? When?"

"When I was like seven or eight."

"Wow, Christos, it's really nice. And that's so cool that you did a painting with your dad!" I envied that he had, or *used* to have, such a close relationship with his father.

All I could imagine doing with my own dad was drawing up a balance sheet. Even then, he'd be controlling everything, correcting me and telling me how I was doing everything wrong.

"Yeah," Christos continued, "my parents were still together at the time. I used to love hanging around in my dad's studio. I'd be in the corner drawing or painting on an easel he'd bought for me. He'd set up fruit or stacks of books or whatever for me to practice still lifes. He'd always be checking in to see what I was doing. Looking back, I think he was getting bored with his abstract work and loved having me as a distraction. It was only another couple years before my mom took off.

"Anyway, the day me and my dad did this painting," he motioned at the big painting on the wall, "he came over to watch me work for awhile. I remember I was working on a still life of a vase of flowers and a little tin box and a tea kettle. It's still hanging in my grandpa's bedroom, by the way. My dad told me to give it to Grandpa for a birthday present.

"Anyway, my dad's watching me work, and he says, '*Agoráki mou*, help me fix my painting. It's no good. Yours is so much better.' I told him I couldn't fix it, I didn't know how."

Christos paused from his memory to look at me directly. "You gotta remember, I'd seen all of my dad's paintings at this point. Not just the abstract stuff he sold for crazy money, but also his realistic work. He was and is so amazingly talented, it would blow you away if you saw his realistic work in person. So, when he tells me to fix his painting? I'm ready to crap my pants. In my eyes, my dad was the greatest painter on the planet, and all I would do was fuck it up. I mean, I'm working on my own little still life, sweating bullets, trying to get it right—"

I interrupted him. "I'm sure your painting turned out awesome, Christos."

He grinned dimples and nodded. "Yeah, it was pretty damn good for an eight-year-old."

"Cocky bastard," I swatted his arm.

"You love me for it."

I did. I kissed him on his cheek. "But I want to hear the rest of your story."

"Okay, so I walk over to my dad's canvas and look at it. At that age, I was never sure what to make of abstract art. I was so focused on trying to do realistic stuff, like my dad."

"So what did you do?" I was totally curious.

"Well, my dad said, 'Look at it for awhile. Take your time to soak it in. When you're ready, grab a brush and some paint and add something. You'll know what to do.' So I stared at it, like he'd said.

After awhile, I grabbed a big brush, loaded it with cadmium orange, and carefully made those shapes right there."

Christos pointed at the complex orange pattern of slashes curving across the right side of the painting.

I was in awe of the connection he'd shared with his dad. "Wow, that was like fifteen years ago, and you remember all of that?"

"Hey, getting to paint on my dad's painting was a big deal. It was like getting the keys to the kingdom."

"So, how come your dad didn't sell it, like his other paintings?"

"Funny you ask. The next time my dad had a show, this was the featured piece. Everyone was talking about it. When my dad told them that I had helped, they creamed all over themselves. Started calling me a prodigy right there on the spot. People offered exorbitant amounts of cash for the painting. They wanted me to sign my name to it too. But at the end of the night, my dad refused to sell it. He wanted to keep it for himself. It's been hanging in my grandfather's house ever since, right here in this room."

I was in awe of Christos' story. Nothing remotely this grand or romantic or exciting, or this *loving* ever happened in *my* family. All I could picture was my mom or dad shouting at me that I was going to ruin something whenever I'd tried to help them out on some project or other around the house.

But at least I had Christos in my life, I reminded myself. He was as grand, romantic and loving as his story about his father's painting. Maybe more so.

Christos was the sensational celebrity in *my* life.

I sighed deeply, trying to clear my welling emotions. I looked around the room again, taking in the rest of the decor. "Well, this is an awesome bedroom you've got here," I said, trying to shift the subject into territory that wouldn't make me want to break down in tears. "And in your grandfather's house, no less."

"Yup. I hate the idea of him living alone, plus the studio is downstairs. It's convenient. And hey, it's free, so I can't complain."

I felt yet another pinch of jealousy. Make that a Vise-Grip of jealousy. I wished that my parents were equally understanding, that their house was an awesome artist's mansion within walking distance of the beach, and that I had my own breathtaking studio. Oh well. Maybe with the money I earned as a cashier at the campus art museum I could afford something, ahhh, similar.

Yeah, right.

"What's wrong, *agápi mou*?" Christos asked, cupping my cheek in his hand. "Something's bothering you."

"It's nothing," I demurred.

"You're thinking about your parents, aren't you?"

"Yeah. Sort of." I leaned into his chest. I felt like I was spoiling our mood.

"Don't worry about it, *agápi mou*. You're part of my family now. My domain is yours. My family is yours. Let me show you."

"What do you mean?"

"Downstairs." He opened the bedroom door and nodded toward the hallway, "Your surprise."

We went downstairs together.

Chapter 17

SAMANTHA

Spiridon stood at the stove in the kitchen, tending to food.

"Hey, *Pappoús*," Christos said to him.

"Your lamb is almost ready, Christos," Spiridon said.

"Thanks, *Pappoús*," he said.

"I kept an eye on it while you were upstairs. Hello, Samantha. Good to see you again," he smiled at me.

I blushed instantly. How long had Spiridon been inside the house? How loud had Christos and I been? How much had Spiridon heard? I tried to hide behind Christos, almost like a little kid hiding behind their parent's legs.

"Give me a hug, *koritsáki mou*," Spiridon said, grabbing me from behind Christos. "I haven't seen you since December!" His arms swallowed me up.

I hugged him back, surprised by the warmth of his affection. He barely knew me, and yet his hug felt more loving than any I'd ever received from my parents. When he released me, he was smiling, and I almost thought his eyes were tearing up.

"How have you been treating my grandson, huh? Have you been good to him?" He wrapped an arm around Christos and rubbed his other hand against Christos' stomach.

Yeah, my parents would never act like that around me. I could imagine myself flinching in a combination of surprise and discomfort if they ever tried.

"She's been treating me like a king," Christos said.

"Show her your present, *paidí mou*," Spiridon grinned at Christos.

"He helped me with it," Christos said to me. "That's why he's all excited."

"With what?" I asked.

"Come on, I'll show you," Christos said, leading me to the studio.

When we were out of the kitchen, I asked, "What was that your grandfather called me?"

"*Koritsáki mou*? It means 'my little girl.' I told you, you're family now." Christos rubbed my back as he said it.

I was going to cry. I sniffled back my tears as we walked into the studio, all the way to the end.

There was a little work space set up in the back that hadn't been there before. An angled drafting table with a lamp clamped to the desktop was surrounded by trays full of pencils, pens, erasers, markers, rulers, everything you might need to draw. Next to it was a small easel. By small, I meant small in comparison to the other ones in the studio. But it was more than big enough for any painting I could ever imagine painting, and it looked brand new. Beside the easel was a table on wheels with paint brushes in jars, tubes of paint, a palette, clean rags, everything.

"What's this," I asked. "It all looks brand new."

"It is. And it's yours. You need your own workspace."

My eyes goggled. "What?! I can't accept this. It's too much."

"Don't worry about it. It won't cost you a thing," he winked.

I was overwhelmed. "I can't, Christos."

"Why not?"

"I don't know. It's just so much."

"So?"

I opened my mouth, then closed it.

"If it makes you feel any better, I buy art supplies all the time. I would need to buy this stuff anyway, sooner or later. If you want, think of it as my stuff, and I'm letting you borrow it."

"I can't—"

"Sure you can."

"Christos!"

He ignored my protest. "Now you can do all your art studies right beside me. While I'm busy working, you'll be twenty feet away."

That sounded pretty awesome.

"We set it up this afternoon," Spiridon said, now standing beside us. "I hope you like it. Is the easel big enough? Christos insisted it would be, but I wasn't sure."

I gaped at Spiridon. What was I going to say?

"Here's a key," Spiridon said, holding a brass key out to me. "For the front door. You can come and go whenever you want."

I tried my best, but the tears poured out of me.

I couldn't speak, I could only sob softly.

Christos reached out and hugged me and stroked my hair. "It's all yours, *agápi mou*."

Spiridon patted my shoulder. "Make yourself at home, *koritsáki mou*."

I realized at that moment that I could now accurately describe what heaven was like.

"Dinner, anyone?" Spiridon asked.

SAMANTHA

Dinner was a Greek cucumber salad with kalamata olives and feta cheese, and roasted lamb with yogurt sauce over rice.

"Wow, this is really good," I said. "Are you sure you made it, Christos," I jabbed, having recovered from my earlier tears in the studio.

"Totally," Christos insisted.

"He did," Spiridon assured. "I just made sure nothing burned while you two were, ahem, upstairs."

I sank down in my chair. Was there room for me to slide under the kitchen table?

Spiridon chuckled. "I didn't hear a thing," he smiled.

I literally slid under the table.

Christos and Spiridon laughed.

I wondered if I could wait down there, staring at their knees, until they forgot I was there and they left the room to go looking for me. Probably not. I struggled back into my chair, the legs squeaking on the kitchen floor, further embarrassing me. My face was hot, my cheeks redder than ever.

"Don't worry about it, *koritsáki mou*," Spiridon said. "We're all grownups." He lifted a bite of lamb to his mouth and chomped it down. "I was young once too, you know. I remember what it was like."

I held my napkin in front of my face. I wanted to beg them both to stop. But I also didn't. They weren't at all uncomfortable with the topic. They both behaved as if sex and love were a normal part of life, something that normal people could talk about instead of hiding it and pretending it didn't exist, skulking around the topic like it was offensive, which was stupid.

There was nothing stupid about love and sex.

Where had my parents gone wrong? They never talked about sex, unless it was the topic of birth control or STDs. And they NEVER talked about love. I mean, never. Zero times. I suddenly wondered if perhaps I had been a test-tube baby. Probably.

"Christos told me you changed your major to art?" Spiridon asked.

I lowered my napkin to my lap. "Yeah. I did."

"That must be exciting," he said.

"It is. I dropped my accounting class and added Figurative Sculpting."

"I bet that Marjorie Bittinger is your instructor, right?" Spiridon asked.

"Yeah," I smiled. "Have you met her, Christos?"

Christos was chewing on salad, and wiped his mouth with his napkin when he was finished. Mr. Manners, as always. "Yeah, once. She's a tough nut."

I chuckled. "I think she has it in for me."

"Really?" Christos asked before taking a swallow of milk.

"Yeah, she took an instant hating to me when I walked in late the first day. And, I think she has a crush on the model. Do you know a guy named Hunter Blakeley?"

"No," Christos answered.

"Well, I think Major Marjorie has a thing for him big time. I think she sees me as competition."

"Major Marjorie," Spiridon chuckled and smiled, "that sounds like her."

"What's her issue?" Christos asked.

I suddenly felt like I'd let the genie out of the bottle. Or maybe the fart out of the jar. Was I going to be in trouble for answering this honestly? I sighed. After holding in so many secrets in high school, I was tired of it. I trusted Christos wouldn't freak out. He wasn't a Lamian Damian. "This Hunter guy was hitting on me during the breaks, and I think it made Professor Bittinger jealous," I said nervously.

"No surprise there," Christos said smiling. "I'd be jealous of you too, if I wasn't me." He winked at me.

I smiled at him while I chewed on some lamb. I waited a few moments to see if Christos said anything else on the topic of Hunter Blakeley. Nope. He didn't seem to care. Wait, did that mean he didn't care at all? I was suddenly confused. Wasn't a guy supposed to bang his chest and hoot and holler and fight for you?

Christos was watching me closely. "Don't worry, *agápi mou*. If this Hunter guy doesn't leave you alone..."

I expected Christos to say something violent like he'd beat Hunter up or challenge him to a duel.

"...I'll set him up with Bittinger. She's a good looking woman, and I hear she's a wild cat in the sack."

Spiridon chuckled. "Send her my way first," he grinned. "I'll set her straight."

I gawked at Spiridon. My grandparents never talked like that!

"I'll bust that Hunter character's head myself," Spiridon finished. He leveled a gaze at me. "You tell him Spiridon Manos is still young and spry, and he better not lay a finger on you," he chuckled.

Christos grinned. "He's not joking. He can still throw a wicked uppercut. I know from experience."

"And don't you forget it, *paidí*." Spiridon said to Christos shrewdly.

When we finished eating, I cleared the table and did the dishes while Spiridon and Christos chatted and joked with me from the table. I so loved being in their house.

When everything was rinsed and in the dishwasher or put away in the fridge, I leaned against the countertop, watching the two of them.

"So, *Pappoús*, did I tell you that Brandon's phone is ringing off the hook?" Christos asked. "Seems like everybody wants my paintings after my show."

"The Charboneaus do good work," Spiridon said. "I knew choosing them for your first solo show was a wise decision. And that Franco Viviano acted like there was no art market in San Diego."

Franco was the guy Christos had introduced me to in Los Angeles, the owner of Spada Gallery, which sold Nikolos Manos' paintings. I felt like I was listening to some private, upper echelon art talk or big back-room deal making bull session.

"Yeah," Christos continued, "Brandon's got buyers lining up. He keeps raising the prices every time someone new calls begging for my work."

"Congratulations, Christos. You've worked hard to get this far. You deserve it."

"I totally forgot!" I blurted. "I need to look for a job!"

Christos and Spiridon turned to face me.

"I'm sorry, I totally interrupted you guys," I said. All their deal-making money talk reminded me that I wasn't in nearly such an enviable financial position. It was such a dramatic contrast between Christos' situation and mine. I had rent to worry about, and groceries, and everything else.

"No worries," Christos said, slightly confused. "I thought you said you found a job at the museum?"

"Yeah," I sighed, "but it's only like ten hours a week. I'm still looking for a second job to pay all my bills."

"Do you want to use the internet here?" Christos suggested. "See what you can find?"

"Uhhh," the idea of looking for a minimum wage part-time job while surrounded by the Manos Mansion and the Manos family's love was somehow depressing, like the good vibes were only fleeting for me, and my reality was back in my lonely one-bedroom apartment.

"I'll grab my laptop and you can work right here on the kitchen table with us," Christos said.

"Stay, *koritsáki mou*," Spiridon said warmly.

I wanted to cry again. Compared to the way my parents had thrown me to the wolves, I felt like this was a hero's homecoming.

"I should go home and do it there," I said, holding back my tears. "I have Sociology and History homework anyway."

"Do you want me to come with you?" Christos asked.

"No, I, I bah-better go," I hitched, heading out the kitchen and toward the front door, hoping to reach my car before tears fell.

SAMANTHA

I was almost to my VW when Christos ran outside behind me.

"Where are you going?" he asked.

"Home," I said, grabbing the door handle of my VW.

"Why don't you move in with me?"

"What?! I couldn't do that!" I yanked my car door open, my tears threatening to spill.

"Sure you could."

"No, Christos." I dropped into the driver's seat.

He squatted down beside the open door and smiled at me with his comforting blue eyes.

Why was I panicking? The man I was desperately in love with was asking me to live with him. Wasn't I supposed to be excited and thrilled instead of scared? Maybe if he'd asked five months from now.

"Why not?" he asked, his brows tight.

Despite all the things Christos and I had been through together, it just seemed too soon.

To say that my life had become a whirlwind of change, both good and bad, was the understatement of my short life. I don't think I'd experienced so much dramatic change so quickly ever before.

Why was Christos' offer making me so nervous?

For one thing, I imagined there'd need to be some kind of Manos family conference where everyone sat around in a meeting hall voting on whether or not the family could withstand the terrible impact of me moving into their house.

At least, that's what I imagined would happen if I asked *my* parents to let Christos move into *their* house. Not that I'd ever subject Christos to such a horrid punishment.

Maybe the other thing that bothered me was that if I'd ever entertained thoughts about living with Christos, it was picturing him in my little one bedroom apartment. A romantic little place for a romantic little couple making their way in the world together.

But that wasn't reality.

Reality was the Manos Mansion and Christos' family having buckets of money to throw around, and they were already pouring some onto my head. Sure, taking a cash bath under a shower of Benjamin Franklins had a certain appeal. But, I don't know, I somehow felt indebted just thinking about it. And look where that had gotten me with my parents.

They'd hung me out to dry while the family greenbacks evaporated under the heat of their ultimatums. I think my long face betrayed my sadness and sense of parental abandonment to Christos.

"Look, Samantha," Christos soothed, "my grandfather has plenty of room. He's always talking about how the house is too big for just me and him."

"Oh, I couldn't impose." It sounded like a weak excuse.

"You saw him in there. He loves you, Samantha. He's basically calling you his daughter. How much more of an invitation do you need?"

I couldn't deny his logic. But it felt wrong. It felt scary. The question for me was whether I was scared for a good reason, or scared simply because this was all so new and overwhelming. Was it possible that unconditional love could make a person nervous? Probably. It was doing it to me. I'd never felt it so strongly since meeting Christos, and now I was getting it from his grandfather. I mean, *both* of them had set up that studio space for me.

For *me*.

I was freaking out.

My heart jackrabbited into my throat.

I needed to get out of there before I had a heart attack.

"I'm sorry, Christos," my voice quivered. "I really need to go. I need some time to think about all this."

"Take all the time you need, *agápi mou*," he said softly. "I'm not going anywhere. You still have the key to the house, right?"

"Yeah."

"Let me see it."

Did he want it back? I panicked, despite my confusion and reluctance. Giving it to him would either be a relief or the biggest disappointment of my life. I fished it from the pocket of my jeans and handed it to him with a shaky hand.

He took it and also took my key ring from my hand. Then he worked the Manos house key around my key ring. "For safe keeping," he said. "I love you, Samantha. Whatever you decide, whenever you decide it, will be perfect. I will wait as long as you need me to." He cracked a dimpled grin. "Besides, you live so close, we're practically next door neighbors."

He handed my keys back to me.

"Okay," I said randomly. I twisted my car key in the ignition and started my VW. The engine purred to life. "I should go."

He leaned into the car and kissed me softly on the forehead.

"You sure you don't want me to come over and help you look for a job at your apartment?"

"I—"

"Or, we could go to a coffee shop someplace close, for a change of scenery. They'll have wi-fi."

I winced. "I don't know, I just, I—"

He stroked my cheek lovingly. "Samantha, remember. You have options. You don't need to stress about getting a second job. One is plenty. You have a ton of work ahead of you with all your classes. You shouldn't spend half your waking hours working in a convenience store or an office supply store, or whatever, when you shouldn't have to. You should be focusing on your studies more than anything else."

"I know, but—"

He held a finger to my lips. "It's okay," he nodded reassuringly, then stroked my chin with his thumb. "I totally get it. Go home, relax, do what you need to do." He smiled at me confidently and stood up. "Drive safe."

I gave him a wave and he closed my door.

I drove home and pulled out my laptop. I searched the job websites with fresh confidence.

Knowing I had some kind of a safety net had filled me with renewed vigor, but I wanted to do this on my own. I needed to prove to myself, and to my parents, that I could handle all my classes and studies, *and* find a decent part-time job that would allow me to pay all my bills myself, all while maintaining a relationship with the most wonderful man in the world.

Things were going to be great. I was going to show my parents what I could do when I put my mind to it.

I shook my head and laughed to myself.

I mean, seriously, what were the chances I'd be stuck working the late shift at a fast-food joint or some crappy convenience store?

I was totally going to find an awesome job.

Chapter 18

SAMANTHA

Ten days later, I stood behind the counter of the local Grab-n-Dash, an all night convenience store. It was still early in the afternoon, but I was already zombie-tired and had raccoon circles around my eyes.

When the manager had hired me, he'd said I couldn't work the late shift because it was too dangerous. So he gave me the afternoon shift.

Nothing like two jobs and four classes and tons of homework to tire a girl out.

The neon-urine colored uniform shirt with the Grab-n-Dash logo I had to wear was a nightmare unto itself. Made from some sort of material that only bunched and wrinkled, it made me look like a Chinese paper lantern, or the person with the lowest score on Project Runway's alternative materials challenge.

So not flattering.

Worse, the shirt trapped odors like a sponge, and I had to hand-wash it in my kitchen sink every night after work or else it smelled like grilled hot dogs.

My manager said the bright color was exciting for the customers. Yeah, maybe if it triggered seizures. I'm telling you, looking at it too long made your eyes vibrate. Beyond that, I couldn't see what was so exciting about it.

Oh yeah. I forgot to mention the equally glowing Grab-n-Dash baseball cap. My pony tail stuck out the opening in the back.

Super sexy.

But hey, I was getting paid nine bucks an hour to whore out the Grab-n-Dash mantra to everyone who walked through the doors.

"Welcome to Grab-n-Dash. How can I brighten your day?"

I had to say it every damn time.

Wasn't the blinding yellow shirt and cap enough?

My customers were teenagers off from school during the first half of my shift, and people coming home from work during the second.

The school kids always stared at me. I was never entirely sure why. One of them, who couldn't have been more than twelve years old, talked like a cross between rappers 50 Cent and Eminem. I dubbed him Eminickle, because he was about a tenth the size of 50 Cent. Eminickle asked me out every time he came in. Flattered, but no. He hadn't even hit puberty, from what I could tell.

The working stiffs were either angry and clearly irritated after a long day of work, or exhausted and mellow because they were too tired to care.

All were jonesing for sugary snacks, cigarettes, energy drinks, lottery tickets, or beer. The high school kids wanted beer and cigarettes too, but they were S.O.L.

I totally felt their pain. I suspected working at the Grab-n-Dash would inevitably turn me into a chain smoker or closet drunk. Maybe my parents were onto something by making me get a crappy job.

I hated them.

:-P

When the shop was slow, things were no better. Like now. Grab-n-Dash was a wasteland. Devoid of all activity. I stared at the clock hanging on the far wall.

The second hand seemed frozen.

I waited for it to tick. Was it stuck? I didn't remember it being stuck. It had worked earlier. Come on, move, stupid second hand! I stared at it as hard as I could. It wasn't going anywhere. I kept staring. One of us was going to blink sooner or later.

MOVE!

Nothing.

MOOOOOOOOOVE!!!!

Click.

Finally! What took you so damn long?

Okay, one second down. How many more to go? I did a quick mental approximation. My dad was right. My math skills were *always* handy. Twenty thousand? I wasn't going to make it to the end of my shift at this rate.

Amongst sundry automotive items like motor oil, wiper blades, and air fresheners, we also sold radiator fluid. You know, antifreeze. Customers actually bought it now and then. I'd heard it was sweet, and dogs would drink it, not realizing it was lethally poisonous, and it killed you slowly and painfully.

I considered pouring myself a glass.

Mmmm.

So neon green. I bet it would match my shirt and cap.

Groan.

I stared at the ICEE machines. They hummed hypnotically, always tempting me to nap while standing up. They weren't helping my focus. But I refused to fall under their sleepy spell. That didn't stop me from thinking about their cool sugary treasure waiting to tickle my tongue.

I'd always wanted to do that thing where you stuck your head under the spigot and filled your mouth until you got brain freeze.

I glanced from side to side. The store was empty.

Now would be a good time to try.

As I walked out from behind the counter to give it a try, the front door's alarm-bell bing-bonged as a new customer walked inside.

I skulked back to my post at the register. My ICEE high would have to wait.

In the past, I'd thought the sound of those bing-bong bells was kind of cute. I remember, whenever I'd walk through the doors in some random store and heard that bing-bong, I'd go back-and-forth a bunch of times, just to hear the sound. The cheery bell sounded cartoony and funny to me. I'd never understood why store clerks always glared at me when I did it.

Now I did.

I hated that fucking bell.

During peak hours, it went off every two seconds. Recently, I'd started hearing it in my sleep.

I focused on my new customer, who was still nothing more than a silhouette in the blinding afternoon sunlight coming through the front windows.

I couldn't make out any details yet.

On my first day of work, I'd felt ethically obligated to warn my boss that the name Grab-n-Dash was basically an invitation to shoplift. He utterly denied it.

Since that day, I knew for a fact that at least ten candy bars, seven bottles of water, and a bottle of aspirin had been stolen. Did I catch the snack burglars? No. My manager told me about it at the end of my first week.

I encouraged him to change the name of the store.

He said no.

I had shrugged.

He had jabbed his finger in my face, almost jamming it up my nostril. "No more shoplifters, young lady!" He had very bushy eyebrows.

I had almost laughed, because of his eyebrows, but I wanted to keep my job. Because I totally loved it.

Sigh.

Anyway, now I was hawk-eyed for shoplifters.

Everyone who came in was a candidate for Crook of the Week.

As the new customer ventured further into the store, I could finally make him out. He was a disheveled homeless man, grimy from head to toe. He moved so slowly, I didn't think he'd try to nab anything while I was watching. But I was going to need to mop up after he left. Ew.

He shuffled through the aisles, literally walking up and down each one. Twice. He was doing laps, almost like a rat in a maze. That's how I felt when I was here.

The man continued to wander aimlessly.

Was he lost?

I hoped not, otherwise I was afraid I'd have to call an exterminator.

Thankfully, he eventually made it to the refrigerators in back. He grabbed a twelve-pack of beer. Would it be his lunch, because he was a late riser, or an early dinner? It didn't matter to me. More power to him.

He shuffled up to the register.

"Welcome to Grab-n-Dash. How can I brighten your day?" Yeah, I had to say it to *every*one.

He grunted.

Whatever.

I was supposed to card anyone who looked under the age of sixty. I'm pretty sure this guy was over a hundred.

I rang up his twelver of Budweiser.

"$6.99, please," I beamed.

The guy was squinting at me. They all did. It was the shirt. It had no brightness control. Deal with it.

The man reached into his pants, and I mean, into his pants, like, right down the front, into his cash drawer, if you know what I'm saying.

He pulled out a greasy wad of bills. Like, *literally* greasy. Dark, stained like they'd been buried in a deposit of petroleum under the earth's crust for at least a billion years, the same amount of time the bills must have spent in this man's crusty pants.

He tore off a small wad and dropped it on the counter.

Um, no?

I really needed one of those radiation-proof containment-boxes you see in TV shows, the ones with the windows where you stick your arms inside the rubber gloves attached to the sides? Yeah, those. Maybe I could ask my manager to build one around the Grab-n-Dash cash counter? Or not.

I eyed the black wad on the counter with some measure of revulsion. By some measure, I meant a number higher than modern mathematics has yet been able to count.

Was it even money? Did I have to find out?

I wondered if I could just pick it up with the hot dog tongs and drop it in the register? I would totally throw the tongs away after using them instead of hanging them back on the side of the hot-dog griller. I wasn't gross. But I suspected my manager would freak out if he found the tongs in the garbage. I didn't need him yelling at me and adding more stress to my life.

I needed another solution.

I looked between the man, his dirty money, the man, his dirty money.

I couldn't bring myself to touch the blackened ball.

"I need change," he rasped.

I was ready to sob.

Then, genius struck.

I grabbed my purse from under the counter and pulled out my own comparatively immaculate cash. "You know what?! Today is your lucky day!!"

He blinked.

"Your beer is free!!!!" I sang.

"Did I win something?" he grunted doubtfully.

"No! I'm paying for it!" I smiled as widely as possible, until my cheeks hurt. I'm pretty sure what I was doing was illegal, since it was beer. Fuck it. My generosity was above the law. I was the Robin Hood of beer, and this man would pay for beer over my dead body.

"Oh, I can't take your money, young lady," he rasped, then nudged the wad toward me with his grimy hands. The ball of bills tumbled toward me, almost toppling over the edge of the counter.

I winced, thinking I would have to pick it up. I reminded myself I still had those hot-dog tongs in case of emergency.

"I can pay," he rasped.

"Oh, uh, I meant, YOU'RE THE WINNER!!!"

"Huh?" he was confused.

"You're the, uh, millionth customer today! And every millionth customer gets a free twelve pack of Budweiser!" I'm sure I sounded as sane as Charles Manson at that point.

"Really," he smiled. "You don't say?"

"I do say, I really do!" I grit my teeth into the biggest smile I could. "Take it!"

"Thank you, young lady." He picked up the twelve-pack.

Was he going to take the money? I think it was burning a hole into the countertop. Because it was radioactive. "Your money, sir? You don't want to forget your money!" *Please don't forget your money!!!*

He smiled at me, revealing one tooth. "Thank you, young lady. You're a peach. You really are."

"You're welcome!!" I grimaced.

He set the twelve-pack down, scooped up the wad, pulled the waistband of his dirty cash drawer open, and dropped his wad inside. I know, it was as wrong as it sounded.

The poor man shambled outside.

Toward the end of my shift, the busy after-work crowd had thinned to nothing. I eyed the ICEE machine.

I really needed a brain freeze, otherwise my brain was going to instruct me to drink that antifreeze before the end of my shift. Again, I checked that the coast was clear. I tiptoed over to the ICEE dispenser. Not that anyone would've heard me.

I leaned my head under it. It was sort of awkward, but I was determined to get my mouth beneath the spout without wrapping my lips around it. Blue-raspberry, here I come. I was going to drown myself in it and brain freeze away my boredom.

I grabbed the lever with my hand and—

"Sam, what are you doing?!" Romeo laughed.

I twisted around and managed to bang my forehead against the spigot. "Ow!!"

"You okay?"

"Yeah." I rubbed my forehead.

"Shouldn't you use a cup?" he smiled.

"Uh...we have to pay for them."

"You don't get free ICEEs?"

"No."

"Your boss is a miser."

"He has bushy eyebrows," I said. "Didn't Scrooge have bushy eyebrows? I think the ghosts of Christmas past, present, and future visited me today."

"Oh, Sam, that's terrible. This situation *definitely* calls for an ICEE," Romeo smiled and leaned under the blue-raspberry spout. He turned the lever before I could stop him. Blue-raspberry funneled into his mouth. "Ahh, eah, at's oooo oooood." He sounded exactly like Homer Simpson.

I broke into laughter.

Romeo kept going, swallowing more and more and more ICEE slush. "Stop, Romeo! You're going to hurt yourself!" I pushed the lever closed.

Romeo stood back up, an ICEE-eating grin on his face. His eyes were watering.

"Are you okay?" I asked, concerned.

Looking around nervously, he choked out a cough.

He looked back at me, eyes glazed.

"Romeo? Are you okay?" I was getting worried.

He blinked several times forcefully, then his face pinched to a pinpoint. "Owwwwww!!" he hollered in extreme pain. "My head!!!!"

I burst out laughing. Sometimes, when doing something stupid, it was safer to let the idiots go first. "Do you want some hot coffee or something?" I offered compassionately.

Romeo shook his head like a wet dog. His lips flapped and he made a "Gugga-gugga-gugga" noise, then winced and jammed the heels of his hands into his eyes. "My eyes feel like someone's stabbing them!"

"Let me get you some hot water." I filled a coffee cup with hot water, then added cold water from the soda machine until it wasn't scalding. "Drink this."

Romeo gulped it down.

"Hold some in your mouth," I said, "to warm your, ah, brain?"

He did. A look of relief washed over his face.

"Don't choke on it," I cautioned.

He swallowed it carefully down.

"Better?"

He nodded. "Remind me never to do that again."

"Will do. Where's Kamiko?" She and Romeo always seemed to be joined at the hip, but not in the way we all know Romeo liked to join at hips.

"Kamiko has some lab for Biology. I think she said they're dissecting unicorns today. So, how's the old Grab-n-Dash treating you, Sam?"

I returned to my seat behind the cash register. "Fantastic," I said sarcastically.

"Sorry," he said sympathetically. "Are you at least managing to get some studying done?"

"No. I'm not supposed to. Anyway, it's usually pretty busy. I doubt I could concentrate."

"Sam, I know you need the money, because of your parents and all, and I'd totally offer to have you live with me in the dorms, but I wouldn't want you ruining my reputation. I mean, if people saw a girl sleeping in my room, they'd think I was *straight*," he said, as if sniffing dirty sweat socks.

I giggled. "Thanks anyway. I'm doing okay. As long as I don't have any other bad news drop into my lap this quarter, I'll be fine," I smiled nervously.

Because, it *was* possible that things could get worse, no matter how unlikely that seemed.

I crossed my fingers and sighed to myself. I sure hoped not. I didn't think I could handle anything else.

When business started to pick up, Romeo left. I thanked him for keeping me company, but he knew I needed to work.

Despite the frenzy of customers over the remainder of my shift, a sense of loneliness permeated my bones and a growing worry filled my belly. Something was wrong, but I couldn't put my finger on what it was. I texted Christos, but never received a reply.

When I finished my shift at seven, I called him. But all I received in answer was a text.

Slammed busy at studio. Talk later.

I really, *really* hoped this wasn't becoming a routine with us.

SAMANTHA

Another week had gone by and nothing had changed. Christos was always busy at his studio. I was always busy at work, or in class, or studying.

I was overwhelmed. I slept poorly and my stress level was pushed to the max. It was starting to mess with my head. I noticed it recently in sculpting class.

It was that stupid Hunter Blakeley.

Not that he was doing anything different. He still hit on me with annoying regularity, but I blew him off with equal frequency. It wasn't him.

It was the sculpting.

Sculpting was some kind of crazy voodoo magic, I'm telling you. Making a sculpture of a naked person standing right in front of you connected you to their body in an intimate way, whether you wanted it to or not. In Life Drawing last quarter, this hadn't been a problem. One reason was that none of the male models had been hot, other than Christos.

Yes Hunter was hot, but I think sculpting him made my anxiety worse than if I'd been drawing him.

In drawing, you put down charcoal on paper in a visual representation of what you were looking at. Your contact with the two-dimensional drawing surface was through the tip of your pencil.

Sculpting, on the other hand, required that you use your hands and fingers to shape the three-dimensional sculpture. To touch it. Lately, I'd started noticing that weird voodoo magic at work. On me.

The more I worked over my sculpture of Hunter, touching it, massaging it, and caressing the clay into an emulation of Hunter's musculature, the more it sort of felt like, well…like I was touching Hunter. And I had the eerie feeling *he* somehow felt it. Stupid, I know.

The moment I finally realized this, I had gasped quietly and pulled my fingers away from my sculpture, as if I'd been touching his naked flesh.

I had been about to reshape the inner thigh of Sculpture Hunter's right leg, right up near his…yes. His package, which hung from my sculpture in a 1/3rd scale representation of his actual… package.

You had to include the clay package because if you didn't, it constantly threw your proportions off. Most of the other students had a little clay blob to represent the man bits, as did I. Romeo, of course, had made his totally lifelike down to every mushroomy detail.

But even with my blobby, nondescript lump hanging between Sculpture Hunter's legs, there was that final, distinctive moment when I'd felt like I was about to bump the side of my hand into Hunter's *actual* package as I slid my fingers between the thighs of Sculpture Hunter.

I suddenly stopped myself, feeling like I was about to cheat on Christos somehow. I couldn't explain it.

Was I *attracted* to Hunter? I shuddered.

No.

There was no way.

I took a deep breath and looked around the room at the other students. All were busy working away, their faces intense with concentration.

Was I the only one having trouble with this part?

I steeled myself. I could do this. It was just a class assignment, right? Just lumps and blobs of clay. Nothing more.

Right?

I took a deep breath and tried again. I ran my fingers up the inside of Sculpture Hunter's legs. It wasn't so bad. I pressed my fingers more firmly against Sculpture Hunter's thighs, right near his blobby package.

That was when I noticed Hunter smirking right at me. Like he'd felt my touch.

OMG! Had he?

I yanked my hands away.

My face boiled with embarrassment as I grabbed a sculpting tool and busily worked over Sculpture Hunter's left foot. I felt my cheeks flashing like fire engine lights.

That big toe on Sculpture Hunter was WAY too big! Better trim it down before it ruined everything! Big toes! Only thinking about big toes!

I tried not to notice that Hunter's smile had widened.

Oh, boy. He'd caught me good. I'm sure he would take this as an invitation to hit on me with new purpose.

The moment class was over that day, I bolted out of the classroom. I needed to get away from everyone.

I didn't even wait for Romeo.

I needed some fresh air.

Badly.

I feared something monumental in my life was shifting. I didn't understand it at all. But I knew one thing:

I didn't like the feeling that was making my hands shake one bit.

Change was coming.

SAMANTHA

When I reached the Student Center, I texted Madison to see if she was around campus still.

At the library she texted back, *fourth floor.*

C u there in five.

I walked to the library and took the elevator to the fourth floor. The Main Library had windows all the way around and had a great view of all of San Diego. Studying in it was like having your own corner office in a high-rise building. The skies were clear and I could see for miles.

I circled the fourth floor until I found Madison in one of the study rooms. At this point in the quarter, there was little competition for study space. I walked in and closed the door behind me. Madison was surrounded by her books and her laptop on the large table.

"What up, Mads!"

"Hey, Sam!" she smiled. "How's SDU's star artist doing today?" She held up her hand for a high-five.

I gave it a friendly smack. "Artist, maybe," I sighed as I sat down. "I don't know about the star part."

"Don't deny it, Sam, you know you're totally rockin' the lady balls since changing your major to Art."

I grimaced. "Okay, I know some women say 'lady balls' all the time nowadays, but seriously, can you explain it? I mean, do guys go around saying 'Dude, you're totally rocking the man clitoris!' or 'Dude, I've got brass man-labia hanging between my legs!'? No! Because no guy would *ever* say that. It doesn't make any sense."

Madison smiled thoughtfully. "You're right, Sam. You're absolutely right. No more lady balls for either one of us." We exchanged another high-five. "Maybe you should change your major to Gender Studies," she joked.

"You might be onto something."

Madison giggled. "But I *have* been with one guy who had a man-clitoris, or a very small willy-nilly. Emphasis on the nilly part."

"You so did not say that!" I guffawed.

Another high-five.

"It's not Jake, is it?" I asked, suddenly mortified.

"No!" Madison protested. "Jake totally has man balls and a man dick. No woman parts whatsoever."

"Oh, phew. I was ready to feel bad for you."

"Nope, Jake's good to go. And go, and go, and go."

I leaned into her, giggling.

"Keep it down in here, this is a library and some people are trying to study," Hunter said, his head sticking through the door.

I frowned, "What are you doing here?" How the hell did he find me? Um, stalker?

"I needed to look something up," he smiled.

"You're not even a student here," I said.

"Am I missing something?" Madison asked.

"Oh, uh, this is Hunter Blakeley," I said sourly, "he's the model in my sculpting class."

He took that as his cue to walk completely into the study room and close the door behind him.

"Ooh," Madison twinkled her nose, "does that mean Sam gets to look at you naked?"

"Mads!" I bumped her knee under the table with mine.

She took the hint and said no more.

Hunter didn't waste any time picking up the slack. "It's all part of the job description."

"What is your job, anyway?" I asked. "Do you actually do anything besides model for Bittinger's class and stalk me?"

"Of course I do," he said casually.

"Do what?" I sneered. "Stalk tons of other uninterested young women?"

"No," he smiled, undeterred, "outside of class, I model for all kinds of things. Some pretty high profile work."

"Like what?" Madison asked innocently.

He chuckled. "You're probably not going to believe this…"

He was probably right.

"You know how when you buy underwear for guys," he grinned proudly, "there's always a photo of some dude with amazing abs and a huge, uh, package printed on the, uh, package?"

"Yeah?" I said. Not that I bought men's underwear, but I'd seen the "packages" he was talking about.

"I'm that guy," Hunter smiled.

I frowned. It seemed too ridiculous to be true. But I knew firsthand that he was certainly large enough to fill a pair of briefs.

"You're the package guy?" Madison gawked.

"Totally." He nodded and smiled. "I still have residuals coming in from underwear I did four years ago."

The study room had windows that faced into the library, so other students could see us inside. Hunter glanced around cautiously, as if he was about to reveal secret intelligence vital to the preservation of the United States of America, and didn't want any stray SDU students hearing what he had to say and selling the information to the Taliban. When Hunter was sure the coast was clear, he leaned toward Madison and me and muttered conspiratorially, "The dirty secret none of the underwear manufacturers want you to know is, I'm 'that guy' for *all* of them." He stood up to his full height, which was over six feet, and nodded, very proud of himself.

I rolled my eyes. I was in the midst of a celebrity. Groan. I considered begging him for an autograph. But…no.

"I also do ads for fitness equipment," Hunter winked.

"Sorry, haven't seen any of those," I said. Hunter was starting to strike me as the sort of guy who spent more time in front of a mirror than any woman ever would.

"Me neither," Madison said, picking up on my vibe.

"Well, I also do runway work," he said, "but that's seasonal."

When I pictured Hunter doing runway work, I imagined him at the airport with the DJ headphones and the glowing red sticks, waving in jumbo jets, wearing only tighty-whiteys and work boots. I snickered, but tried to cover it up.

Hunter flashed his amber eyes at us. "What? Did I miss something?" he smiled hopefully.

Mine and Madison's deflating interest was shriveling up his ego. I realized we needed to let him off the hook before he shriveled up any further and lost his dick modeling contracts.

Crinkling my nose, I said, "We kind of need to study, Hunter."

"I can come back later," he offered hopefully. "Maybe walk you to your car?"

As nice as the guy seemed, he tried way too hard, and he didn't listen. I think I'd told him I wasn't interested, oh, I don't know, every time I saw him? Okay, one more time.

"Hunter, you're a sweet guy. But I'm not going out with you, no matter how many times you offer to walk me to my car. Please respect the fact that I have a boyfriend."

"I do. But you have the wrong one."

I dropped my head into my forearms on the table. I had walked right into that one. "Please, Hunter, I'm begging you—"

"That's more like it," he chuckled. "I like it when you beg."

"—to go away." I laughed that desperate laugh when you don't want to be rude, but you can't think of anything else to say to make a person go away.

He nodded confidently. "No worries. I'll see you in Bittinger's class." He winked at me when he walked out.

Why did he always have to wink?

"Wow, what a stalker," Madison said. "Cute stalker, but man, he was desperate. Or head-over heels for you know who!" she grinned.

I dropped my head back into my hands. "No, please no. I've tried to be nice, but no matter what I tell him, he keeps coming back."

"You're not sending him mixed signals, are you?"

"What?! No! Not at all. I've told him over and over again I'm not interested."

"Maybe you're telling him too forcefully," Madison suggested.

"I'd rather not tell him at all, but he won't leave me alone," I groaned as I pulled my laptop out of my book bag and turned it on.

"He was pretty hot," Madison said thoughtfully.

"You think so?"

"Are you blind? Of course he was."

"But," I said nervously, "isn't it weird to be attracted to another guy when you're dating Jake?"

"Wait, are you saying you're attracted to this guy Hunter?" Madison gasped. "What about Christos?"

"What? No! Don't turn this around on me! I'm totally attracted to Christos. He's uber hot. Hunter isn't even close." I took a relaxing breath. "But I mean, Hunter *is* good looking. How could I not notice when he stands naked ten feet away from me every time I have sculpting class?"

Madison gave me a long, considering look. After a minute, she spoke, "Sam, relax. When you fall in love, the rest of the world doesn't cease to exist. It's still filled with attractive people. If you happen to notice that some random guy is hot, who cares?"

"I'm sorry, Mads. You're right. I guess it's just bugging me because I'm being forced to stare at the same random guy naked, several hours at a stretch. Twice a week. For ten weeks straight."

"Don't worry, Sam. You'll be over him sooner or later. His cock will become invisible to you," she grinned.

"Like someone lopped it off?" I smiled hopefully.

"That's not a bad idea," she giggled. "But no, eventually you just won't care anymore. Staring at Hunter's hickory dickory will become business as usual."

I laughed. "That is *so* wrong."

"What, it's made of wood, isn't it?" she giggled.

Madison putting the idea of wood into the same notion as Hunter's unmentionables was having the wrong effect. "Not helping," I warned.

Madison cackled at me. "Fine, then pretend it's made of broken glass."

I winced. "Ew!"

"Ok, how about a red-hot rod of iron?"

"Not helping!"

"Okay, fine! Pretend his thing is a gun and bullets come out," she giggled. "But make sure his safety is on when he's cocked and loaded!"

"Mads! Stop!"

We both broke into laughter.

Chapter 19

SAMANTHA

As much as I wanted to, I still hadn't agreed to move in with Christos. I felt like I was too young and it was too soon. No matter how much I missed seeing him, no matter how hard I had to work to pay my bills, moving in seemed too big a step.

The other pressing problem was my parents. How could I possibly tell them? They'd go thermo-nuclear. I couldn't imagine telling them. But if I *did* move in with Christos, I would have to. My parents had co-signed my lease on my apartment, and at the very least, they would deserve to know my new address, in case of emergencies, or whatever.

Groan.

Moving in would have to wait.

Fortunately, in the mean time, Christos and I had solved the problem of not seeing each other enough by me coming over to work at the studio space he'd made for me.

I loved it. Now I was seeing Christos several days a week, and Spiridon as well, who obviously loved having me around too.

The only downside to this arrangement was working in the studio alongside Christos proved a bit more of a challenge than I'd planned.

I hadn't factored in the constant supply of nude cuties parading through.

Whenever Christos had a naked model sitting in front of him, thrusting her bouncy bits in his face, and by extension mine, I had to restrain my urge to storm over and throw blankets over the women on a minute-by-minute basis.

Sigh.

But I reminded myself, Christos was making art. Not hosting a live sex show. Yes, there was a difference. Not that I'd been to a live sex show, but I'm pretty sure they were more exciting than a nude woman sitting frozen in one position for four hours, minus the brief breaks.

Double Sigh. I would get used to it. It was art, not porn. Art!

Art!!

Seriously, it didn't bother me.

Not one bit.

Besides, who was I to judge? I stared at naked Hunter all the time these days, and he *did* throw himself at me constantly, yet Christos didn't care. I could picture Lame Damian freaking out if he'd found out I'd been staring at a hot guy like Hunter naked twice a week.

Sigh. I didn't want to be a Lamian. Believe it or not, Christos trusted me. Imagine that. I realized I owed it to him to trust him too. It helped I was on hand to keep an eye on him.

JUST in case.

Because I was in *NO* way jealous.

Seriously.

Not jealous at *ALL*.

>:-|

The model today was Isabella. She'd been around a lot lately. Her body was perfect, as in, not one flaw. Her skin had neither freckle nor mole. Her dark hair was luxuriant, her cheekbones delicate and symmetrical, her eyes alluring and radiant, her mouth inviting and plump. Her proportions were perfect, her breasts full, her waist tiny, her hips womanly.

Not one bit jealous! Not a molecule of jealousy in me. If I walked through a jealousy detector, like, the most sensitive jealousy detector *ever* invented, it wouldn't beep and sirens wouldn't go off.

Because I. Wasn't. Jealous.

I did my best to ignore Isabella. She ignored me with casual ease. Snooty bitch. I mean, she was a terrific model. Never moved a muscle. Totally professional.

I was convinced that Isabella was toying with me every time she came to the studio. She tried to lay claim to Christos in little ways. Touching him on the shoulder during breaks, offering to get him water, instead of him doing it for her. Giggling like a porn star at everything he said. Even when he said things to her like, "(*picture Christos holding his mouth open while no sound came out*)."

You get the idea.

Constantly.

Me and her were best friends.

Fake Smile!

To Christos' credit, he handled everything completely professionally. He never seemed nervous, never worried that I was keeping an eye on him.

During one of the rare breaks when Isabella *wasn't* hovering around him, Christos walked over to where I sat at my easel, working on my painting of an arrangement of three Calla Lilies.

"Wow, that's coming along great, *agápi mou*. I love your composition, the way you've painted the corner of the window behind the lilies, framing the vase."

"Thanks, Christos," I smiled.

He scrutinized the painting more closely. "Nice brushwork on the petals. And you really nailed the warm and cool of the white. Normally, people just squeeze white paint out of the tube. But I can see you've mixed in hints of lemon yellow for the cool whites and cadmium yellow deep for the warm whites. Excellent," he smiled and pecked me on the lips. "You're a natural, like I've always said."

"Wow," I smiled, "you never miss anything when it comes to painting."

But I think he might have missed my Isabella-induced all-day discomfort. I had a tinge of worry that Christos' peck on my lips was too brief, too distant, like he didn't want to look too familiar with me in front of Isabella.

Crap. I realized I was making myself miserable by making things up, looking for problems that probably weren't there. Isabella wasn't even in the room. So there was nothing for me to worry about, right?

"Is it just me, or is Isabella not picking up on my signals?"

Dread punched my heart. Signals? As in, *Hey baby, as soon as my dumpy girlfriend Samantha isn't looking, we should totally jump each other like jaguars.* And Isabella would purr like Catwoman, *Rawr!*

I so needed to murder her before she left today. I wondered if you could find instructions on the internet for how to cut a car's brake lines? Wasn't that what they always did on TV shows?

"Samantha? You there?" Christos asked.

"Oh, sorry. What were you saying?" I asked guiltily.

"I just said, I've told Isabella a hundred times I have a girlfriend, who I love, who is sitting twenty feet away from us. Chick can't take a hint. And by hint I mean hammer, because, Jesus Christ, what part of 'girlfriend sitting right over there' is she not picking up on?" Christos smirked and smiled at me while caressing my cheek with his thumb.

Oh, *that's* what my boyfriend was saying.

He continued, "You'd think by now Isabella would've realized that she's so not in your league, and would've just given up on me. I guess some rare women aren't cursed with the female 'I'm ugly' gene, and end up over-rating themselves."

Was he talking about the same Isabella I had dagger eyes for? The perfect one he was painting?

"Not everyone can be as blessed by beauty as you, *agápi mou*," he smiled.

Wait, was Christos bullshitting me? I searched his eyes.

All I saw was honesty and love.

I was an idiot for doubting him and...*swoon*.

I wondered if Christos could send Isabella home early today. Not because I was jealous, but because I desperately needed to jump him right at that moment.

Isabella walked back into the studio from the back deck, where she had spent her break looking at the view.

"More painting?" Isabella asked.

Party pooper. I sighed. Back to my painting of Calla Lilies. At least they were turning out nice.

"You know what?" Christos asked.

"Yes?" Isabella said hopefully.

"Why don't we finish up early today. I'm feeling a bit tired."

Christos had read my mind. Take *that* you, uh, nice lady model.

"No!" Isabella pouted.

Home wrecker.

"Sorry, Isabella," Christos said. "I really need a break myself. We can pick up next time."

"Okay, Christos," she said in her thick accent. "I do whatever you say." Yes, she fanned her eyelashes at him.

I was now officially above looking daggers at her anymore.

Christos ushered Isabella out as quickly as he could. She dragged her feet like a kid being told it was bedtime. To me, she seemed as pouty as a seven-year-old, so it was an apt description. Was she like this all the time with Christos?

Probably.

I needed to research brake lines tonight.

When Christos finally got Isabella out of the house, I decided to surprise him when he came back in the studio. I'd become more adventurous in the past few weeks, all because of Christos. He was always encouraging me, reminding me how wonderful I was, how beautiful I was. His words were starting to sink in.

Maybe now was a good time to experiment with a little adventure.

I walked over to the painting he was doing of Isabella. It was gigantic, and it was truly amazing. He'd finished the face, and had painted a good deal of the body. The palette lying in front of the easel was covered in smears of paint. Brushes soaked in jars, paint-stained paper towels filled a small trash can.

I was in awe of Christos' talent. I felt like watching him work was as close as anyone would ever come to being in the studio of a Rembrandt or a Vermeer or a Velazquez. Christos was a living master of oil painting, yet he was still so young. And he was all mine.

I eyed the divan where Isabella had been posing in the nude all afternoon. I was going to take off all my clothes and lie down on it. I wanted to be waiting for Christos when he came back into the room.

Was I marking my territory? If Christos and I had sex on the divan in the next two minutes, I suppose you could say that I was. Fuck it.

This was *my* studio, bitches! :-P

I untied my painting smock and hung it over the back of Christos' chair in front of the easel. Then I pulled my sweater and t-shirt up together. When it was over my head, and my nearly-naked torso was exposed to the world, save for my bra, I heard voices in the house, heading toward the studio.

Shit!

Christos and…a woman's voice!

Double shit!

I yanked my shirt and sweater back on, mussing my scrunchie. Hair fell out of my pony-tail in random strands around my face. I grabbed my painting smock and tied it on as I trotted over to my own easel and plopped down, smoothing my hair and hurriedly redoing my scrunchie.

I almost got caught naked! I was never doing that again!

My cheeks burned, but hopefully my blush would be the only evidence of my indiscrete impulses.

Christos walked into the studio.

Followed by Tiffany Queenston-Micehouse. Wow, she really knew how to rain on my parade. She was a practiced expert. I ducked behind my easel, hoping she wouldn't see me and pull out a handgun or maybe a flamethrower.

The studio was a maze of paintings and easels between the entrance and me, so she might not notice me in the back.

"Who was that girl outside," Tiffany asked Christos at the far end of the studio.

"Isabella? She's one of the models Brandon sent me. Down from L.A. I think she does work for Vogue and all the other fashion mags."

"She sure is beautiful," Tiffany said. "Brandon knows how to pick 'em."

"I guess," Christos said.

"But Isabella isn't as beautiful as me, right?" Tiffany purred while inspecting the painting of Isabella, her back facing me. She turned slightly and thrust her ass out at Christos. In nature, that was called presenting.

Bitch!

"No one's as beautiful as you, Tiffany," Christos said sarcastically, glancing at me between the frames of several easels while rolling his eyes and shaking his head. He pointed at Tiffany's jutting butt and raised his eyebrows in a "can you believe her?" look.

I stifled a giggle.

"How beautiful *am* I?" Tiffany asked, leaning into Christos' chest.

Double Bitch!

"Do you need some more bait for your hook, or are you going to keep fishing for compliments all day?" Christos asked, audibly frustrated. "You know, fly-casting style, just throwing the lure out there over and over, and *over*, again? Even when this fish isn't biting?"

I did the Happy Dance in my head. Yeah, Christos!

"Fine," Tiffany huffed. "I came on business anyway. Well," her voice went coquette, "business *and* pleasure."

"Do tell," Christos said, perturbed.

"Daddy told me to offer you $75,000 to paint me nude."

"Your dad is so generous. A true prince."

"Well, am I worth it?" Tiffany asked coyly.

"Hey, Samantha," Christos hollered, "do you think seventy-five K is a fair price for me to paint Tiff?"

"Do you have to paint her live, in person day after day, or can you use a photo?" I hollered from my hiding place.

"Huh? Who's here?" Tiffany asked, concerned.

"Yeah, it has to be live, in person," Christos hollered to me.

"Then charge her *two* seventy-five," I giggled.

"Who is that?" Tiffany demanded.

I came out of hiding. "Hey, Tiff," I said casually.

"You," Tiffany scowled the second she saw me. "*You* don't call me Tiff. Understand?"

I ignored her demand. "Make sure she pays cash this time. Up front."

"She's right," Christos said to Tiffany. "Cash up front." He held out his palm

Tiffany looked between Christos and me like a trapped hyena bitch. "I see you've moved your charwoman into the estate. If she has some time off, perhaps she can clean my toilets as well?"

Triple Bitch!

Where was *my* flamethrower! Tiff was going down in a blaze of glory!

"I would never subject Samantha to the shit that comes out of your ass, Tiffany," Christos smiled, "or my worst enemies, for that matter."

Tiffany growled. I don't mean that figuratively. I mean, she literally went, "Gaaarrrr," low in her throat while her lips peeled back over her fangs. I'd never seen a grown woman do that before. Where was my camera?

I giggled, but covered my mouth politely.

"Can I show you the door?" Christos asked her.

"I know my way out."

Tiffany stalked out, slammed the front door behind her, and literally screamed in the driveway.

Me and Christos heard it clear back in the studio.

We both erupted with laughter.

SAMANTHA

Although Christos and I had finally been making time for each other, Kamiko had fallen completely off my radar, with the exception of Oil Painting class.

So Romeo and I made a special effort to swing by her dorm room together in the block of time I had after classes but before my shift at Grab-n-Dash. I had plenty of homework to do that day, but I was sure I could squeeze it in later that evening.

Who needed sleep?

Kamiko ushered me and Romeo into the suite of rooms where she lived in Paiute Hall.

"Hey guys!" she smiled. "I can't wait to show you what I've been doing!"

"Are you making your own Hentai anime porn?" Romeo asked, "The kind with all the penetrating serpents? I'd totally love to see it!"

"No!" she smacked his arm. "I've been working on my submissions for Charboneau Gallery's upcoming Contemporary Artists show."

We all walked through the door to her double room at the back of the suite.

"Where's your roommate?" I asked.

"She went to the library to study."

All of Kamiko's art supplies were crammed onto her side of the room and there was almost no space to move or sit down. Her bed had a tarp over it with a dozen small paintings resting on top.

Romeo leaned over to pick up one of the paintings.

"Be careful," Kamiko said, "most of those are still wet."

Oil paintings could take days or even weeks to dry, depending on how thickly you applied the paint, and you had to be careful not to touch them until they dried. I knew, because a week ago, I'd bumped into one of my studies from class that I'd had drying in my apartment. I had been wearing a white sweater and my elbow had smeared across the canvas and come away looking like unicorn vomit. Bye-bye sweater.

"Where do you sleep?" Romeo asked Kamiko. "With the art?"

"I put the tarp on the floor at night," she said.

"Aren't you afraid you'll step on your paintings when you have to get up to go to the bathroom?"

"I'm careful," Kamiko shrugged her shoulders.

"You're becoming a dorm-room hoarder," Romeo joked.

Ignoring him, Kamiko said, "As soon as they're dry, I'll stack them out of the way."

"You've gone crazy, Kamiko!" I smiled. "You have like, twenty awesome paintings in here!"

The paintings had all manner of subjects. Some I recognized from our Oil Painting class, but most were new. She had painted a variety of outdoor scenes: a sunlit garden, the cliffs by the beach, crashing waves on the shore, sailboats at the marina, even a seagull that was totally lifelike. They were all really good.

"Ever since Brandon told me about the Contemporary Artists show," Kamiko said, "I've been doing studies almost every day. I totally want to get one of my pieces into that show."

"Aren't you worried about taking too much time away from all your pre-med classes?" Romeo asked.

"Yeah," she sighed, "but I can't help myself. Painting is way more fun," she giggled. "Don't tell my parents," she said nervously.

Romeo pulled out his cell phone and mimed dialing. "Bring!," he said. "Bring! Oh, hello, Mrs. Nishimura? Yeah, this is Romeo Fabiano, Kamiko's friend. Yeah, Kamiko is totally bailing on her Biology homework and spending all her time painting. Yeah, she's crazy. Thought you'd like to know." He mimed ending the call and shoved the phone in his pocket. "She said she'd be here with the entire family to intervene in about an hour. Oh, and you have been disowned. But they're still coming anyway. Said something about a caning."

"I thought caning was only in Singapore," I offered.

"Her parents are very multi-cultural," Romeo joked. I knew that Romeo had met Kamiko's family and knew them pretty well.

"They wouldn't do that, would they?" I asked.

"No way!" Kamiko said. "Caning uses a rattan stick. My parents prefer those bamboo samurai swords the kendo guys use. They're called shinai, and have been known to break bones."

"What?!" I was shocked. "You're kidding, right?"

"Half," Kamiko said morosely. "Anyway, which painting do you guys think I should submit to Charboneau?"

"They're all so good," I said.

Kamiko was amazingly talented. I had to keep reminding myself that I was getting better every day too, even though it seemed like Kamiko was always outpacing me.

"She's right," Romeo said. "I can't pick one. Maybe you should take all of them down to show Brandsome."

"That's what I was thinking," Kamiko said. "So I took photos of them all and printed them out." She held out a black portfolio folder filled with color prints of each painting in the plastic sleeves. A business card mounted on the front, printed with elegant script, read, "The Artwork of Kamiko Nishimura." Below her name was her contact information.

"You even made your own business card!" I marveled. "So professional."

"I did it all on my computer," she grinned.

I flipped through it. "Wow, Kamiko. It looks amazing."

"Thanks," she smiled. "I had planned on going by the gallery later this afternoon. Do you guys want to go?"

"I've got section," Romeo said. "I'm having a terrible time with my scene for Playwriting class. I need to talk to the TA and get some suggestions. Right after, I have Acting class."

I shook my head. "I can never get over how awesome your class schedule is, Romeo."

Kamiko looked at me hopefully. "Sam, do you want to go? I'm sort of nervous about showing my work to Brandon."

"That's only because he makes your thighs quiver," Romeo joked.

"He does not!" Kamiko blurted.

"Sounds like love to me," Romeo smiled. "Well, I'm going to run, you guys. Have fun at the gallery. Sam, make sure to keep a tight leash on Kamiko, or she'll jump all over Brandon and ruin her chances of getting in the art show."

"I will not!" Kamiko protested.

Romeo gave me a knowing nod and rolled his eyes. "She's so in love with Brandsome. Bye guys," he waved as he walked out.

Kamiko turned to me with a pleading look on her face. "I am *not* in love with Brandsome."

"I believe you, Kamiko," I giggled.

SAMANTHA

Kamiko and I made the short drive from SDU down to La Jolla in my VW. I took the scenic route along Torrey Pines Road. We parked on the street and made the short walk to Charboneau Gallery.

I hadn't been to the gallery since Christos' show last year. It was drastically different during the day time. There were no crowds, and all new art hung on the walls. The doors were open, but the place seemed empty.

Kamiko and I stood in the middle of the main room, looking around.

"Where is everyone?" I asked.

"I called Brandon this morning and he said he'd be here all afternoon," Kamiko said uncertainly.

We both turned to see Brandon coasting down the stairs.

Kamiko leaned toward me and whispered, "He's so hot!"

Halfway down the stairs, Brandon said enthusiastically, "Greetings, you two!" His face beamed as he looked at us. It had been weeks since New Year's Eve. Kamiko's crush on Brandon was obvious to all of us. He'd been such a gentleman with her, but was he interested?

"How have you been, Samantha?" he asked, extending his hand.

I offered mine and he kissed it. I pulled my hand free as soon as I could. Luckily, Kamiko hadn't noticed. She was too busy gushing over Brandon.

"Kamiko," Brandon said, extending his hand to her, "good to see you."

Kamiko offered her hand, but Brandon merely shook it.

I winced. Oh boy. This was not good. My only hope was for Kamiko to continue crushing so hard she wouldn't notice his focus on me.

"To what do I owe the pleasure?" Brandon asked.

Kamiko blinked. "I called about showing you my samples? For the Contemporary Artists show?" She held up her portfolio.

He didn't actually take the portfolio from her. "That's right," Brandon smiled his snake-charmer smile. "My apologies, things have been intense around here lately."

I wasn't fooled. I needed to strategize my way out of this before Brandon broke Kamiko's heart by throwing himself at me. I wasn't sure if he actually wanted to see her art, or if he was blowing smoke up Kamiko's ass. Maybe the best solution was to extract both of us from the situation.

Had Brandon been completely drunk on New Year's Eve with Kamiko or just being polite? Was there even a remote chance he liked her? I had no way to know.

Brandon motioned toward the stairs. "Why don't we go up to my office and I can look your samples over?"

"Okay," Kamiko beamed.

The three of us went up the staircase and into his office. The walls were covered with dozens of framed paintings in a variety of artistic styles. I guessed they were from the many artists who had sold art through Charboneau Gallery over the years.

Brandon sat behind his desk while me and Kamiko sat in the leather chairs in front of it.

"Samantha, have you seen much of Christos lately?" Brandon asked. "He must be busy with all the new work I'm sending him."

Was he insinuating that Christos was too busy for me? Or just stating the obvious? With Brandon, I told myself it was safe to assume he never did the obvious. The solution: lie through my teeth. "Oh," I said, "I'm not sure. I just know we spend a ton of time together. I sometimes wonder when he even finds time to paint—" Okay, shut up now. Don't make things worse.

I watched Brandon closely while he took in what I'd said.

"Mmm," he poker-faced. He wasn't giving up anything. "So, Kamiko. Your art."

"Yeah!" Kamiko handed him her portfolio.

He flipped through it casually. Was he looking at the paintings at all, or me? I wasn't sure, but his eyes were darting at me way too much.

"What do you think?" Kamiko beamed, on the edge of her seat, her eyebrows a mile high.

He smiled pleasantly. "It's solid work, Kamiko. But it's very standard."

Kamiko's brows fell from the sky and crashed over her eyes in a knitted, garbled line. "Oh," she sighed.

Brandon sighed, "The Contemporary Artist's show at Charboneau Gallery is about new ideas, risky ideas. What you have here are some very skillful studies. They are excellent studies. Fine workmanship. But they're still studies."

Kamiko seemed to be sinking into her chair like it was made of quicksand. Poor thing.

I didn't know what to do.

Brandon quickly sensed Kamiko's change in mood. "I have no doubt you could sell your work to any of a number of different galleries," he said optimistically. "There is always a demand for beautifully rendered traditional imagery."

Kamiko slouched over despondently.

"I could give you some names of other galleries," Brandon said encouragingly. "I could even make some calls myself, put in a good word for you."

I suddenly realized why Kamiko was shutting down. It wasn't the fact that Charboneau Gallery wasn't the right fit for her amazing work. It was that Brandon wasn't interested in her paintings. Her passion. I was willing to bet he wasn't very interested in Kamiko, either, but his cursory dismissal of her art was a harsh enough rejection on its own.

I wanted to reach over and console her, but I was afraid if I did, she'd crack and tears would come gushing out.

"Maybe she could paint something else?" I suggested animatedly. "Couldn't you do something different, Kamiko?" I encouraged.

Kamiko looked at me like she was dying. Painfully.

"I'm sure you could," I said. "I don't know, see what some other artists are doing? Try something different?" I was grasping at straws. "Isn't that right, Brandon?"

His eyes goggled at me like he was helpless.

I wasn't letting him off the hook that easily. "Isn't that *right*, Brandon?" I insisted.

"Oh," he swallowed, "yeah. If Kamiko wanted to prepare some new samples, I would be happy to look at them."

Damn right he would. "Maybe you could give her some ideas about what to paint? *Brandon?*"

"I don't know…" he waffled, "I'm no artist…"

"But maybe you could suggest some artists for her to study? Some artists from past shows maybe?" Christos had suggested as much to me a week ago. I was merely parroting his words back to Brandon.

Kamiko's eyes brightened. "Yeah, I could do that."

Brandon's look of guilt faded as he reached into a desk drawer. "I've got just the thing." He pulled out a beautifully printed booklet. "The catalog from last year's show." He set it on the desk in front of Kamiko, so it faced her, and opened it up. "This will give you an idea of the work we accepted last year."

Kamiko leaned over and started flipping through the pages, growing excitement lighting her face. "I could totally do work like this!"

"But," Brandon cautioned, "it needs to be your own work."

"I wouldn't copy anything," Kamiko said enthusiastically.

"That's not what I meant," Brandon said. "You need to develop a style that is uniquely your own. It's not enough to emulate what you see in this book. You need to originate your own visual language, one that buyers will instantly recognize as distinct from other artists."

Kamiko looked hopeful, but somewhat lost. "Ahh…"

Brandon leaned forward, elbows on his desk. He seemed suddenly in his element. "Kamiko, this is a chance for you to explore, experiment. Go crazy. Try something different. Show me what Kamiko Nishimura can do that no one else can do."

Why hadn't he said that before? He was probably too busy thinking about snake-charming me rather than helping her.

"I guess I can do that," she said tentatively.

"What about your anime?" I offered. I turned to Brandon. "Can she do something with her cartoons?"

"Yes," he said. "She can work some of the stylistic motifs of manga and anime art into her work. The trick will be combining it with a fine art sensibility. But it can be done. Many artists today are doing exactly that."

"You could totally do that," I encouraged, resting my hand on Kamiko's forearm.

She nodded.

"Kamiko," Brandon said confidently, "paint me some new work.

You have plenty of time before the show. Bring me some samples and I will be happy to take a look."

"Okay," she said, now sounding only half shell-shocked.

"Well, I hate to make this a short visit, but I have some pressing business to attend," Brandon said, standing up.

Kamiko shot to her feet. "Thank you, Mr. Charboneau." She shook his hand firmly.

"My pleasure." He turned to me, "Samantha?"

I nodded. I wasn't shaking his hand after how he'd blindsided Kamiko. No matter what he said about her paintings.

"Excuse me you guys," Kamiko sniffed, "I need to use the bathroom before we go."

"It's downstairs," Brandon offered.

Why did I think Kamiko needed an excuse to weep in private? Groan. This visit was a disaster.

Kamiko walked out of the office.

"I'll go with you Kamiko," I said, standing up.

"It's okay," Kamiko said. "I'll be right back."

"Actually," Brandon said, "can I speak with you briefly, Samantha?"

Great. I looked to Kamiko, awaiting approval.

"You go ahead, Sam," she said. "I'll be right back." She left her portfolio on top of Brandon's desk.

I would have to take Kamiko out for ice cream after we left the gallery or go back to my place and share a half-gallon with her in front of some Bravest Warriors or Adventure Time.

Fucking Brandon.

I decided to give him a talking-to the second Kamiko was out of earshot. I listened to her feet shushing down the hall toward the staircase.

It suddenly occurred to me that Brandon was Christos' art dealer. Could I chew Brandon out? Would that create tension between him and Christos? I suddenly felt like I was getting in way over my head. Maybe it would be best if I didn't say anything to Brandon.

Brandon's smile glowed. As much as I didn't want to admit it, he was very handsome. No wonder Kamiko was falling to pieces over his blunt treatment.

"So good to see you again, Samantha," he said.

I smiled politely.

Hello! I was here for Kamiko, not him. Didn't he see that? Maybe he didn't. Or didn't care. I barely knew him, so anything was possible. I had to say *something.*

Still sitting in the chair, I folded my arms across my chest. "Brandon, don't you think you were a little harsh on Kamiko?"

He slid his hands casually into his pockets. "How so?"

"You crushed her. She's worked really hard on those paintings."

He sighed. "Try to understand my position, Samantha. Charboneau has a particular clientele with particular expectations. How would it help me to sell the Charboneau brand if I allowed Kamiko's current work into the show?"

I wasn't really sure what he meant by "brand." This was all new to me.

"Look, there are dozens of galleries in San Diego that carry work like Kamiko's. She's already better than half the artists hanging in those galleries right now. I have no doubt she could make an appointment with any one of them and sell everything in her portfolio. I did her a favor."

"You're missing the point, Brandon." I nearly growled when I said it, but tried to keep my voice calm.

"And what point is that?"

Could I tell him that Kamiko had a crush on him? Would that help, or make things worse? Screw it. "She likes you, Brandon."

Brandon smiled. "I could tell," he said way too confidently. Jerk.

"So why were you so mean?" I demanded.

"Like I said, I was trying to help her out. Steer her in the right direction."

"What, away from you?"

"No," he smirked. "Toward the galleries that will embrace her."

"But you're the one she wants embracing her. You, Brandon. Not the gallery. Don't you get it?" I glared at him. Did he not realize what a jerk he was being? Guys were all the same.

He smiled that irritatingly handsome smile of his. "I do, Samantha. But the problem is, I'm interested in you..." he leaned forward and put his hand on my cheek.

I had been sitting on the edge of my chair, so I slid back into it all the way, trying to escape. Brandon followed. His nose was inches from mine. I couldn't slide back any further in the chair unless I literally crawled over the back of it.

Brandon continued in a low voice, "...not her—"

Suddenly, Brandon's smile froze. He straightened up stiffly and slipped his hands in his pockets. "Oh, hey, Kamiko," he said flatly.

I whipped around, practically falling out of the chair. Shit! How long had she been standing there? Judging from the tears in her eyes and the way she ran down the hall sobbing, I would guess long enough.

From where Kamiko had been standing, I'm sure it looked like Brandon was about to kiss me, but Kamiko wouldn't have seen the grimace on my face.

"Kamiko!" I shouted. "It's not what you think!" But she was already pounding down the stairs. She probably hadn't heard me. If she had, I feared she didn't believe me. I stood up from the chair, about to run after Kamiko. "You're such a jerk, Brandon!"

He frowned. "Why, because I'm not interested in her?" he scoffed. "Is that a crime?"

"No! But..." I sighed heavily, "...you're still a jerk!" I ran after Kamiko, but stopped halfway down the hall. I ran back to grab her portfolio off the top of the desk. I glared at Brandon as I picked it up.

"What?" he asked defensively.

I eyed the show catalog Brandon had taken out for Kamiko. I didn't know if she was going to care, but I snatched it for her, just in case.

When I reached the bottom of the stairs and the gallery floor, Kamiko was gone. I ran out the front doors and onto the sidewalk. I looked in both directions, but I didn't see her anywhere.

It was getting dark, and quite a few people walked up and down the sidewalks. There were shops everywhere, and four-way intersections at both ends of the short block. She could be anywhere.

Crap. I walked to where my car was parked. Maybe she'd be waiting there. Nope, there was no sign of her when I reached my VW.

I dialed her on my phone. No answer.

I left a message, "It's me. It's not what you think, Kamiko. Brandon was putting the moves on me. He surprised me right before you walked in, I didn't have time to react. I'm totally not into him…" I almost added that I was with Christos, but I suspected that reminding her I had an awesome boyfriend shortly after stupid Brandsome had thrown her heart in the garbage was a bad idea. "…and I'm really sorry about how Brandon was treating you." I wasn't sure if saying that made things worse or better. I ended my call, afraid my message wouldn't do any good. Sigh.

Over the next hour, I called Kamiko three times while waiting at my car. She never answered.

Maybe she called Romeo for a ride? I called his phone, but he didn't answer. Moments later, I got a text back from him that said,

in class. call u later.

Kamiko probably hadn't contacted Romeo. If she had, he would've mentioned it in the text. I hoped. Was she taking a bus back to campus? It was five miles back to SDU. For all I knew, she was going to walk.

I felt terrible. I hoped she wasn't going to stay mad at me. If anyone, she should be mad at Brandon.

I sighed heavily.

How did guys always manage to ruin everything?

I waited another thirty minutes and called Kamiko twice more before leaving.

I went back to campus to her dorm room. Her roommate let me in the suite and told me Kamiko hadn't been to the room.

Where was she?

I couldn't wait around. I had to be at the Grab-n-Dash in twenty minutes.

Crap!

SAMANTHA

I made it to Grab-n-Dash with a minute to spare. The lull in customers that greeted me was a stark contrast after my drama over the last two hours.

The first thing I did was try calling Kamiko again. I felt terrible. I worried she thought I was trying to steal Brandon from her. But that didn't make sense. She knew I was dating Christos.

No matter how many times I called, Kamiko never answered. I was worried about her.

When the customers started coming in, I did my best to put

Kamiko out of my mind and focus on my work.

An hour later, my ongoing exhaustion hit me like a brick. I could barely keep my eyes open during customer lulls, and when it was busy, I felt wired and delicate, like a fragile glass version of myself.

Every night, I still went through job websites unsuccessfully and never got enough sleep. I was starting to wish the math tutoring had panned out, but no luck there either.

I knew Grab-n-Dash wasn't a long term option. Not only was it physically tiring, but it was emotionally draining as well. There was this depressing quality about it I couldn't identify. Maybe it was the fact that I knew being a convenience store clerk wasn't the sort of job my parents would be proud of. They'd probably chuckle and tell me they'd told me so.

Eye roll.

I wondered how long I could keep up my pace with four classes and two jobs. Could I maintain it through the end of the quarter, until Spring Break? *And* keep my grades up? What about Spring Quarter after that? Would a week's rest from classes be enough to rejuvenate me?

I feared it would not.

At the moment, the only thing keeping my tired eyes open was the hot-dog odor wafting off my neon-urine uniform shirt. No matter how many times I'd washed it, the smell wouldn't go away. I'd begged my boss for a new one several times.

His response was always the same, "It's not in the quarterly budget," he'd say sarcastically while his prickly eyebrows caterpillared over his glasses.

Silly me. I'd forgotten that Grab-n-Dash was a Fortune 500 company with very tight margins to maintain if it hoped to meet shareholder expectations on a quarterly basis.

So I diligently hand-washed my uniform shirt nightly, air-dried it from the walkway balcony railing outside my front door every night, and stuffed it in a garbage bag when it was dry to trap the smell. Every morning, I prayed I'd wake to discover that someone had stolen my shirt off the railing, but I think the criminals were smarter than that, as were the homeless people who had minimal standards to maintain when it came to personal odor.

Hot dogs.

Yeah, I was never eating one again.

The front doors bing-bonged as Eminickle, my favorite illicit twelve-year-old Lothario, walked into Grab-n-Dash with his posse, 2 Small Crew.

"What up, girl," Eminickle said. "You sure look foxy today!"

I smirked down at him. I think he was just shy of three feet tall. Perhaps shorter. And that was standing on his tiptoes. Was he really twelve? Maybe he was six?

"Hey, Eminickle," I said.

"You know you call me dat cuz you know I'm yo number one playa," he said suavely.

"Um, no? I think it's because one is your shoe size."

"Oh, snap!" his buddy to the right said. This buddy had red-hair, freckles, braces, and wore a T-shirt with an eight-bit Space Invader on the front.

"Come on, girl," Eminickle said, "let me be your baby daddy!"

"Get her, dawg!" his other buddy said. This one had big glasses and a Jew-fro. His t-shirt had a picture of a rabbi holding a pair of six-pointed throwing stars of David, posing like a ninja, above a logo that said "Jew-Jitsu."

They were harmless.

I would never tell them how much I thoroughly enjoyed their friendly visits. They were a pleasant distraction from the regular customers.

Eminickle and his crew raided the candy display and filled ICEEs at the machine before bringing their treasured treats up to the counter like they held golden jewels and silver chalices in their hands.

I rang everything up.

"I got y'all covered, boys," Eminickle said generously, pulling out his velcro wallet to pay. It had an Angry Birds logo silkscreened on the outside. He handed me a ten dollar bill, which covered everything.

I made him change and slid it over the counter.

He lifted up the remaining dollar bill and held it out to me. "For you, girl, because you is so damn fine."

"Save it for milk tomorrow at school," I sneered.

His buddies cackled.

"Down in flames, dawg!" Space Invaders said.

"A'ight, I get it," Eminickle said to me confidently. "You playin' hard to get. But I can tell, I'm growing on you."

"Like a zit," I said.

His friends erupted with laughter.

"Any time you wanna *pop* me, girl," Eminickle winked at me, "and I *know* you know what I mean... you let me know. A'ight?"

"Gross!" I don't know how, but he made zits into sexual innuendo. *So* not hot. Sigh. *Kids today.* I rolled my eyes at the three of them. "Don't you guys have homework to do?"

"See you next time, foxy momma," Eminickle winked as he and his buddies walked out.

I waved sarcastically and rolled my eyes.

Once Eminickle and 2 Small Crew were gone, my tiredness set back in.

I eyed the coffee machine. Did I need a fourth cup?

No, caffeine wasn't helping. All it did at this point was make my hands shake and my eyelids quiver.

I checked the clock on the far wall. Yup, it was running backward.

I really needed to find a different job.

Chapter 20

SAMANTHA

As mid-terms neared, I felt the crushing weight of looming disaster hovering over my life. Not only had my friendship with Kamiko gone off the rails, but my grades were falling into the crapper as well.

On the plus side, Oil Painting was most likely an A. Professor Cogdill was a great teacher, and very supportive. Check.

Sociology 2, on the other hand, was looking like a solid B. Not what I wanted. My parents wouldn't be happy about anything less than an A. Unfortunately, Professor Tutan-yawn-yawn kept putting me to sleep, no matter how hard I tried to focus. The energy drain from my two jobs wasn't helping.

History was heading toward a C. That freaked me out. I hadn't had a C since junior high. Maybe I could pull it up to a B by the end of the quarter, but no hope of an A. Groan.

Figurative Sculpting was a wild card. I needed to actually go to Bittinger's office hours to find out exactly where I stood.

I wasn't looking forward to a friendly visit with the Bitchinger.

Luckily, her office hours were not on the same day as classes. Maybe she wouldn't be so bitchy without Hunter in the room making gaga eyes at me while ignoring her.

I walked across campus in the morning and into the Visual Arts building to her office. I'd made sure to arrive well before her posted office hours. I wanted to be waiting on *her*, not the other way around. I needed all the advantages I could get.

As I hoped, she wasn't there.

I slid down against the wall and pulled out my sketchbook to doodle while I waited. I almost started cartooning her, but I knew I'd get carried away and she'd walk up at the exact moment I finished an insulting picture of her.

I could see the cartoon in my mind. Marjorie would have a sour look on her pretty face and the body of a mangy dog from the waist down. She would be sitting behind a little roadside stand, waiting for the next willing idiot to come along and pay for her unique brand of cheap grief. The signage scrawled on the front of the stand would read:

"Insults and Aggravation. 5¢."

"The Bitch is In."

With a grin on my face, I started drawing Doggy van Peltinger. I couldn't resist. Maybe I needed to be a cartoonist.

Of course, that was the moment Marjorie Bittinger chose to walk down the hall. My drawing would have to wait. I stuffed my sketchbook in my book bag and stood up.

"Good morning, Miss Smith," Professor Bittinger said as she pulled a ring of keys out of her purse and opened her office door. "I assume you're here to inquire about mid-term grades?" She smirked.

"Um, yeah."

She walked into the office and dropped her bags behind her desk. I sat down at one of the chairs in front of her desk. Her office had very clean, precise decoration. Three small pedestals along the wall had bronze sculptures of heads on top of them, each one of a different handsome young man. I didn't recognize any of the people, but they were all very well done, and the men looked super-sexy. "Are those heads your work?" I asked.

"You mean the busts?"

"Yeah." I guess that's what they were called.

"Yes." Still standing behind her desk, she rifled through a folder, looking for something. Maybe she'd find some social niceties inside, because I could tell she'd forgotten to bring hers with her this morning. A moment later she tugged out several sheets of paper and slapped them on the desk. "Your file."

How did she manage to make me feel like I was sitting in the Principal's Office, about to receive a bawling-out for in-class antics? Detention or expulsion to follow?

Marjorie sat down and slid a pair of reading glasses onto her face. Even in glasses, she projected an elegant beauty. Why was it that people's insides and outsides could be so poorly matched?

Marjorie flipped back and forth between two pages, reading,

flipping, reading. She pulled off her glasses, folded them up, and put them away before lacing her fingers primly on top of her desk. "Currently, your grade is a D."

"A *D*?" I was shocked.

She pressed her lips together. "Minus."

"What?" That was impossible. At worst, I was expecting a B. I was working my butt off in her class, and my sculptures were as good as anybody else's. I had assumed that, like Life Drawing, sculpture class would be graded on progress. "Why is it so low?"

"Because your work is shoddy and heavy-handed."

"Heavy-handed? What does that mean?"

She smiled with ample superiority. "If you want to become a mason and pour cement for a living, you're doing a terrific job."

"But I'm learning," I hoped I didn't sound like I was whining. "Isn't this a beginning-level class?"

"I would hope to see a finer level of execution in a college level course." She leaned forward, going in for the kill, all smiles. "Not all of us have what it takes to become a figurative sculptor, Miss Smith. Perhaps you should consider a ceramics class. Ashtrays and painted plates might be more your speed."

More my speed? She was making it sound like I wasn't smart enough or talented enough to join her club. What an epic bitch. I felt myself starting to tear up. Then everything clicked into place.

I leveled a look at her. "You're trying to push me out of your class."

Marjorie's perfectly plucked brows knotted together in a nasty, nervous bunch.

"It's Hunter, isn't it?" I asked.

"What?" she scoffed.

Even I knew how to recognize bald-faced denial. "You like him. That's why you hired him as your model. You wanted him to be closer to you. But he's interested in me. And it's driving you nuts."

"That is ridiculous! I've never heard such—"

"That's why you want me to drop your class," I continued forcefully, "or give up, or whatever. That's why you've been so hard on me since day one. I'm competition, and you're jealous." I smiled my own superior smile. *Take that, you Epic Bitchinger!*

"I don't know where you get your crazy ideas, Miss Smith, but I assure you, your grade is a reflection of you performance in class, *not* some sort of teenaged love-triangle."

"You know," I said calmly, "one of the things I read about in Sociology, during the gender studies portion, was sexual harassment. I was curious, so I looked up sexual harassment policies here at SDU online. Do you know what a 'hostile learning environment' is, Professor Bittinger?"

"This is absurd, I don't have to listen to—"

"You're right, you don't have to listen. But I see how you drool all over Hunter, and how you treat me worse than the other students. I'm the only one you single out for no reason."

"I do no such thing, Miss Smith."

"Then I'm sure you won't care if I speak with the Dean about this. I bet he'll be more than happy to hear me out."

Marjorie's eyes were wide and literally shaking with fear.

I stood up and slung my book bag over my shoulder. "See you in class, Professor."

I smiled to myself as I walked out.

SAMANTHA

I was pleasantly surprised when I next attended Figurative Sculpting.

Professor Marjorie Bittinger was a new woman. You could even call her nice. I was able to focus entirely on my sculpture, and got a lot of work done.

Romeo, of course, was happy to distract.

At one point, when no one was looking, he caressed the butt of his Hunter sculpture and made bedroom faces at me, which for Romeo meant his tongue hanging out and his eyelids quivering. I giggled, expecting Major Bitchinger to be looking over my shoulder as usual, she had me trained, but she wasn't. She was on the far side of the studio, helping another student.

What a relief.

I sighed contently. It seemed I would be enjoying a more forgiving classroom environment. One that was altogether non-hostile. Points for me.

Yay!

Hunter, on the other hand, was the same old laser-focused predator. Every single break was an opportunity for him to put new moves on me. Was he ever going to let me out of his sights?

The other thing I'd learned about sexual harassment at SDU was that the same rules applied to professors were also applied to Teaching Assistants. But Hunter wasn't a TA. He was almost like a guest speaker, or contractor, for the school. I didn't know if he had to follow similar rules or not. Maybe I needed to give him a lecture anyway, like I had Marjorie?

Something told me Hunter wouldn't listen. Hunter did what Hunter wanted.

Besides, now that Major Marjorie was off my back, Hunter's stalking didn't seem like as big of a deal. He was a nuisance, but at least he was polite about it. He was harmless.

Wasn't he?

When class was over, Romeo and I packed up our tools and walked out of the studio together.

"You know what I hate about sculpting class?" Romeo asked.

"I thought you loved sculpting," I smiled.

"I do, but it's a love-hate thing."

"What do you mean?"

"Well, the truth is, I'm so embarrassed to say this, but, well…" He sounded really nervous.

"It's okay, Romeo. Say whatever it is."

He gave me a pleading look. "If you hadn't noticed, I have a 'thing' for Hunter."

I giggled. "No, I hadn't noticed that," I said sarcastically.

"Sam, I'm serious!" Romeo whined.

"Okay," I relented. "Yes, so you think Hunter is hot? So what?"

"No, Sam. You don't get it. I think I'm in love with him."

We came to a stop on the pathway leading through the Eucalyptus grove outside the Visual Arts building

I looked at Romeo sympathetically. His face was genuinely desperate. Not fake Romeo comedy-desperate, but the real thing. I felt terrible for him.

"Oh, Romeo," I said, "I don't think Hunter is gay."

"I know, but it doesn't change the way I feel."

"I don't know what to tell you Romeo. I think you're going to be disappointed, no matter what happens."

"Maybe he's bi?"

"I have no idea. But he doesn't seem like it to me," I said

cautiously.

Romeo looked pathetically disappointed. "You really think so?"

"I'm sorry, Romeo. But yeah, I really don't think Hunter is—"

"Hunter is what?" Hunter smiled, walking up behind us on the pathway.

Oh, great. Hunter was always butting in like clockwork. I think I was finally over it. "Nothing," I sighed.

"Come on, what?" Hunter smiled. He had his aviator glasses on again, even though the sky was gray and overcast. "What do you think about me? I really want to know."

I smiled to myself. I could *so* run with that. I could tell Hunter he was an egotistical jerk, he was shallow, he didn't know when to quit, and being a dick model for underwear packaging was lame. Instead, I said, "I was just saying you were a good model for sculpting. It's easy to see all your muscles."

"I know," Hunter smiled, his teeth shining prettily.

I saw Romeo swooning out of the corner of my eye. Why couldn't Hunter be into Romeo instead of me? Then everyone could go about their business and live happily ever after.

"When are you going to let me take you out, Sam?" Hunter prodded.

"You could take *me* out," Romeo said hopefully.

Hunter rolled his eyes at Romeo, clearly frustrated at him. I'd have thought that Hunter would be immune to Romeo's constant overtures by now. I guess not. They were getting to him. So why couldn't Hunter see that his hitting on me was just as tiresome? Too much testosterone applied to the classically one-track male mind was the likely answer.

Nothing I could do about that.

"Come on, Sam," Hunter said, his voice rough with self-doubt, "let me take you out. Just once. I'll show you a good time, I promise," he pleaded.

I couldn't believe it. Hunter's confidence was finally starting to slip. It had only taken what, two months? He at least deserved an A for effort. But I wasn't handing out any prizes. I sighed. "No, Hunter. There's only one man in my life. In fact, he's the love of my life."

Hunter smiled his perfect smile. But this time, it looked sort of shark-like. "You sure?" he asked.

Yeah, he was getting frazzled. But he wasn't giving up.

It was time for me to burst his bubble for good. I was tired of his game. Because that's all it was. He didn't listen. Ever. "What do you mean, am I sure? How many ways do I have to say it, Hunter? I'm involved. Off the market. Seeing someone. Going steady. Get the picture?"

Hunter raised an eyebrow. He still had some fight left in him.

"I'm totally available," Romeo said nervously. "*On* the market. Seeing *nobody*."

Hunter was temporarily distracted by Romeo's antics.

I took that as my opportunity to escape. I started walking away quickly.

Hunter followed a second later. When he caught up to me, he flashed his sharkish grin, "We can still hang out, as friends, right?"

Wow, he sounded desperate. "No," I said firmly, walking fast.

Romeo trotted to catch up with us. "I'm right here!" he hollered to Hunter, who ignored him. "Totally willing to be more than friends!"

Poor Romeo. I stopped, waiting for him to catch up.

Romeo caught his foot on a bump in the pavement and nearly blundered into Hunter.

Hunter's brows clenched together and he growled at Romeo, "Dude, back the fuck off!! I'm not a fag!!"

Romeo regained his footing and stopped beside me. He was totally taken aback by Hunter's words. For the first time since I'd met him, the constant glee went out of his eyes. He straightened stiffly, and pretended to examine his fingernails.

"What's wrong with you?" I demanded of Hunter. "Don't talk to my friend that way!"

Hunter's brows relaxed and his lips widened into an easy smile. The way he went from angry to smiling his shark-smile reminded me of Lame Damian. Why was I not surprised?

Hunter ran his hand through his shaggy hair. "Sorry, dude, I didn't mean that," Hunter said smoothly, as if it was no big deal.

"We should go," I said to Romeo. I held out my hand to him, almost like a parent. I needed to get him out of here.

"Okay," Romeo said softly.

I took his hand and led him around Hunter.

"Wait, I'm sorry!" Hunter called, trotting to catch up.

"Samantha, hold on a second!"

He clapped a hand on Romeo's shoulder.

Romeo flinched.

"I'm sorry, man," Hunter said. "I didn't mean to call you a fah —" He stopped himself, flustered. "I shouldn't have said that."

Romeo stopped and stared at Hunter. Romeo's face was tight. He and I both looked at Hunter expectantly.

"Ahh, I don't know what to say," Hunter stammered. "Uh, I apologize?"

Romeo was still stone cold.

"Try it a different way," I said to Hunter.

He was confused. "Try what a different way?"

"Your apology?"

He growled petulantly, "How many different ways do I have to say it?"

"As many ways as I had to tell you I had a boyfriend?" I sneered.

"Huh?" Hunter was dumbfounded.

I rolled my eyes, "Don't you remember how many times I've had to say 'no' to you over the last two months, Hunter? I was starting to think I was going to have to file a restraining order against *you*. Because you never give up." I suddenly realized what I was saying to Hunter was what I had wanted to say to Damian Wolfram for the last three years, but never got to. Lecturing Damian in effigy felt great. I wanted to do more of it. I smiled inwardly. No more stupid jerks were going to walk over me. "Hunter, maybe you should try apologizing to people you hurt at least as often as you try to get in a girl's pants."

Hunter chuckled. "No way."

Like that was a surprise. "Let's go," I said to Romeo.

I turned down the path with Romeo and walked right into Christos.

"Christos!" I was so happy to see him. "What are you doing on campus?"

"I decided to hit the Rec Center gym. I haven't worked out in a couple weeks. Needed to blow off some stress," he smiled as he slid his thumb across my cheek. "More importantly, I knew you'd be coming out of class about the time I finished up."

I liked the sound of that.

Christos wore a heather-gray hoodie, the hood pulled over his head. The sweatshirt was unzipped, revealing his naked chest and Fearless tattoo, and his stunning abs. He glistened with sweat, sexy as hell.

Yeah, Christos put Hunter to shame in the looks department. Pretty was nice, but ruggedly sexy was ten times better.

"Where's your shirt?" I asked Christos.

"Too hot," he smirked.

Too hot was right. His blue eyes beamed into my heart. I noticed his jeans rode low on his narrow hips, revealing the tapering wedge of his lower abs. Shiver.

"Do you work out dressed like this?" I asked.

"No," he chuckled. "Too many of the women at the gym were having heart attacks, so the management makes me keep my hoodie zipped while I'm lifting."

That was my Christos.

"Hey, C-Man," Romeo said abjectly.

"What up, Romeo," Christos smiled, obviously happy to see him. "How you been, my man?"

"Oh, uh," Romeo still sounded distraught after the blow from Hunter. "I'm okay."

I felt terrible for Romeo. I wasn't sure what might cheer him up. He was always so energetic and happy, I'd never seen this side of him before. Maybe he needed ice cream. It always worked for me.

"Is this your boyfriend?" Hunter demanded petulantly.

I'd forgotten he was there. Damn. Too bad. "Yes, Hunter, this is my *boyfriend* Christos."

Christos extended a hand without a second thought. "What up, man. You must be the model from Samantha's sculpting class?" He was smiling at Hunter. "She says you do good work."

Hunter stared at Christos' extended hand, but didn't shake it. "Yeah, I'm the model."

I could tell Christos sensed Hunter's edginess, so he lowered his arm. "Samantha told me you're a friend of Marjorie Bittinger?"

"She did, did she? What else did she tell you?" Hunter sounded like a spoiled baby. Was he intimidated by Christos?

Christos chuckled confidently. "She also mentioned that Marjorie has a thing for you."

Hunter scoffed. "So?"

"So?" Christos grinned. "Marjorie is a total cougar fox. Why aren't you hitting that shit?"

I suddenly realized what Christos was doing to Hunter. He was a freakin' genius. Rather than confronting Hunter like a defensive silver-back gorilla who only knew how to jump around and bang his chest or fight, Christos was trying to steer Hunter toward the path of least resistance. No matter how much I disliked Marjorie Bittinger, I could honestly say that she was an attractive woman, and she couldn't have been older than 40. I thought every guy had an older woman fantasy.

With Marjorie literally begging for Hunter's attention, I couldn't figure out why Hunter was wasting his time on me. Thrill of the hunt? Maybe that was all. Hunter liked hard-to-get. Sadly, impossible to get was all I could ever be for him. Did that mean he would try *harder*? I hoped not. I really didn't want to deal with him anymore, not after how he'd treated Romeo.

I leaned into Christos, nuzzling my cheek against his chest. Wow, even straight out of the gym he smelled like man-candy to me. I inhaled deeply.

Hunter chewed his lower lip, flashing some canine as he glanced between me and Christos.

"Dude," Christos offered to Hunter, "if I wasn't totally in love with Samantha, I'd be knocking on Marjorie's door myself."

"Be my guest," Hunter said. "You take Marjorie, I'll take your girlfriend."

Christos blurted out a short laugh. "Sorry, bro. No dice. Samantha's with me." Christos smiled, not a hint of doubt in his tone.

"For now," Hunter growled.

"Dude, relax," Christos smiled. "I see what you're trying to do. You're trying to get me all worked up, maybe get me to throw a punch at you."

A dark smile crept across Hunter's face.

"But I'm not in the mood. I just finished working out. I want to go have dinner with my girlfriend, and my good friend Romeo."

Romeo brightened when he heard that.

"So do us a favor," Christos continued, "go find Marjorie, and take her out to dinner. From what Samantha has told me, you'll probably have her in bed before dessert." He paused thoughtfully.

"You know how they say that women reach the sexual peak between thirty-five and forty-five?"

Hunter didn't answer. Instead, his smile darkened further.

Christos continued, "By that statistic, Marjorie is peaking. Like, totally at her best. You'll probably bang her ten times tonight. I always preferred fucking over fighting anyway. Go get Marjorie, man," Christos said with total sincerity, "You'll have a blast."

Hunter nodded sarcastically. He took a step forward, his weight on the balls of his feet. "You're a pussy. You're afraid to fight."

Hunter was insane.

CHRISTOS

"Do I look afraid?" I asked Hunter, holding my ground.

Hunter chuckled at me. "Yeah, I totally smell pussy." He took another step toward me.

I sighed. I was out on bail. I didn't need this shit. "Dude, I'm not going to fight you."

"Because you're all bark and no bite, bitch."

"Come on, Hunter. When have I barked at you? I'm trying to help you out. Me and Samantha are tight. Marjorie Bittinger, who is hot and ready to fuck your shit, is waiting for you back in the Visual Arts building."

Hunter frowned. "How do you know that?"

Christos sighed, "Because I know where the sculpting studio is, where Marjorie teaches. So quit stalling, and go get her, man."

Hunter shook his head slowly, his grin widening into a predatory smile. All fangs.

I rolled my eyes at him. I would be happy to tear this guy up, but there was no way I was doing it on campus, in front of Samantha and Romeo. If Hunter wanted to sign a waiver and go into the ring, I'd be all over it. But I could tell he was psyching himself up, trying to convince himself that I was afraid, and now was his opportunity to get me out of his way and get to Samantha.

Really?

Hunter took another step forward.

"Samantha, Romeo," I said, "Please back up. Hunter is not going to be happy until he gets his way."

"What?" Samantha gasped. "No, don't, Christos."

"It's okay," I reassured. "This will be quick." I pulled off my hoodie and tossed it to Samantha. Maybe if Hunter saw me pumped up, fresh from the gym, saw all my ink on my arms, he might finally back down.

"Quick for you," Hunter snarled at me.

Nope, he was an idiot. I rested my hands on my hips casually. "Please, dude," I laughed, "do something already."

Hunter's hands curled into fists. He wasn't sure what to do.

"Now or never," I said.

Hunter took a step forward, but he was still a mile away from being a threat.

"Okay, man, I'm tired of waiting. I've got shit to do." I turned to Samantha, knowing what was coming.

Hunter charged my back.

I sank and pivoted on the ball of one foot while sliding my other leg out with my toes curled up to hook around his ankle.

I tripped him.

Hunter spilled into the dirt on the side of the trail, kicking up dust and fallen Eucalyptus leaves.

Romeo and Samantha laughed.

"Chill, you guys," I said. "Let's go."

Hunter sat up, his face covered with dirt.

I hoped he'd skinned his knees like the child he was.

With my arm around Samantha and Romeo at our side, the three of us walked down the pathway together.

"You guys hungry?" I asked, taking my hoodie from Samantha and sliding my arms through the sleeves.

"Hungry for you!" Samantha said when we were out of Hunter's earshot. "Rawr!"

I chuckled.

"Me too!" Romeo said. "Double rawr!"

"We need to find you a man, Romeo," I said.

Romeo smiled bashfully at me. "How about you, C-Man?"

"Dude, you would totally break my shit in half," I smiled confidently. "I meant a man who could actually handle you." I winked at Romeo and slapped him good-naturedly on the back.

Romeo laughed. "You hear that, Sam? Christos has finally confirmed what I've been telling you all along. I'm too much of a man for even the manliest men!" Romeo pumped his fist and jumped, bicycling his feet in the air.

Samantha chuckled at him.

"What do you guys want to eat?" I asked. "I'm buying."

"You!" Samantha and Romeo chorused before looking at each other and laughing.

We walked to the Student Center together.

Chapter 21

SAMANTHA

The next day at school was a long one. I had classes all day and a shift at the art museum afterward.

When I got off work, I was exhausted and starving. At least with my two jobs, I felt like I had enough money to eat right. No more protein bars for lunch and Mac & Cheese or Ramen for dinner.

On the way home from SDU, I treated myself to take-out in the form of a Carne Asada burrito with extra guacamole from Roberto's.

Of all the various "-berto's" taquerias in San Diego: Royberto's, Rolberto's, Rigoberto's, Alberto's, Tio-Alberto's, Filiburto's, Gualberto's, Nolberto's, and all the rest, Roberto's was by far the best.

Even though it seemed like most everything else in my life was dragging me down, at least I didn't have to go hungry.

When I got to my apartment I dropped my bags by the door, grabbed a plate for my burrito, and sat down at my kitchen table. I pulled my burrito out of its paper sack and unwrapped it. My mouth was watering in anticipation. I'd been looking forward to this all afternoon.

As I lifted the savory burrito to my mouth, my phone bleeped. I set my burrito down and got up to pull my phone out of my purse.

My parents. Great. I suddenly had indigestion.

I answered on speaker phone. "Hello?" I sat back down at the kitchen table and took a huge bite of burrito. I was too hungry to wait any longer, even if it was my parents.

"Hello, Sam? It's your father."

Duh. Who else could he be? "Hey, Dad," I mumbled around food. Mmmm, Carne Asada.

"Do we have a bad connection? It's hard to understand you."

"I'm eating."

"What?!"

"I'm eating!!"

"Oh. Well, your mother and I wanted to check in on how things are going. Hold on, let me get her on the other line."

I rolled my eyes. I couldn't wait.

"Hello, Sam," Mom said.

"Hey," I said.

"She sounds garbled," Mom said. "Is there a bad connection, Bill?"

I rolled my eyes again.

"She's eating, I think," my dad said.

"Don't you know it's impolite to talk with your mouth full?"

I chewed, rather than answer.

"Sam?" she asked.

"I'm chewing, Mom!" I mumbled over my extra-helping of exasperation.

"Mind your manners, young lady," my mom barked.

"Can't you wait to eat until after the call?" dad asked.

"I'm starving," I argued.

"Your tone, Samantha," Mom warned icily. She only used my full name when she was pissed. Good.

My dad cleared his throat, trying to lighten the mood. Good luck. "So, uh, Sam? Have you found a job?"

"Two."

"Two?" he asked, confused. "Two what?"

"Two jobs!" I hollered. Man, they were killing me. Somebody get them some Q-tips.

"Samantha!" my mom growled.

I took another huge bite and chewed, pretending I was grinding my mom's nastiness between my teeth.

"I can only assume that you've taken two because neither one pays sufficiently to cover your expenses?" my dad asked.

Damn, he was right.

"What, may I ask, are your *two* jobs?" Mom said sarcastically.

"I work at the art museum on campus and a convenience store."

Mom chuckled. "A *convenience* store?"

O. M. G. She was as rude as Tiffany Kingston-Whitehouse tonight. "So? It pays."

"How much?" Dad asked.

"Do we have to go into this?" I asked, swallowing and wiping guacamole from my lips with a napkin.

"Your mother and I just want to make sure your jobs pay sufficiently to cover your living expenses," Dad said.

"The museum pays ten an hour, and the convenience store pays eight-fifty. I have enough hours at both jobs to cover all my expenses. After taxes. Happy now?" I said snidely.

"Well that's good to hear," my dad said.

Nothing from my mom on the subject.

That was it? Geez, a congratulations would've been nice.

"Have you changed your major back to Accounting?" Dad asked. He was all business tonight.

"No," I said.

"Oh?" my dad said thoughtfully.

That was strange. I'd expected my dad to be on the warpath when I told him.

I smelled a trap.

"You must be pretty busy with two jobs and classes," Dad said.

"I guess." I still smelled that trap.

"Sam," my dad said with a distinct smile in his voice, "all you have to do is change your major back, and your mother and I will be glad to cover all your expenses once again."

Spring! There went his trap.

"Think how nice it will be not to have to work two jobs," he continued. "You can focus on your classes and have time left over to relax with your friends."

Yeah, my dad sounded like the devil. He had that nice guy voice the devil always used when he was telling you how great everything would be after you signed away your soul in blood.

"I'm not changing my major back," I said calmly.

There was a long, long pause from my parents. I enjoyed the silence, but I knew it wouldn't last.

"Well," Mom blurted with a cackle, "I hope you like working at a *convenience* store. I'm sure their retirement benefits are stellar."

"I'm not going to work there for the rest of my life, Mom."

"What," she scoffed, "are you going to be an *artist*?"

"Now, Linda," my dad said, trying to calm her. "Sam *is* working. Two jobs, no less. We should cut her some slack."

That sort of surprised me. He was usually on Mom's side.

"No, Bill. Your daughter is making terrible choices. And you know what? I bet it's that Christos character."

"I don't think—" my dad said.

My mom interrupted him. "It *is* him, isn't it, Sam?"

I was shocked into silence.

"I'm right," Mom said. "I *knew* it. He's filling your head with all these crazy ideas about being an artist, isn't he, Samantha?"

"No!" I protested. I pushed back my chair from my dining room table and began pacing the living room. I felt like I was suddenly on dangerous ground, and wanted to move, like I needed to run away from my parents. What else was new? Sigh.

My mom's tone suddenly went friendly, which scared me. "Samantha, are you telling me that you're no longer seeing Christos? Or have you found some other boy to waste your time on?"

"No! I mean, yes, I'm still seeing Christos!"

My mom chuckled throatily. "That's what I thought. Bill, your daughter is spending so much time with this *boy* Christos, she's lost her head. I knew it was going to happen sooner or later."

There was something so disgusting about the way my mom had said it, like she was calling me a dirty harlot, just because I was in love. There was nothing dirty about my relationship with Christos. "You don't know what you're talking about, Mom," I growled.

"I don't?" she chuckled.

"Calm down, both of you," my dad said in an even tone. "Whether or not Sam is dating anyone is not what's at issue. Sam has shown initiative, Linda. She has secured two jobs and is paying her bills. As long as she keeps her grades up, her personal life is irrelevant."

Geez, did my dad think I was a robot? A computer to be programmed and set about a specific task? The way he'd called my personal life "irrelevant" spoke volumes. Groan. At least he was getting my mom off my back.

"Further," Dad continued, "there's no sense in her withdrawing from her current classes this late in the term, only to have to repeat them later. Sam, can you apply both your Oil Painting and Figurative Sculpting credits toward your General Education requirements?"

"Yeah," I muttered.

"Excellent. I believe that, when combined with Figurative Drawing from last quarter, you will have completed your Humanities series, correct?" Dad was on the ball, as always.

"Yeah," I said.

"Good," my dad continued, "do you know if Managerial Accounting will be available next term? Or is it only offered once per academic year?"

"I don't know," I groaned. I didn't care either.

"Can you check?" he asked.

"I guess," I moaned. All I wanted to do was get my parents off my back for the evening. I'd had enough of them.

"If all goes as planned," my dad said in a positive tone, "you can register for the appropriate classes for Spring Quarter and resume your Accounting curriculum. Then you will be back on track to complete your major in four years."

That was my parents. Making plans for me without asking how I felt about them. I was so done with this conversation.

"Do you find that acceptable, Linda?" my dad asked.

My mom sighed on the other end of the phone. "As long as she follows through, I'm fine with it," she said to my dad. "But if we find out you have *not* changed your major back to Accounting, Samantha, your father and I will be having a very long discussion about whether or not we should continue paying for your education at SDU at all."

She let that sink in.

"Fine," I said. Were we done yet?

"And if I find out your grades are slipping because you're spending too much time with that *Christos*," Mom hissed, "rest assured, young lady, there will be hell to pay."

"Your mother is right, Sam," my dad said. "We're not funding your stay at SDU so you can meet young men. You're there to procure a degree. Period. You will have plenty of time for men when you are older."

"Fine," I spat. "Can I go so I can finish my dinner now?" I sounded whiny. I didn't care.

"Yes," my dad said curtly.

"Bye," I sing-songed sarcastically.

"Good night," my dad said.

"Remember what I said, Samantha Anna Smith," my mom hissed. "Hell to pay."

I thought to myself, *Wow, I love you too, Mom.*

When they didn't say anything else, I rolled my eyes and pressed END on my phone and dropped it on my coffee table.

What was it with my parents *both* talking like they were minions of Satan? Or Satan himself? Which led me to the obvious question, did Satan have a wife? And was she the one in charge of the whole operation?

I didn't know, but if Satan's wife was anything like my mom, I was convinced she ran the show.

Whatever.

I glanced at my scrumptious Roberto's Carne Asada burrito on the kitchen table.

My appetite was gone.

Thanks, Mom and Dad.

SAMANTHA

The next afternoon, I was back behind the counter for another brain-draining shift at Grab-n-Dash. I did my best to keep a smile on my face.

Sadly, as usual, this job and my neon-urine hot-dog-smelling uniform reminded me of all the things going wrong in my life. Yes, many things were going right, like in the Christos department, but a lot of it was Groansville.

I was pretty sure my History and Sociology grades were slipping further, and I was tired all the time. How was I going to get my grades up if I was too tired to concentrate?

Worse, my parents had become complete strangers. I mean, like, worse than they'd *ever* been in the past. Maybe because I'd always followed their rules. Now that I was making choices for myself, it had become clear they didn't understand me at all. They didn't realize that Accounting had always been the wrong place for me. Why couldn't they see that?

When it came to my love for Christos, I was certain my mom and dad couldn't even begin to understand. They didn't have what Christos and I had. To me, they seemed like loveless roommates.

But Christos and I were in love.

Deeply in love.

Couldn't my parents at least respect that, even if they didn't understand it?

I wanted to live my life my way, not theirs.

Thinking about it any further was going to make me either throw up or break down in tears. Sadly, neither would set the right mood when a customer came in and I needed to say, "Welcome to Grab-n-Dash. How can I brighten your day?"

I tried to block everything out and focus on work.

Fortunately, it wasn't long before the afternoon rush kicked in, distracting me from my gloomy mood. Customers rolled through the doors every thirty seconds. I generally had a line of people three-deep waiting to pay.

I was so busy cashing out the customers, I was surprised when I looked up into the eyes of Tiffany Shithouse-Mousetrap. For once, she smiled.

"You've finally found your calling, haven't you?" she gloated while looking me over. "Nice baseball cap and matching shirt. The yellow goes with your teeth." She held a 32 ounce cup of soda in her hand.

"Welcome to Grab-n-Dash. How can I brighten your day?" I winced as I said it.

Tiffany looked at me with rampant superiority. I saw the wheels behind her eyes turning. "You want to brighten my day? How about this?" She peeled the lid off her 32 ounce cup of cola.

"No, don't—!" I held up my hand at the last second.

She jerked the cup right at me and 32 ounces of cola with minimal ice splashed onto my shirt and rained all over my shoes and the tiled floor.

"My day is definitely brighter now," Tiffany smiled and walked out, dropping her cup on the floor. The bitch didn't even pay.

I needed a mop. My shirt was sopping wet.

The other customers in line gave me conciliatory looks. I was ready to burst into tears, but I dutifully rang up each person in line. At some point, I realized tears were running down my face against my will, but I rang everyone up anyway.

When there was a lull in the customers, I stepped out from behind the cash counter and prepared to go into the back to find a mop or crawl into a corner and bawl my eyes out properly.

"Samantha?"

I hadn't even heard the door bing-bong.

"Christos? What are you doing here?"

"I decided to surprise you as soon as Isabella left for the day." He held a small but classy pink sunflower bouquet in his hands. I'd never seen anything like it. It was perfect.

More tears. But this time, it was the good kind.

He set them on the counter in front of me. When he saw my dirty shirt, he said, "What happened, *agápi mou*? You look like you've been through the ringer."

"Would you believe Tiffany threw her soda in my face?" I sniffed, trying not to cry again.

"What?!" he asked in total disbelief.

"Yeah, like twenty minutes ago," I wiped my runny nose on the back of my hand. "I need a tissue."

He grabbed a napkin from beside the hot dog stand and handed it to me over the counter.

It smelled like hot dogs. I was used to it. "Thank you, Christos."

He leaned over the counter. "This is ridiculous, Samantha. We're barely seeing each other anymore. I'm dying without you. Painting all these nude women every day has gone from hollow to desperately lonely. It's so much better when you're there to keep me company. It's like I'm painting for us, not for my rabid customers. When you're there, I don't care what I'm doing. I have a blast."

"I feel the same way," I said.

"Do you want me to eject the painting career, and get a job with you here at the Grab-n-Dash?" he joked, all smiles. "I totally would, if it would make you happy."

"No, I'd never ask you to work here. The people who come in here are animals." I smiled when I pictured Eminickle and 2 Small Crew. Well, not all of my customers. Just the Tiffanies.

"You sure? I think I'd look hot in a...what color is that again? Your shirt?"

"I don't know, but I think it's radioactive, which means, if somehow I have cancer, my shirt is curing me. If it doesn't kill me first."

"*Agápi mou*," he snickered, "this is the wrong place for you." He reached over the counter again and cupped my cheek. Frowning, he realized how awkward and unromantic it was with the counter between us. "Wait, hold on a second. I need to do this right." He backed up from the counter and looked around, examining the rack of candy behind him until he found what he was looking for. He grabbed two packages and moved the bouquet he'd brought for me to the side, then vaulted over the counter like an Olympic athlete, and dropped to one knee.

He peeled open the wrapper on one of those giant candy rings. It was red.

"Cherry!" I smiled. "My favorite."

He slid the candy ring on my finger and looked up at me earnestly.

The waterworks in my eyes started up all over again. OMG, what the hell was he going to say?

"Samantha Smith, will you…"

OMG, OMG, OMG!!!!

"…move in with me?"

"Yes!"

He stood up and I jumped into his arms.

Home at last. My mom had *no* idea what existed between me and Christos. How could she? My dad was nothing like Christos. Maybe that's why their marriage was the way it was. Well, my mom wasn't a prize in the romance department either. She preferred tax day over Valentine's Day, I was pretty sure. I suddenly felt a pinch of compassion for my parents. Maybe neither of them had any idea what true love could be.

Christos hugged me tightly and smooched me on the lips. I felt something in his hand pressing into my back. "What's that?" I asked.

He held up a box of candy cigarettes. "For later, after we have celebratory sex in your new home."

"You are the biggest dork I've ever loved," I smiled through tears.

"The *only* dork you've ever loved, *agápi mou…*"

We kissed passionately for a long time, I think until my shift was over. I didn't care. I loved my dork *and* his dork.

SAMANTHA

That night after work, Christos and I had dinner at the Manos house with Spiridon. We all sat in the kitchen while Spiridon cooked. He refused to let me do anything.

Spiridon made lamb kebabs. On the side was Tzatziki, which Spiridon explained was Greek yogurt with cucumbers and garlic, dolmades, which I had learned to love, and Kolokithopita, which were fried zucchini fritters.

I shoveled up some Tzatziki off my plate with a triangle of pita bread and took a bite. So yummy.

"We're celebrating your moving into our house, *Samoula*," Spiridon said from where he stood at the stove.

I wrinkled my nose. "What's a Samoula?" I asked.

Christos chuckled. "It's a Greek nickname for Samantha, right *Pappoús*?"

Spiridon turned around and smiled at me. "Yes. Now that you're moving in with us, *Samoula*, you're going to have to learn not only to eat Greek, but to speak Greek, think Greek, and live Greek. You did warn her about us, right Christos?" Spiridon winked at his grandson.

"Are you kidding, *Pappoús*?" Christos laughed. "If I'd told her what she was getting herself into, she would've run screaming back to Washington D.C.!"

"I would not," I chuckled. I hadn't even moved in yet, and already I felt completely at home in the Manos' house, like I'd live here for years.

For the first time in my life, I felt a hint of what a home *could* be. Home was a grounded place. A place I'd dreamt of since I was a little girl, but never known firsthand. Home was a comforting, supportive environment.

I thought about my little corner of the art studio at the back of Spiridon's house.

Home was also a nurturing environment. A place to help me grow, to allow me to become a woman. A place where I could gently set aside the girl within me and embrace the woman I was meant to be.

Sure, I recognized that my parents had done much to raise me. They had provided, they had directed. They had controlled. They had tried to make me a robot. A drone I never wanted to be.

I wanted to jump into life and discover things.

Christos had helped me do exactly that. It was as if he swam in a sparkling, magical ocean, and was constantly asking me to dive in with him and explore a vast, unknown world of exciting, enchanting possibility.

And now I had.

I was jumping in, all the way.

As the three of us ate together and filled our bellies with nourishing food while laughter filled our hearts, I felt like I was finally in the right place.

Finally home.

Christos had awoken me from a nightmare that had haunted me for my entire life.

Now I was alive.

I was awake, and I was never going back to sleep.

I was ready to live.

With Christos by my side.

After wiping his face with a napkin, Christos asked, "Do you still have those candy cigarettes?"

"I do," I smiled. "They're in my purse."

"Good, because you're going to need them."

"When?" I asked coquettishly.

"Right after dinner," Christos grinned. "Well, more like three hours after we finish dinner."

"I have to wait that long?" I would never have had this conversation in front of my parents. I didn't even think twice about how raunchy I must have sounded to Spiridon, who was sitting across the table from me.

"For the cigarettes, yes," Christos clarified, "but no, we're starting as soon as I clear the table." He smiled his cockiest grin.

"Gosh, would you look at the time?" Spiridon said, standing up from the table. "I totally forgot I was meeting an old friend for drinks tonight."

"Oh?" Christos asked. "Who?"

"Walt Childress," Spiridon said.

"You mean Professor Childress?" I asked.

"One and the same," Spiridon said.

"Really," Christos smiled. "When was the last time you two hung out?"

"It's been ages," Spiridon mused.

I grinned, "Then I bet you two will have plenty of fun tonight."

Spiridon chuckled, "If we don't punch each other out the second we say hello, I'm sure we will."

"You guys won't fight," Christos smiled warmly.

"Probably not," Spiridon said. "We're both too old to bother. I'll probably be gone for awhile. Which means you two can have the house to yourselves." He left the room while Christos and I cleaned up.

When Spiridon came downstairs, all dressed to go out, he said "Don't do anything I wouldn't do, you two." He slid the sleeve of his jacket back over his watch and glanced at the time. "I'll be gone, oh, let's say, four hours? That should be long enough, no?" He winked at both of us.

I burst out laughing. He totally knew we were going to have sex. And I didn't care! I couldn't believe it. My parents would've slapped a chastity belt around me if they'd been here.

Christos chuckled and wrapped his arm around my waist. "Bye, *Pappoús*. Say hi to Walt for me."

"Me too," I said.

"Will do," Spiridon said. "Have fun," he waved, then walked out the front door.

Christos turned to face me, encircling me with his arms. He gazed down at me with his lustrous blue eyes, those glowing jewels that had captured my heart the moment I'd seen them in September.

"I love you, Christos."

"I love you, *agápi mou*."

My life was perfect. It couldn't get any better

He leaned down to kiss me.

I was wrong. It could get better. Much better.

Our lips met and our tongues slid together.

We kissed for awhile in the kitchen.

"You know what I love about eating garlic?" Christos asked.

"What's that?" I frowned, expecting the worst.

"When we both have it, neither of us seems to care," he chuckled.

"I was thinking the same thing," I giggled, and pushed away from him.

"Where are you going?" he asked, his lashes lowering seductively.

"Catch me if you can!" I turned and ran out of the kitchen, through the living room, and upstairs to his bedroom.

I was giggling the entire way. He was right behind me, pounding down the upstairs hallway.

I dove onto the bed and tumbled into the sheets.

He stood in the doorway, hunched over. "I'm going to eat you up, little girl," he growled.

"Please do," I said confidently.

He vaulted across the room, flying through the air.

"Christos!" I shrieked, scooting back from the edge of the bed.

He slammed onto the mattress, laughing and bouncing like a kid. "I'm ravenous, *agápi mou*. I haven't had a thing to eat all day."

"You just had dinner!"

"That was an appetizer. You're the main course."

He crawled over the bed and started tickling me.

"Christos! Stop!"

"Why?" he smiled. "I love getting you worked up."

I pulled a blanket up to my chin. "I already am."

"Then I'm going to have to rip your clothes off," he leered.

"Please do."

He slowly pulled the covers down my chest. My heart raced. My thighs quivered. I was completely dressed, but I knew my womanhood was wet and ready.

He pulled my shoes off, one by one. Then lifted my shirt over my head and dropped it on the floor. Bra next. This was so easy. Why had I ever been shy?

My full breasts spilled out, my nipples instantly hard in the cool room. Christos lunged at one breast with his mouth and sucked on my nipple while squeezing and kneading both breasts passionately with each hand.

I leaned back on the pillows as he consumed me.

"I need more," he growled.

"Take it. Take me. Take everything. You have all of me, Christos."

He grinned his cocky grin. "And you have all of me, *agápi mou*." He unzipped my jeans and pulled them off. He smirked. "When are we going to get you some sexy underwear? You're all about the cotton panties. I'm picturing thongs and G-strings to go with your perfect body," he grinned.

"Maybe for Valentine's Day?"

His eyes flashed. He took a deep breath, and sat back on his heels.

"Is something wrong?" I asked, concerned.

"No," he smiled. "Everything's fine. I just need to take my boots off." He turned and sat on the edge of the bed, and slipped them slowly off. "Hold on, I need to use the bathroom."

"Are you okay?" I asked, now decisively worried.

"No, I just need to take a leak. I've had to go for an hour."

"Why didn't you say something, silly?" I swatted his arm.

"I'm saying something now," he flashed his dimpled grin, stood up, and went into the bathroom.

CHRISTOS

As soon as I closed my bathroom door, I turned on the water faucet. I leaned both hands on the sink, hanging my head. Fuck me.

My trial was on Valentine's Day.

Fuck.

She didn't know.

I still hadn't told her.

How could I?

All of the good feelings spinning through my heart, through Samantha's heart, flowing like love was supposed to flow: strong, powerful, eternal, all of it was going to come to a shrieking halt in a matter of days.

I didn't want to ruin the mood. Not tonight.

This would be our Valentine's Day celebration.

For me, anyway. I knew she'd be disappointed on the 14th. What girl didn't want Valentine's Day to be magical?

But how the fuck were you supposed to do that when you spent the entire day in a courtroom, watching your life hang in the balance?

I tried to push my misery out of my head.

Focus on the present moment.

Right now.

With Samantha.

"Are you okay in there, Christos?" Samantha asked through the door.

"Yeah, I'm good. I'll be out in a second." I flushed the empty toilet bowl for effect.

I looked at myself in the mirror. I pictured Samantha's amazing eyes. The naked, honest love I saw in them every time she looked at me. The love I wanted to protect from all the harm in the world.

My heart swelled as I thought about our love.

My grin returned. Cocky as ever.

Were my eyes watering?

Agápi mou...you have no idea how much I love you...

I hoped Samantha wouldn't notice, it might ruin the mood. She was always looking at my eyes, so I'd have to distract her from them.

SAMANTHA

Christos strolled out of the bathroom, completely naked, a cocky smirk on his face and his jumblies hanging out.

Wow! I clapped my hands to my cheeks. "Oh my god! I hadn't been expecting Mr. Naked! Where did Christos go?"

"You like?" he grinned.

"Of course I like! I *love!*"

He chuckled while walking over to the bed and climbed on top of the covers.

I ripped my panties off. "Don't need those anymore!"

"What do you mean?"

"It's thongs from here on out!" I said proudly.

"Don't rush into things," Christos chuckled.

"Hey, if I'm going to be as sexy as you are, I need the proper undergarments."

"I can live with that," he smiled.

"I have a surprise for you," I said, holding my arms out to him.

He leaned back slightly, his eyes narrowing. "What's that?" he asked cautiously.

Why was he so nervous? It wasn't like him. Oh well, I had the cure for that. "I started taking the pill two weeks ago." Christos had also told me a month ago that he had himself regularly tested for STDs, and was totally clean. We were now free to enjoy each other's bodies uninhibited. There was nothing left to interfere with the mingling of our bodies in physical love. "We don't need to use a condom!"

His eyes goggled. "What?"

"Did I say something wrong?" Now I was totally freaking out. Something felt really off, but I had no idea what it was.

"No, you said everything right," he smiled.

"I did?" I was so confused.

"Look," he said, pointing at his crotch.

I only realized at that moment that this was the first time I'd been naked with Christos and he hadn't had an erection from the get-go. He'd been flaccid when he'd walked out of the bathroom a moment ago. Before I had a chance to wonder why, his cock grew to full, straining attention in seven seconds.

"Holy shit!" I blurted. "I didn't know it could work that fast!"

"It only requires the proper motivation."

I was grinning from ear to ear as Christos crawled on top of me.

"Well," I said seductively, "two can play at that game."

"Really," he said cockily as he slid his fingers between my legs, and slipped them inside me. "You weren't kidding," he said, amazed. "You're soaking wet, woman."

"Only for you, *agápi mou*," I said.

Christos grinned like a kid. "Did you just call me *agápi mou*?"

"I did. Your grandfather said I needed to start speaking Greek, didn't he?"

"That he did," Christos chuckled.

"When are you going to teach me more Greek?"

"How about now?"

I felt the head of his cock pressing against my drenched folds.

"Oh," I moaned. "Teach me all the Greek you want, Christos. I'm ready for you to fill me up with all the Greek you can."

He laughed and dropped his head onto the pillow, burying his face next to my ear.

I laughed with him and wrapped my legs around his waist.

He slid right in.

"Whoa," he moaned. "You're too much, *agápi mou*," he whispered into my ear, which he promptly licked.

Between the sweet pressure of his cock filling me up and his warm breath on my ear, I was in heaven.

"I love you, Christos," I moaned as he pumped slowly in and out.

He moaned in the throes of his own ecstasy. "You have no idea how fucking *good* you feel, *agápi mou*, no idea."

"I think I have a pretty good idea," I quivered as my core clamped down around him.

He pushed himself slowly, deeply into me, and moaned. His hands reached beneath me and squeezed my ass, like he was trying to push himself more deeply into me than he ever had before.

It was luscious, it was flesh ecstasy, it was the greatest pleasure I'd ever known.

I was vaguely aware of the fact that Christos slid his hardness in and out of my softness for a long, long, time. I expected him to come. I'd always heard that guys came fast when they weren't wearing a condom.

Not Christos.

His stamina was beyond anything I'd ever imagined. At first, I almost wondered if he was feeling anything at all, but he sucked in deep hisses of breath and blew them out so frequently, I knew he was as overwhelmed with pleasure as I was.

"It feels so fucking good, *agápi mou*, I've never felt anything this good. Ever..." he groaned.

I moaned in response. It was all I could do.

He continued his hypnotic, mesmerizing rhythm of fucking me deep, long, hard, and so, so good.

I came multiple times while Christos pushed and pushed. My pleasure built in waves that swept from head to toe, stealing away all of my tension, all of my fear. I swam with Christos in that magical ocean I'd dreamed about.

The ocean that was *us*...

Finally, after what I actually believed was over an entire hour, I felt Christos begin to throb inside me. Every stroke seemed to be a Herculean effort for him. He literally shouted each time he pushed into my wetness. I vaguely felt that the sheets beneath me were soaked with my liquid love for this amazing man.

With every stroke, his body quaked.

"Aaahhh!" he yelled.

Again and again he forced himself deeper inside me until I thought he was going to shatter into a billion pieces.

"Aaaahhhh!!!!" he shouted.

The muscles deep inside me spasmed and grabbed his cock, not wanting to let him out.

Ever.

I started to have a titanic orgasm. Waves of pleasure pounded through my body.

"AAAAHHHH!!!!" he screamed.

His back arched and he forced his mammoth manhood into me deeper than ever before. And he came.

He *came*.

He threw his head back and roared, shaking the entire room.

"*AAAAAAHHHHHH!!!!!!*"

I felt his cock firing his cum into me.

It sent me over the edge. I came with him and screamed.

The muscles of my vagina clenched around him, milking out every last drop of his potent, slippery elixir. I wanted all of it, deep inside me.

All of it.

My body was trembling, vibrating, shaking in an overwhelming orgasm that wouldn't stop, my legs squeezing, my core hot and tight and wet, my love burning, exploding, overtaking all as Christos poured his love into me.

My rippling orgasm kept going and going.

I screamed ecstasy.

My heart raced. My eyes squeezed shut. My body consumed his, taking all that he had to give.

Our oceans of love had become one as our mutual wetness blended together forever.

Chapter 22

SAMANTHA

Christos and I woke up in each other's arms.

"Morning," he smiled down at me.

Sunlight peeked through the curtains, lining the edge of Christos' chiseled features in gold. He looked like a painting of a mystical hero. I couldn't help but smile widely.

"What?" he grinned.

I was afraid to open my mouth, certain my morning breath would ruin the moment. We'd had garlic galore the night before, when we ate all that Tzatziki. I imagined that if any low-flying birds were to pass by as I opened my mouth, they'd drop from the sky, with X's for eyes and land on their backs with their stiffened claws sticking straight up.

Christos leaned down and tried to kiss me. Obviously, he had no compassion for animals. I turned my head away, worried about those birds.

Christos snaked on top of me and kissed me on the mouth anyway, but I kept my lips locked.

He pulled back a few inches and chuckled. "You're worried about your breath, aren't you?"

I frowned, but knew he was onto me. I nodded guiltily.

He grinned. "Don't sweat it, *agápi mou*. At your worst, you're a hundred times sweeter than any woman on this planet." He leaned down for a kiss.

I shook my head.

He tickled my ribs and I burst out laughing.

His lips were on top of mine and we kissed passionately. I was learning that laughter always changed my mind. So what if we smelled like a garlic factory? If Christos didn't care, why should I?

The next thing I knew, he was between my thighs, his hot, hard manhood pressing against my already wet entrance.

"Oh!" I smiled.

"Morning sex?"

"Anything for you," I grinned, "*agápi mou…*"

"Man, hearing you say that totally turns me on every time. You even have the accent down pretty good. Say it again," he smiled.

"Anything for you," I purred, "*agápi mou. Agápi mou, agápi mou!*" I giggled.

"*Every*thing for you, *agápi mou*," he murmured, cocking his dimpled grin seductively as he slid himself inside of me.

He began a steady rhythm as our bodies twirled together in heady ecstasy. It seemed to go on for at least an hour before we both enjoyed powerful, exhilarating, and seemingly endless orgasms.

After, we showered together.

"What are your plans for today?" Christos asked as he reached around me with both arms and circled his soapy hands against my ass.

"I'm going to tell my apartment manager I'm moving out on the way to campus." It was increasingly difficult for me to concentrate with his hypnotizing hands in motion. "I've…uh, got, *oh*, classes," *moan*, "after…" I shook my head. "What are you doing?"

"Who, me?" he asked innocently.

"Do we have time?"

"You tell me," he murmured.

We were pressed together, chest to chest. His hard-on forced between us, a friendly visitor.

I didn't think we had time for another marathon round of love-making in the shower, but maybe we had time for a little something. "I think the first thing on *my* agenda is taking care of Little Christos," I giggled.

"Oh, you *so* did not call him little," he chuckled.

"Well, I only meant by comparison to the rest of your magnificent self." I circled my hands around his massive, soap-slick chest.

"I think you hurt his feelings," Christos moped.

"What?" I looked down. Sure enough, Little Christos was shrinking. "No!" I cried.

Christos laughed heartily. "He's going back into his shell."

"How do you do that? Did I do that?" I was confused. Had I

turned Christos off?

"You have to apologize," Christos grinned.

"I'm not apologizing to your penis!" I shouted. "What is it with men talking to their dicks like people?!"

Christos threw his head back and laughed. Water coursed down his face and drizzled into mine. My eyes automatically squinted until he tipped his face back down to gaze into my eyes.

"I have a ton to do anyway," Christos smiled. "My girlfriend's moving in with me soon, so I've got to get the place ready."

"Your *girlfriend*?" I smiled seductively.

"Yeah, she's the best. Amazing in bed. Don't even bother trying to top her, she's way too good." His arms wrapped around my waist and he kissed me passionately as water cascaded around us, swallowing us in a warm embrace.

"She's good in bed, huh?" I asked skeptically.

"None better," Christos smiled.

"I bet I could show her a thing or two," I teased.

"Oh yeah?" Little Christos stood up and demanded my full attention once again.

"Yeah," I smiled devilishly. I wrapped my fingers around the head of Christos' cock and slid my soapy hands over the tip, squeezing and sliding and massaging.

Christos' head tipped back and he moaned loud and long. His knees buckled slightly and he stepped backward until his shoulders touched the wall. I continued my slippery assault on the softness of his hard cock. His eyes rolled back into his head as his lips peeled back over his teeth.

I worked my hand around the head of his cock, not entirely sure what I was doing. "Like this?"

"Fuck," he snarled, "keep doing that."

"Your wish is my command, master," I joked.

Christos bent forward and laughed hard, leaning his forehead into mine. "I'm pretty sure you're the one in charge at the moment," Christos snickered.

I couldn't help but giggle in response. I started sliding my hand up and down his length. I cupped Christos' balls with my other hand. They were so soft compared to his penis. I caressed them as I pumped his shaft.

Christos' snickers stiffened into hisses. "Fuck, Samantha, that is fucking paradise. Keep doing that."

I did.

He threw his head back again, his whole body arching with intense pleasure.

"Samantha," he moaned, "don't fucking stop."

Spray from the shower-head poured around us, steaming up the entire stall with sultry fog. I felt his cock expand in my hand. It was burning hot. It was so big, I had to encircle its length with both my hands. How did all of it fit inside me? I didn't know, but I was suddenly wet between my legs and desperately wanted to put his penis back where it belonged.

Inside *me*.

Before I could figure out how to do that, he moaned. "Aaaaahhhhhh..." His head twitched repeatedly back as his cock stood taller, prouder, hotter, harder. Without warning, it jolted in my hand.

Mission control, we have lift off!

"FUUUUCCCCKKKK!!!!" Christos shouted.

A thick rope of semen jetted out of his cock.

"AAAAAHHHHH!!!!" he shouted again.

More and more come gushed out of him, splashing on the shower floor.

"Oh my god!" I blurted. "There's so much!" Not that I had much to compare it too, but it was a lot more than I had expected.

Christos was lost somewhere. Knowing that I had taken him on this journey was about the coolest thing I'd ever done in the bedroom, er, I meant the shower. *I'd* done it. *I'd* made him come.

Me.

Wow.

I kept wringing the head of his cock with my fingers and pumping the shaft with my other hand, wondering how far I could take things. Christos' body was sagging against the shower wall. Then suddenly, he lurched forward as my fingers again slid over the head of his cock.

"Fuck! Stop!"

I yanked my hand away, suddenly worried I'd broken something. "I'm sorry! What did I do?"

He slung his arm over my shoulder and kissed my cheek. "The head gets super sensitive after I come. I mean, like, a million times more sensitive."

"Oh. Is that bad?" I asked, concerned.

He kissed me briefly. "No, it's all good." He chuckled throatily. "I mean, crazy, insanely good."

"Do you want me to stop?"

"No. Just, let me relax, and keep doing it, just go slow."

"Are you sure?"

"Totally," he moaned.

I started up again, slowly. Every time the ring of my circled fingers squeezed down the head of him, his entire body shivered. I worried he was going to fall to the tiles and hurt himself, he shook so hard.

"More?" I asked uncertainly.

"Uh, uh, uh, uh, uh," was all he could say.

Eventually, he knelt down on the tiled floor, and I had to release him from my grasp. He hadn't come again, but I swear he'd had a five-minute orgasm or something.

"Are you okay?" I asked tentatively.

"I'm about to pass out," he whispered hoarsely.

Was that a good thing? I wasn't sure what to do next.

"I'm fine," he reassured. "Just went to the moon for awhile. Fuck, Samantha, you are a fucking natural at that."

Christos was kneeling in front of me and leaned his cheek against my stomach. His arms wrapped around my ass and he pulled me into a strangely intimate embrace, his mouth inches above my womanhood.

Wow. I couldn't believe it. I'd literally brought this insurmountable mountain of a man to his knees.

Me.

Whoa.

I couldn't get over how this magical man was teaching me things about *myself*, things I would never have guessed, as if he knew me better than I knew myself. In many ways, I thought maybe he did. Almost daily he showed me who I *could* be, if I only gave myself a chance and took the risk to try. I'd had no idea.

I could only begin to imagine who I might become with Christos in my life. With him, the stars were the limit.

I suddenly felt overwhelming emotion pour through my body. I loved Christos so much, I wasn't sure what I would do without him. A powerful protective urge welled up into my chest, heating my heart, filling my body with a womanly fire. This was *my* man. Mine.

I would do anything to keep him safe.

Anything.

I was desperately scared life would snatch him from my arms. I squeezed him as tightly as I could, my hands cradling his head against my belly.

"*Agápi mou*," I whispered passionately.

"I love you," Christos said.

Why was I suddenly so terrified?

SAMANTHA

After we cleaned up from our shower, we went downstairs.

Spiridon was sitting in the kitchen, sipping coffee. "Good morning, *Samoula!*" He smiled from ear to ear. My parents never smiled in the morning.

And I never looked at them ten minutes after having tons of sex. Heck, I don't think I could be in the same *city* as my parents for at least ten days after what Christos and I had done upstairs. My face boiled over. Hopefully Spiridon thought it was from the shower. Er, I mean, from taking a shower, alone, like a proper girl. Crap, I needed to run out the front door and drive off before embarrassment caused me to spontaneously combust.

"Hey, *Pappoús*," Christos said. He didn't seem the slightest bit uncomfortable. "How was Walt?" He walked up to his grandfather, leaned over with an arm around the man, and kissed the top of his head.

Wow, I would never kiss my dad or mom like that under any circumstances. Had I woken up in the Twilight Zone? Without giving it a second thought, I wrapped my arms around Spiridon and gave him a huge hug. "Morning!"

He rubbed my back while he said, "Good morning to you too, *koritsáki mou!*"

My embarrassment disappeared as quickly as it had overtaken me a moment ago. I didn't feel weird at all. Probably because Spiridon didn't act weird. He probably didn't even give what Christos and I were doing a second thought. I could easily get used to this.

My parents, on the other hand, would be prodding for cracks in my defenses, snooping around for whatever inappropriate behavior I had most recently engaged in. I was so done with that kind of treatment.

Christos made us breakfast while Spiridon and I sat at the table.

"Walt was terrific," Spiridon said. "We had a good talk. Mended some fences."

"That's great," Christos said.

What was the mystery behind the history between Walt Childress and Spiridon Manos? I still had no idea. It didn't seem like any answer would be forthcoming over breakfast.

Afterward, I drove to my apartment in my VW and told the manager about moving out. He told me I had to give a 30-day notice in writing, and I had to pay the pro-rated amount for the days in March I hadn't yet paid for. Oh well, at least I was moving out.

As much as I wanted to, I couldn't quit Grab-n-Dash right away, but I was happy to keep my job at the Eleanor M. Westbrook art museum for the rest of the academic year. It seemed like I got more studying done for Sociology and History at the museum than I did anywhere else anyway, so that was okay. I was all about killing two birds with one low-stress on-campus job.

I left my apartment and drove to campus by myself. For the first time since I'd started at SDU, my drive didn't feel one bit lonely.

I was totally wrapped up in the warm embrace of Christos and his welcoming grandfather. I had never experienced this sense of pervasive peace growing up. My life had always been tense, nervous, filled with problems and worries and frustrations.

I started to wonder if perhaps all those concerns my parents labored under were nothing more than their own creations. It's not like they were broke, or had major health problems, or dangerous jobs. They just didn't seem happy. Like they didn't know *how* to be happy.

Was it that simple?

I didn't really know. But I did know that I was starting to feel a happiness and contentment that was worth its weight in gold. No, strike that. At this rate, I think my happiness was verging on priceless. I had discovered the greatest treasure a person could hope to find in life.

Unconditional love from my second family.

I was beaming with a huge smile when I parked on campus at SDU and walked to Oil Painting class.

SAMANTHA

My happiness bubble burst when I walked into the Oil Painting studio in the Visual Arts building.

Kamiko had set up at an easel between two other students. Up until the fiasco with Brandsome at Charboneau Gallery, she had always set up next to me and Romeo. Ever since then, she'd set herself up so that there was no room for me or even Romeo.

I felt terrible about the whole thing. I'd tried to apologize to her about Brandsome via texts, emails, stopping by her dorm room, anything I could think of. But she wasn't ready to talk. All I could do was give her space.

I set up my paints, brushes and palette at a free easel, and saved the space next to me for Romeo. He was running late today. When he finally came in, he set his book bag down next to me and pulled out his supplies.

"Hey, Sam," he said, somewhat flustered.

"I think this is the first time I've ever made it to class before you," I said in a friendly voice.

"I was up late working on another scene for Playwriting. I had to get it just right," he smiled. His expression dropped when he saw Kamiko ignoring us on the other side of the room. "I see that Kamiko still looks like a wounded bunny rabbit. Poor thing."

"Yeah," I sighed. I had already told Romeo in detail what had happened at Charboneau with Brandon and how he broke Kamiko's heart. "You told Kamiko I was sorry again, right?"

"Yeah. I've told her a hundred times how bad you feel," Romeo said.

"And you told her that Brandon had totally come on to me? Not the other way around?"

"Yes, Sam," Romeo reassured compassionately. "I don't think she's actually mad at you. More than anything, I think she's just sad. You know how it is, Kamiko's so busy with studying, she never gets out, never dates, and that hot bastard Brandsome had to go and send her a bunch of mixed signals on New Year's Eve. She's probably been making secret wedding plans ever since."

"Doesn't she tell you everything?" I asked.

"Usually. I mean, she's been prattling on about Brandsome non-stop for weeks. But I know Kamiko. I'm starting to think she was holding something back. I guess I didn't realize how bad she had it for the guy."

"Oh," I said.

"Yeah, I'm a little worried about her," he said. "She's been secluding herself more and more lately. It's not good for her."

"Is there anything we can do?" I asked. "I mean, I know she's not talking to me, but I want to help somehow."

"If you've got any of that love potion you used on Christos left over, maybe we can trick Brandsome into drinking some," Romeo joked.

I shook my head and rolled my eyes. "I wish I did," I smiled forlornly.

"Wait, I know!" Romeo said. "Professor Bittinger is a witch! Maybe she can stir up a fresh batch in her cauldron!"

I smiled. "Sadly, I think if she knew how to brew potions, she would've already used one on Hunter."

"You're right," Romeo sighed. "I guess all we can do is give Kamiko time to get over it."

"Yeah," I said. I glanced at the clock on the wall. We still had a few minutes until class started. Professor Cogdill still hadn't arrived. I looked around the room and saw that all the students were chatting or setting up. All had a lightness of spirit and purpose. Except Kamiko.

She sat on a stool, slumped over, totally miserable. She was breaking my heart. I walked over to her.

"Hey, Kamiko," I said quietly.

She looked up at me with heavy eyes that revealed an equally heavy heart. She didn't respond.

"I, um, Kamiko? I just wanted to say again I'm really sorry about what happened. It wasn't my fault. Brandon came onto me, and when you left I told him what a jerk he was for treating you like that." I sounded nervous, and the proximity of the other students wasn't helping. At least they were engaged with setting up, or were chatting with the other students nearby. I wished this conversation had been private, but I hadn't been able to find a better location. I was desperate.

Kamiko stared back at me, her face long. She looked completely miserable. Was I making things worse? Should I leave her alone? I glanced back at Romeo. He shrugged his shoulders sympathetically. He didn't know what the answer was either.

I squeezed around Kamiko's easel until I was standing beside her. I put my hand tenderly on her shoulder. "I'm sorry, Kamiko. I really am. I don't know what else to say. But it makes me sad to see you hurting like this."

Kamiko had to crane her head to look up at me. The naked heartbreak in her tearing eyes almost broke mine.

"I'm so sorry," I said. I wanted to hug her. I leaned tentatively toward her.

She shrugged me off and turned back to stare at her feet.

I let my hand slide from her shoulder as I walked back toward my easel. I was ready to cry. I needed to step outside for a minute. When I opened the door to the studio, Professor Cogdill came walking in.

"Thank you, Miss Smith," he beamed. "You must have X-Ray vision to have seen me coming through a solid door," he quipped.

I stammered, "Oh, uh, no, I…"

He smiled back. "It's okay, your secret's safe with me," he winked. "Ready to start painting?"

"Yeah," I muttered. I would have to save my cry over Kamiko's distress until after class. It made me so sad to see her like this, but there was nothing I could do. Romeo was right. She needed time to heal. I just wanted to help take away her pain somehow. But I couldn't. I could only offer support which she didn't necessarily have to take.

Maybe she just hurt so bad because she thought the whole world was against her. I could totally relate.

I knew what it was like to have strict parents like hers. Hers were pushing hard for her to become a doctor as soon as she possibly could. But all you had to do was take one look at all the paintings covering her dorm room to realize that maybe medicine wasn't the path for her.

Sadly, no matter what I did, I couldn't change her situation. It was her struggle between herself and her parents. Would she grab hold of her dreams and never let them go, or would she succumb to the demands of her family?

I almost felt guilty for having Christos in my life. He was the one light that had guided me into safe harbor from the tumultuous, miserable life I had lived back in Washington D.C. under both the iron influence of my parents and the rejection of my peers.

For all I knew, Kamiko was wishing that Brandon Charboneau would be her Christos, her savior from a bleary future she didn't want, her guide out of the prison of her parents' dictatorial demands. And now Brandon had closed that door for her.

As I returned to my painting easel next to Romeo, I silently thanked my good fortune that I had Christos in my life. I feared that without him, I would be as distraught and lost as Kamiko was right at that moment.

I shivered and pushed my dark thoughts away, determined not to fall prey to my own morbid worries.

Besides, I had my own issues left to deal with. When Oil Painting was over, I would have to go to Sculpting and face Hunter Blakeley. I still hadn't seen him since the incident with Christos.

SAMANTHA

Romeo had lunch with Kamiko after Oil Painting, just the two of them. He told me was getting worried about her, and wanted to check in with her privately. I understood.

I bought a sandwich at the Student Center convenience store and went to the Central Fountain to eat in solitude.

I sat down on a bench and unwrapped my sandwich. I couldn't believe how warm it was for February. My heavy winter coats were all packed away in the back of my closet in my apartment. I didn't think I'd ever need them in San Diego. The thought brought a smile to my face.

While I chewed on a bite of my sandwich, I glanced around and noticed someone carrying a huge bouquet of flowers along one of the walkways that connected to the Central Fountain.

I wondered who the flowers could be for. Maybe they were going to some professor's office, a gift from a secret admirer, delivered by some singing telegram man? Maybe some graduate student was about to propose marriage to another graduate student who was a T.A, and the guy with the flowers was going to walk into his girlfriend's section in front of a bunch of undergrads, and get down on one knee? I smiled. The romantic possibilities were endless.

I smiled to myself as the massive bouquet and whoever was carrying them approached the fountain. I felt increasingly nervous as the flowers got closer and closer. By now, I would've expected the person holding them to have turned and headed off toward their destination.

But the flower man kept coming, until he stopped right at my feet.

Gulp.

I couldn't see around the bouquet. Who was it?

Christos?

The flower man lowered the bouquet.

Hunter Blakeley.

Oh, great.

I had a moment to thank the fact that Kamiko wasn't here to witness yet another guy throwing himself at me. Not that Hunter was right for Kamiko. Hunter was right for himself, and that was about it.

"Hey, Sam," Hunter smiled.

Yes he was handsome. For once, he didn't have his aviator sunglasses on and his amber eyes seemed to glow like warm embers in the overcast light.

"Hey, Hunter." Did I sound like I was groaning? I didn't want to be rude, but I didn't exactly want to be polite to Hunter, either. Not after how he'd treated Romeo and Christos. Screw it. Maybe I needed to be rude.

"I bought these for you," Hunter smiled, setting the bouquet down on the bench next to me. "Think of it as a peace offering. For what I said to your friend," Hunter smiled.

Did he expect me to thank him? After what he'd said and done? I glared at him. "He has a name, you know," I growled.

Hunter's smile dimmed slightly.

"You don't even know his name, do you?" I shook my head. "You're a jerk, Hunter."

"Would it help if I said I'm sorry?" he asked.

"Not to me, it wouldn't. Besides, I can see right through you,

Hunter. You're not here because you care about my friend's feelings. His name is Romeo, by the way. Maybe you can remember that and apologize to him the next time you see him."

Hunter scoffed at my suggestion.

"Yeah," I smirked, "that's what I thought. You're just making a play for me, Hunter."

His mouth opened to protest.

"Zip it," I barked. "Let me try this one more time. You have met my boyfriend. He is a real person. We are in love. And...I. Am. Not. Interested. Okay?"

"But—"

"Do I need to hire a skywriter to put it up in smoke clouds for all of San Diego to see? 'Samantha Smith has a boyfriend. She is not going to date Hunter Blakeley. Or go out with him. Ever.'" Did I sound harsh? Maybe I did, because I was mad. I wasn't going to let Hunter get away with being charming when I knew it was all an act. A Lame Damian sort of act.

The quivering smile on Hunter's face gave it all away. He was forcing himself to smile. Trying to hide his anger. Not because he thought his anger was inappropriate or undeserved in this situation, but because he knew it worked against his goal of getting in my pants. That was it. I believed he lacked any genuine compassion. Any he may have given would have just been for show.

I gave Hunter a flat smile. "You should probably go," I said. "No, never mind, I'm leaving." I packed up my sandwich, grabbed my book bag, and walked away, leaving Hunter and his ridiculous bouquet at the Central Fountain.

I wasn't at all surprised when Hunter showed up in Sculpting class an hour later without the bouquet. Maybe he smartened up and gave it to Marjorie. Somehow, I doubted it. I was, however, completely surprised that Hunter didn't speak to me during any of the breaks during class, and didn't follow me after class.

Had he finally gotten the message? I hoped so. Because I had far more important things to worry about than Hunter Blakeley. As I drove home from campus, I thought about the fact that I needed to actually call my parents and tell them I was moving out of my apartment, and didn't need their bribery money to become an Accountant.

I was done with that.

I was going to be an artist.

When I pulled into my apartment and clomped upstairs, I was determined to figure out exactly what to say to them to set them at ease. My stomach flipped and dropped at the thought.

After distracting myself for several hours with homework, I decided I needed some advice about handling my parents.

I decided to give Christos a call. He would know what to say, even if all he had to offer was encouragement.

Unfortunately, he didn't answer his phone.

I left a message and hoped he'd call back soon.

Too bad I didn't hear back from Christos until late the next day.

Chapter 23

CHRISTOS

After spending another day in my studio with Isabella, I sent her home and picked up the mail. I opened an invoice from Russell Merriweather's law firm. There were way too many zeroes in the amount after the dollar sign.

At the rate I was blowing through my cash, I was going to be broke before my trial was over. Oh well. Being broke beat going to prison.

I walked to the hand-carved mahogany liquor cabinet in the living room and debated having a drink. Whiskey sounded really good. As I reached for a clean glass, an image of Samantha flashed through my head, followed by a picture of my mom walking out the front door of my parents' house for the last time.

After releasing a heavy sigh, I set down the glass and decided to go for a jog up the hill to my grandad's bench instead. I always loved sitting up there and enjoyed the view. It was meditative and exactly what I needed to relax.

I changed to running clothes and walked out the front door of the house, ready to get my blood pumping.

A black Mercedes convertible whipped off the street and drove up my driveway.

Tiffany.

Great.

Her dad was in the car with her.

Even worse.

The shining car rolled to a stop right in front of me. Tiffany was all smiles, "Hey Christos."

"Hey, Tiffany," I sighed. "Hey, Mr. Kingston-Whitehouse." I hated calling him that. I think he liked that I, and probably everyone else who knew him, hated calling him that. His first name was hyphenated too. Westin-Conrad. No shit. All those syllables. It took two weeks just to say the guy's damn name. Westin-Conrad Kingston-Whitehouse the *Filth*.

Filthy, as in dirty.

For short, I thought of him as Wes-Con.

The only difference between Wes-Con and your average street criminal was the expensive team of lawyers he kept on retainer. Fucking nouveau American Royalty.

Anyway, I knew for a fact Wes-Con never drove himself anywhere. He always had a chauffeur. But Tiffany loved to drive, so I'm sure she'd offered to take the wheel for Dear Old Dad.

Wes-Con would do anything for Daddy's little girl.

"To what do I owe the pleasure?" I asked while opening Tiffany's door for her. Like I said, it was a gentleman thing.

She was all tan legs and about an inch of skirt. Her pastel top was equally minimalistic, showcasing more of her lusciously tan shoulders and delicate neckline.

Tiffany gave me her hand, like she couldn't stand up without my help. I indulged. It was easier than making an issue out of it. She stood and I closed the door.

Wes-Con gave me a wide-eyed look when I didn't dash around to open his door, like he was stuck inside Tiff's convertible. He could get out of his own damn car. Believe it or not, he unbuckled his own seatbelt, but he fumbled with the door handle, like he'd forgotten how door handles worked from lack of practice, before climbing out of the car. He played off his ignorance like it was normal.

He wore standard-issue Martha's Vineyard golfer's attire. Had nobody told him this was San Diego?

"Christos," he said, walking around the car, his hand already out and ready to do some greasing. Wes-Con shook firmly, and held my elbow with his other hand. It was this bizarre, upscale authoritarian thing, like he was saying, "you are now under my control."

Okay.

"Good to see you, young man," he said.

I smiled at him. "Likewise. Come inside. Can I offer you two something to drink?" I knew how to play the game too.

"That would be fantastic," Wes-Con said.

I could tell Tiffany was deferring to her dad. That definitely meant they'd strategized in advance. I remembered reading somewhere that you should never fight a war on two fronts. It had fucked Napoleon, and it had fucked the Germans in World War II. I had a feeling I wasn't going to fare much better with two Kingston-Whitehouses going for my throat.

Oh well, into the lion's den. At least it was my den. I led them into the Manos house.

"How is Spiridon?" Wes-Con asked.

"He's doing good," I nodded.

"Is he painting again?"

"Not really. I think he's retired."

"It's a damn shame," Wes-Con said. "Your grandfather is a living legend in the world of landscape paintings."

Although I wished that was a simple compliment well-earned by my grandfather, I sensed it was merely an opening stratagem. *Set your opponent at ease. When their defenses are down, attack with great force.* I think Sun Tzu or somebody said that.

I walked over to the liquor cabinet in the living room. I guess I wasn't getting away from it as easily as I'd hoped. "What can I get you to drink?"

Unlike most people, for whom that meant water or iced tea or soda, for Wes-Con, it only meant liquor. The harder the better. I could respect that.

"Do you have any scotch?" Wes-Con asked.

"Of course." I poured two glasses of thirty-year-old Glenfiddich single-malt, neat. I knew for Wes-Con, this was the cheap stuff. He could deal. "You want one, Tiff?"

"No, thanks. Do you have any Zima?"

"Fresh out," I quipped. Nobody drank that shit anymore.

"Never mind," she snooted.

I handed Wes-Con his glass and we clinked before swallowing.

"Excellent," Wes-Con said.

It should be, at five-hundred a bottle.

"Tiffany tells me there's been a problem with her painting?"

He didn't waste any time. Down to business. I smiled. "Yeah, something about a missing check?" I believed in hitting hard and hitting first.

"I can write you a check right now, from my personal account, if you'd like." Wes-Con pulled a checkbook out of his blazer and started writing with a thousand-dollar gold pen. I knew Wes-Con was like a samurai warrior with that checkbook of his. Once he took it out, he meant to use it. "I believe the amount was $25,000?"

I knew his check would clear. That was never the issue. We both knew it. Wes-Con just liked to hold onto his money until you showed up outside his front door in the middle of the night with the pitchforks and torches and the rest of the indentured servants. Then he made nice, handed you thirty pieces of silver, threw you some table scraps, and told everyone not to come back until they'd been deloused.

He could keep his bribe.

"Oh, that's not necessary, Mr. Kingston-Whitehouse," I said smoothly.

"Nonsense, young man. I can't very well expect you to do work and not get paid."

Yes he could, and did.

He tore the check from the check book and handed it to me. Mother fucker. He was good. But he made one crucial mistake. He was trying to buy me for his daughter. And we both knew it.

Problem was, I was not for sale. Especially when it came to the Kingston-Whitehouses.

Wes-Con held the check out to me expectantly. It hovered between us like a victory flag. He was acting like he was Neil Fucking Armstrong about to plant that shit on the moon.

"I'm sorry, Mr. Kingston-Whitehouse. I can't take your money. It's the principle of it. Think of my painting as a personal gift from me to your daughter. A token for all our years of friendship, and the friendship between our two families." My shit-shovel was moving a hundred miles an hour. "It looks splendid hanging in your yacht, by the way."

Wes-Con drilled my eyes with his. "I insist." It was all he said.

He could drill all he wanted. He wasn't going to strike oil with me. "I couldn't."

The check hovered. Wes-Con's hand twitched imperceptibly.

I wasn't going to grab it, and I knew he wouldn't let it fall to the floor. Mainly out of respect, partially, because I don't think he could stomach the idea of letting his money touch the ground, like some miscreant would rush out from beneath the couch, snatch it up, and run to the bank with it.

More importantly, he would never deign to simply set it down and say something like, "I'll leave it on the counter," or whatever. Because he wanted me to *take* it. If I *took* it, we both knew it meant he owned a piece of me.

No dice.

He tucked the check into his blazer. But the checkbook was still out. He wanted blood. "No matter," he grinned like a lizard, "I would also like to discuss the manner of an additional painting for Tiffany."

I shot Tiffany a warning glare. She and I had already been through this.

She opened her mouth to speak but clamped it shut when she saw me glaring.

After a moment, I chuckled. "Tiffany and I discussed this on your yacht, Mr. Kingston-Whitehouse. On New Year's Eve. Isn't that right, Tiffany?"

"We did," she smiled viciously, "and—"

I cut her off. "And the answer is still no." I was standing firm. No nude painting of Tiffany.

Wes-Con's Cheshire grin came out. The trouble with perfect teeth, and I meant the kind that cost north of a hundred grand, was that they were *too* perfect. Like he had two-times too many of them or something.

"What's your price, Christos?" Wes-Con smiled.

What I always loved about a good fight was that there's not always a definitive moment when the tables turned. Sometimes, the superior fighter just wore his opponent down inch by inch.

I shook my head.

Wes-Con's smile cranked up another kilowatt, "I believe Tiffany had discussed with you the figure of fifty thousand cash, direct to you."

I shook my head.

"One hundred thousand."

I was going to string this out.

A knockout fight where the loser dropped to the mat in the first round was always a big thrill, but it was never as sweet as when two heavyweights went head-to-head all the way to the twelfth, pounding the shit out of each other until the loser finally went to his knee in the last minute of the fight, down but not out, struggling to get back up before the final bell. Both fighters would be all battered and bloody afterward, and you knew both contenders were the meanest sons of bitches on the planet.

But one of them was meaner.

That guy was me.

I flashed a thin grin at Wes-Con, toying with him, pushing to see if he would stay standing all the way to the bell.

Wes-Con wasn't throwing in the towel. His smile stretched a little wider. "One-fifty."

I could respect that, but I shook my head. It wasn't the twelfth.

Wes-Con's smile went all the way. "Two."

This time I didn't shake my head.

Just when I thought Wes-Con's smile couldn't go any wider, it stretched another half-millimeter. His cheeks quivered. I think he was cramping up. "Two-fifty."

I stood my ground. I wasn't for sale to anybody, no matter how much I needed the money.

His eyes twitched. Wes-Con was about to go DefCon. I saw a single drop of sweat on the corner of his forehead. That was his towel going into the ring. But it wasn't even the twelfth round. I'd thought Wes-Con had way more cash than that, especially when it came to his daughter. Guess not.

They say that every man had his price.

I didn't. Not when my love for Samantha was on the line.

The battle won, I said casually, "Would you guys like to see the new work?" Meaning, a sneak-peek at my unveiled, upcoming paintings. You always wanted to offer them a token gift after you ransacked their shit. A gift that said, "Hey, your ass has been kicked, but it doesn't mean we can't still be friends."

"I think we better be going," Wes-Con said, sliding his checkbook back into his blazer, where it joined the useless check for $25,000. Had there been any samurai warriors on hand, they would've broken that gold pen of his on principle.

I was merciful. His pen would remain intact.

"*Daddy!!*" Tiffany shrieked with anger. "*You promised me that painting!!!!*"

You know how they say behind every powerful king is a powerful queen? Sometimes all you needed was a princess. They were the worst.

"No, Tiffany," I said.

Unfortunately for Tiffany, Wes-Con had just become my vassal on this issue. At least she still had her yacht to go cry on. Or she could make Wes-Con buy her something for a couple-hundred grand.

"*Daddy!!*" she screeched. "*I want my painting!!!!*"

I shook my head. She was still referring to it as hers. Her entitlement was legendary.

Westin-Conrad Kingston-Whitehouse flicked his eyes at his daughter briefly, then gave me a plaintive, horrified look. I think it was meant to be a private moment between us men.

I actually felt bad for the guy.

I showed them the door and offered them waters for the road. Both declined. Maybe I should've offered Wes-Con some earplugs. Poor guy.

When they were long gone, I returned to the liquor cabinet and poured myself a fat glass of the cheap stuff and pounded half of it in one go.

I walked out to the studio and looked at my nearly-completed painting of Isabella. I was not liking what I saw. It was verging on hack work. The problem with showing hack work was that if you did too much of it, no one wanted to pay a premium price for your art anymore. Not long after that, nobody wanted your art at all. We're talking garage sales and thrift store pricing.

I sighed heavily.

Maybe I was rushing the painting because Brandon was calling every day asking about my status. I had a backlog of paintings to get through for the show. Maybe I could spend more time on the Isabella canvas, turn it into something special.

Or not.

As of yet, no pre-sale money had come in. Brandon had said something about building anticipation to push the prices up before closing any sales. That meant no more money for yours truly until after the show, which was likely to be months away.

Russell Merriweather's invoice for services rendered would have to wait, but I could only string him along based on our friendship for so long before I looked like a bum. Russell had bills of his own to pay.

With my trial date breathing down my neck, I wondered how

much painting I would get done if I landed in jail. I'm sure the corrections officers would be more than happy to set up a private studio in my cell.

Yeah, right.

With storm clouds hovering over my financial horizon and shit closing in around me from multiple directions, Wes-Con's $250,000 was money I could've used.

But there was no way I was selling out Samantha for any amount.

I tipped back my glass of whisky and downed the rest of it before walking back to the liquor cabinet for more.

Maybe there was an escape hatch from this mess I wasn't seeing yet.

There was *always* a way out of any dilemma, even if it was the most drastic one.

SAMANTHA

When I got my mid-term grade for History that day, it turned out I was bombing the class worse than I'd thought. My overall grade was now hovering around a C-minus. The last thing I wanted was a D on my transcript.

Fortunately, I had paid Major Marjorie another visit in her office hours and she had confirmed that my grade would now most certainly be a B, if not higher. That worked for me.

But a D in History? Even *I* wouldn't be happy with that. My parents, of course, would put out a contract on my life if they found out I got a D. Knowing my mom, should probably put one out on Christos, too.

Hell to pay...

I needed to start hitting the books twice as hard. I don't know where I was going to find the time. The only answer was less sleep. Even though I'd agreed to move in with him, Christos and I really hadn't been spending much time together lately, even when it came to working together in his studio. We were both simply too busy. It was a total drag.

Luckily for me, I didn't have a shift at either the museum or Grab-n-Dash today. I was free to focus my entire afternoon and evening on the political exploits and daring deeds of the American Presidents. Yipee! Not.

But I *was* morbidly surprised to discover that many past American Presidents were far from nice people. Many had been involved in all kinds of back-door nastiness. I mean, I'd heard that Abraham Lincoln had secretly hunted vampires, but I didn't know that some of the previous presidents had *been* vampires. Seriously. I read it on the internet somewhere.

Groan.

The truth was, I doing anything I could think of to make my reading more interesting for myself, but I kept imagining political cartoons of everything I read, which wasn't actually helping my comprehension and retention.

Maybe I needed some ice cream? I was convinced it helped me remember things better. I stood up to go raid my freezer.

My cell phone rang.

My first thought was that it was Christos calling to tell me not to get any ice cream and that he was coming over to cook me dinner. The idea made me smile.

Then I saw it was parents.

There went my smile.

"Hello?"

"Good evening, Sam," my dad said.

"Hello, Sam," Mom said.

"To what do I owe this pleasure?" I asked sarcastically.

"Your mother and I were calling to find out if you had registered for Spring Quarter classes yet?"

Registration was just around the corner.

"Not yet," I sighed.

"Well, I wanted to be the first to break the good news," my dad said.

"What's that?" I asked, pretty sure my parents' idea of good news didn't match up with mine.

"I noticed in the online schedule of classes that Managerial Accounting is indeed offered Spring Quarter. Isn't that terrific, Sam?"

Wow, my parents were totally stalking me. I rolled my eyes to myself. They were so not getting me.

"Now you can change your major back and continue with your Accounting classes without falling behind," Dad said with a smile.

I steeled myself. It was time to put this issue to bed once and for all, even if it killed me. "I'm not changing my major."

"And why, pray tell, are you not?" my mom asked snidely.

"Because I don't want to?" I sneered.

"I told you, Bill," my mom growled, "it's that *Christos*. He's putting all these silly ideas in our daughter's head."

"No, Mom," I said confidently, "if you remember, Art was *my* idea. Remember you guys said I couldn't go to art school because it was too expensive? Well, SDU isn't too expensive, and it turns out the university has a great art program. For the same price as an Accounting major."

"We're not throwing away good money on an *art* education!" my mom scoffed.

"I have to agree with your mother on that," my dad said.

I shook my head. "It's not throwing away. There's all kinds of jobs for people in the arts."

"I'll bet," my mom huffed dismissively.

"Mom, you don't know what you're talking about. I—"

"Pardon me?" my mom barked.

I tried to calm myself. "Mom, the more I learn about art, the more I see there are jobs out there."

"If there were so many *art* jobs, what are you doing working at a convenience store?" Mom sniveled.

"I don't know, Mom, but it's not like there were a bunch of accounting jobs for undergraduates either. I scoured the job websites and never found a single one for someone who's only taken two accounting classes."

Mom was silent.

"She has a point, Linda," my dad said.

I was shocked into silence again. That was probably the first time in my life my dad had conceded that I wasn't an idiot.

"I don't care *what* sort of point she has," Mom growled, "I'm not happy about this whole art thing. And I don't care *what* you say, Samantha, it's this Christos who's put you up to this. You were never this defiant before he came along. I'm telling you, Bill, this Christos is steering our daughter in all the wrong directions."

I sighed and wondered if now was the time to tell them that I planned on moving in with Christos, on top of everything else?

Hmmm. Maybe not.

I eyed the END button on my phone.

Maybe I needed to terminate this call before my parents made plans to terminate me.

"That boy has you wrapped around his finger, doesn't he, Sam?" my mom said, her words suddenly dripping with foul judgment.

Why did I suddenly feel like guided missiles were pointed at my heart?

"I bet you two are having plenty of sex, aren't you?" she sneered. "Well, I hope you're using protection."

I was shocked into silence. Not because we were discussing sex and birth control. That was nothing new. It was the pure hatred pouring out of my mom's mouth like a fire hose. Or maybe a sewage hose. I never imagined she could be *this* harsh.

"I knew he looked reckless the second I saw him with his leather jacket and his tattoos," she sneered. "Ever since you met that young man, you've turned reckless yourself, Samantha. He's bringing you down to his level, and he's going to ruin your life. Mark my words," she said ominously, "whether it's two weeks or two months, that Christos character is going to lose interest in you. He'll forget your name in no time, and in a few years, he won't even remember having slept with you. Then where will you be? Huh? Tell me that."

"He's not like that," I argued, suddenly on the verge of crying, "Christos loves me!" I hated that I was shouting like an irrational teenager, but my mom was always good at clawing my heart.

"Sure he does," Mom snapped venomously, "that's what they *all* say,"

"All?" my dad asked, confused. "All *who*? Linda, what are you —"

Mom cut Dad off definitively, saying, "I bet your *Christos* is no better than that Damian," she hissed.

"*You don't know anything about Christos!!!*" I wailed at the phone.

"I may not know him, Sam," my mom said confidently, "but I've known men *like* him."

"You have?" my dad asked. "That's news to me, Linda, I—"

"Shut up, Bill," my mom barked at him.

Whoa, Mom. I'd never heard her this crazy. She had lost it. "You're wrong, Mom," I said through my tears, finding new strength. "Christos asked me to move in with him."

Mom chuffed out a harsh laugh. "You're pregnant, aren't you?"

"What?! No!" I protested.

"Not yet you aren't," she shouted stridently. *"But you will be! Give it six months, maybe a year, and he'll knock you up! Then he'll be gone! Just like that! Make sure you have enough saved up for the abortion!"*

Mom had gone crazy. Why did I think she was talking about herself all of a sudden? That didn't seem remotely possible. I couldn't picture my mom getting knocked up without a business plan in place.

Whatever.

All I knew for sure was that I suddenly felt like I was the parent of a tantrum-throwing infant. Oddly, this gave me a measure of confidence I'd never felt with my mom before. Her heightened irrationality allowed me to remain calm. "I'm using birth control, Mom. I'm being responsible."

"I knew it!" she cheered. *"You're having sex!"*

"So? People have sex all the time. It's not the end of the world. Anyway, that's not the point. The point is, Christos asked me to move into his grandfather's house."

"So you're going to be freeloading?"

"It's not like that! They're good people."

"And we're not?"

"No, Mom. You don't understand." I was getting confused. My mom had pulled herself in and was going for logic. I was on dangerous footing.

"We have supported you your entire life, and you think you can just waltz into some random family and they'll take care of you like your father and I have?"

I paused to think through my words carefully. I worried I was getting in over my head. But I wasn't giving up. "Yes."

"Hah!" my mom blurted. "And pray tell, Sam, why is that?"

"Because Christos loves me," I reiterated calmly. I knew I was repeating myself, but it was the truth. What more did anyone need to know than that? It was all I needed to know.

Long, loud, laughter erupted from my mom. She went on for at least an entire minute. "You, you think *love* is going to fix everything, Sam? You think this puppy love crush you have on Christos is going to bring world peace? Heal all of mankind's ills? I've got news for you, Sam, *it doesn't work that way.* Let me put it another way, Sam. Are you listening?"

I refused to answer her.

"Sam, Christos does *NOT* love you—"

I stabbed the END button on my phone.

I'd never hung up on my parents before, but I'd never been this freaked out by them either. I set the phone down on the coffee table and backed away from it, afraid it might attack me. I imagined my parents' arms reaching out at me through the screen on my phone, trying to choke me from three-thousand miles away.

That was silly. I smiled at my own lunacy.

My apartment was deathly silent and suddenly seemed cavernous. I'd never felt so alone in my entire life, as if their parental support had evaporated over the course of that brief call.

Forever.

When the phone rang, I jumped. It was the ringer for my parents.

Of course they were calling back. They were probably furious. I'd never disobeyed them this blatantly before. I half-expected them to call 911 and have the cops send over a car to round me up and take me downtown for Disobeying a Parent's Orders.

The phone continued to ring. Each time, the shrill sound stabbed my brain and I had to fight my deeply conditioned urge to answer. It took everything I had not to. The funny thing was, my parents weren't even in the room, yet I felt nineteen years of parenting compelling me to answer.

My hand reached out...

Who the heck was moving my arm? I was being remote-controlled!

No!

I wouldn't do it!

Fortunately, my phone went to voicemail after the fourth ring. I heaved a sigh of relief. I felt like I'd narrowly escaped with my life.

I was afraid if they called back a second time, I might answer. Against my will. And if I did that, I feared I might very well cave to their orders. After nineteen years, they had that much power over me, for good or bad.

I covered my face with my hands and sobbed.

I wanted to throw up.

I ran to the bathroom and my burrito missiled right out of my stomach.

I needed Christos. He was the only one who could set my heart at ease. After brushing the barf out of my mouth with my toothbrush, I walked into my living room and reached for my phone to call him.

I nearly had a heart attack when it rang in my hands.

CHRISTOS

I sat in my grandfather's studio, kicked back in an old office chair, a fresh glass of whiskey in one hand, my phone in the other.

I was nicely buzzed.

Maybe a bit drunk.

The thing about being a cocky bastard was that I could *appreciate* I was a cocky bastard. I enjoyed it. I hadn't always been one. I'd had to earn it.

The proof was in my phone.

I scrolled through dozens of unanswered messages from as many hot women, all of which had come in on my phone in the last twelve hours. By hot, I didn't mean Nebraska hot. I meant L.A. hot. Hollywood hot. There was a difference.

The messages:

Tiffany: *What do I have to do to get you to paint me nude again? If it's not the money, tell me. I'll give you anything you want. Anything.*

Paisley: *Adonis! When are we going to go blading (and other things) again?*

Skylar: *I need you Adonis. It's been months. Why haven't you called? Remember Onyx? I'll never forget it...*

I'd forgotten it. Who the hell was Skylar, again?

Mercedes: *I'm in town, Adonis. I'm staying at the Hotel Del until Saturday. My room number is...*

Tiffany: *Please, Christos. Anything you want. Do I have to spell it out for you? S-E-X. Oops, I meant, A-N-Y-T-H-I-N-G ;-)*

That one was kind of funny. Tiffany was a clever girl, despite her personality flaws.

Destiny: *I'm having two of my girlfriends over this weekend, Adonis. Do you want to come and party with the three of us? Clothing optional.*

There were another twenty or thirty just like these. Yeah, some of them were stripper names, some of whom were actual strippers, but not all. Chicks like that seemed to find me wherever I went.

I thought about the fact that any guy I knew would kill to have their own phone filled up with blatant propositions like mine. The only problem? Those dudes still wouldn't have been me.

Imagine if I found some Maynard on campus, you know the kind with the thick glasses and 4.0 GPA, and gave him my phone? Imagine the look on Mercedes's face when Maynard knocked on her door at the Hotel Del later tonight.

He'd tell her, "Christos sent me."

She'd freak.

I chuckled to myself.

Shit, knowing Mercedes, she'd probably quote Maynard a price. Maynard would be the one with the look of utter confusion on his face. But if he had two-hundred bucks cash on him, Mercedes would give him a dance routine that would spin his head around. She was a Vegas Showgirl and knew how to move. I was sorely tempted to track down the closest guy at SDU who fit the Maynard bill, pay the two-hundred myself, and give him a show from Mercedes he'd never forget.

I was nothing if not generous.

Anyway, now that Samantha was in my life, I could chuckle at the fact that I used to be "that guy," the one who, three months after becoming exclusive with Samantha, was still getting dozens of requests from hotties who wanted more of my patented cock-doctoring. Hey, it wasn't my fault those girls were all sick for me.

I had every right to be a cocky bastard.

Without giving it a second thought, I punched buttons on my phone and deleted all of the messages.

That Maynard guy was on his own.

I called Samantha.

"Christos!" she answered.

The biggest, most genuine grin I'd ever grinned widened across my lips. "I missed you, *agápi mou*." I sounded only slightly slurry from drinking.

Who needed cocky when you had Samantha? Thank fucking Christ, because I was sick of all that posing that led to having a phone filled with meaningless messages from meaningless women.

"Christos!" she sobbed. "I need you to come over right now!

Please!"

The sound of her panic got me freaking out in a heartbeat. "Are you okay? Samantha! Are you hurt? What's wrong?"

"My parents..."

"What? Are they okay? Did they get in an accident? Samantha, what's wrong? Talk to me?"

"They're evil..." she sobbed.

Shit. That wasn't what I was expecting. "I'll be right over," I said quietly.

I ran outside and hopped in my Camaro. I stuck to the speed limit and came to a full stop at all STOP signs. I knew I was on the edge of legal to be driving and didn't need a fucking DUI.

Fifteen minutes later, I was running up the stairs at Sam's apartment. I knocked on the door and she opened it quietly.

She was crying, her mascara running. I'd never seen her looking this miserable. She held out her arms for me like a little girl.

I enfolded her with mine and pulled her into my chest. "Shh, *agápi mou*. I'm here. Everything's going to be all right. I'm here."

She broke into fresh sobs in my arms. I stroked her hair while she cried it out. After a time, she calmed. "Do you want some water?"

She nodded silently.

I filled a glass in her kitchen and led her to the couch. "Sit down, *agápi mou*."

She swallowed some water. I noticed the remains of a burrito on her coffee table. It reminded me I was hungry. I might have to eat it later.

"My mom is evil, Christos," she cried, hitching tears. "She, she said you're going to, to, to *leave* me and forget my name."

"That's craziness, Samantha," I chuckled.

"Don't laugh," she pleaded.

"Sorry. It's just, hearing you say that doesn't make any sense to me because I'm not going anywhere, no matter what your mom says."

She looked at me with naked fear in her eyes. "I hope so, because I feel like my parents are abandoning me. Without you, I'd feel like I have no one. I couldn't bear to lose you, Christos. Not even for a second."

Hearing her words tightened my heart. I hoped to fuck I didn't turn out to be a liar the day after my trial was over. No matter how badly I wanted to keep my promise to her, I might not be able to.

I spent the night with Samantha in her bed. She curled against me like a frightened child. Did she somehow sense that no matter how strong my arms were, they might not be able to protect her from my past?

Luckily, she went quickly to sleep. She must've been exhausted.

I tried to block out my own chaotic thoughts, and get some sleep too. But the reality of my shitstorm life kept battering me awake.

In the morning, I was drained.

Chapter 24

CHRISTOS

Samantha slept hard.

I didn't.

I was jittery all night, kept waking up, and tossed until 8:00 a.m. when I checked my phone. I had a message. A very important one. I couldn't take the call here.

Russell Merriweather.

He only called when things got worse. It wasn't like he was going to tell me the District Attorney had decided to give up. Those guys were pit bulls and had their jaws clamped around me good.

I was antsy to hear his message. I treated bad news like Band-Aids. Better to get it over with quick.

But I wasn't going to make Samantha wake to an empty bed. So I paced the apartment. Sat on the couch for awhile. Pulled the remainder of her burrito out of the fridge where I'd stashed it last night. Downed it in two bites. Drank some water. Twiddled my thumbs.

Fucking-A, this was driving me nuts.

What did Russell need to tell me?

When Sam finally awoke, I was sitting on the edge of her bed, fully dressed. "Sam, I need to go." I felt like an asshole saying it. She needed me. It was obvious. But I needed to check my message.

"Why? What's wrong?"

"It's…" I didn't want to tell her. "I've just got some stuff to do. At the studio," I lied.

Her eyes searched mine. "What is it, Christos? You can tell me."

No, I couldn't. Then everything would shatter around both of us. "It's nothing, *agápi mou*. I promise." Man, I was a fucking liar.

"Do you want breakfast?" she offered.

"No, I'm cool. I really need to jet."

"Please stay."

The look in her eyes tore me apart. I wanted to tell her everything. I wanted to tell her nothing, hoping my problems would go away. She didn't need to be worrying about this.

"Please, Christos," she begged.

"I have to go, *agápi mou*."

"Okay," she nodded reluctantly.

I felt like shit when I walked out her front door.

I climbed in my Camaro and drove east toward the Five. I stopped at a gas station before getting on the freeway and checked my message from Russell.

"Christos, the Deputy District Attorney has made a plea offer. We should discuss this face to face. This is a big decision, whichever way you go. Come by my offices tomorrow, any time."

I cruised onto the freeway and lurched through traffic. I had plenty of time to sweat bullets in my car while I thought about whatever plea bargain was on the table.

My guts were churning by the time I reached downtown. Too bad traffic was so heavy. If the road had been empty, I would've floored it all the way there.

After I passed SDU, I noticed the same landmarks that had taunted me back on the day the cops had driven me to jail, the day I'd met Sam in September. The surfer mural in Pacific Beach. The humpback whale mural in Mission Bay. At least this time I wasn't caged in a squad car. Just caged in traffic.

I considered sliding my Camaro onto the empty shoulder and flooring it. But it was broad daylight.

And I was out on bail for aggravated assault and battery.

Fuck it. I was tired of rolling through traffic like an old man. I dropped the Camaro into second and revved the engine. It rumbled reassuringly, ready to tear up the road as I diagonaled across lanes toward the shoulder on the right.

Samantha's eyes filled my mind. The sad eyes she'd given me when I'd left her apartment a half hour ago.

Fuck.

I couldn't afford to be stupid. Not like when I was younger and didn't give a shit. I had something to live for now, some*one* who needed me.

Samantha.

I huffed out a breath and slid the shifter back into third. My Camaro remained in the slow lane as I continued to cruise along at the same sluggish pace everyone else was going.

Traffic turtled along all the way downtown. I pulled off on Front Street and headed toward Russell's offices.

I parked in the underground garage and marched up the stairs like I was going to a hanging. Every step got taller as my boots got heavier. I felt like I was going to collapse by the time I reached the 20th.

I walked through the double doors into Russell's offices.

"Good Morning, Christos," Rhonda said. "I'll let Russell know you're here. He should be out in a minute."

"Thanks, Rhonda." I walked over to the picture window and stared out at the San Diego bay once again. It was shrouded in fog. Appropriately moody.

"Christos," Russell said as he walked into the lobby. He wasn't his usual jovial self. "Come on back to my office, son."

Man, had somebody died? Or was everyone mourning my impending funeral?

I walked into Russell's office and dropped into the chair. He closed the door behind us and sat down.

"How have you been holding up, son?" Russell asked compassionately.

"Holding," I said with a half-assed laugh.

He nodded understanding. I'm sure he saw in my eyes the weight I was carrying. "I'll cut right to it. The Deputy District Attorney is offering you twelve months in county jail for a guilty plea. With time off for good behavior, you're looking at maybe nine months."

I ground my jaw. Nine months of lock-up. Nine months of calling Samantha collect from a jail phone? Nine months of her making weekly visits with all the other inmate's wives and girlfriends? Sitting in the visitor's bunker with a wall of steel and glass between the innocents and the convicts? Nine months looking her in the eyes trying to pretend I wasn't miserable and stressed and living in a stinking pit?

I'd been on both sides of that window wall. Good buddies of mine had been in the can over the years for fighting, DUIs, all that immature young men's bullshit.

Watching your friends on the inside struggling not to rot away from the emotional squalor that took hold of the inmates was not fun. Wondering every time you visited if your good friend was going to have a bloody eyeball with a detached retina or maybe be missing some teeth he'd had the week before. Or maybe, your buddy might not even show up to get on the short phone because he was in the infirmary for getting his leg kicked in by three guys in the shower, and he couldn't walk.

Yeah, fun shit.

If I got locked up, my time on the inside was going to be bad enough. But thinking about how miserable Samantha was going to be made it worse.

I didn't want to put her through any of it. She needed to focus on good things, on her classes, on her art. Not my bullshit.

Maybe I needed to let her go.

Russell cleared his throat. "Christos, I want you to know I negotiated my ass off with the D.D.A. trying to reduce the offered sentence. But Schlosser would not budge. He thinks he has this case all buttoned up. If we go to trial, he's going to nail you to the wall on reasonableness and avoidance. You're in a tough spot, son. Nine months in jail on a plea bargain is still nine months. But if we go to trial, and the jury finds you guilty on all counts, you could be looking at up to four years in prison." Russell took a deep breath. "I've gone head-to-head with Schlosser before. He's tough as nails, and he's chomping at the bit on this one. If he wins, he's going to push the judge for the maximum sentence."

I nodded silently.

"It's a gamble either way," Russell offered. He watched me carefully. "I wish I had better news, Christos. Take some time to think this over. Discuss it with your family. You don't have to make a decision until a few days before the trial."

Somebody wake me up and tell me this shit was just a nightmare.

CHRISTOS

I cruised homeward on the Five in my Camaro, keeping it to the speed limit. Master of Puppets by Metallica was pounding out of my sound system at concert-level decibels. If I couldn't speed, at least I could give my ears a good pounding.

My phone vibrated in my pocket. I pulled it out to check the call. Fucking Brandon. I didn't want to talk to him. Fuck it. May as well get it over with. I'd have to talk to him sooner or later.

I turned down the tunes on my MP3 player and pressed TALK on my phone.

"Hey, man," I said.

"Christos, always good to hear your voice," he said.

"Yeah," I said curtly.

"How are the paintings coming along?"

Man, he asked me that at least once a day. "Great."

"Do you have an estimated delivery date on any of them yet?

"The one of Avery is done. So are the ones of Jacqueline and Becca. Isabella is in progress, so is Sophia, and I started in on the one of Victoria and one of Hannah."

"Only three are complete?" Brandon sighed. "We're going to need a lot more than that."

Did he *think* I didn't fucking know that? I grit my teeth. "I know."

"When can we expect to set a date for your next solo show?"

He said "we" like "we" were hunched over the fucking easel seven days a week. I'd squeezed in a seventh day of painting when it had finally sunk in that my trial was not going to wait for my ass to finish my paintings at a leisurely six-day-a-week pace.

"Shit, Brandon. I don't fucking know. Why don't you come down to the studio and help out. I'll hand you a fucking brush and you can stretch canvases and paint backgrounds and shit, like Rubens used to have his studio grunts do."

Brandon chuckled mellowly. "Point taken."

Damn right, point taken.

Brandon sighed. "We can't keep the customers waiting forever, Christos. Eventually, they'll lose interest and move on to the next big thing."

I twisted the steering wheel in my grip. If I wasn't careful, I might rip the wheel off the fucking steering column and throw it out the window while I tooled down the freeway at sixty-five. "I'm working as fast as I can, Brandon. There's only so many hours in a day."

"I understand. How's the painting of Isabella coming along?

She's an amazingly beautiful woman. I'm thinking your portrait of her will likely be the center-piece of your show."

"It's coming." Too bad I thought it looked like a poster for a porno.

"What does that mean?"

I slid my hand down my stubbled face. "I don't know how to say this, but I'm not liking it."

"Do you want me to call New York? Or Europe? Find some more exotic models?"

Flying models out from the east coast or across the Atlantic meant escalating model fees. They'd need hotels, meals, pampering (we're talking top-end models here), the works. All that shit would cost me an arm and a leg, and since I only had two of each, I was reluctant to start spilling more of my blood paying more bills. The L.A. models would have to do.

"No," I said. "I'll make it work. I'll tweak some things on the Isabella portrait, maybe change up the background, and it'll be great," I lied.

"I don't think changing the background will make much of a difference," Brandon scoffed. "Are you having trouble capturing her likeness?" He hadn't seen the painting yet, so he didn't know.

"Fuck no." It looked like a goddamned full-color holographic photo of her.

"You're not going to find a more beautiful model on the west coast than Isabella…"

"I know."

"…unless you can convince Samantha to sit for you."

That again. I had to agree. But I didn't think I could convince her. Not with all the shit she was juggling. She needed to focus on her art career, not mine.

"No," was all I said on that topic.

"Fine. If you change your mind about the European models, let me know. I've been looking through some Russian agency books and there's three or four stand-outs you might want to consider."

"Email me the photos and I'll check them out."

"Terrific. I'll do that as soon as we're off the phone."

"Sure," I sighed. I never thought I'd say it, but I was fucking sick of hot chicks. I wanted to chuck all of them out of my life and make more room for the only one that mattered.

Agápi mou…

"Excellent," Brandon said in a smiling voice. "Call me if you need anything."

How about an all-expenses-paid trip to the nearest firing squad?

"Will do," I said before ending the call. I just about threw my phone out the window, but stopped myself at the last second.

I cranked the volume back up on Metallica and drove straight to the nearest bar.

CHRISTOS

That night, I called Jake.

I needed a break from all the shit coming down on me. Jake was the perfect distraction. I picked him up from his place in my Camaro. I'd pretty much sobered up from hitting the bar in the morning.

Whatever.

At least I wasn't on my bike.

Jake and I decided to head downtown and grab dinner at Dick's Last Resort in the Gaslamp Quarter. The wait-staff at Dick's treated the customers like shit, on purpose. It wasn't a great destination for date-night, but was perfect for me and Jake to catch up.

After our obnoxious waiter had bitched us out and thrown our silverware, napkins, and paper place-mats at us, we ordered beers. The waiter brought them back a few minutes later, two Corona's with lime wedges shoved in the necks of the bottles.

Jake and I clinked beers.

"Long time no see, bro," Jake said.

"No shit," I nodded. "I've been super busy."

"That's an understatement," Jake said, pausing to gulp down some Corona. "Before I forget, Sebastian and his crew keep bugging my ass about bringing you out to hit some waves. Maybe go down to Ensenada some weekend."

"Sebastian? You mean that military kid with a prick for a dad?" Sebastian was seventeen when I'd met him, so he would always be a "kid" at any age.

"Yeah," Jake grinned. "Sebastian told me he had some score to settle with you about stealing his tube-ride last time at La Jolla Shores."

I remembered the moment well. Me and Sebastian had shared a good laugh over it afterward. But that was a year ago. I chuckled, "I haven't seen that dude in forever. He still with that MILF?"

Jake smiled. "You mean Caro?"

"Yeah. Her." I smiled, picturing her in my mind. "She was a total fox."

"Dude, Caro's not a MILF. She doesn't have any kids. She's a HILF," Jake grinned.

I almost choked on my beer. "HILF? That's lame, man. What the fuck is a HILF?"

"Hottie I'd Like to Fuck."

"Duh," I smiled at my own ignorance, then nodded at Jake knowingly. "Total HILF," I said, lifting my beer to clink bottles with Jake.

"To Sebastian and his HILF Caro," Jake smiled.

Jake and I ordered burgers when the waiter returned.

While we waited for our food, my phone rang in my pocket, playing the chorus of Before Your Love by Kelly Clarkson. My new ringtone for Samantha.

"Dude," Jake grimaced and smiled, "what kind of gay shit is that?"

"That's my ringtone for Samantha," I grinned.

"Dude, you're so gone for that girl. Your only ringtone used to be 'Battery' by Metallica."

"That was before I met Samantha." I answered my phone. "*Agápi mou.* How are you?"

"Fine," Samantha said, "now that I'm hearing your voice."

"What's up?"

"I've been trying to call you all day," she said softly. "Is everything all right?"

"I'm good," I lied. I felt like a total prick. Samantha was probably still freaking out about her parents. As much as I wanted to be by her side to reassure her that I would always be there for her, after meeting with Russell today, I couldn't say it with a straight face. Not sober, anyway. "Just out with Jake," I said casually. "We're chillin' at Dick's Last Resort. Getting burgers and brews."

"Dick's Last Resort? That sounds awful. Is that a strip club?" Samantha snickered.

"No, it's a burger joint in the Gaslamp."

"You sure? I hope you brought lots of singles to tip the, uh, waitresses," Samantha sneered.

"I promise, the fat guy with a double-chin who's serving us is fully clothed," I grinned over at Jake. He'd seen the guy.

Jake cocked me a smile.

"I hope so!" Samantha groaned. "Anyway, I just wanted to make sure everything is all right?"

"Yeah, I'm good, *agápi mou*. Are you okay?"

She sighed. "I'm fine. I just, I sort of needed to talk to you some more about my parents. I'm still freaked out, I guess."

Fuck. She wasn't going to let me off the hook. "Do you want to talk about it tonight? I can come over later, after me and Jake finish our burgers. How's that sound?" I felt like a huge douche. I winced, wishing all my problems would go away so I could do the right thing by Samantha at that moment.

The sad truth was my problems weren't going anywhere.

My shit was booming inside my head like thunderclaps. I really needed to pound out some of my stress, or I was going to explode. I wasn't in any shape to listen to Samantha and be supportive. How could you listen to somebody else's problems when you had your own thunderclouds shooting thunder and lightning between your ears every fifteen seconds? I had to deal with my own stress first, and I did it the best way I knew how at the time: drinks with Jake.

There was a long pause, then Samantha finally answered, "Okay. I'll be waiting."

Man, I felt like a shithead. "You sure?"

"Yeah," she sighed. "It can wait. I'll be okay. I'll be doing homework at my apartment all evening, so if you want to stop by when you're finished, I'd love to see you."

"Me too, *agápi mou*. I'll come by as soon as we're done. I love you."

"I love you too," Samantha said before ending the call.

Thankfully, the waiter showed up with our food before I had to explain any of that to Jake.

After we ate, we pounded more beers at Dick's before bouncing.

Outside, we strolled the busy streets of the Gaslamp Quarter. It was San Diego's most active night-spot destination. You could walk from bar to bar all night and never hit the same spot twice. Perfect for pub crawling.

I was leaning toward getting hammered tonight.

"Where do you want to hit next?" Jake asked.

"First place I smell beer," I said.

"How's the trial shit going?" Jake asked.

I stopped on the sidewalk, threw my head back, and laughed. It was not a happy laugh. It turned into a roar of frustration.

"Sorry, dude," Jake said. "Wrong topic."

I sighed. "Don't sweat it. It's not like that shit isn't on my mind twenty-four seven, now that my trial date is days away."

"How you coping?"

"Ask me again when I have a beer in my hand."

"Totally, bro," he smiled.

We wandered along the block, passing people strolling the sidewalk in both directions.

"How about some frozen yogurt?" Jake joked, nodding toward a storefront.

"Yeah," I laughed, "I could definitely go for some low-fat, sugar-free shit right now," I said sarcastically. "My doctor tells me I need to take better care of my health."

We found a dingy bar with hipster smokers hovering around the entrance. The kind of place with no windows, no sign, save the red-and-white plaque in the doorway that read "NOTICE: NO PERSONS UNDER 21 ALLOWED."

"Perfect," I grimaced.

We went inside.

It was dark. The lights hanging over the pool tables and the soft glow behind the bar were the only illumination. We grabbed barstools.

"What'll it be?" a middle-aged bartender asked, all business. He had silver hair fluffed back in an old-school style and a silver goatee.

I turned to Jake. "I've already had a bunch of beers. What's that shit people say?" I grumbled, "Beer before liquor, never sicker. Liquor before beer, you're in the clear?"

"That's how I remember it," Jake said.

"Fuck the rules," I said to the bartender.

The bartender snorted.

"You got any Wild Turkey?" I asked.

The bartender nodded.

"You want one, Jake?" I asked.

"Whatever he's having," Jake said to the bartender.

"Two shots of Wild Turkey," I said to the bartender.

"Is that two and two," the bartender pointed two fingers at me, then at Jake, "or just two total?"

"That makes six," I grinned, amused with myself. "Three each."

The bartender smirked. "Let me know when you need the bucket below the bar," he said before walking off.

"Dude," Jake said sarcastically, "You sure you don't want to order a few more shots before he runs off?"

I smirked at Jake and shook my head, ignoring his comment. "So, how's Madison?"

"She's awesome. She's some kind of business genius, man. Once I told her about starting a clothing line, she jumped all over it. She handed me a business plan two weeks later."

The bartender brought over a tray with six full shot-glasses and set the tray in front of us. "Bottom's up, boys," he nodded, then walked off to help another customer a few seats down.

Jake and I each raised a shot glass, clinked, and pounded.

Did I think about the fact that my dad first started drinking when the pressure of painting for a bunch of demanding rich fucks started getting to him? No. Did I think about the fact that I was probably going to be in jail inside of ten days? Fuck no. I just drank my drink. I didn't want to think about any of it.

"Good shit," Jake said.

"The best," I said. "When are you and Madison getting married?"

Jake laughed. "Whenever she says yes."

"You ask her already?"

"No, but damn, she's great, man. I can't imagine a tighter girlfriend."

"She's tight all right," I said. "And she's a good person, I can tell. Hold on to that shit, man." I raised a fresh shot glass to Jake. "To you and Madison."

He raised his own and we clinked. "To me and Mads," he said.

We pounded.

"Sam's pretty damn awesome herself," Jake said. "Gimme a minute, and we'll raise that last shot to her."

"You pussing out on me, bro?" I jabbed.

"No, just wanna keep the drinks in my stomach and not put them in that guy's bucket," he smiled. "They're costing *you* good money."

"Me? *I'm* fucking paying?"

"When you order six fucking shots for the first round, you are," he smirked

"Totally," I smiled back.

"Dude, not to be a bitch," Jake said cautiously, "but I haven't seen you drink like this for a long time. It's the trial, isn't it?"

I sighed heavily. "Yeah."

"Is your lawyer having any luck?"

"Man, I'm spending a fuck-load on Merriweather. He's got the best people all over that shit. But it isn't getting me anywhere."

"What are you gonna do?"

"Roll the dice."

"You mean go to trial?"

"Fuck yeah. I'd rather take a risk than sign up for nine to twelve months down at Thunderdome."

"What's Thunderdome?"

"That's what they call the jail down past Otay. Where I'd be going. And that's not even the prison, which is worse. I could end up there if I'm found guilty for everything."

Jake was silent.

I didn't blame him. "At least I'm out on bail instead of sitting in that hole awaiting trial." I picked up the third shot. "Here's to fucking making bail," I said sourly.

Jake picked up his shot but rested his hand on my forearm. "No, we don't drink to that shit, man. Like I said earlier, we drink to you and Samantha. To good shit."

I looked him in the eyes. He was right. I needed to crawl out of the cesspool in my head. "To Samantha."

"To *you* and Samantha," Jake said, clinking his shot glass against mine.

"To me and Samantha." I threw my shot back.

SAMANTHA

I set my Sociology reading down and rubbed my eyes. They

were crossing from staring at the page all evening. How long had I been reading and re-reading the same paragraph? I had no idea, but I did know I hadn't the foggiest idea what the paragraph said.

All I could think about was calling Christos. I was worried about him. He had seemed off. I didn't know what it was, but for the last two days, he'd taken a sudden, dark turn.

When he'd come over last night, after my blowout call with my parents, he'd smelled like alcohol.

I knew that smell.

I used to smell like that, back in high school.

Emo. Goth. Suicide Watch...

Christos was hiding something. But what?

Another woman? That stupid Isabella? I'd claw the bitches eyes out.

Bitch. Slut. Whore...

But I didn't think that was it. In truth, I had no idea what it could be. I'd believed that telling Christos I wanted to move in with him was going to magically fix all my problems. I guess I never considered *his* problems. But what problems did he actually have? None that I knew of.

Unless...

Did it have something to do with me moving in?

Oh, no. Was my mom right?

Had I somehow scared Christos off, now that I'd agreed to live with him? It couldn't be. He'd seemed so excited the night I'd told him. So what was wrong? Was it possible he was having second thoughts? I wasn't sure, but I knew he was pulling away.

Oh, God, please no.

Maybe I'd been stupid to think Christos was so perfect. He was human, after all. He had to have some flaws somewhere.

Whatever they were, I would love him and accept him. If he would only tell me. The not knowing was driving me crazy.

I jumped up from my couch and grabbed my phone. My finger hovered over the speed dial for Christos.

I was going to call him again and ask him to come over right away. I desperately wanted to sort things out with him.

But he was out with Jake.

Groan! I suddenly felt guilty at the thought of calling. I knew Christos needed a break. He'd been working hard on new paintings ever since New Year's Eve. He never took any breaks, other than when he was with me, and that wasn't nearly often enough, considering how busy I was with my jobs and classes.

Maybe he just needed space. For tonight.

I reluctantly set my phone down on the coffee table and went to my kitchen.

I'd been a good girl lately. I'd barely touched my ice cream in weeks. I pulled a pint of Double Dark Chocolate Devil's Delight out of my freezer, grabbed a spoon, then went back to my couch.

Ice Cream always helped me study. That's the only reason I was going to eat any. Because Sociology 2 deserved no less.

I would not let Sociology 2 down at any cost.

I swear, my worries about Christos had nothing to do with my sudden urge for an ice cream splurge.

I wondered if perhaps the red cartoon devil printed on the side of the ice cream carton would be waiting for me at the bottom of the tub when I reached it.

Nope, just cardboard.

CHRISTOS

Jake and I stumbled out of the bar a couple hours later. I'd lost count of how much I'd had to drink after the beers at Dick's and those shots of Wild Turkey.

Whatever.

We cruised the streets, trying to sober up.

Neither one of us was in any shape to drive.

"Maybe you should call Sam," Jake belched.

"Naw, we'll be fine in a while." I didn't want to tell him that I felt like a dipshit for getting so loaded, and I didn't want Samantha to see me like this.

"I can call Mads," Jake said.

"We'll be fine, just give it some time. There's an all-night coffee shop around here somewhere. We can sit in it and suck back espressos until the booze bleeds out." At this rate it was going to be sunrise before I saw Samantha.

We strolled through the thinning crowds on the sidewalk in the Gaslamp.

As we turned onto Fourth Street, we passed by Horton Plaza. "I fucking love that place, man," I slurred. "It's like the Disneyland of fucking shopping malls."

Jake snickered. "Dude, you're fucking wasted."

"I'm fucking wasted," I smiled.

We continued down Fourth until we hit the Hooters on the corner of Market Street.

We paused.

I cocked a thumb toward the Hooters. "Wanna get some more drinks?"

"And have a bunch of PG-13 strippers wearing those road-crew orange shorts hit on us all night? That shit is comedy, but I'm all good," Jake smiled. "Hey, didn't you used to bang one of the waitresses who worked here?"

"Probably," I sputtered, meaning it.

Jake cackled, knowing I was telling the truth.

Jake and I both turned as the doors to Hooters opened and a group of rowdy guys poured onto the sidewalk. They were laughing and shouting and making a bunch of noise.

One of them was that guy Hunter Fucking Blakeley. He had his arms around two bar babes. They were clearly into him. He was clearly into them. Both bar babes looked toasted. Both were pretty damn hot in their tight skirts and tops. Neither were in Samantha's league, but both were hot enough for a magazine cover.

They were gazing up at Hunter like he was Brad Fucking Pitt or some shit.

I could fix that.

I stood my ground as Hunter's buddies parted around me and Jake like we were our own fucking continent, and they had no choice but to flow elsewhere.

I made sure to stare Hunter right in the eyes.

It didn't take long.

"I know you," Hunter said. "Where do I know you from?"

"From my girlfriend," I growled.

He stopped. "Oh yeah! You're Sam's man. You were too pussy to fight me the other day."

He could spin that shit however he wanted. But that wasn't my point. I was strategizing.

It took about three seconds for his two honeys to turn their greedy eyes on my shit.

"Is this your friend?" the brunette asked Hunter.

Hunter had some game. "Yeah, sure," he said confidently. He wasn't ruffled yet.

Yet.

"What's his name?" the blonde asked.

Hunter didn't seem inclined to answer.

Both of the girls were drooling at me openly.

Despite the chill air, I wore a short-sleeve black V-neck. My tatted arms were cocked and loaded. I twitched both arms, making the muscles pop and stand out like hard-chiseled granite, all striated and rugged.

"Mmmm," the blonde said. She literally released her grip on Hunter and stepped up to me. She slid her hand down my chest and abs. "I like," she purred.

I was used to this shit. When I turned it on, like now, chicks went fucking nuts.

"What's your name, honey?" she asked.

"Adonis," I said. Fuck yeah, Adonis.

"Sounds like a hero's name or something," she said.

Fuck yeah, it did. "What's your name?" I asked her.

"MacKenzie," the blonde murmured. "Check him out, Kylie," she said to her friend. "He's yummy," she purred.

Kylie the brunette was now gaping at me.

I cocked my dimpled grin at her.

As if hypnotized, her hands relaxed from touching Hunter and drifted slowly to her sides. She leaned away from him like she was hypnotized and floated toward me on her heels. She grabbed my belt with one hand and slid her other into my front pocket.

"Oh my god," she whispered, her fingers gliding across my dick through the material.

The thing was, this shit only worked when you did it for real. I was hard as a fucking rock.

"He's huge, MacKenzie," Kylie said to her friend, sounding astonished, like she'd just met God.

Hunter glared at me.

His buddies circled around me and Jake. There were three of them. Four on two. Jake could fight. We were going to be fine.

I could feel the tension on the street corner.

MacKenzie and Kylie hung off me like they were my harem.

The second I'd seen Hunter walk out the door of the Hooters, I'd wanted to kick his ass. But this was better.

"You guys ready to go?" Hunter asked the two girls who were humping my legs.

They looked at him like he was a ghost or maybe a gust of wind.

One of them broke into a stripper laugh. That was all either of them had to say on the subject of going anywhere with Hunter and his boys.

"Shall we?" I said to the girls. I nodded toward Jake. He opened the door.

I walked inside Hooters with MacKenzie and Kylie on my arms. Jake followed.

Hunter and his buddies were left out in the cold.

It was winter, after all.

Chapter 25

SAMANTHA

I was totally disgusted with myself for downing the entire pint of ice cream, I couldn't even begin to think about calling Christos to come over. I imagined burping up the taste of ice cream in his face while asking him if something was wrong.

It didn't seem like the right tone.

I went for a jog instead. Slowly, at first, until I was certain I wouldn't puke, then settling into a normal pace until I'd run four miles.

I came back to my apartment, hoping there would be a message from Christos telling me he was on his way over. Nope, he still hadn't called.

I took a shower and got ready for bed.

I considered driving to his house and surprising him by waiting in his bed. As much as I liked the idea, I felt like I should at least call first. I didn't know the number to the Manos house, or Spiridon's cell phone number, or if he even had one. I didn't want to just show up unannounced. Although I suspected Spiridon probably wouldn't care if I did, it still seemed rude.

I laid down on my bed with damp hair. My phone lay on the night table beside me, the ringer set to low, in case Christos tried to call. I did my best to keep my eyes open while willing my phone to ring.

Ring, damn it!

It didn't work.

I woke up in the morning to an empty bed.

CHRISTOS

Inside Hooters, Jake and I had to buy drinks for MacKenzie and

Kylie. We would've looked like dicks if we hadn't.

Me and Jake drank colas. It was as good as coffee, I guess. And we both drank plenty of water on the side. Didn't need a hangover tomorrow.

It turned out that MacKenzie and Kylie were not really drunk. I kept an eye on what they drank, and noticed neither did much more than sip. They were kind of fun to talk to. Both went to USD, over in Morena, just east of Mission Bay. They were law students, and they were pretty fucking sharp. Me and Jake couldn't believe it. Not that they were smart, but that they were so good at pretending to be stupid drunk chicks, because it was a total act.

When it was last call at Hooters, I hit the Men's room and drained for what seemed like an hour. At least I was down to a light buzz. I could probably drive.

Me and Jake walked the girls to their car, like gentlemen.

"You guys okay to drive?" I asked.

Kylie held up keys to her Audi and jangled them. "I'm as sober as a judge," she joked.

"Then you better not drive," I smiled.

"Touché," she smiled. "I'm fine."

"Since you're law students," Jake said, "You can represent yourselves in court if you get DUIs."

"You guys *could* drive us home. In your car," MacKenzie said.

"Sorry ladies," I said. "Me and Jake are sworn to our girlfriends. We may as well be married."

"He's right," Jake smiled.

MacKenzie shook her head. "You guys are two of the good ones," she sighed.

"Damn right," I smiled my cocky grin.

"If either one of you men ever ends up single, look us up," Kylie said.

"Yeah," MacKenzie blurted to Kylie, "I think either of them would be more than enough for the both of us."

Jake chuckled.

"Will do," I grinned. "But don't wait around. Go find some eligible bachelors. I'm sure there's some around San Diego somewhere."

They waved after climbing into their Audi, then drove off.

Me and Jake turned around on the dark city sidewalk and

headed back to my Camaro. At the end of the block we ran right into Hunter and his boys.

"Fuck, Hunter," I smiled casually, "how long have you been waiting for us?" I laughed. "We were in Hooters for three hours. You must want a beating real bad."

Hunter ground his jaw and curled his lips over his teeth.

"Dude," Jake said calmly, "I don't think this is a good idea."

I knew what Jake was thinking. My trial. Me out on bail. If there was the slightest chance of cops driving by, or Hunter crawling to the cops after getting his ass beat, I was in for a good reaming. Bail revoked. Sitting in jail until trial. The new charges I would get for pounding Hunter would be further evidence used against me in my pending trial.

Jake had a point.

"I *knew* you were a pussy," Hunter sneered.

I smirked at him. "I thought I taught you a lesson the other day, Hunter." The question was, did I need to give him the graduate course on why he should not fuck with me? And would I stop myself before I murdered him? Fuck it. He deserved a full-ride scholarship. I was tired of his shit. "I'll give you a free swing. Go for it, Hunter."

I stood tall, waiting.

Hunter glanced at his buddies. They nodded. They were ready to rumble. His buddies were pretty big. Thick-necked gym rats. One of them was busy cracking his knuckles while making fists. Another lowered his center of gravity into a crouch. He maybe knew what he was doing.

Did Hunter?

"Throw it, bitch," I said.

Hunter was considering.

I knew Jake was down. He turned to a forty-five degree angle facing the other guys. Fighting stance. He shook his arms loosely and cross-stepped to the side, lining himself up so that Hunter's second buddy, the one beside him, blocked the path of the third guy behind him. It would give Jake more time to take down the second guy before the third guy in back could get at him.

That left me with Hunter and the fourth guy.

"Are we cracking heads?" Jake asked me quietly. It was his way of saying he had my back while giving me a final chance to walk away from this bullshit. He didn't really care what we did. But we both knew the wisest path to tread in this situation.

Fuck wisdom.

"I'll let Hunter make that call," I grunted.

I watched Hunter swallow hard.

This bomb was about to go off.

I glared at Hunter. There was no way I was going to throw the first punch.

Please, I thought to myself, *let me take you out. Please, come on, please.*

Hunter was psyching himself up.

Shit, was this going to take all week? I was ready yesterday.

Hunter dropped into a boxer's stance and fainted left with a jab a split-second later. I saw where this was going. Wrong move. His torso twisted as his shoulder tensed to deliver a hard right.

Too slow. I snapped forward on the balls of my feet and slapped his lead hand down before he launched his fist. The backs of my knuckles crashed down on his nose. At the same time, the toe of my boot slammed into his shin. Boxers never expected a simultaneous strike to come from that low. Their nervous systems weren't accustomed to dealing with a low attack when their hands were busy.

Hunter tumbled to the ground, shocked. He was on his ass, staring up at me wide-eyed. He probably wasn't even hurt. But he would have a bloody nose in about five seconds.

"Who's next?" I asked calmly.

Jake laughed and glared at Hunter's three pals. "Any time, ladies."

Hunter's buddies stared at me and Jake like antelopes staring down the barrel of a lion. They knew they were outclassed. The two smaller ones picked Hunter up by the arms.

"Let's go," Hunter grunted, pulling free from his friend's helping hands, as if their grips were acid. He wiped his forearm under his nose, smearing blood.

"Better get that shit looked at," I said. With any luck, I hadn't actually broken his nose. I couldn't tell in this light.

Fuck, I hoped he didn't call the cops.

Was he that much of a pussy?

Only time would tell.

SAMANTHA

In the morning, I texted Christos, just to make sure he was all right.

I started to worry when I hadn't heard back from him after I had breakfast, but I had to get to campus for classes. I finally received a text from him during Sociology 2.

Late night with Jake. Just woke up. Sorry. I love you. Talk tonight?

I replied, *Dinner at my apartment?*

I'll be there. What time? he replied.

7pm?

Ok. I'll bring food. ILY

ILY2 <3 <3 <3

I put my phone away and did my best to focus on the lecture. Knowing Christos was all right, I actually managed to take decent notes for once, and not just waste class time doodling in my sketchbook.

I met Madison for lunch at the Student Center after class. We got in line to get Mexican food.

"Do you and Christos have any plans for Valentine's Day?" Madison asked while we waited to order food.

"Oh, I don't know. I hadn't asked him," I said taken off guard. I hadn't even thought about it.

"How can you not have Valentine's plans?" Madison goggled. "I've been bugging Jake about it for three weeks! He keeps putting me off by saying it's a surprise. I think that's guy code for 'I haven't thought of anything yet.'"

"Totally," I smiled.

"So, do you think Christos is planning something?"

"I don't know. I've been so worried about my parents…" I stopped myself. I hadn't told her about their freak out, and I really didn't feel like going into it.

"What about your parents?" Madison probed. "Are they okay? Did something happen to them?"

"No, it's nothing. Just the usual petty parental annoyances," I said nervously.

"Ok, girlfriend, you're holding out on me. I can tell. What's going on? Is there something I should know?"

I grinned at Madison. I shrugged.

"Tell me, Sam! I'm on a need-to-know basis. As your BFF, I *demand* to know." She folded her arms across her chest.

"Ah…" I smiled nervously.

She arched an eyebrow. "Sam?"

"Fine," I grimaced reluctantly, "I told them about moving in with Christos and they freaked—"

"What?! You never told me about moving in with Christos!"

I hadn't. My life had become so crazy, I was barely keeping my best friends in the loop anymore. Romeo didn't know either, and Kamiko probably didn't want to know. "Sorry, Mads. I was afraid I'd jinx things if I talked about it before it actually happened," I said sheepishly.

Madison swallowed me in a huge hug. "That's awesome, Sam! I'm so happy for you!" She was jumping up and down with her arms around me while we waited in line.

I couldn't help myself, I started jumping with her, overtaken by her enthusiasm.

People stared at us like we were crazy teenagers, which we basically were.

I started giggling. "It's pretty awesome."

Slowly, we stopped jumping.

Madison asked, "Are you guys getting an apartment, or what?"

"No, the plan is for me to move into his house, with him and his grandfather." I used the word "plan" because everything was still so up in the air. I *really* hoped I wasn't jinxing myself talking about it.

"Really? Wow! That's totally cool."

I sort of expected Madison to ask if Spiridon was okay with things, but I realized that was how my parents saw the world, not other people. Because I could totally imagine Madison's parents inviting me to move in with them if I needed a place to stay without giving it a second thought. More and more, it seemed like my family was the strangest family that ever existed.

"Maybe now you can quit your Grab-n-Dash job," Madison said. "I know how much you hated that place."

"Yeah, it was not conducive to my sanity," I smiled.

"So what about Valentine's Day? Maybe Christos is going to

throw you a surprise Valentine's Day thing at the house! Like, a Moving In on Valentine's Day celebration!" Madison's eyes were wide with excitement. "You should totally do it! It would be *so* romantic!"

It would. But was any of it going to happen? The sudden knot in my stomach made me wonder. I'd turned in my 30-day notice already. Was it too late to cancel that, just in case?

Just in case my mom was right.

No, please no.

A wave of nausea rippled through me as Madison and I made it up to the cashier at the Mexican restaurant. Right now, not even fish tacos sounded good.

Hopefully, Christos would set my mind at ease over dinner later.

SAMANTHA

Christos surprised me by bringing sushi on the back of his motorcycle to my apartment at seven o'clock on the dot.

I hadn't had sushi in forever. It was perfect. We sat at my dinner table in the kitchen, sitting next to each other.

"I'm so sorry about last night, *agápi mou*," Christos said. "Jake and I were out pretty late, and I was sauced. We had to wait it out till we got sober enough to drive home." He chop-sticked a piece of dragon roll into his mouth.

"You should've called," I said, setting down my bite of tuna sashimi. "I would've come and picked you guys up."

"Nah," he said, wiping his mouth with a napkin, "it was late. I didn't want to wake you." He smiled.

"Next time, call me. No matter how late," I said forcefully.

"Will do," he smiled and leaned over to give me a peck on the lips.

"I'm here for you too, you know," I said seriously.

He gazed into my eyes for a long time. I expected a cocky response, but all he did was nod.

Fishing for information, I said, "So, Madison tells me Jake has some big surprise planned for Valentine's Day."

"I'm not surprised," Christos smiled. "Jake is totally in love with her."

Did he look uncomfortable when he'd said that, or was it just me? I wasn't sure. Whatever it was, this was Christos' cue to say suggestive but ambiguous things about how awesome *our* Valentine's Day was going to be. Silence hung between us. I waited.

We looked at each other. He smiled and picked up another piece of dragon roll with his chopsticks and popped it in his mouth.

Okay, so Valentine's Day for me and Christos was top secret? Did that mean it would be that much more awesome? Or was bad news brewing and I was going to be the last to know?

I needed a change of subject.

"Any more calls from your parents?" Christos asked.

Not the subject I was looking for.

"No," I said. "I mean, they've left a bunch of voicemails I haven't listened to and emails I haven't read. They're probably all death-threats. knowing my parents."

"Sorry to hear that. Maybe you need to call them and clear the air. Let them know you're okay. They're probably worried about you."

I huffed a laugh, "Yeah, they're worried I'm not following orders."

"Was it that bad?" Christos said while dipping tuna sashimi in soy sauce and wasabi with his chopsticks. He popped the raw tuna in his mouth and chewed.

"Yeah," I sighed. "I told you they're evil."

Christos set down his chopsticks and wiped his mouth with a napkin. "Look, *agápi mou*, I know it's the last thing you want to hear from me, but maybe you just need to call them and set things straight. I'll be right here for support, like when you told them you changed majors. What do you say?"

I wanted to say that last time my parents had thrown me to the lions with their decision to stop paying for my apartment and this time they might throw me to the tigers, bears, sharks, and carnivorous dinosaurs, oh my!

Which led me to my real concern. Now that I'd given a 30-day notice to my apartment manager, I needed to make absolutely sure I wasn't walking a high wire without a net. "Christos, before I call them," I said tentatively, "I have to ask you one thing."

"Anything, *agápi mou*," he said before drinking some water.

I looked into his eyes. They were so sincere, it gave me the courage to press forward. "I feel silly for asking this, and please don't hate me, but…are we moving in together?"

He frowned. "What do you mean?"

Was I sensing doubt? Screw it, I needed to get this over with. "I mean, are you totally sure it's cool for me to move in with you and Spiridon? Cuz if it's not, I totally—"

He put a reassuring hand on my thigh. "*Agápi mou*, I meant what I said. And so did my grandpa. You can move into the house for as long as you want."

"You're sure?" I asked hopefully. It really did seem too good an offer to be true.

"Yes."

I was wrong. It was true. "Okay, good. I just needed to make sure. My mom said some nasty things that made me, I don't know, nervous about the whole thing."

"Like what?"

"You don't want to know," I chuckled nervously.

"Sounds to me like you need to call them, *agápi mou*. I can tell them myself that you have a place to live for as long as you want. I mean, I spent two weeks at their house. Why wouldn't my family extend the same courtesy to you?"

"That's right!" I smiled. "But, it's for more than two weeks," I winced.

"So what?" He'd said it with such confidence, I couldn't possibly doubt him.

"Okay, I'll call them!" I cleared our dinner plates from the table, wiped it down with a damp sponge, and washed my hands in the sink.

I was drying my hands on a dish towel when Christos grinned at me.

"Ready to rip that Band-Aid off?" he asked.

"Do you have to make it sound like this situation is a bloody wound?"

He chuckled. "Okay. Uh, are you ready to call your parents and tell them what they've won?"

"What, like a sweepstakes? That doesn't make any sense."

"Yeah it does. They have an awesome daughter who's taking charge of her own life in admirable ways. Sounds like the big win to me."

I giggled. "You always know the right things to say, *agápi mou*," I said.

"You keep talking with that sexy Greek accent you've picked up, and we won't make it to the phone call," he said suggestively.

"Fine by me!"

He laughed. "I knew you were trying to distract me. Call them, Samantha. Let's get this over with. How bad can they be?"

I took a shaky breath. I didn't want to make any predictions lest they come true. "Fine," I said and grabbed my phone. I plopped down on the couch and Christos sat next to me.

"Here goes nothing," I said as I dialed and set the phone to speaker.

"Hello?" my mom said.

I sighed, wishing my dad had answered. He would've given me a slight buffer before everything went nuts. "Hey, Mom."

"To what do we owe this honor?" she said sarcastically. "Considering you didn't bother to answer any of our previous messages."

I rolled my eyes at Christos. He took my hand and held it.

"Sam?" my mom asked.

"I'm *here*," I said rolling my eyes, already sounding whinier than I'd planned.

"What do you want?" she snapped bluntly. She was never *this* bad.

"You might want to get Dad on the phone."

"Why," my mom chuckled, "are you eloping with that *Christos*? Getting married in Las Vegas? Or have you already gotten hitched and dropped out of school?"

Wow, she sure knew how to set me at ease. I wondered if the State Department needed any more diplomats to bridge gaps between warring nations and rekindle world peace. I'd totally recommend my mom. Not. "No, Mom," I sighed. "Just get Dad. Please?"

"Fine." She put the phone down. A minute later the other phone line clicked on.

"Hello?" my dad said. "Sam?"

"Hey, Dad," I sighed. Would he be as bad as Mom?

"Is everything all right?" he asked. "Your mother and I were worrying about you."

More like yelling about me, would be my guess.

My mom was back on the phone, "So what was your big announcement?" she grated.

Here went nothing. Or everything. "I'm moving in with Christos. I gave my 30-day notice to the manager at my apartment."

"You *what?!*" Mom shouted.

Christos squeezed my hand supportively.

"I'm moving in with Christos," I said confidently. Ironically, my mom's sudden anger strengthened my resolve.

My dad started nervously, "Sam, are you sure this is a guh—"

Like she'd been on a time-delay fuse, my mom blew up again, "*Over my dead body you will!!*"

Maybe I shouldn't have told them?

"*You will NOT move into that young man's house! I will not have you throw your life away on a whim for some two-bit tough!*"

I goggled at Christos. He raised his eyebrows sympathetically and winced. So it wasn't just me. My mom was a lunatic, like I'd always suspected.

"I'm not throwing my life away, Mom!" I pleaded. Why did I have to plead at a moment like this? I didn't know, but that's what I was doing. "Christos is a good person! I'm going to live with him and his grandfather. Both of them are working artists! They make their livings selling art. They're showing me how to do it too!"

"I don't know what kind of a hippie commune this Christos and his grandfather have," my mom said acidly, having calmed from stark raving lunacy to simmering insanity, "but I'm sure it sounds much better than it actually is. You can't pay the gas and electric bill with peace and love, Samantha. But if you like taking cold showers, that's your prerogative," my mom said with finality.

"You have no idea what you're talking about, Mom! They're not hippies! They live in a mansion. I mean, an actual mansion. It has a gazillion bedrooms. And the last time I took a shower there, it was really hot, and it never ran out of water, like when I shower after you and Dad get ready for work."

In my experience, there was nothing quite as annoying as running out of hot water and shivering in the shower because your dad was too cheap to set the central house thermostat to a reasonable temperature. Not even my mom could change Dad's mind about that. Our house was an icebox most of the winter. I swear, one time, I woke up and saw icicles dangling from the ceiling in my bedroom as my breath puffed out of my mouth in cold clouds.

"That's all well and good, Samantha," my mom continued, "but —"

I cut her off. "Yes, mom. It *is* well and good. It's nicer than your house. And I'm moving in with them. Christos' grandfather Spiridon is a very nice man, and he—"

"Spiridon?" my mom scoffed. "What kind of a hippie name is that?"

She was going too far. "It's Greek, mom. Look it up. It's a real name. And he's nice." I was getting flustered. My mom was turning this into an insult-a-thon. I wasn't going to stoop into the sewer with her.

"Perhaps you two should both calm down," my dad suggested.

"*I am calm!!*" my mom shouted.

Really? Not from where I was sitting three thousand miles away. I stifled a chuckle.

"I will *not* have our daughter moving in with some strange young man in flagrant disregard of our orders, Bill!" Mom growled.

I sighed heavily. If my parents were this unreasonable, maybe I didn't need them in my life at all. "I'm moving in with Christos. I'm not going to be an accountant, and I'm going to live my life."

After a minute of silence, Mom said, "Bill? Do you have anything to say? Because now would be a good time. I can't get through to your daughter."

In a cold tone, my dad said, "Sam, is this course of action your preference?"

Wow, was Dad suddenly taking my side? Was he being reasonable? "Yuh, yes," I stammered.

"Fine. If you no longer require our assistance regarding your living arrangements, I think I can speak for both your mother and I when I say that we would be more than happy to cease all funding of your college education, if that's your preference."

I was shocked silent.

My parents paid a substantial portion of my tuition. If they stopped paying entirely, I wouldn't be able to cover the difference with my two jobs. I'd have to take out more loans, but I didn't know if I could actually get a large enough loan to make up the difference.

If my parents stopped paying, my entire life would be thrown into a blizzard of change and uncertainty.

Was I ready for that sort of chaos? I'd been through plenty in the last five months. Did I want to make things worse?

I looked at Christos. He rubbed my knee sympathetically.

"Answer your father, young lady," Mom said viciously. "Do what we say, or pay your own way," she chuckled at her own cleverness. She sounded like she was gloating. My mom was the biggest bitch I'd ever met, hands down.

"Don't be flip, Linda," my dad said with calm confidence. "Sam, all you have to do is change your major back to Accounting and explain to your landlord that your 30-day notice was a mistake, and all of this will go away."

My Dad Satan was back to his usual tricks.

"Fine." For the second time in my life, I hung up on my parents. The irrational fear that this was the last time I would ever talk to them suddenly seized me. "That went well," I joked to Christos sarcastically. Agony hit me a second later and my heart snapped in half.

I threw myself into Christos' arms and wailed. His arms wrapped protectively around me as he pulled me into his chest.

"It's okay, *agápi mou*," he murmured, "I'm here."

I felt completely betrayed by my parents. For once, my life was going good. For once, my dreams were turning into reality. But, as always, my parents stridently objected to what *I* wanted. They were trying to manipulate me with bribes and threats. Was that parenting? Weren't you supposed to trust at some point that your children would find their own way?

My parents didn't.

No matter what I did, they fought me every step of the way. Why were they always the biggest obstacle I faced in my life?

I thanked fate for bringing Christos to me.

I sobbed in his arms.

"Oh, Christos, I don't know what I'd do without you!"

Chapter 26

CHRISTOS

I held Samantha in my arms. "I'm so sorry, *agápi mou*," I whispered.

She shook with tears and burrowed her face into my chest.

Samantha's parents were truly insane. Did they not realize their life plan for their daughter was all wrong and was making her miserable? What kind of fucked up people were they?

My parents had never treated me like this. Not even close.

In a perfect world, I would've moved Samantha into my house this weekend, and told her I had plenty of cash to cover her living expenses and whatever tuition she had left over.

But I didn't live in a perfect world.

In my world, I was going to trial on Friday. I could be in jail by Saturday. I wouldn't be able to help her move in. And the money? Shit, after I finished paying Russell for defending my ass in court, I wasn't going to have *any* money left.

That was my world.

"I'm so lucky, Christos," Samantha wept, "I'd be freaking out right now if you weren't here."

I kissed the top of her head gently.

How was I going to tell her I might not be here in five days?

I couldn't do it. I couldn't let her down. Not right now. She was still reeling from her fucking parents.

I felt jitters in my feet. This always happened when shit hit the fan. I wanted to take action. Bust some heads. Knock shit over. Or, fuck, the opposite. Go build something. Throw up walls and nail shit together, bolt stuff down. But none of that would make a fucking difference. My trial date was barreling toward me and I was chained to the train tracks.

All I could do was wait.

Samantha clutched my shirt in her little fists and sobbed. "Oh, Christos..."

Fuck, I couldn't do shit to help her.

I tried to calm myself. If I didn't, I was going to missile through the ceiling. This was killing me. I needed to think this through. I needed to help Samantha somehow.

What were my real options?

On the plus side, I had my grandpa. I even had my dad. No, fuck that. I wasn't calling my dad. But my *grand*pa would make sure Samantha got moved into the house no matter what. He would make sure Samantha had a roof and ate three squares every day. At least the basics were covered. Samantha was safe physically.

That took a huge load off.

But what about mentally?

That's what was worrying me, big time. I knew my grandpa would be supportive, but I couldn't expect him to be Samantha's personal grief counselor, not when her parents were trying to shove their bullshit down her throat. I imagined my grandpa wouldn't want to butt his nose into their family business, especially without my input.

Problem was, Samantha desperately needed *some*one to butt in and tell her parents they were fucking lunatics. That's where I came in.

I wanted to help her fight the inevitable battles that were coming just down the road on her journey to becoming an artist, the ones every artist faced, *and* the ones she faced against her parents.

How was I going to do that from a jail cell?

And what was Samantha going to do when her tuition bills came due? Throw it in and do what her parents wanted? I wouldn't blame her if she did. Cast adrift like she was, who wouldn't be scared shitless? Most people would grab the life preserver her parents were throwing out, no matter what strings were attached.

The idea of Samantha sinking her dreams while saving her skin like that broke my heart.

Worse, I was on the verge of bailing out right after her parents had kicked her heart to the curb.

What kind of a fucking prick did that make me? I tensed as revulsion broiled in my stomach. I suddenly realized I was becoming my mom. Running out when shit got hard, just like she'd done to my dad.

Fuck me.

I vaulted from the couch, tumbling Samantha into the cushions.

"I've got to get out of here," I growled through clenched teeth.

"What is it, Christos?" Samantha pleaded, tears streaming down her face.

"My life is fucked," I said hoarsely, pulling on my hair with both fists, like if I ripped the top of my head off, all my frustration would blow out, releasing the pressure in my head. Too bad it didn't work. My skull was still capped and I was ready to blow. "It's always been fucked."

She blinked at me, panic setting in. "I don't understand?! What's wrong?!" She stood up slowly and walked over to me tentatively, almost like I was dangerous.

I ground my jaw. I'm sure she was completely freaked. We'd gone from her parents losing their shit to me losing mine two minutes later. But she had no idea why. I had a brief moment to laugh at myself. I was going insane. How could I tell her the truth now? It would only make things worse.

"Please tell me, Christos," she said, wiping tears from her eyes.

I could tell she was desperate and confused.

She didn't want to lose me and I didn't want to abandon her. But chances were good that's how it would play out. I would be walking down a concrete hallway in days to spend years behind bars. What good would I be to Samantha then? Every time she came to visit me, she'd be thinking about how her mom was right, how I was a fuck-up. Because, when you got right down to it, that's who went to jail.

Two-bit toughs.

Fuck-ups.

Like me.

I stood in Samantha's living room with my head hanging between my shoulders. It may as well have been hanging from a noose based on how good I felt about myself at that moment.

She wrapped her arms carefully around me and hugged me tightly. "Whatever it is," she begged, "I'll understand. I can't help you unless you tell me. We can get through *anything* if we do it together."

I grit my teeth, holding in a laugh. That was the problem, wasn't it? How together can you be with phone calls and inmate visits? You can't. It's a ghost of a relationship. You could wish the person on the outside well, but you literally couldn't be there to catch them when they fell.

"Please, Christos," she said in a trembling voice.

My heart was about to snap in half.

I wanted to bolt. I wanted to stay.

Fuck!!

"*Agápi mou*," she said, holding her hand to my cheek, gazing up at me. "Tell me. Please."

The look of love in her eyes was breaking my fucking heart. I was a fucking piece of shit for holding back on her. She'd given me everything and I wasn't giving her *anything*.

"I'm here, *agápi mou*," she said.

Man, the tables sure had turned.

I hissed a hard sigh as my heart calmed.

I'd held out on her long enough. It was grinding us both down. She deserved better. At the very least, she deserved to know the truth.

I ran a frustrated hand through my hair and said, "Remember last year, before we starting going out, I told you my life was a shit storm waiting to happen?"

"Yeah? I never understood that," she said skeptically, as if it couldn't possibly be true. "You have a grandfather who loves you, you live in an awesome house, and you have all that new work from Brandon. Your life and career is what I dream of having twenty years from now, if I'm lucky."

I stifled a laugh.

The grass was always greener, wasn't it? I didn't want to spoil the fantasy for her. I was pretty sure every job had aspects that drove people nuts, but that wasn't the bitter truth I needed to reveal to the love of my life right now.

I took a deep breath.

It was one thing to tell someone that dream jobs had thorns, but another when you had to tell your beloved you were a bad person. "I never told you *why* my life was about to become a shit storm."

She gazed up at me courageously, ready for anything. I was in awe of her strength. Maybe I was the idiot, and telling her really would somehow fix things.

"I've been awaiting trial for the last several months," I said. "I've been out on bail since the day I met you. There's a good chance I'm going to end up in jail. Or prison." I winced, ready for her to tell me what a fuck-up I was.

"For what?" she asked with zero judgment.

It was then that I realized the person judging me most harshly had always been myself. Looking into Samantha's eyes, I saw only her belief in me. It gave me the courage to continue. "For aggravated assault and battery," I answered.

"What does that mean?" she asked.

"It means I punched a guy out," I said, expecting the worst.

"How come you never said anything?" Her brows cinched together and she looked heartbroken.

"Because of the look on your face right now," I muttered, sensing her acceptance had gone up in smoke a second ago.

"All you did was punch a guy out?" she asked skeptically, holding both my hands in hers.

I nodded. "One punch."

"Did he die or something?"

"No," I smiled.

She hugged me tightly. "Christos, it doesn't matter. It sounds like it was nothing. You should've told me. I still love you. You have no idea how much I love you."

The thing was, there was way more to my story than punching out *one* guy *one* time. "That's because you don't know me, Samantha," I said quietly. "You don't know about my past."

"What past?"

Up to this point had been the warm-up. Now it was time for her to hear the cold, hard truth. "All the times I've been locked up. There have been many. I'm a convict, Samantha."

She scoffed. "What, like a drug dealer or gangs or something?"

"No, not like that. But I'm a guy who's been in jail enough times that it's normal. I'm on a first-name basis with more criminals and corrections officers than I can count."

"What have you been in jail for?"

"For racing and doing crazy shit on my motorcycle, some of which has caused other people to get seriously injured and in one case, killed."

"Oh my god," Samantha gasped, holding a hand in front of her mouth. "Wuh—what happened?" she stammered. "Did…did you, I don't know, run him off the road or something?"

"No. But I may as well have. Guy tried to keep up with me on a canyon road, but he didn't have the skills to follow. High-sided his bike right over a guard rail at sixty miles an hour. Tumbled down a rocky hillside. He was probably dead by the time he hit the bottom two-hundred feet below."

Her face knotted with horror as she backed up a step and hugged her elbows against her chest.

Who wouldn't be horrified? I know I had been. I couldn't sleep for three days after the guy died.

"Oh, no," Samantha said. "That's…that's *awful*, Christos."

"Yeah," I sighed. "It is."

"But you didn't cause the accident, right?"

I clutched my fists in front of me, squeezing the air in frustration. "You're missing the point, Samantha. The thing is, I was watching the guy in my rearview for three miles. He was lagging farther and farther behind after every turn. He started trying to make up lost ground by coming into the corners too hot. All I would've had to do was slow my bike down, let him catch up, keep a pace he could safely manage. If I'd done that, we would've been toasting beers at the end of the day. But I didn't. I had an ego about the whole thing. I wasn't gonna let some hothead beat my shit, no fucking way."

Holding fingers against her lips, Samantha searched my eyes. "When did this happen?"

I could see her wheels turning. She was desperately trying to make sense of this. But there was no sense to be made.

I indulged her. "Three years ago," I sighed.

She took a step toward me, resting one hand on my arm. "Oh, Christos. You were nineteen. You were just a kid. *I'm* nineteen. I still do stupid things all the time. If that guy hadn't followed you that day, the next time, he would've followed someone *else* he shouldn't have been following. It wasn't your fault."

"But that's not what happened," I argued, shaking my splayed hands in front of me. "He died when he was following *me*," I sneered, dropping my arms to my side in defeat, "because *I* got too competitive. Not some other rider. I wasn't thinking to myself, 'Oh, this young fellow is terribly outclassed. The responsible thing for me to do as a grown-up is take the poor boy aside and set him straight before he injures himself. Teach him to mind his own limits, and follow the rules of the road responsibly.' Nope. I was just thinking that his sorry ass wasn't going to catch me. Now he's dead."

Samantha chewed on her bottom lip and frowned. She was silent.

Because there wasn't a good argument in this case, was there? That's why they called it *reckless* driving and *criminal* negligence.

I rubbed my hand across my face and tipped my head back in frustration.

"And that's just the tip of my iceberg," I sighed. "I've been in so many punch-ups, I've lost count. I've hurt a lot of people, put them in hospitals countless times. Broken bones, knocked out teeth, all because deep down," I was seething now, "I'm a fucking *hot*-head who didn't know how to control my shit for *years* before I met you."

A pained, disgusted grimace stretched across Samantha's face. Her arms dangled uselessly at her sides.

I'm sure any desire she'd had left to hug me or tell me everything was going to be all right evaporated when the truth came out. I couldn't blame her. I was disgusted with myself too. Because I knew that beneath my shiny, chromed-up good looks, I was a monster.

She took a hesitant step back, toward the coffee table. If she was backing away from me, I couldn't blame her. When you smelled trouble, that's what a smart person did.

"But you never started any of those fights, right?" Samantha asked seriously.

I had another can of disappointment for her. I pulled it out of my back pocket and popped the top.

I huffed out a laugh, "Yeah."

She was frowning and chewing her lip again. "What do you mean, yeah?" she asked.

"I mean, I've started tons of fights. Shit, even the ones I didn't? I could've walked away. But I decided to stay and fight. I wasn't going to let anybody out-man my shit."

"Christos, that isn't like you," she frowned sternly.

Sadly, she was in total denial. Because I knew the truth. I could be a fucking prick when I was trying to deal with the rage that had boiled in my veins for a decade…since my mom…

Mom…

Samantha shook her head definitively. "That's not the man I know," she said passionately, "the man I fell in love with."

And there went my silver lining, my hope that this would all work out. Because she hadn't fallen in love with the real me. She'd fallen in love with the thin veneer I'd pasted over my brutish past in the last two years. She didn't want to know about my shit. Fuck, *I* didn't want to know about my past, but I was fucking stuck with it. I chuckled to myself. What difference did it make if I got locked up after my upcoming trial? I would forever be chained down by my history.

I sneered at her. "That's because I'm really not the man you think you know. I'm a fuck-up, Samantha."

"That's not true."

"It's not?"

"No," she protested softly. "I *know* you."

"No you don't," I laughed. "I'm not a Boy Scout, Samantha. I'm the bad guy."

"But you never start fights!" she pleaded. "You're always protecting me."

I chuckled. "Maybe now. Two years ago? I was the asshole. I was the guy starting shit everywhere I went."

"I can't picture you doing that," she whispered.

"That doesn't mean I didn't." I was ready to jump out of my skin.

I wanted to ram my head into the wall. I should've told her sooner that I was a Class-A fuck-up and let the chips fall, instead of jumping into a relationship with her. Then she could've calmly decided to keep her distance. That would've been okay. I could still have mentored her. But I'd been too much of a coward to tell her. A fucking yellow-backed coward.

Samantha had needed a guide through her art career when I'd met her, not a fucked-up lover.

But I had been so head-over for her after only a few short weeks, I'd let my heart overrun my good sense. I'd let my greedy need take over. The next thing I knew, after spending a month or two with her, I loved her so much, the idea of scaring her off by telling her the truth about my past and my impending trial had freaked me to the point I just buried everything.

For the last five months, it had felt so good being the good guy she thought I was. Maybe I thought her love for me as the good guy would make my bad guy go away, like he had never existed.

How wrong I was.

Now I had the most amazing woman I'd ever met staring at me like I was the fucking monster I'd always been.

At least now she knew the truth.

I was Jekyll & Hyde.

Too bad Samantha had fallen in love with Jekyll, because I was Hyde to the core.

I couldn't hide my Hyde anymore.

I took a deep breath and stared at her. May as well put the final nail in this shit and bury it. She didn't need me bringing her down.

I said, "Remember when you were talking about Jake's surprise Valentine's Day plans for Madison?"

"Yeah?" she said, her voice quivering nervously.

I opened my mouth to finish things off while glancing at Samantha's innocent, tear-stained face.

"Tell me, *agápi mou*," she said softly.

I couldn't do it.

I couldn't break her heart any further than I already had. I couldn't tell her that what Jake had planned for Madison on Valentine's Day would be a million times more awesome than sitting in court behind me, watching the burners heat up under my ass. Shit, Jake could buy Madison one of those boxes of candy hearts with the messages printed on them and mail it to her a week late, and that would still be way better than Samantha sitting in the back of the court room with me on February 14th.

Man, I was a fucking prick.

Sharp as a tack, Samantha said, "What about Valentine's Day?"

I couldn't tell her.

"Is…is your *trial* on Valentine's Day?"

After an interminable guilty silence, I nodded.

"Oh, Christos," she said. Her eyes were tearing up again. She held one hand to her mouth, as if to cover her shame. There was this sad tone to her voice that made me want to chuck biscuits all over her carpet.

That was when my final surprise came.

Clarity.

I finally saw it in the form of one of those forty-foot earthquake waves that washes inland for miles and destroys everything in its path. That wave was Samantha's parents.

If they found out I was in jail, it would confirm *everything* her mom had said on the phone about me. It would be hard, ugly proof. Then they would go to war for their daughter.

The thing Samantha didn't realize was her parents cared about her. A lot. Sure, they were thick-skulled about it, thinking a stable 9-to-5 was the path to satisfaction.

They may've been misguided, but they cared. That's why they weren't going to tolerate their daughter dating a two-bit tough in lock-up.

No fucking way.

Earlier, on the phone, Samantha's mom had been a momma bear backed into a corner. She wasn't giving up her daughter to me.

I wouldn't put it past her to hop on a plane to San Diego to stage an intervention on Samantha's behalf. Round her daughter up and take her back home to D.C., just to get her away from me for good.

Shit, if some guy like me was dating my daughter, I'd probably do the same thing.

There was only one way to fix this.

I stalked over to the door and yanked it open. "I have to go."

"No, Christos, wait!" She grabbed after me, but I slipped free. "Don't leave! I need you!"

I couldn't bear to look her in the eyes. My heart was already broken into too many pieces.

I was out the door and hopping on my bike seconds later.

CHRISTOS

The lane lines on the freeway machine-gunned at me like tracer bullets.

My Ducati screamed between my legs. I was tucked beneath the fairing as wind pounded the front of the bike.

It was three in the morning and I was doing 175mph on the Five.

The pain inside me was so big, nobody could save me from it. My only option was to speed away from everything, go so fast, nothing could catch me.

Somewhere far behind me were my problems.

Samantha's broken heart. There was no way I could fix that, not unless I could magically rewrite history and erase my past.

Her parents. Something in my gut told me they were coming for her. They weren't gonna let this two-bit fuck-up take their daughter away. No way.

My pending trial, two days away. The possibility of jail time, maybe even prison time.

In all three cases, I had no control over the outcome. Everything was up to the people around me. It was driving me nuts. But there was one thing I *could* control.

I could control my fate.

The only thing stopping me from high-speed death on this freeway was *me*.

This I could control.

My bike. The pavement. I was in my element.

I ignored the demons behind me as I concentrated on the road ahead. The surface was damp but not wet. It had drizzled just before sundown, hours ago. Traffic had dried twin wheel-tracks into each lane. The tracks were about two feet wide. As long as I kept my bike inside the track, I was on dry road.

If I hit the wet strips on either side at 175? I didn't fucking care.

All I could think about was keeping my bike in the dry track. There was no time to think about anything else.

At this speed, the lazy curves of the freeway became dangerously sharp. If I kept my eyes trained in the distance, I could time things tightly enough.

If you went the speed limit, the ride from Samantha's apartment to Pacific Beach took about twenty minutes. I'd made it in seven. I got off the freeway at Garnet to turn around. The cops always got heavier near downtown.

A minute later, I was back on the freeway heading north, and winding through the gears past one-forty.

I eased up carefully on the throttle as I hit the curve around Mount Soledad. As soon as the road straightened at La Jolla Village, I opened the throttle back up and blasted past SDU. When I shot beneath the overpass at La Jolla Village Drive, there was a brief concussion as the cement roadway overhead smacked the roar of my Ducati's engine back at me.

This section of straightaway was about three miles long. I cleared it in just over a minute. I had hoped to catch air over the top of the grade at Genesee, but the pitch was too shallow, even at 175.

I relaxed the throttle again as I neared the merge with the 805. I scrubbed off some speed and toed the shifter while blowing past two cars heading into the turn. I think I was still holding one-thirty as I rounded the curve.

The bike leaned as I hit the apex of the turn and feathered the gas. As I started coming out of it, I brought the bike up to standing while winding out the throttle.

The engine screamed as I worked my way back up the gears and arrowed across four lanes, cutting a razor line between an eighteen wheeler and an SUV.

I rocketed northward with the hounds of hell nipping at my heels.

They couldn't catch me.

SAMANTHA

I dreamt of a fallen angel.

I woke up in the middle of the night, gasping for air.

Alone.

"Christos?" I asked the emptiness that enveloped me.

My darkened apartment was empty. I shook off my nightmare and reached for my phone, sensing deep in my heart that something was wrong with Christos. I dialed his number for the fiftieth time that night. It rang four times, then went to voicemail.

For the fiftieth time.

I had tried following him when he'd left my apartment earlier, but there was no way I was going to catch his Ducati with my VW.

After driving all over my neighborhood for thirty minutes, feeling lost only blocks away from my own apartment, I'd given up and gone home.

I had then texted and called Christos repeatedly, but he'd never answered. Eventually, I'd given up trying, exhausted from the worry.

After the draining conversation with my parents, the frightening conversation with Christos, and the panicked calls to his phone, I'd had zero energy left. I was so exhausted, I didn't even consider ice cream before crawling into bed and sobbing myself to sleep.

Now that I was awake, the images from my nightmare still haunted me.

A fallen angel.

Darkness.

Alone.

I couldn't just sit still. I needed to make sure Christos was okay. Maybe he'd finally gone back to his house?

I needed to check. I threw on clothes and ran to my car. If I could see him with my own eyes, see that he was safe, everything would be all right.

As long as I still had Christos, *everything* would be all right. I didn't care about his trial, or jail, or my parents. None of it mattered if I had Christos.

He had no idea how deeply I loved him. He wasn't a criminal. He was a beautiful man.

He was my angel.

My savior.

I needed him.

I drove to the Manos' house fearing the worst. I told myself it was nothing, just nerves. I tried to imagine the soothing calm I would feel the second I laid eyes on Christos. He would be sleeping peacefully in his bed. I would crawl into bed with him and curl up beside him. I would whisper to him that everything was going to be all right, that we would get through this dark journey together.

As long as I could feel his touch, his warmth, and his love, I would be fine.

We were going to be okay. No matter what.

I shook my head, smiling to myself as I turned onto Christos' street. Any second, I was going to pull into his driveway and see his motorcycle parked beside the house.

When I drove up, the driveway was empty. That was okay. His motorcycle was probably in the garage.

I'm sure he was fine.

Dread.

When I parked my VW, I jumped out and ran into the entry court. I pounded on the front door. There was no answer.

I ran out of the entry court and looked up at the front of the house. All of the windows were dark, each one a black pit echoing the dread in my heart.

Dread.

I ran back to the front door and pulled out the key Spiridon had given me. I had never had to use it because either he or Christos had always been in the house.

Dread.

The door creaked open ominously as I crept inside. The entry hall and living room were dark. Only a light in the kitchen cut through the gloom.

"Christos?" I called nervously. "Spiridon?"

My words were sucked into the darkness of the house. It was eerie being inside this place alone. The sense of emptiness was heavy and foreboding.

I went from room to room, calling out.

"Christos? Are you here? Is anybody home?"

Dread.

The studio was cavernous and empty when I flipped the lights on. It had never seemed so barren. I don't know why, but I half-expected to find Christos curled up in a corner, staring into oblivion like a mad man. I dismissed the notion as crazy. Yet I feared my dark vision was preferable to what the storm in my stomach told me I was going to find.

There was no one downstairs.

I trudged up the staircase to the second floor, lifting each heavy foot, almost afraid to go farther, to find out what awaited in the darkness. Images of what I would find flashed through my mind.

Christos in a pool of blood, his body torn and broken beyond repair...

I cringed, pushing away my terrible thoughts. I tried to focus on something else. My mind went straight to...

Bitch. Slut. Whore.

No!

I got rid of you!

Emo. Goth. Suicide Watch...

Leave me alone!

Suicide Watch...

My old pain, my damage. It was all still there. I had never healed any of it. I'd wanted to think I had. But it had barely been two months since I broke my silence about Taylor Lamberth.

Who was I trying to fool? I was still broken.

The stress of this moment had brought it all crashing back. And it was going to rip my head and heart apart.

Suicide…

The only thing that could possibly hold me together was Christos. I had to find him. And he was…

An insane laugh was about to rattle out of my throat. I stifled it down, worried that if I allowed it to escape my body, it would take my sanity with it.

I took a deep breath, trying to calm myself. I was acting crazy. *This* was crazy. Christos was fine. He was probably out with Jake or, or, or…

No!

Christos was fine.

He was fine!

I walked calmly down the upstairs hallway, toward his bedroom. The door was closed.

I winced as I touched the doorknob, fearing what I'd find inside.

I could do this.

Christos was fine.

Christos was…

—I yanked open the door—

…not in the room.

I checked the bathroom, just to be sure. Empty.

I searched the rest of the upstairs.

"Christos? Spiridon?"

No one was home.

I returned to Christos' bedroom and sat down on his bed. I tried calling him. He didn't answer. I sent him a text,

<3 Please call me. I love you. <3

I'm sure he was fine.

I crossed my legs and leaned my forearms on one knee, slumped over, preparing to wait. My foot started bouncing. Christos was probably out someplace having a good time with Jake again. He was…

Christos' sketchbook caught my eye. It rested on the night-table beside his bed. I leaned over and picked it up. There was a pen keeping place in the middle of the book.

I opened the sketchbook all the way.

The marked page was the last one with anything on it.
On it were written the following words:

"Alone
I must brave this day
Alone
I have sealed my fate
Alone
I will touch the sky
Alone
I must die"

Beneath those words was the date. Today's date.
Oh no.
Suicide…
"Christos?" I whispered to the empty room.
Dread.

Epilogue

CHRISTOS

I stood on the edge of an abyss. Not a metaphorical one.

A real one.

Ten stories below me, cement death called my name. I gazed down at it like an old friend. I'd been up here, balanced on this exact railing, countless times in the last six years.

This was my favorite destination when the pain in my life became too much.

After speeding up and down the Five freeway at 175mph had failed to produce any novel results this evening, I'd come here.

The dormitory building was called Nyyhmy Hall. Its sister dormitory, Paiute Hall, stood next to it. Both were named after indigenous tribes that inhabited the area surrounding Mono Lake, located just east of Yosemite Valley.

These dormitories were the main housing for undergraduates who attended Ansel Adams College, one of the sub-colleges that comprised San Diego University. Adams, as the students called it, was named after the pioneering environmentalist photographer Ansel Adams.

Each of SDU's sub-colleges had their own particular architecture, educational requirements, and student culture. Samantha's cute little friend Kamiko attended Adams. When I was an undergraduate, I'd attended Adams too, because I'd liked its hippie, naturalist vibe.

That's when I'd discovered the tenth-floor balcony in Nyyhmy.

I knew for a fact that a small number of SDU students had jumped to their deaths from this very balcony. The pressure of college and the metamorphosis into an adult was an intense process for lots of kids at SDU.

I understood where they were coming from.

I was surprised that after all these years, you could still open the tenth-floor sliding glass doors that let out onto the balcony. There was no safety cage, like on the observation deck of the Empire State Building. Sure, this balcony wasn't an 86-story drop, but ten stories would still kill you, and both buildings had their own brooding history of human melancholy.

I took a deep breath and looked at the twinkling lights far below.

I was standing here to remind myself I wasn't dead, that life hadn't killed me yet.

It was a control thing.

I'd come up here to remind myself who was in control of *my* life. Not the courts, not the jurors, not my clients, not Brandon.

Me.

Whenever I stood on this railing, I always took my boots off and did it barefoot. Boots made your feet blind, and you had way more control with your toes free. Most people didn't realize that toes and fingers had a lot in common. But when your toes spent a lifetime locked up in cumbersome footwear, you forget how to use them.

My toes were quite adept at gripping the 4-inch cold steel-tube railing mounted in the waist-high cement wall that was the dividing line between a glorious view of the Pacific Ocean and a three-second trip to oblivion.

The only reason guys like me became daredevils was because they were running away from something. Usually that something lived inside them. I knew of what I spoke.

Ever since my mom had left, it had been like this.

Pain was a powerful motivator.

A body wanted to run away from pain. If a flame was burning you, you pulled away. But you couldn't pull away when the pain was inside you.

That's why I needed to come up here and remind myself that *I* was still in control.

I could make the pain go away in an instant, if I wanted to.

Or, as long as my balance was good enough to keep my ass from slipping to my death, I held the keys to my future.

I did.

No one else. *I* was in control of my life.

The only problem with my logic was that not killing myself, while it seemed like the ultimate control, was not the same as controlling my pain.

I could ride my bike at 175mph all night long or stand on this railing until the sun came up.

But it didn't change the simple fact that a jury of twelve was going to decide whether or not to fuck my life up. Then Samantha and her parents would know I was a piece of shit.

If she was going to lose me, maybe it was best if she thought I was a fuck-up. Then it would be easier for her to let go.

Pain hit me again, like every cell in my stomach had exploded simultaneously with black cancer, and I was consuming myself in a dark demise of self-destruction.

My smart phone jangled in my pocket. Before Your Love by Kelly Clarkson played from it. Samantha's ringtone.

I started to slip.

Hello, cement.

I adjusted my hips and spine while my arms made small, erratic circles, until I recovered my balance. I loved that feeling when my stomach climbed up to my throat.

It meant I was still alive.

I stood motionless until my phone went to voicemail.

Telling Samantha everything earlier had been a mistake. It was too much to ask of her with all the shit her parents were heaping on her. It may have helped me release some of the wildfire tormenting me from the inside out, but now I felt selfish, like all I had done was burn her life into ashes, just like mine. What did it matter if I felt better? Her future was what mattered.

Mine was in the toilet.

I didn't want her worrying about me. I was a waste of time. I wanted Samantha to be free from my agony so she could build her own life.

No reason to drag her down with my shit.

I lifted one foot off the railing and raised my leg to the side, shifting my hips over my knee to counter-balance my weight.

Nobody was going to control my fate except me.

A cool breeze rustled the tops of the Eucalyptus trees far below. My standing calf buzzed with tension as I levered myself up onto the ball of my foot.

I was in control.

No one else.

When I closed my eyes, it felt like flying.
I'll always love you...
...Agápi mou...

Want to get an email when the sequel is released?

Sign up here: **http://eepurl.com/B7crf**

Find out what happens next in:

the sequel to RECKLESS

coming early 2014

Personal thanks from Devon Hartford:

Thank you, dear reader, for taking the time to live with Samantha, Christos, and the gang for awhile! If you enjoyed Reckless, please leave some positive feedback on Amazon, Goodreads, or any book blogs you frequent. Be sure to tell your friends about it!

If you want to drop me a line, you can find me at any of the links below. I love to hear what you have to say, and I love to talk books!

-Devon

Like me on Facebook: at Devon Hartford, NA & YA novelist

Friend me on Facebook at Devon Hartford

Follow me on Twitter @DevonHartford

Follow me on WordPress at devonhartford.com

ABOUT THE AUTHOR

Devon Hartford spent most of his life in Southern California, frequenting many of the locations in Reckless. Devon also paints. His background in the arts was the inspiration for this book.

OTHER BOOKS BY DEVON HARTFORD:

Fearless (The Story of Samantha Smith #1)

ACKNOWLEDGMENTS

First and foremost I need to thank fellow New Adult author Elle Casey. She has gone above and beyond in her efforts to help me promote this series and get it into the hands of you, the reader. You should definitely check out her work!

Secondly, thanks to all my passionate and fantastic beta readers: Jenn Hedge, Beta Speed Queen, The REAL Julie England, Krystal C., Sarah Welsh (a.k.a. Princess Frilly-Bottoms of the Land of Willow), Natasha Slater, Ginger B., Kirsten Isa Goddess, Emaleth Morrigan (mermaid), Kimber, Sandye, Steffini Walker Texas Ranger, and Mandy Jamerson for invaluable feedback and encouragement!

A special thanks to Delia Gosa Steele, a.k.a. Deecabulary, the official caretaker of the phrases "I'm trippin' monkey nuts!" "uber goober" and "meatmonster."

Thanks to Andrew Coopman, the official curator of the term "cum dumpster."

Chrissy Zent Sharp for bringing twat-waffles and peens to my attention, and for awesome book pimpery via The Book Whore-der's Delights. Be sure to check them out if you're a Romance reader.

Special thanks to author Jane Harvey-Berrick for expert typo-sniping and for allowing me to host the guest appearance of Sebastian and Caro. You can read more about their story in Jane's novel *The Education of Sebastian*.

And thanks to everybody else who has helped make this book a reality!

www.ingramcontent.com/pod-product-compliance
Lightning Source LLC
Chambersburg PA
CBHW050901250626
47155CB00001B/57